Spirit Lake

Christine DeSmet

Hard Shell Word Factory

Many thanks to my critique group in Madison, Wisconsin,
who allow me to write creatively and try new things all the time.
Thanks to my family for their support
and for always asking how the writing is going.

Most important, thanks to Bob,
who's been my rock and gourmet chef since Day One
when I said I wanted to write fiction and I disappeared into the
computer room, never to be seen again.

© 2000, Christine DeSmet
Trade paperback published May 2001
ISBN: 0-7599-0391-3
Published March 2000
ISBN: 1-58200-544-3

Hard Shell Word Factory
PO Box 161
Amherst Jct. WI 54407
books@hardshell.com
http://www.hardshell.com
Cover art © 2000, Mary Z. Wolf

Chapter 1

BOARDING A TRAIN was going to be difficult for Cole Wescott. Especially since he didn't have a ticket. Then there were the guys shooting at him.

Cole hauled fast through the railyard's main gate, his boots sliding on the cinders and gravel. The June fog rolled its gray plumes around the boxcars and Cole like hot breath from a relentless hunting dog. With a backpack slapping up and down against his shoulder blades, Cole raced on, slipping deeper into the murky maze of steel tracks and trains crisscrossing Miami's downtown past Biscayne Boulevard just after midnight.

A dry desperation overwhelmed him. Find an open car. Hop on. Get out of here without detection.

Little over a week ago he was diving off the sunny Keys, pulling up encrusted treasure from a sunken World War II ship, and looking forward to a weekend speedboat race. Normal, relaxing danger. Now, he looked forward to an illegal trainride cross-country to ditch hitmen in order to dig up the truth behind his brother's death. A simple midnight run.

Cole sweated just thinking about his brother's final missive. Mike's letter from the bank's safety box said he'd hidden crucial information in the one place nobody would think of and Cole never wanted to see again—a whistlestop called Dresden, Wisconsin. Or was it *her* he never wanted to see again? Love can be messy sometimes, like a Pandora's box better left behind with the lid slammed shut.

Stumbling on the cinders, Cole quickly scrambled up, shoving the backpack in place. The mementos inside included the papers and a map Mike had left him in the bank. Cole was loathe to return to Dresden, a patch of northwoods filled with bears...and *her.*

She'd be a woman now, past innocence. Probably married to the richest man in town, with the big house and kids, volunteering in the church and school. Not involved with trouble anymore.

A muffled click echoed through the fog. A gun being cocked? Or was it only tons of metal adjusting its own weight on the tracks?

If the hitmen didn't splice him, the trains might.

Perspiration trickled down the back of his neck.

Footsteps crunched nearby, planted step by step in the cinders.

Cole felt his way along the boxcar, fingers feverishly scrabbling along dew-studded steel. He found the front corner of the car, straddled the coupling, then leaped across two sets of rails.

Sweat bathed him now, dripping off an eyebrow. His thoughts mutated strangely, back to glimpses of a sun-drenched meadow—anything but this railyard—and him and her, laughing, wearing nothing but the sunshine's sheen, glorying in that limbo between adolescence and adulthood.

How would she look and sound after fifteen years?

He'd changed a lot. People never picked him out of his old yearbooks. He liked it that way, scars and all. Helped him keep that Pandora's box shut.

Groping alongside a boxcar, he discovered the lettering CSXT, sighed with relief, then prayed for an open door. Cole knew from his research that this line headed through Tallahassee, Pensacola, then Mobile to New Orleans. From there he'd pick up the Southern Pacific to Phoenix. He'd head for Sacramento, maybe stay a day or two there to catch a newspaper's sports page and see if anyone missed him, then double back on the northern route, loop through Chicago and up to Oshkosh riding on the Wisconsin Central.

Nobody wanting to kill him could follow that route, could they? Mike—the level-headed brother and detail man of the two Wescotts—had warned Cole constantly about hopping trains for fun. Now, instead of an adventure, this would be the ride of Cole's life.

Picking up his pace, he inspected tons of murky brown and red steel beside him on the tracks but failed to find an open cavity big enough to hide a man. The rail companies had learned to foil hobos and vandals by redesigning and enclosing train cars. He'd be lucky to find an open auto carrier where he could break in and snuggle down for a ride in a backseat.

He stopped, holding his labored breath again to listen to the night. The metallic clanks of a rail car rumbled some distance away. Sweating, he fingered Mike's hunting knife sheathed in his pocket.

Voices drifted to him through the fog.

Running again, he slipped on a wet rail but refused to fall. He clutched his chest pocket, crinkling the photo of the mysterious man who might help him avenge Mike's death. The photo had been in the lock box, right on top but with no note, as if Mike had hastily deposited it there. As if he'd been watched.

Quaking from a thousand thoughts, Cole almost slammed into a huge boxcar oozing past from out of the white soup.

"Jesus," he whispered, feet pedaling backward, his stomach churning. He swiped at the sweat collecting on his chin stubble.

Several cars slid by. Cole adjusted the backpack to one shoulder.

Voices came from the other side of the slow-moving train. It would pull away like a curtain, revealing what? A gun in his face?

Cole spun in the opposite direction and sprinted until another line of boxcars halted him. They moved laboriously. Rumbling. No open doors. No holes. Nothing to grab onto. Nothing to leap into.

Click. Ping! The cinders exploded at his feet.

He catapulted across the track, then tossed his body and backpack under a resting grain car, forcing himself to roll under and out.

Another shot split the railyard rhythms of rocking, creaking steel.

He dashed into a narrow cinder alley between two trains.

A whistle blew. Then air whooshed from brakes up ahead, and the cars next to him jerked with a deafening bang and began grinding forward.

Running hard, in time with the cranking train axles, he barely felt the bullet.

It grazed him from the left side and hit his chest pocket and right upper arm. Warmth seeped onto his skin under his shirt. He kept running.

Then a second "pop" ripped his eardrums.

A sting erupted in the calf of his right leg.

He flung himself at the side of the next car, digging his fingers into a slit in the steel to hold on, knowing he could no longer run. The moving train would have to save him.

The stench of cattle manure curled into his nostrils. The boxcar flinched, threatening to shake him off. He grabbed for any bolt, board or strap, calling on every muscle in his shoulders and forearms to drag him upward one slat at a time, despite the smarting pain making his leg feel like a cement block.

He heard a shout, and then, "Get him!"

With adrenaline engorging his arms, Cole surged up to the top edge of the moving car and then an arm dipped into hollow air. An open hatch!

To get his bearings, he clung for a moment on the top slat,

squinting over the edge to see beneath him. Seeing....

Bulls. Used-up bulls, huge beasts on their way from Florida ranches to who knows where and what, their graying muzzles adding steam to the fog, their pointed horns decidedly uninviting.

Another gunblast chinked the steel near his butt.

Cole swung up and over, diving through the hatch and into the fray of hide and horns...and yet one more Cole Wescott adventure.

LAUREL HASTINGS gloried in the peacefulness of her surroundings. She'd lived all her life in the woodland of northern Wisconsin and it never ceased to please her sensibilities.

She stood in the screened breezeway behind her cabin proper, drawing in a lungful of crisp night air, and listening, holding tight to a wiggling bundle in her arms.

Years ago, the piney smells of night, the maple leaves rattling on a breeze and the low call of nighthawks had been her healing salve. Now, she simply counted them as part of her home decor. Some people's houses sported designer wallpaper and sound systems. Her ambiance came from merely opening windows or walking outdoors.

Laurel watched a June bug walk down the outside of her breezeway screen. A breeze off Spirit Lake caught tendrils of her waist-length hair, tickling her sweater sleeves and fluttering about the little one she cradled, reminding her that June was hurrying on and wild animals needed time to run, time to mate and time to raise a family before autumn's howl set in.

It was late, maybe midnight, maybe more morning. She never kept track of time in conscious ways anymore. She rarely turned on a light in the dark. To check the sun's position against a watch, or to scar the night with high wattages seemed rude to the natural course she'd allowed her life to take. The darkness meted out protectiveness, and a world that followed a slow, meandering pace she enjoyed immensely. Her animals needed that peace, too.

As a wildlife animal rehabilitator, she was often rousted from bed at odd hours. Time and lamplight didn't matter when her heart quickly hurried her into the outdoors to tend to animals in need. Wounded animals needed darkness and quiet in order to heal.

Tonight, Sheriff John Petski had called and asked her to check out a possible trapped and hurt animal, reported to him by tourists on a late-night nature walk who heard horrible screechings at the old mansion across the bay. Laurel thought of herself as brave and strong, but the idea of going near that abandoned three-story Victorian always brought a shiver over her.

She glanced at the eyesore across the bay. Moonlight glinted in her eyes, but it reflected off the round, porthole window in the third story of the clapboard and shuttered hulk.

She would never have moved out here, right across from it, except that her father had built this cabin years ago and it remained perfect for her needs in sheltering wild animals away from people noises. The breezeway connected her cabin to the animal shed, a busy place full of life in comparison to what stood across the bay.

The boarded up mansion had been abandoned for years. Most of the windows were broken, save the round one at the top. Moonlight played off the round window like the eerie, watchful beam of a lighthouse. Behind the old glass, though, her imagination always saw eyes looking at her from the past, reminding her that under the cloak of contentment, Laurel Hastings was as much an empty shell as the old house.

Tonight she put on a defiant, wicked grin and thrust her chin at the old place. She'd finally convinced the town board and sheriff to have it officially condemned and then razed. Still, a bone-chilling loneliness, a sense of loss, washed across her when she imagined the old place wiped away. She had been inside that sprawling house years ago, when it thrived with cookie smells and rhyming ditties, sounds of dishes clattering in the big kitchen, and laughter. *His laughter.* She forced her gaze away.

She peered down at the ball of red fur in her arms and hugged it.

"You're coming along just fine, Rusty. Soon I'll let you go live where you belong."

The young fox seemed to sense it and burrowed his nose into her heavy sweater.

Laurel laughed. "None of that, Rusty. I admit you may have gotten a little soft living here these past weeks, but you'll do fine. Just don't go getting caught in a trap again. Lucky for you, old Slater Johnsrud found you when he was out looking for that loose cow of his."

For close to eight years Laurel had operated the wildlife rehab center from this base in the northern Wisconsin forest. The profession proved to be a savior. After losing too many loved ones in a short span of years, she needed a bright spot of hope, a respite from relationships with men.

Laurel's heart still recalled the sense of betrayal, but she wasn't one to dwell on the negatives. She even smiled now, her cheekbone sensing the rapid heartbeat of the baby animal in her arms. It needed her. She was continually awed by the definition of love. At times love demanded so little, like simply a cuddle. And now, even scientists confirmed that the sense of touch, of being close physically held magic to prolong lives and cure illnesses.

Weekends were her busiest time for administering her special sense of touch. Those special days bustled in a tourist area like northern Wisconsin. Road traffic increased, and she'd invariably receive from some good samaritan a dog or raccoon that had been hit. Her Saturdays and Sundays often found her setting broken bones while other people lazed about in fishing boats or went water skiing, hiking or tracking the area's burgeoning but small wolf and elk populations.

After settling Rusty back in his cage, she went back to the cabin to trade her bulky sweater for a more serviceable sweatshirt that wouldn't snag—no telling what she'd find out there tonight—and lined windbreaker. She'd need the windbreaker to ward off the chill of the fog they invariably got each night and morning, a fog seeping in already, filling in the edges of the shadows.

She headed down the incline to the dock. Nighthawks crisscrossed overhead as always, their quiet screeching calls singing in a rhythm like a mother's lullaby.

Laurel climbed in the boat, her boots clunking against the aluminum, its sound echoing back across the bay. She lived on the densely-wooded north finger of Spirit Lake, the area's longest and deepest lake. Her cabin sat five miles up from the summer tourist haven of Dresden. The lake spread seven miles farther south of Dresden and abutted the national forestland along most of its southern shoreline.

Laurel untied the second rope, tossed it in the small craft, then settled next to the small trolling motor, her eyes scanning the open lake.

She eagerly awaited springtime with its wakeup call to life. Everyone she loved had died during snowcover. She tolerated the long winter, which lasted here through April, but she was always eager for Mother Nature to flick her apron at the last gasp of cold air. Like an obedient child, winter stepped aside overnight to let the verdant flush of summer dance into the room with fern fronds unfurling and unruly bear cubs tumbling out behind new fawns. She got almost giddy with nature's transformation. Close to happy. Certainly contented.

She was about to crank the motor when she paused to smile at a train whistle echoing through the woodland. The Wisconsin Central skirted about a mile south of here and always signaled its approach to the trestle spanning the Deer Creek gorge. The whistle blasted again, long and mournful, yet soothing. Trains flowed on, as did the current in the lake, as had Laurel in the past fifteen years. Nothing could shake her peaceful existence anymore.

She yanked the motor's rope. After a cough and a sputter, the engine slow-danced Laurel across the moonlit bay, its waters glassy quiet. Even the fish slept. She kept watch over this environment for Jim Swenson, the local agent of the Department of Natural Resources. Jim often brought her the animals that needed tending, but she and Jim also worked together on a variety of projects. She was proud of spearheading the construction of the new drainage ponds next to the farmland upstream in order to improve the quality of the lakewater. As a thank you, the state had recently honored her with a plaque from the governor and a grant of money to re-establish native aspen and birch groves along Spirit Lake by fall, a project Jim would oversee. One of those groves would replace the hateful old mansion, the only scar remaining from what happened fifteen years ago.

She eased the boat into the shoreline just below the mansion. A few old posts from a dock still swayed in the water, defying rot and nature. She planned to remove them after the fire department burned down the clapboard mess.

Climbing out, she grabbed the boat's rope, then struggled up the steep, grassy embankment to loop the rope on a scraggly sumac bush.

As Laurel reached the top of the embankment, two orphan raccoons she'd raised last summer tumbled through the tall, weedy grass of what was once a finely-groomed yard to greet her.

"Roxy. Roger. You heard my old motor, didn't you? It's good to see you."

She didn't touch them, knowing they were mostly wild creatures now and could nip at her. If they were completely wild, she would harbor fear of them coming at her, not only because of rabies. Raccoons were actually fierce animals. They'd been known to turn on even the biggest dog attempting to tree them and kill the dog. Now though, the half-tame, half-wild Roxy and Roger stood on their hind legs, stretching their front paws up expectantly.

"No more treats from me. You have to work for a meal now. Scoot. Go find some yummy snails or minnows to dine on."

Seeing she meant to disappoint them, they plunked themselves on all fours and tumbled off through a deer trail in the waist-high scrub and grass. Since the path led toward the mansion, Laurel followed.

Finally standing at the bottom of the front steps, she crossed her arms, rubbing her hands up and down her arms, shuddering at the round window three stories above. From this angle, it was but a slice, dark and bleak. Abandoned. She understood such a thing. Another chill riddled her, but intent on seeking out the reported injured animal, she stepped up to the front door under the verandah.

The floorboards swayed and squeaked, but she heard no other noises from within. She found the carved wood door still solid, and the sheriff's condemnation sign hung on it from a small nail.

Just as she was about to shoulder open the door, Roxy and Roger scurried back around her feet, fussing in agitation.

"What's the matter—"

A man's faint cursing drew her gaze to the overgrown gravel lane. She ducked down, her nerves prickling, on alert. She then peeked over the tops of the dried grass and brush pressing against the verandah's railing.

In the meager light, the man limped along, a tall silhouette above the brush, with broad shoulders outlined in the moonlight. The breeze caught shaggy shoulder-length hair. He continued cursing at the brush slowing his progress, flailing at it with a knife that glinted haphazardly with his movements.

Laurel crouched lower. She had to get out of here and call the sheriff.

The man moaned, his guttural curses scratching the quiet before he disappeared from Laurel's view.

She slipped inside the front door, figuring she'd go through the house, skirt around back and escape in her boat. Finding a deadbolt handle, she turned it to lock the door behind her, but its loud screech terrified her. Had he heard her?

Kneeling, she peered through the slit between the windowsill and the plywood boarding up the window.

Still yards away, the man limped into shorter grass and proceeded to pull up a pant's leg and poke with the knife at rags wound around shin and calf. He cursed again.

When he stood straight again, moonlight etched deep lines on his face. He inspected the knife, a dagger really, probably with a college degree in sharpness.

Stumbling backward, Laurel stepped on a loose floorboard, flailed out to grab anything, but felt the next board give way and send her lickety-split downward through the floor.

COLE HALTED. Pain raged in his leg, but he swore he'd heard something odd beyond the blood pounding in his head. The damn nighthawks seemed to always cry out just as his head pain crescendoed.

The flesh of his calf wanted to explode. Hopping on and off trains for a week had aggravated the wound miserably. To top it off, getting off the Central a few minutes ago had proven almost fatal. He'd leaped too soon past the trestle over the gorge and rolled all the way down to the creek. The icy water soaked through the rags wrapped around his bad leg, chilling him to the bone and adding more pounds of weight for him to drag. He'd struggled for what seemed hours to get back up that bank. Now his shoulder, which had been healing nicely, also burned with the sensation of hot needles shooting back and forth. *Yeah, Mike, I admit it, buddy, hopping trains is dangerous. No wonder it's not covered by HMOs.*

Tired, he could barely focus his eyes. Was it the right place? He hadn't expected something quite this rundown. In the dark it appeared gray, devoid of life and personality, as Cole felt right now. Didn't it used to be yellow with white trim and green shutters? A couple of shutters clung to some second-story windows, waiting to fall like leaves in the next big wind. And where was that corner post on the verandah? The one... he and a red-haired soulmate would run at, catch and twirl around before flinging themselves out into the lawn?

His heart pounded a ragged beat.

This was the place. *Why Mike? Why make me come back here?*

He looked up, raking a hand through his long hair, detecting a burr or two he'd have to contend with later. But they didn't cause the flinch at the corner of his mouth, or the tug in his chest.

The third-story window was intact. He smiled.

When they were tikes, he and Mike called that room their pirate ship. A flash of blue light hit the window, then thunder rolled from off in the distance, and for an instant, he remembered a pair of fiery emerald eyes and a sea of red hair. They hadn't meant to roll her daddy's new Olds in the ditch, but she'd been laughing at the breeze coming in through the windows. Like him, she loved to go fast. With everything.

He broke out in a cold sweat.

Then an icy raindrop knifed the back of his neck, resurrecting the ache in his leg that proceeded to ripple across his weary hide. He groaned. Just what he needed—the dampness from cold rain and wind to keep him miserable down to his bone marrow. At least he'd have a roof over his head tonight. He'd suffered with less amenities in the past week, starting with perching his butt on the hip of a dancing bull and balancing there for a night that stretched forever.

Retrieving his backpack from the grass, he tossed it at the front door, then tried to step up the front steps. To his frustration, the pain in his leg buggered him so much the right leg went limp, giving way under his weight. Without a railing he was reduced to crawling and dragging himself up the steps and across the splintery boards on his knees.

Once at the door, he grabbed the doorknob and used it to help himself stand again. His throbbing leg wobbled, threatening to topple him. He had to do something about the leg, and soon, but he couldn't afford the time until he retrieved whatever was inside this house.

He leaned his face close to the sign. Then scoffed. So the place was condemned. Surprising, and perfect.

Cole had assumed the family sold the property long ago. Hadn't his great-aunt Flora Tilden gone to the quiet retirement home shortly after the trouble involving Cole? Out of embarrassment?

The surprise of it aside, the condemnation was also perfect because nobody would be bothering him while he searched for Mike's evidence that would confirm his killer. Cole'd be in and out of here within hours, undetected and alive. He wanted the betrayer and murderer to become fishbait for what he'd done, for ripping out the hearts of Mike's lovely wife and kid left in the wake. And he'd gotten away with it. Cole Wescott intended to change that.

The breeze switched, colder, gustier. His leg's calf muscle seized up, and to touch it felt like he was hammering spikes into the bone. He slammed a fist against the door, leaning his weary body into it, stretching the leg. Finally, the pain subsided enough to turn the front door's knob.

But the wood wouldn't budge. His shoulders sagged. Not a single thing about this trip had gone right. Why start now, he groaned inwardly. Then he noticed the plywood on the nearby window looked loose. With his good arm, he ripped it off its rusted nails, but the effort of crawling over the sill just about made him want to cut his right leg off.

A rolling thunderclap hurried the moonlight behind a curtain. With it pitch black, he edged toward the front door to get his bearings, but a board creaked underfoot.

And a voice cracked, "Watch out—"

He spun around.

"—for the hole!"

Too late. His trip across country just got worse.

Chapter 2

LAUREL WATCHED in horror when the body fell through the half-light of the hole in the floor above her. The man bounced on the same stack of boxes she'd hit, but he tumbled off cockeyed and his head hit the floor with a crack.

She inched toward him, then thought better of getting too close. She remembered the knife. In the dark, the man lay like an inky, twisted pile of laundry. He smelled of oil and creek clay, and danger.

Backing up, she pulled at the boards on the cellar steps until she found a loose one. Yanking it up, she held the two-by-four in front of her like a baseball bat before shuffling toward him.

An occasional flicker of lightning made him look...dead.

Kneeling, she still held the board in one hand but laid a finger on his neck to check him. He moaned and she shrunk back, her heartbeat kicking in faster. She gripped the two-by-four with both hands, wiggling it in front of her.

His eyelids flickered open. "What," he said in a scratchy whisper, "the hell happened?"

Laurel didn't like the way he squinted out from under hair and mud with one eye, its white orb almost disembodied in the darkness of the basement. The other eye remained closed.

"What're you doing here? Who are you?"

He growled, "I could ask the same of you."

He attempted to roll away from her. Was he getting up? Panicking, she snapped, "Don't move."

"A friendly B & B you run here."

"Don't mess with me. Now where's that knife?"

He coughed, but she stood her ground, brandishing the two-by-four. Nerves jangled her stomach. Her eyes roved over his inky visage, searching for the knife. He'd landed with the bad leg askew and the good leg twisted back from the knee. He didn't seem inclined to answer her, if his low moan meant anything.

Her doctoring instincts getting the better of her, she offered, "Throw away your knife and I'll help you with that leg."

"Throw away my only weapon?" he muttered. "I sure as hell wouldn't do that with you standing over me with a piece of lumber. You going to stand all night like that?"

Something about his wryness stirred her insides to attention. There was a familiarity. Had she encountered him before? Was he that wretched railroad hobo from last year with the bad teeth come back to beg again? She shivered. All the more reason to hang tight to her weapon. "What if I do?"

He lay back, a hulking shadow, crooking an arm across his eyes before groaning again. She didn't know what to make of him, other than he was hurting and needed help. She stepped toward him.

"Get away!" he barked.

She snapped her weapon into place, but then a groan oozed out of him with more anguish attached to it than Laurel could take.

She lowered her voice, as she always did when approaching a vicious animal with its paw caught in a trap. "What's wrong with your leg?"

"Nothing an amputation couldn't cure."

"Let me look at it."

"In this light?"

Lightning flickered a blue wash across them, reflecting in the centers of his eyes, like the moon would do on the round window high above them. She shivered at the strange familiarity.

He tried to pull himself up but only managed to hit his head against the back wall. His cry of pain was so sharp it forced Laurel to ignore his warning look. Dropping the two-by-four with a clunk on the cement floor, she rushed to his twisted leg and unfolded it for him.

"Ouch, damn you," he growled, "I said get away."

Wary of the still-hidden knife, she retreated to sit on a stairstep. She clung to her two-by-four again, watching.

He lay with his eyes closed for what seemed like forever. She held back a dozen questions. Who was he? Where had he come from? How had he gotten so seriously hurt? Gooseflesh prickled across her skin. Maybe she didn't want to know anything.

Between clenched teeth he finally said, "We can't get out, can we?"

"I tried the cellar door already."

"No knob."

"How'd you know?"

His sigh unnerved her more. "Because I happen to identify with old rusted things falling off right now, okay? My leg's next. Watch out when it rolls your way."

She flinched at his grisliness, backing her seat up to the next wood step away from him, trying to think of a way out. The boxes were empty cardboard, too old and weakened by the dampness to let her stack them and climb back through the hole. The door above her wouldn't budge. There had to be a way.

He grumbled, "At least you don't talk much."

The scratchy assuredness of his voice caught her off-guard again. It pricked her memory, bothering her. Had this man perhaps asked her for the time sometime on the street? Had he been following her? Stalking? She clung to the two-by-four. "I'm known for my quiet bedside manner."

"A doctor?"

"Actually, I patch animals. I was out here looking for a wounded and trapped animal."

"I ache, I can growl and I'm stuck in a basement. Do I qualify for your HMO?"

She almost smiled. "If you were a raccoon, I might know how to treat you. I can get you to the hospital though."

"No thanks," he grunted.

Laurel grunted right back. "It's a free service for people like you."

"People like me?"

"People in need. Down on their luck."

"Yeah, that's me," he sighed.

The sophisticated timbre of his lowered voice niggled its familiarity at her again.

Thunder rumbled, punishing the old house above their heads. Its wood creaked. A loose shutter rattled.

"Damn storm," he said. "But then I love being drenched and having that barometric pressure shoot pins up my leg."

The sarcasm again.

"I call storms heavenly bread-making. The sky's gathering up all that humidity like my mother gathers up the edges of bread dough, pounding and pounding at it until it gives up. We get a lot of 'em this time of year. You got a headache?"

"Thanks for reminding me. Almost forgot it with all your attempts at poetry making me hungry."

"Are you always this rude?"

"So shoot me. Everybody else has had a shot."

For a long time then, darkness stretched on with the loaded minutes, with her watching him while a storm built above them outside. When lavender and blue hues flashed down the hole in the ceiling, she tried to get a better look at him. Fairly large man. Long legs. Filthy dirty. Smudged, bewhiskered face.

She almost jumped when he whispered, "You going to heal me by staring at me?"

He closed his eyes again, bedeviling her with his nonchalance. She clutched the board harder.

She waited for him to rouse himself again, but he'd either fallen asleep or passed out from his pain. The latter worried her.

At a hint of a snore, she shuffled over one footstep at a time, keeping the board in one hand just in case he came to and lunged at her with the knife, wherever it was. Wiping a hand against her pant's leg, she lowered her palm, waiting for a lightning flash. When it came, she found his forehead. He was burning up!

Concerned, she ran her fingers over his nearest hand to check his body temperature. The back of his hand was broad, the knuckles roughened with scratches, as were the long and sinewy fingers. They were icy cold. She thought about picking up the hand and blowing her warm breath on the fingers, but then fear gripped her. He could wake up and grab her too easily.

Then, when his breathing grew shallower, her ingrained need to help the injured—no matter how dangerous they might be—drove away the fear. She put down the two-by-four weapon, lifted his hands one by one, sandwiching them between her own to blow gently on them. He slept on, obviously exhausted, a slight snore punctuating the night between the thunder now and then.

Outside, rain spattered the house. A chilly breeze dropped down from the gaping hole. June nights in northern Wisconsin could still dip to near-freezing temperatures. A quick shiver rippled through her. She'd seen enough sick animals die of hypothermia to know this man was in danger of the same thing. If he were a bird, she'd cradle him in her hands to warm him.

She refused to be defeated. The boxes almost spoke to her, and she groped at them in the darkness, ripping them apart into flat sheets before piling them in a double layer over his feet and legs and chest. She sneezed at their mustiness, and when he didn't wake up, she eased a couple of box flaps under his head to cushion him.

She fumbled for his jacket's zipper, to make sure he was zipped against the cold. When her hands slid underneath the fabric, its fine texture and that of the shirt underneath made her pause. This man couldn't be a hobo, could he? They didn't usually dress this well.

She leaned close to him, taking another hard look at his face between flashes of the storm. With muddied whiskers, hair plastered on his forehead and more creek mud everywhere else, he looked ghoulish. Touching his hands again, their coldness gave her the creeps. She could not let this man die, whoever he might be.

With quick resolve and knowledge of outdoor survival tactics, she stripped off her jacket, laid it over his chest and snuggled into the crook of his shoulder to share her heat. She drew the sheets of cardboard up over them again, then reached out to secure the two-by-four into one hand.

His oily train smell begged her to sneeze. She held her nose until the urge passed. His bristly chin scratched her forehead.

His heartbeat almost roused her out. It pulsated strong in her ear, replete with life pouring into her in an unsettling way she hadn't expected. She had forgotten what it was like to fall asleep next to a man's heartbeat. It soothed.

And scared her. No way could she let herself fall asleep next to a drifter with a knife.

But his hurt—the pain in that familiar voice—spoke to her across the quiet. She hated listening to the wail of pain, especially when it reminded her of the nightmares men had caused her in the past.

She wasn't about to sleep. Fixing up his leg as best she could would speed him on his way in the morning. The more she thought about that, the more the idea took hold.

As she eased out from under their shared jacket and cardboard, reality set in: She was about to "pat down" this man for his weapon.

Then she recalled the deep timbre in the voice, the hint of cockiness in the words he chose. She squinted again at his long form splayed before her, his heartbeat still booming in her brain's memory. Her own heart swelled to match the beat, searching for the memory of the feel of nighttime with a man, when a woman eased alongside him in bed, and peace stole over with the breeze rustling the curtains of her cabin window.

And that's how she'd been betrayed before. By falling for the neediness in a man. She sucked in her breath, held it, let her lungs burn her back to reality before she took a more even draught of air.

The reality was, she reminded herself, that this was a giant of a

man, a rude, strange man. *Who has a knife.*
And you better well find it before morning.

WHEN COLE jerked awake, fear blasted a cold wind through him.
Disoriented, he thought at first his boss had tossed him in a dungeon.
Where was he?

Then he heard shallow breathing, felt lips fluttering ever so softly
against his neck. He tensed. Ah, yes, now he remembered the woman
with the lumber aimed at his head. So what the hell was she doing
sleeping in the crook of his shoulder?

Turning his head, he narrowed his eyelids at the woman. Dawn
brought with it a meager shaft of light through the hole in the floor
above them. When his gaze caught the soft tilt to the eyebrows and the
lush lips, perspiration beaded his forehead.

Was it really her? Couldn't be.

When the vague scent of wildflowers in her hair tossed his
memory back to a meadow of long ago, he thought he might be having
a heart attack.

This was no stranger at all. He had to get the hell out of here. And
fast.

Escape remained elusive. He lay for a long time looking over at
the impossibly high hole in the basement ceiling, knowing the door was
jammed and his leg hurt like hell. When Laurel finally stirred, Cole
closed his eyes and turned his face away, pretending to sleep. He could
not allow her to recognize him.

She left his side, and when the steps creaked, he watched her
climb the cellar stairs and try the door again. He turned his head away
just before she crept back down.

He waited for her to come look at him, to recognize him and
explode. Instead, he heard her...jumping? Flickering an eyelid half
open, he spied her leaping at the opening in the floor above.

Was it really Laurel? Now he wasn't sure. Fifteen years changed
people, especially if they started out gangly as teenagers. This woman
wasn't gangly. She was, well, curvier and he wished she'd quit
jumping up and down that way. It was enough to cause him a
meltdown.

The hair confused him, too. This woman's dark, flowing velvet
curtain of red hair—get a grip, man—defied the short-cropped carrot-
top he remembered. His Laurel had sported hair so short she could
have snuck onto a boys' softball team, and she was the kind to do it.

And where was the cussing? His Laurel would have been jawing up a storm of expletives at not being able to reach that broken floorboard hanging over the beam up there. Maybe it wasn't Laurel. He hoped. He kept his eyes averted, half-hidden.

He cleared his throat, and she glanced over, his heart skidding to a momentary halt. With hair spilling over a shoulder, hands resting on slim, bluejean-clad hips, and squared shoulders barely holding up an oversized blue sweatshirt, this version of Laurel looked seductive. Scary. The freckles were gone, but there was no mistaking those emerald eyes. They had meant business when they snagged his attention fifteen years ago and they meant business now.

She asked, "Could I use your belt, please?"

Her soft-spoken voice caught him off-guard. Maybe this wasn't Laurel. His Laurel had always commanded and teased, bubbling with energy. This woman was sedate, controlled, some animal doctor or lion tamer thing she'd said. His head hurt. Did growing up change people this much? It did. All he had to do was look at himself. With the way she glanced at him, all businesslike, he could tell she didn't recognize him either.

Still, a bundle of nerves inside his gut said to keep his voice raspy and low, disguised. "Why do you need my belt?"

"If I can hook that flooring screw up there with the buckle, I might be able to pull myself up. I'll call the sheriff for help to come help me get you outta here."

Panic stunned him to silence surer than her two-by-four ever would. Sheriff? Not John Petski, he hoped. There was still that matter of the banged up mailboxes from fifteen years ago festering in Cole's brain. He'd been asked to leave town so fast he hadn't settled the damages. He didn't doubt there might be an old warrant for his arrest still floating around on the sheriff's desk.

She stood there with her hand out, waiting, not amused by his reticence. Heat washed down his half-hidden face.

He struggled to sit up but the world took on an unexpected spin. It spun Laurel right to him.

"Lay back," she said, gently pushing him down to the floor. He quickly turned his head away from her. She fussed some more. "I didn't mean for you to get up so fast. You knocked your head good last night and you're bound to have a doozy of a headache."

That wildflower essence hit him again, shuffling the heat from his face down the rest of him. His head rested on a stack of old cardboard she must have fashioned into a pillow sometime during the night. Her hands seemed everywhere at once, fluttering like butterflies. She laid her jacket in place again, patting and tucking it over his shoulders and arms and smoothing it down his chest and belly. A slight tightening gripped his groin.

"You warm enough?" she asked.

"Sure," he grunted, thinking an icy splash of that creek water he'd fallen into would feel good about now.

He didn't remember Laurel being the fussing kind and it kept niggling at him how much she'd changed. She'd been a tomboy, damnit. Fun and giggly. Never serious. This woman had a two-by-four weapon within reach somewhere and a focused demeanor to match.

She sent a furtive glance right at his belt buckle. "May I?"

More heat waves crashed over him until they settled in one delicate spot. Suddenly the tightening there told him he didn't want her long fingers filching for a belt.

"You sure your idea will work?" he grumbled.

"You think I'm too heavy for the belt?"

Now that was the sassiness he remembered. "It's an old belt. And it's seen a lot of country."

"An expensive one, too. Nice feel to the leather."

"How did you—"

"Now give it up. I'll buy you a new one." Before he could protest more, she'd unbuckled him and he was forced to finish the job or suffer embarrassment.

She set about tossing the belt buckle at the broken boards above them. She was tireless, which impressed Cole, but she needed more height. Cole rolled out of his makeshift nest and lumbered up. The world tipped, but he fought to steady himself.

She picked up the two-by-four weapon and glowered at him. Cole looked down at her, a surprise itself. As teenagers they were about the same height. Right now she didn't seem to appreciate the growth spurt that had hit him back then. Her weapon wiggled back and forth, right under his nose as if it were an irritating mosquito, something else irritating he didn't like about Wisconsin's northwoods.

He turned away to pick up her jacket from his makeshift bed, then dangled the jacket off the end of his outstretched arm.

"Here," he growled, "put it on. You'll catch cold."

She snatched the garment away, then waved the board at him. "Go sit down."

"I could hoist you up closer."

"You're weaving like a drunk."

"Did we drink last night?" Muzzy, he squinted at her. "What did we do last night?"

Her face squirreled up in repugnance. "Absolutely nothing and that's the way I liked it, thank you very much."

"But I am listing to the starboard side a bit much."

"Just don't fall," she snapped. "Not after all I've gone through to make sure you survived the night."

So she took her doctoring seriously. She was worried about his health. He was right up there with some vermin she healed on other days of the week. That amused him, but confound it, he had to get rid of her before she discovered who he was.

Again she set to slapping the belt up at the screw sticking out of the crossbeam. She said, "Please. Sit down. I'll be out and back with help in a jiffy."

"Won't be necessary. I was just passing through."

"More like dropping in."

He wanted to chuckle in the worst way, but restrained himself. Instead, he lunged to catch the belt. When he did, she stiffened, stumbling away from him, almost tripping over her two-by-four. Grimacing against a sharp pain in his leg, he stooped over and picked up the board, tossing it to her. "You forgot something. Didn't mean to scare you."

She wiggled the board menacingly at him. "Keep your distance."

"Look. I'm not going to hurt you. I want outta here too."

Finally, her shoulders rose and fell in a sigh. "Okay."

If she recognized him, she sure played it cool. His whooziness returned, but he gritted his teeth against the temptation of mentioning anything that might draw her close to his face again.

He said, "I'll hoist you up. You find that screw or something to grab onto. Then use this shoulder to step on." He nodded toward his healthy shoulder.

She stepped over, her head at an odd tilt when she looked at him. Following his orders, though, she allowed him to lift her, all that sweet, thick hair of hers showering back into his face, making him smile.

Soon she peered back down from above, freed. "I'll go get some tools to undo that door," she said, her hair raining down over one shoulder at him.

Afraid she'd bring that sheriff, he sniped, "No!"

She sucked in her breath. Her wildflower smell wafted over him again, almost buckling his knees. Not daring to look up into her face, he said, "Get my knife. I left it with my backpack on the verandah."

"So that's where it is."

A fever slammed through him again like a Florida hurricane. "Sounds like you had busy hands while I slept."

She blushed. "Oh, don't worry. Everything was strictly professional. What do I do with the knife?"

"That door is probably swollen. If you can pry the knife in, I might be able to bust the door loose by pushing at it from this side. Try the hinges, too. See if you can loosen them with the knife."

"You can't make it up those steps and shove at that door without falling."

"Then you hop back down here, lift me up through the hole, and you can shoulder the door while I carve."

"Very funny. I was concerned for your health."

"Are you always this worried about an old hobo? Your life can't be that dull, lady."

She quickly looked away, but he'd seen the odd wince tie up the corner of her mouth before she could stop it. He found that reaction curious, but then her shoulders grew rigid again. "I want you out and on your way, is all. I've got better things to do with my life than watch you hit your head on the cellar floor. You're filthy and you don't belong here."

For some reason, her brusqueness wounded him. He grumbled at her though, "All the women tell me that."

"Stuff it," she said, almost sounding the way he remembered her. He grinned to himself.

The cellar door soon budged for them, and Cole staggered onto the verandah but she quickly stood sentry in the weedy yard, clutching his knife, her eyes wide with fright again.

Never in his life had his mere presence frightened a woman. As a speedboat racer spending plenty of time on famous beaches, he was used to the opposite reaction from women.

He couldn't take his eyes off the way the morning's rays set her hair aflame. She was a treasure. Or a Pandora's box, he reminded himself. Don't touch. *She's not the reason you're here, buddy. You don't want to hurt her. Don't get her involved.* Except to help his head. It ached right now. Bigtime.

"Do you have any aspirin on you?" he asked.

"I could take you to Dresden in my boat," she said, to his surprise.

"No thanks." He didn't need to accidentally run into her father or the sheriff. Another Pandora's box.

"A fever with that leg isn't something to ignore."

"I'll give it a good dunking in the cold lake. That should do the trick."

Aghast, she lowered the knife a little. "That won't keep the swelling down forever."

He grunted, keeping his voice low. "I'll catch some rest and be on my way. A few days okay?"

"Better make it sooner than that," she said, gesturing with the knife.

"And why's that?"

"Because the fire department's coming out soon to burn this place down. They're just waiting for the final say-so from the sheriff and a local attorney."

His brain came alert. The condemnation sign. "When?"

"They could choose to burn it just about any day now. It has to be gone before the end of summer."

His mind raced. Any day? What if he needed more time? And what about the legal papers on this place, folded now in his pack next to him? Come to think of it, he hadn't read them carefully. He assumed Mike knew what he was doing. Would he have to see this sheriff after all, and now an attorney?

Panicked, Cole fished for information. "Doesn't somebody own the place?"

She scoffed and pulled her jacket closer around her, the knife still in her hand. "An older lady owned it a long time ago, but she's dead now. There's been plenty of public notice in the papers, but nobody wants to pay the back taxes for, well, that thing."

The hand with the knife jabbed at the rotting house. Her obvious disdain for the property ruffled him. Didn't she remember how it used to look? He wanted to ask, but couldn't. Then there was his pride. This house had been in his family. Great-aunt Flora Tilden had come to them via a brief marriage, but still, she had been shirt-tail relation.

He probed some more, playing the innocent. "The old woman, she lived alone? No relatives to pay the taxes?"

"Nobody who cares."

That stung. Instinctively, Cole knew she wasn't condemning just a house. She was condemning his whole family. No. Try him. Just him. Guilt rose and he wanted to rush off the verandah, take Laurel in his arms and explain away the years. But he couldn't. He didn't want to drag her into his messed up life again.

She turned and started a stiff walk through the tall grass and brush, fading into the mist hanging over the lake.

Clenching his jaw against the pulsations in his leg, he limped after her. Reaching the top of the embankment, he peered down at Laurel in her small craft. After three yanks, her boat coughed and started.

"Could use a tune-up." It came out of his mouth before he could stop himself. "I could do that for you."

She glanced up, scorn deepening the shadows across her eyes. "Don't hang out here. You hear me?"

A definite warning. The chill of it tightened the imaginary vise on his leg until he couldn't breathe. "A couple of days." He felt like he could sleep for a whole week.

"Two days," she snapped, turning her face back to the water. "Then I call the sheriff about your trespassing."

Then she motored away, and he watched her until she became a murky, watercolor rendition of herself. When the boat's sputtering stopped on the opposite shore, he arched a brow. So she lived in the log cabin. Alone? He remembered when her father started building it. Cole helped lay flat rocks for a walkway, but he never got to finish the job.

Fire lanced through his calf then. He leaned down...and found his leg wrapped in a woman's undershirt under his jeans. So that's what those busy hands had done last night. He shook his head, thinking about her comforting a stranger even as she must have feared for her life. Didn't she learn anything from what happened fifteen years ago?

He straightened up, turning to stare at the old house. That "thing," she'd called it. The reason he'd returned. Or was it? He could have hired a detective to scour the place first, but he hadn't.

No, it wasn't just the house he'd come back to explore. He'd come back because of his own feelings of emptiness that had gnawed at him since the day he'd left this place. Like wearing the wrong size clothes, he'd walked through life uncomfortably, making do with a murky memory that never quite allowed him to touch it.

He shivered again. Then the heat came with the new memory of the grown woman lying beside him last night.

He closed his eyes against a damnedable thought.

He wanted to take her up to the attic in that old house before him now, crush her in his arms, and kiss her until all of his ills were cured.

Opening his eyes, he looked at the decrepit house again. It was the reality. Maybe deep down, where his heart met his soul and the heat of truth was unbearable, he knew he'd wanted to see Laurel Hastings again. But she was a woman he could never have.

He swung back around to catch a last glimpse of her, but the fog had swallowed her up. Just like his dreams.

But her sweet scent lingered on the damp air, teasing him, swirling about his body, swelling him toward a new ache. How could he want her like this after so many years?

He parted his lips, tasting the soft brush of satiny fog. Tasting her.

And that would have to do. Tomorrow, he must be gone.

Chapter 3

AT HOME, LAUREL couldn't get into her usual efficient rhythm.

Out in the animal shed, she spilled water while trying to refill pans for bigger animals like Rusty and drippers for the smaller ones like the baby squirrels. She knew why she was clumsy and she hated it: that man over there. His festered leg, that fever she'd felt under her palm, his refusal to let her take him to a doctor—none of it would leave her. Especially his wry humor. And his voice...something about his voice still bothered her.

Should she call the sheriff? Should she go back over there with provisions? He needed more than aspirin. He didn't want more than aspirin. The stranger in need had tied her in knots.

She decided fixing formula for the baby squirrels would calm her. But at the kitchen counter, she glanced at the man's knife sitting there and proceeded to break egg shells into the homogenized milk. She had a devil of a time fishing them out. Then when she took the hand beater to the mixture, the bowl almost tipped over and she noticed she'd already whipped the mixture to an airy froth no baby could possibly have.

While rinsing the beater under the sink faucet, she acknowledged being rattled. "You just spent the night worrying and tending a man who hopped off a train. You have the right to feel odd this morning."

Looking back on it gave her the creeps. The drifter could have killed her.

"But he didn't," she muttered again.

He had a hint of anger about him.

"No, that was droll sarcasm." She grabbed the dish towel and dried the beater.

But he was shiftless, never looking her in the eye.

"But no, that was him squinting, a normal reaction to pain." She plunked the beater down and sagged back against the counter. "And you just left him over there? How could you do that?"

Stop being silly, she chided inwardly. She identified with anything injured, although a possible convict hopping off the train was stretching it. He may be hurting, but she didn't want any tall, muscular, dark-haired growling stranger around. And since when do you notice all that detail? Just how lonely are you, Laurel Hastings?

She shoved off the counter, tidying things, making busy work to calm herself. He didn't try to harm you, said a voice in her head. He even had a sense of humor. That thought rattled her more. What if he was just down on his luck? What about that infection he had? Blood poisoning started that way, zipped right into a person's organs, rendering the person...dead. If not tended to.

She rushed to her living room viewing scope. For wildlife watching she kept a long-barreled lens mounted on a tall tripod at the picture window overlooking the lake. She placed her eyeball into position.

She didn't see him. Relief flowed through her. Good. He heeded her warning and left. She wouldn't have to call the sheriff. She wouldn't have to—as her mother called her doctoring profession— "worry and tend."

But she worried while going about chores in the animal shed. After feeding the squirrels, she moved to Rusty's cage. The white splint reminded her of the man's leg. She tugged her lip with her teeth. Staring at Rusty, she knew the man's flesh was probably red as the animal's fur. He needed aspirin, clean bandages....

Stop it.

Why think of him? Was she stung by his refusal to let her help him to a hospital? Yes. And then there were the contradictions: gruffness sandwiched with humor; fine clothes sandwiched with hopping dirty trains.

Curiosity plagued her. On her way back through the breezeway, she noticed a plume of smoke across the way. Startled, she rushed into the house and swung her viewing scope back and forth until she spotted him. Her heartbeat came alive, but a frown followed. He nurtured a sloppy campfire one stick at a time.

"Darn it," she muttered, "stupidity sandwiched with carelessness."

Although last night's rain nourished the new green grass, the tall brown stubble left over from winter quickly dried in the warm sunshine and became easy tinder, often the cause of springtime wildfires here until the new shoots overpowered the old. His campfire could leap to life and her woodland would go up in smoke.

When a horn honked, she frowned, but went to see who was in

her yard. The sheriff. Good. He could keep an eye on the stranger. She'd spent too much "worry and tend" energy on him already.

Sheriff John Petski's grim face pushed aside her good intentions.

"John, what's wrong?" She immediately spotted the small animal cage draped with a towel and dangling off one of his stout arms.

"Got a bad one, for ya, girl." The sheriff, a fixture in town all her life and her father's best friend, could get away with calling her "girl."

He pulled the towel back off a corner. A small barn owl lay in the cage's bottom, one wing akimbo, its eyelids half shut.

Her heart leaped out to it. "What happened?"

"A camper found him lying in a puddle this morning. We had some fierce gusts last night. He's barely there, Laurel."

Laurel shoved her sleeves up. "Put him in the cage next to the hawk, but on the side with the solid wood divider so there's no fuss between them. Turn the heat lamp on for him. I'll go get a clean dropper, and judging from the size of him, I better cut up some raw beef heart and eggs, just in case that will coax him awake."

"Got it, kiddo. Hey, what kind of animal did you find over at the old mansion?"

Befuddled, she said, "There wasn't an animal. Just...an old drifter." Who wasn't old. Who didn't seem like a drifter. Yet, what else could he be?

John raised a fatherly warning finger at her. "Keep an eye on him. The world's filled with too many crazies these days. Call me first thing if he hangs around."

"Sure, John."

The sheriff strode around the cabin toward the animal shed. Laurel hurried inside, threw the chopped beef heart and eggs mixture in a bowl and took it to the living room. Stirring furiously, she leaned into the viewing scope for another peek at her other wildlife.

Her breath caught. The man seemed to be attempting to pitch a small nylon tent, though it kept flopping down. "Oh no," she groaned. "You can't stay."

She put down the owl food to go find John, but his truck already bounced down her wooded driveway. She returned to the scope but the phone rattled and she almost poked her eye out against the eyepiece.

Cradling the cordless phone between ear and shoulder, she picked up the bowl in the kitchen, mixing owl food while heading for the scope. Looking through it, she muttered vaguely, "Yes?"

"Now what kind of greeting is that for your mother? What's

wrong? I hear a scraping noise. Is there something wrong with your phone? I could dial again—"

"Mother, I'm a little busy."

"Not another new animal?"

Laurel ignored her mother's resigned tone and watched the man dip a can into the lake and haul it back up to the small campfire. "Yes. He, uh, came in with the storm."

"Then are you invitin' me out to see him, at least? It's been so long since I've been out there and I'm dying to show you the material for the rental cottage curtains."

"No. Don't come. I mean, he's, uh, not cleaned up yet. Mother, I had a long night—"

"You didn't stay up all hours again?"

"It's my job, mother. Animals call and I go."

"It'd be nice if you'd go out with friends more often. Pretty soon they're going to stop calling. What man would ever put up with..."

They had this conversation at least once a week so Laurel let her attention drift to the man who had just knocked over a pot of water onto his bad leg. She winced. He hopped around on his good leg. She grinned. So used to talking to herself, she slipped and muttered, "He's got to stay off that leg."

"What, dear? What leg? Are you talking about a bird?"

Laurel watched him flailing about like an injured bird. He gripped his bad leg and collapsed onto the ground. She sucked in her breath.

"Laurel?"

"I'm here," she muttered, but she watched the man begin working at her make-shift T-shirt bandage. His whiskery face contorted so deeply that she winced in empathy.

Her mother's voice drifted back. "...So when I get the curtains up that cottage should be rentable again."

The man dropped flat in the grass! Had he fainted?

Laurel raced to the kitchen, bowl in one hand and the phone in the other. She plunked down the bowl of owl food, then addressed the disembodied voice still talking from the receiver. "Oh, mother, I'll be in town a bit later, okay? Love you. Bye."

She grabbed clean linens and her first-aid kit. Before charging out to her boat, she called the sheriff's office. Busy signal. She called Jim Swenson's office, but was told he was out checking storm damage to a stream ten miles up the road. She left a message for him to meet her at the old house anyway, but if he couldn't, the assistant was to call 911 for her.

Racing out the breezeway and through her shed to reassure herself that the owl would live without immediate food, she ran outside and down to her dock.

Within moments, her motor sputtered and pushed her across the bay in what seemed like slow motion. The stranger's grumbly voice rose in the back of her head: "Could use a tune-up." So what did he know about boats anyway, she grumbled inwardly right back. But now she couldn't get her mind off the boat motor. The loud, coughing boat motor that needed fixing. Damn him.

Finally reaching his shoreline, she mounted the slippery embankment, grabbing at the tall grass to pull herself up. At the top, she paused again, wondering why she was courting danger. She knew why, though. She couldn't shake the feeling that there was something different about this man, including his need to keep help at a distance. Even hobos usually took a handout.

She found him a few yards in, sitting in the tall grass with his legs stretched out and his back to her. He was attempting to pull burrs out of his hair. Without a glance her way, he growled, "Get the hell home."

Her mouth went dry. So much for his sense of humor. "Sometimes it takes two hands to separate the wild animal from its trap, or the hair from the burr."

"If I had my knife, I could cut them out."

She licked at her dry lips. "You have no business with a knife that size when you're stumbling around and passing out. You could have fallen on it."

"All hail Mother Theresa," he ground out, his back to her yet.

She grew indignant, but drew in a controlling breath. "You could use her help with your leg."

"You already giftwrapped it. Now go."

"Your churlishness won't scare me."

"Are you so lonely that you have to hover around muddy strangers falling off trains?"

Heat splashed her cheekbones and then hit the pit of her stomach. "I already have one mother, thank you."

"You should listen to her. I could be a dangerous criminal."

Noticing his bare feet, she saw socks hanging nearby over a leaning spike of scrub oak brush. "Criminals don't usually bother laundering their socks. They're too busy running."

He harumphed. "Spilled the water. Then fell over the can. I'll run later."

His backward glance caught the sunlight and her attention. Whirlpools of darkness, his eyes sucked her in and for a moment she thought this a dream and they'd float into the air together. All that in his eyes. They harkened to something familiar within her, yet she couldn't put her finger on the odd feeling.

He looked away, but a bit of electricity remained behind. Something felt terribly wrong, enticing her, yet warning her. Her legs begged her to flee, but she couldn't run before getting a good look at that wounded leg. Or this man. She'd only seen him in the dark or from a distance in the fog. His sleight-of-face routine was beginning to grate on her.

Setting the towels and first-aid kit in the grass, she opened the kit. Her stomach knotted. "Damn. I forgot how low I was on gauze and smaller needles—"

"Stay the hell away from my leg with needles."

His voice had risen and the pitch haunted her. Maybe he just sounded like someone she knew in town. She decided she needed to hurry with this. She extracted the snub-nosed scissors and stared at the back of his head. "At least let me cut those burrs out of your hair before I leave."

"I said get—"

"I muzzle some of my animals to work on them safely."

He snorted. She took that as an assent and stood over him from behind with her scissors. The breeze picked up strands of his blackish hair, the sunlight mining coppery highlights in it. A chill trundled down her spine. She remembered another time, another sunlit day. She shunted the thought aside. The man was spooking her out! Where was Jim Swenson or the sheriff? She snipped under a burr with shaky scissors.

With only the robins chirping for sound, she grew uneasy. "You have a name?"

"A handle, as they say on the rails. Atlas."

"The Greek Titan, holding up the heavens?"

"No. My buddies on the rail lines found my using maps and atlases amusing."

Maps? It triggered a warning and a memory inside her.

Laurel stepped back, staring at his jet hair fluttering above the broad shoulders under his thin jacket. She didn't recognize any of it. Or did she? That voice, in its lighter tones, niggled her again.

"What did you say?" she asked, ready to listen hard, fear and anger trembling below the surface.

"My hobo buddies—"

"Stop there." Suddenly, his tone hit its mark. Queasiness rocked her.

She managed a hoarse whisper. "People use maps because they want to get somewhere. Find more adventure." Her memory dredged up an ancient globe, and a young man showing her all the places he'd lived...and would live. "People use maps to help them run away!"

Watching his back stiffen, she eased away, paralysis climbing over her heart. Ancient rages roiled about in her soul, spilling acidic adrenaline across raw nerve endings.

Between clenched teeth, she railed to the back of his head, "It *is* you!"

She flung herself at his shoulders, shoving him hard. "I never wanted to see you again! Get away from me, Cole Wescott!"

He toppled sideways in the grass to escape her blows, his jacket flying open and papers dumping from his shirt pocket.

Dropping to her knees to pummel him more, she screamed, "You bastard! Why'd you come back? Maybe 'cause you forgot something when you ran out of town fifteen years ago? Like me? Your wife?"

He snagged her wrists, and with strength that surprised her, he rolled over, stilling her on top of his heaving chest.

They lay on the ground, alone in the grass, a prelude they'd danced many times long ago one summer, but now his dark eyes were even darker than she remembered, more mesmerizing. They flung her soul back in agonizing leaps across the years, to hollowed-out nights when all she could do was wonder why he'd been able to leave her and get on with his life so easily.

Her head pounded. She wanted to spit at him. Instead, she forced out, "You're hurting me. But then you're good at that."

When his fingers loosened, she got up, backing several feet away, trying to control her shaky breathing and the palpitations of her stomach.

He got up in a slow fashion that pleased her immeasurably now, and he stayed planted where he was. "I didn't come here to find you, believe me. You're the last person I wanted to see."

Her insides shriveled. What did she expect him to say? "Tell me something new, you, you—"

"Bastard's acceptable."

How could she not have recognized those hawk-like eyes, ready to swoop...or leave at a moment's notice. He dipped his head at a rakish angle, dark brows shading his eyes while they shuttered up and down her body. Her heartbeat tripped despite her resolve. Although she hadn't recognized the man physically at first, he was smooth and that much hadn't changed.

"Don't try that cute, contrite look with me. It may have worked back then, but I'm not taken in with your kind anymore."

"And what kind is that?"

"A man who runs from his responsibilities."

"I'm in trouble this time, Laurel. Real trouble. And I'm not running away from anything, except a bullet or two."

He winced for good measure before sending his gaze to his bad leg. She didn't know what to believe. What's more, she didn't want to care. Let him fill up with infection to his eyeballs and see how it feels to have nobody care what happens to him.

She said, "You were always a trouble-maker."

"That's why we liked each other."

Liked? That's what he'd felt for her back then? Mere like? Laurel retrieved the towels back up from the grass. "Whatever it is this time, I don't want to hear it."

"We were only teenagers that summer." He hobbled toward her, a hand raking through his mass of wavy hair. "We didn't know what we were doing."

She stepped back, refusing to let the swarthy charm work on her again. "That's your excuse? Wayward kids?"

Looking uncomfortable, he asked, "Why'd you come back over here now?"

So he was changing the subject. Damn him. "I thought you might be dead by now. I see I'm too soon. I'll go back and wait."

"Still have the wildlife scope in the picture window?"

She hated that he knew her so well, that he could remember even a single element in her life that brought her pleasure. She was not interested in sharing anything pleasurable with him. Ever again.

Cradling the towels in one arm, Laurel snatched up the first aid kit from the grass. "Petski's jail hasn't changed since the day you dirtied it with your presence and he might appreciate seeing you again."

Shooting her a smoldering look, he swiped up the papers and a photo off the ground and limped over. "Here. I came back because somebody wants to kill me and harm my family, and damn it all, I won't let him destroy us."

Kill? Family? Us?

A sickening flood of numbness gripped her. He shoved the photo at her. A teenager with Cole's same piercing eyes smiled back at her. Pain spiked deep into her heart. She'd heard he'd gotten married, but a son? This old?

When she looked at him, his steady gaze unsettled her more.

"Was I the fool, Cole? You rushed out of my life back to Miami, but did you already have someone else there? Were you thinking of her when we exchanged vows here?"

His eyes deepened under the shadows of his bent brow. From his hesitation, she had answer enough.

He'd borne a son. Soon after he'd left her. At the altar. The ache stabbing her was almost unbearable.

She handed back the photo. "When was he born? And how is your wife? They don't mind you taking off for a quiet week of train hopping?" It was perverse, she knew, to jab at him, but she had to. Her heart demanded retribution.

He eased down to the ground, parting the long grass to sit. "Tyler's mother and I divorced a few years ago and we rarely see her. And he wasn't conceived until after she and I had married."

"We were married—"

"It wasn't legal. Just two kids in love with romance exchanging words in private."

Remembering him promising to make it legal, she gulped back a lump choking her throat.

He eyed her, then shook his head. Pain racked his face. She hoped it was connected to guilt. That much he owed her.

"Tyler's mother and I had known each other a long time. My parents and her parents were friends. The same social circles."

That stung. "Is that it?" She slammed down the towels and first-aid kit. "You needed the family nod before you'd marry a woman? My father would have come around, if you'd been here."

His face fell. "That wasn't it at all."

"Then what was it? Couldn't find your father to talk to him because he was over in England tending to his foodstore chain—"

"Laurel—"

"Then there was your mother's family in some wine country—"

"They lived in Chile. Damnit, I didn't have what you'd consider a normal life like you. I told you about all the traveling in my life. Stephanie was my constant during school, always there, always sure of her course in life. We'd always been friends."

Laurel's jawed clenched so tight she could barely speak. "You never mentioned this Stephanie."

"You're getting this all mixed up. She didn't matter to me. I mean, until after us."

Laurel turned away, ready to be ill. Back then, she'd built up so many scenarios to help justify her anger. Sarcastically, she said, "So you weren't seduced as part of some girl's plot to take your family money? You didn't fall for a starlet or bimbo?"

"No. I'm afraid Stephanie was what I wasn't."

"A responsible, upstanding citizen?"

"Sounds like your daddy's words."

Laurel shuddered, but turned to him, sighing when recalling her father railing at her about Cole back then. "What's wrong in wanting, no, expecting more than just hearing you'd called a couple of times? Then nothing?"

He rose and hobbled over to her until he blocked out the sun. "Whenever I made those phone calls your father got on the line," he muttered, "and told me to quit bothering you."

She stood in his shadow, shivering, angry, stricken by all the news, the flashbacks bursting like bombs in her head...and a man standing before her she didn't recognize except for those deep, dark eyes.

With a finger, he tipped her chin up. A bolt of heat shocked her from head to toe and back again. When had he gotten so tall, and even more dangerous looking? The year after he left? Or yesterday, just to niggle her with a giant ruse, another prank?

"Hey," he said, his voice husky, "I never wanted to hurt you."

Finding it impossible to breathe with him touching her, she pulled away. "What you didn't want was me. Why can't you say it instead of talking about 'what was best for me' as if I were your child? I was your...lover."

She wanted to swallow back the word. A knot had its way in her stomach. Because of him, she'd made choices to avoid putting her heart in vulnerable situations. And here he stood again.

He looked different, standing there patiently. Could she pretend he wasn't the same old trouble?

Could she believe anything he'd just told her?

She picked up her supplies again and headed toward her boat, weary, wanting to escape to the safety of her cabin across the bay. "Excuse me, but I have things to do."

"Laurel?"

The languid way her name rolled off his tongue in a husky whisper halted her in her tracks. Hearing him call to her had once signaled joy. Now, he offered nothing but confusion. She kept her back to him, afraid of looking into his mesmerizing eyes, afraid he might read the secrets of her new life and be disappointed in her. Maybe angry with her own betrayal of him. "I can't get involved in whatever you're doing here."

"I could use your help."

Anger sparked within her again. She faced him, throwing her shoulders back. "No. You're not going to use me. Not anymore."

When she began walking away, she heard him shuffling through the weeds after her. "Laurel, wait."

She picked up her pace, fear riddling her.

Then she heard him stumble. He spilled out a string of expletives that echoed across the clearing.

"Cole?" She swung around, saw the genuine pain wrinkling his whiskery face and brow, and went to him. His injuries worried her all over again, despite her resolve. Worry and tend—a reflex.

He lay in a heap, face contorted, smile now a grimace. Her makeshift bandage—her undershirt—had worked loose under his pant's leg, exposing his calf. All her experience with animals didn't prepare her for the fiery red and mottled skin swollen with infection. Cole was a strong man; he couldn't be this vulnerable. The realization stole her breath.

Gulping, she asked, "What happened to you?"

"Mike was murdered," he grunted, closing his dark eyes against pain.

"Murdered?" It lanced a shiver up and down her spine. Or was this one of his acts?

He opened one eye against the relentless sunshine, and she couldn't mistake the tortured look. "I buried Mike, Laurel. My brother is gone." She watched him torturing a hand into a fist. "Now I'm the prey."

His eyes took on the soulful, instinctual desperation she'd seen in the yellow-tinged eyes of a live wolf caught in a trap, a powerful animal rendered helpless. Needy. She believed him, but that didn't help her nerves. They turned to ice with fear.

She felt herself being sucked in here, too. Her heart flailed against him as if she were thrashing to save herself from drowning in the lake. "You? The prey? How do you know?"

"The killer's my boss."

"What?!"

"Unique downsizing concept. Instead of firing me, he decided to fire at me."

When she glowered at him, he added, "Help me, Laurel Lee."

A hitch in her heartbeat gave her pause.

Nobody had called her that since he had, long ago. *Laurel Lee.* In the meadow. Their meadow. The shrine to so much. Too much.

Against her better judgment, she lowered a plank across the moat of their history. "Let me see that leg. And then I want you to get the hell out of here and never come back."

Chapter 4

AFTER LAUREL finished ripping away the T-shirt bandage, she split the seam of Cole's pant's leg up to his knee to gain easier access to the raw flesh of his calf. A huge, festering wound threaded from the front to the back, threatening her with nausea.

"Cole, you need hospital treatment."

A hand snaked up and gripped her upper arm. "I can't risk being found out. I mean it, Laurel. Some bum with a ripped up leg with a bullet in it sounds like local front-page news to me."

Her pulse quickened under his grip. "Then I'll bring a doctor here."

"All it takes is one slip, and I'm dead. My son will never see me again. You hear me?"

Like talons his fingers dug into her, frightening her more. A shudder thundered through her. His son. How could he be involved in such danger?

"Don't, Cole. You're scaring me."

"I mean to. The man after me doesn't care who gets in his way. Listen to me or you'll get hurt."

"I don't take orders from the likes of you." All she wanted, was to run from him. Staring him down, she attempted to quell her ragged breathing, to no avail.

But something in his dark eyes twitched, and he let go of her to lay back in the grass, groaning. "Just take out the damn bullet. Now."

"I told you, I don't know if I can. You need to be in a hospital."

"You told me you doctor animals."

"All I have in the kit is a short scalpel and a tweezers. I can lance it, but I can't go digging around for a bullet—"

"You're stalling, Laurel Lee. Give me the thing."

Laurel Lee. Her heartbeat pulsated wildly. How dare he call her the endearment that used to make her giggle when he shouted silly limericks and rhymes. *Laurel Lee, come with me.* How dare he use it to attempt to get his way now, to make her stay by him.

He lunged for the first-aid kit, terrifying her. Shoving it out of his reach, she suffered the threat of his narrowing eyes, and snapped, "Don't force your danger on me, not after all these years of nothing between us."

He didn't flinch. "I have no choice."

Their gazes locked, nerves fraying, the breeze rattling the tops of the brown, dried grass against his shoulders. A crow cawed, as if to warn her to send him away. Soon. Before his gaze saw what lay in the bottom of the well inside her soul. Her own secrets. "I'll see what I can do."

He nodded, a grin of relief nudging the wide, firm mouth. "I never would have thought you the doctoring kind."

"Why not?" Her fingers quaked when she considered her task of cutting into Cole. Her Cole.

"You could never sit still for long."

"Neither could you," she said, pushing her palm against his chest. To her surprise, he obeyed and laid back in the grass.

"You used to fidget when I took you to the drive-in."

"It's long closed." She grimaced at the sore leg.

"Too bad. I would have liked to do that again—"

"You're not staying that long," she said, her heart racing. He couldn't stay. He just could not.

"And you drummed your fingers on the restaurant table because I ate too slowly."

The small talk was getting on her nerves. She reached for her scalpel and huddled over his leg. "I did it to bug you. You always ordered two desserts. No girl in her right mind could eat that much and not become wide as a barn."

"Not you, Laurel Lee. You had those skinny long legs—"

"Will you shut up, please." Now she was the one with the fever, her fingers trembling as she gently explored the mottled flesh, trying to find the entry point of the bullet. But the thought niggled her: He remembered those little things about them back then. A feathery warmth tugged at her.

"This is bad, Cole. I shouldn't try this. And you shouldn't want me to. Grab some courage and common sense and get to a hospital."

Popping up to his elbows, he spat through gritted teeth, "I don't give a damn about courage. Mike's play at being captain courageous got him killed. Just do it. All I want is justice."

Justice? It stunned her. It's what she'd dreamed of getting from him for years. The same reckless Cole still lurked under this almost unrecognizable taller, more muscular version of the man she'd fallen in love with once. Now he called recklessness, justice? Maybe he deserved the pain she was about to inflict, at his own insistence.

Sucking in a steadying breath, she poised the scalpel, her other hand gripping his cool, tanned calf muscle.

To his credit, he barely flinched when she lanced the wound. But when she wiped away festering pus and blood with a towel, making him roll over slightly to slosh disinfectant quickly behind, he howled like a dog hit by a car. "Yeoooowww, woman! Have mercy!"

"I was beginning to think you weren't human."

"Got the bullet yet?"

A sickly chill trickled through her. "Still in there."

"Get it, Laurel Lee."

She needed him fixed up and out of her life before the bad memories—and pain—began to thunder back. She knew they would, given time.

She plunged deep into the cut with a tweezers.

"Woman, what the—"

With a great sense of relief, and with the breeze cooling her perspiring forehead, she pried open one of his fists and plunked a ragged, bloody pellet into his palm.

He lolled back on the grass, still wincing. "Thank you. I think."

"You're welcome," she said, relief crawling through her.

She couldn't take her eyes off his whiskery jawline, or the firm muscles of his neck leading like steel bands to the juncture with his shoulders. Her lips parted, tingling, remembering how tentatively she'd kissed him once upon a time in the hollow of his neck. How they'd lay in grass just like this, pointing out faces in the clouds. She realized, deep down, she longed to taste his skin, his firm mouth, to lay there beside him. To compare the sensations. Then and now.

When she picked up her only needle and began poking at his flesh to suture, he cursed, "Nurse Nightmare, what tool is that? A pitchfork?"

"I usually use these on raccoons, possums and dogs. Of course, they're laid on the bench in the animal shed and knocked out with medication or tied down."

"Sounds positively comfy."

"I'll only take a couple of necessary stitches here. You need major human antibiotics and another go at those stitches with more appropriate equipment."

"Your equipment's fine, doc."

Heat flashed like last night's storm across her cheeks. "Your equipment could find itself out of order if blood poisoning sets in. You might do well to listen to me."

"Thanks, doc. Your bedside manner's improving. I'll write a letter recommending you get a raise."

His mirth and cockeyed smile pierced a part of her heart she'd closed years ago. But she refused to trust anything about him. Quickly grabbing the T-shirt and what little tape she had left in her kit, she began securing the T-shirt and a towel over the wound by winding the tape over it and around his calf.

"It'll hurt for a few days, even a week or two," she said, her fingers trembling under his watchful gaze.

"You've got a tender touch," he mused. "Always had."

The tape slipped from her hands, and she had to retrieve it from the grass. Her heartbeat sped up. "I have to go into town today. Want me to pick up anything for you? Food to replenish that pack before you move on?"

"Don't bother. I've got some dried soups."

"That's all? You expect to heal this thing on the strength of dried soup? You're pitiful, Cole, definitely no common sense."

Pushing her hands away, he finished the taping job himself. "So I'm a loser. Isn't that what your daddy predicted of me? He'd love to see me finally get that shotgun blast he was thinking about. To protect his lovely daughter."

The derision stilled the breeze.

Struggling up to one knee, he reached for his socks hanging on the nearby weeds. When he writhed in pain, her instincts made her snatch them from his fumbling hands.

She thrust him unceremoniously back onto the grass, and plunged to her knees at his feet, already readying the sock, her stomach knotting. "Damn you, Cole. If I have to dress you to get you away from me for good, I will!"

His sharp whistle stopped her as he sat up. "That's almost like the old Laurel Lee! Even had a cuss word in there."

Breathless, flushed with embarrassment, she didn't dare look him in the eye. She started nudging the sock over the first row of toes. "I'm sorry for raising my voice again."

"Hey, don't think of it. You're right. I come back like some ghost. You have a right to be upset and raise a voice at me."

There he went again, getting all polite after the storm, tossing her emotions all over the place. And she was buying into it! She yearned to push him away, to pay him back for leaving her. Pulling the sock over his ankle, her fingers grazed his steely calf muscles with their springy hair. Oh, he was real, all right. The raw maleness of him sent sparks right up her arms.

His chuckle caught her off guard.

"What's so amusing now?" she charged.

"Remember how we'd dress each other after a good swim in the pond?"

With heat scissoring through her again, she handed him his other sock. "Don't go down memory lane with me."

He shoved the sock right back. "Please? My leg's throbbing. I don't want to wrestle to reach down to my ugly toes."

Against her better judgment, she grabbed the sock, then slipped it on him. "They're not so ugly."

"You always called my big toe Mr. Potato Head."

"Did not," she said, smiling, despite herself.

"Didn't you stub yours on the new sidewalk outside the hardware store one day? The owner came out and yelled at us—"

"At *you*, for writing dirty words in the dust on his window."

"And your bare foot slipped off the bike pedal."

"At least we escaped."

"Blood all over the sidewalk. You put mud on your toe to stop the bleeding. A doctor in the making."

Her eyes found his and that warm summer's day. Her throat constricted. "The new owner is a guy about our age, in his 30s, Gary Christianson. Keeps his windows clean."

Groping for a safer subject, she sat back in the grass and asked, "Who'd want to harm Mike? He was always so quiet and polite, knew what he wanted out of life, even as a teenager."

"Nothing like me?"

Shrugging, she drew her legs up, wrapping her arms around her knees to set her chin there, following his pained gaze to Spirit Lake, seeing the anger darken him.

After a shudder, she asked, "Who's this man, Cole? The murderer?"

"My brother and I worked for Marco Rojas, an entrepreneur from Venezuela." He spelled out the name. "He hated it when people didn't know enough about Spanish to know the 'J' is pronounced silently like an 'h.' 'Ro-hoss the boss' became our mantra."

"So you worked for an egomaniac, but a very rich one."

"Always suspicious and jealous of people with the same kind of money."

"Afraid perhaps, that they'd find out he was a fraud?"

He harumphed. "I hadn't thought of it that way, but perhaps."

"Which makes him very dangerous. Like a rabid animal pushed into a corner," she offered. "Where'd 'Ro-Hoss' get his big bucks?"

"We've been lucky, hauling up a lot of pieces that museums and collectors pay big for."

Laurel couldn't deny the thrilling sense of awe threading through her. "You're a modern day explorer. A Cousteau, a Titanic raiser."

"Don't make it sound too romantic. The flip side of that was our racing. Mike lost an eye a few years back. Got hit by another boat when his split apart. I was ahead of them, and didn't see it happen. And now this."

Her insides lurched for him.

He continued, "Mike began running a Miami marina for Rojas while I continued racing the hydroboats. Mike managed all the books. He knew everything."

"Too much?"

"Enough to make Mike come up here and hide something about Rojas's operations."

Shivering, she glanced over her shoulder at the old place. The idea of someone lurking about inside the clapboard hulk without her knowledge spooked her. Then a new thought struck: what if she'd razed the place already, destroying Cole's precious evidence? She shuddered to think how that would have left things for Cole.

"When was your brother here?"

"Almost two weeks ago now. When he returned, he and Rojas didn't see eye to eye on anything anymore. That's when..."

When Cole's tanned face turned ashen, she hurried to him, feeling his forehead, her heart pounding. "You should be lying down and resting. I just put you through a lot with that scalpel."

Cole swiped up her hands, clutching them for dear life in his fists, stilling her breathing again.

His gaze scorched her. "Forget about my health. Listen to me," he hissed, shaking her captured wrists to punctuate his words. "He's dead because of me. I was so damn angry that Mike wasn't telling me what was going on. He even warned me, said he thought Rojas was involved in something no good, that he was going to prove it.

"We argued, right there on the dock before a race. I insisted on knowing right there what he'd found out. Mike told me to shut up. I'd never seen him like that. We always shared everything. But not this for some reason."

"Maybe he didn't have all the evidence he thought he needed," she offered.

"But I kept badgering him. Made a scene." His chest heaved up and down, his breathing so fiercely charged it felt as if he'd suck her in. "And to shut me up he took off in the speedboat I was about to warm up. He never did things like that. Nothing careless in his whole life. He was a good man. A good father, too."

When he unhanded her, Laurel reeled from the raw love for his brother rimming his eyes. She couldn't move. "I'm sorry."

"The man I worked for had rigged the boat. I'm sure of it. It blew up out in the water. My brother, gone, just like that."

His hands had turned to ice, and she rubbed them instinctively to warm them. "I'm sorry."

Stumbling up, he limped away, but stopped only a few feet from her because of the pain. She heard the pain on his sigh, saw it in the way his shoulders rose with several deep breaths.

Scanning Spirit Lake toward the western horizon, he muttered, "Don't feel sorry for a man who should have saved his brother and who wishes another man dead. Don't allow yourself to—"

"Become involved. I know." But looking at his broad shoulders, sagging now, Laurel hurt for him.

When he weaved on the bad leg, she quickly slid beside him, acting as his crutch, not minding that she fit perfectly under his arm and alongside his firm body. Not minding that he needed her. Even for only the moment. "It could have been an accident. The authorities, they could—"

"The authorities!" He almost knocked them down. "Mike couldn't trust them and he wasn't ready to trust me yet with whatever it is he found. There's something about this whole mess that calls for a lot more than simple solutions."

A quick glance showed blood seeping through his thick bandage. She needed to calm him down. "Where's your son?"

"Tyler's with Mike's wife, or widow now. Karen. And his cousin Tim. They're in hiding. I made sure they moved the same day Mike was killed."

Quaking, she began gathering up her supplies from the grass, remembering how his lack of good judgment got them in trouble years ago.

"You should be with your son. Not here."

Cole turned her around roughly to face his piercing hawk-like eyes. "I didn't have a choice, Laurel. Mike chose this old place, not me. I can only pray for a little time before Rojas finds someone who will tell him about this property, because he'll come here if he has to."

"And then what? A final shootout? Listen to yourself. Don't you care about anybody? You'll put me in danger, everyone in Dresden and who lives around Spirit Lake? What about your son? The authorities should be the ones taking care of your boss, not you. Go home to your son where you belong!"

With the first-aid kit, she turned to go, but he grabbed her, tossing the kit aside and whirling her back into his arms. "Don't leave like this."

Her heartbeat skittered into a higher gear. "Leaving's your habit, not mine. You can verify that habit with your son I bet."

"Laurel, why are you so bitter? What the hell happened after I left?"

"You left me with an...aftertaste," she said, her stomach churning with the dread of him pressing her for too much. "You left my whole family with a bad taste."

He caught a fistful of her long hair whipping in the breeze, gentling it back against her face until his knuckles grazed her cheekbone, sending thunderbolts through her. "Listen to me," he said in a tone gone guttural. "I tried to square things by sending money to your father to pay for what I did to his car."

"I didn't know that." The fragrant spring air brought the scent of his heated skin along with her next breath, threatening to buckle her legs.

"Your father kept returning the envelopes to me unopened."

"Sounds like him. I'm sorry."

"Did you go to college?" Letting her hair fall from his fist, he combed it back into place with his fingers.

She shivered. He didn't seem to notice. "I started out studying plants. They didn't talk back or cause trouble."

At his chuckle, she flicked her gaze up to meet his. The dark eyes softened, inviting her in.

"And the animals?" he asked.

"I switched to environmental studies, and in the field labs I discovered I had a gift for working with animals. They responded to me."

"As I always have," he muttered, rubbing a thumb along her jawline, leaving sparks in his wake. "The way we made love then, it was real."

She sucked in her breath and tried to jerk away, but he held her tight, bringing her back into his shadow. The cardinals and robins chirped from the nearby woodland, almost serenading them.

His dark eyes narrowed. "Every night riding the rails, freezing my ass off trying to sleep in a cold metal boxcar, I kept thinking about coming here, dreading it, but at the same time remembering how warm it felt lying next to you under the sun, and how hot our skin got, and how we knew how to cool ourselves in the pond, and how much we didn't have a worry in the world."

Melting under his gaze, she remembered too, but she'd changed. Strength of maturity buoyed her now. "Why, Cole? Why are you telling me these things?"

The cardinals and robins stopped their cacophony, as if they should listen to the hawk, too.

"Because there's an emptiness in my gut. It settled in that day Mike died and hasn't left. And I don't know where it's leading me, except that I know there's been an emptiness involving you and me, and yes, our choices were mixed up and we were young, too young, and hell, but it's a mess, and you're right about it being a mess."

The heat of him mingled with her own charged breathing, filling her lungs with the earthy tang about him, spilling the essence of him into her veins as if he were suddenly her lifeblood. His arms—stronger than anything she'd remembered—drew her even more tightly against him, until her breasts tingled against the vibrations of his heartbeat.

"Emptiness," she said, her mouth dry and helpless against the truth, "waits and waits for something to fill it."

"Something, or someone? I need a friend, Laurel Lee."

"Only a friend?" Her heartbeat went ragged at the yearning softening his already-velvet eyes.

"Please," he murmured, his breath feathering across her cheekbones, sending the same soft tickle through her middle. "I'm scared as hell."

His head descended, his firm lips parting in their hunger.

HIS KISS SWEPT her into the clouds, where she rode with the birds, and smelled sweet clover wafting up from the meadow below. Her body grew ticklishly light, her nipples hardening where they brushed against his heaving chest as he carried her higher.

Then he landed with her. A crash landing.

Snapping open her eyes, she found him five steps away already, limping toward the nylon heap that looked like it might become a tent.

Stomping over, kicking aside the tall grass, she demanded, "Don't you dare tell me you didn't feel anything—"

"Damnit, I'm sorry," he snapped, without looking up. "I shouldn't have done that." He gathered tent stakes and crouched down, giving her his back again.

"Sorry doesn't cut it anymore." She snatched up a tent stake he was laboring to reach and thrust it at him. "And why are you building this tent? You can sleep in that old mansion over there."

"Too much dust and crud. Not good for my lungs."

"Swell. Clean lungs will be appreciated by the killer once he gets here."

Disgusted at herself for railing at him again, she turned to soak up every soothing, rippling inch of Spirit Lake. When he surprised her by ushering up beside her, cradling her elbow in his rough palm, the unbidden heat hummed along her skin again.

"What're you doing?" he asked.

"Finding my control before I head back."

Their breathing grew shallower while they watched the undulating water, and listened to the occasional duck quaking before taking flight. After a moment, he tugged on her hair. "Not sure I can get used to this sedate you."

"It's best you don't get used to it."

Turning back to his flat tent, he gingerly crouched down again. "You're right. I can't botch this for Mike. I've botched a lot of things in my life."

He left that hanging in the air, but she refused to respond. Finally, after listening to him grunt over one of the stakes, trying to shove it into the ground with no leverage because of his bad leg, she glanced about for a rock. Spotting one, she got it, then handed it down to him. When he frowned up at her, she said, "To help you pound in the stakes. In this soft ground, you're going to need to go deep."

"I'll keep that in mind," he replied, his mouth curling up in a sly smile.

She pursed her lips, refusing to play along.

He asked, "Now tell me, oh wise Miss Hastings, why do I tend to botch things? Something you seem to have observed."

"Long ago I concluded you're only capable of concentrating on one thing at a time, to a fault."

He hiked up one eyebrow at her. "How so?"

"You liked being with me, until you got in trouble. Then you had to focus on running away from trouble. Then, you had to focus on making a marriage to Stephanie work since ours didn't, but then other things must have impinged on that marriage, too. So you had to leave that in order to focus on something else, such as the racing."

He slammed the rock down hard on the top of the stake, spiking it cleanly into the earth.

Flinching, she continued, "You like projects. You concentrate on one adventurous project at a time."

"You haven't seen or heard from me in fifteen years and you know all this?"

"I did plenty of reading about men after that summer. There are men who consider women projects. They focus all their energies until they've fixed them to their liking. And then they move on."

"I wasn't that way." Plopping back in the grass, he stared up at her slackjawed.

"You didn't try to remake my wardrobe or anything—"

"For cryin' out loud, you hated getting dressed up. You were a tomboy."

"You never stopped focusing on your little adventures to ask what I liked and didn't like. You saw one side, the side that could be coaxed into doing stupid shenanigans and you focused on that."

"I didn't care if you wore a dress!" He struggled to his feet, grabbing a tent stake and the rock before heading for another corner of the tent.

"That's my point. You didn't care enough about all the other sides of me. I finally convinced myself that I was glad I never married you with society's legal paper back then. That reality and a family takes juggling and you can't juggle more than one ball in the air at a time. You're always in a crisis, and as each crisis hits, you forget all else."

"You're nuts." He dropped the rock and barely missed his toe.

"No, not anymore. If a tomboy suffices to feed your little plots to get in trouble, why risk messing up the fun by seeing another side to her, right? It's probably the same reason you wanted me to butcher your leg instead of going to a hospital. I'm at hand and easy to focus on. I'm no trouble and you face no responsibility with me. Even a quick kiss to satisfy your curiosity—hit and run—only proved it to me that you haven't changed a lick over the years."

"This is the most ridiculous psycho-babble I've ever heard."

She knew she should just leave, but he had her ire up now. Her pride wouldn't let go. "You asked my opinion but you don't really care what I say, do you? You just go on your merry way. Never mind the feelings of others swirling around you."

"Laurel, come on. That's not me anymore."

"It's not?" She scoffed. "You expressed undying love to me, but when trouble came, boom, you're gone. On your merry way. Now years later you drop everything, even your son, to avenge your brother's death."

"I love my son."

A stabbing ache hit her heart. "Oh? You're here and he's in hiding. Quaint proof of your love."

"My life's at stake."

"And that makes you a hero in your son's eyes? What if you get killed? Where's the responsibility and love in that?"

He scrambled up, cursing his sore leg to get to her. His eyes simmered with fury when he stabbed the air with a fist. "I didn't plan this misadventure, but I won't get killed. I'm not stupid."

She plucked the first aid kit from the grass and backed away. "You guaranteed that to your son?"

"Damn you, I can't guarantee anything."

"Pity the next woman who falls for you."

"You'll come back over here again?"

She turned to go but he caught her arm. Electricity skipped along her skin. "I doctored your leg and that's all you'll get from me. If you'll excuse me I have to check on an owl. At least it's not interested in pecking my heart out."

Releasing her, he grunted, "You're way too controlled."

Except for my thudding heartbeat. "Unlike you, I've changed. Now go to the hospital and get that leg looked at. Don't worry about being recognized. If I didn't recognize you at first, I'm sure you can put on an act again and get away with it."

He grinned defiantly. "That bothers you, doesn't it? I recognized you first, even with your longer hair, how you've filled out nicely—"

"Save it," she snapped, turning with the first aid kit to head for her boat.

His sudden, hearty and free-flowing laughter seemed to settle the ancient, irritating dust that had been stirred up between them. She rescued her nerves with a calming breath. But her heart's yielding toward him still scared her. "Tell them you're Atlas, a homeless man with the world on his shoulders, just for the drama of it. You'll get free treatment and be able to leave my lake tomorrow."

She couldn't escape to her boat fast enough. But the weeds rustled behind her. "Stop following me."

"I need a ride to the hospital."

"Not in my boat. The DNR warden will be here any minute. Hitch with Jim Swenson."

Feeling his gaze boring into her back, she slipped and slid down the muddy bank and into her boat. He stood high above, truly like some Greek god lording over his dominion. She dared glance up. A mistake. The sun formed a halo around him, throwing his tanned face into coppery, handsome silhouette. It took her three yanks on the cord to start the old motor, embarrassing for her. When she backed the aluminum boat away from shore, he stuck a hand tentatively in the air, then waved. She could even see his white teeth.

He was smiling, darn him.

She wished he hadn't done that, because it felt intimate and wondrous. Cheery even. But part of his act. Always, the act. If only he'd given her even the smile and wave fifteen years ago, a simple gesture of good-bye in person. Instead, he'd left her dangling with only hope and dreams for company.

Out in the middle of the bay, with its sweet water smells and the lapping of the ripples, she allowed herself to tremble. All over. Every inch, every follicle. He had no rights to anything anymore. Not her secrets, her triumphs and what she'd made of her life.

Or did he?

One visit to the meadow and beyond and he'd have too many questions.

Chapter 5

FORMING TIGHT fists, he watched her boat bob up and down, navigating the small waves. Her red hair whipped about like nautical flags warning of a storm. A smart sailor heeded such readings and headed in the opposite direction. Cole could not. Maybe he was nothing more than a surly pirate. She'd certainly pointed out a few faults more befitting of a pirate than...the father—the hero—she insinuated he wasn't for his son.

He itched to follow after her and prove somehow he wasn't the selfish lout she believed him to be.

Her small shape soon climbed onto the far dock. With her scarlet hair she could have been one of the cardinals going about its business against the green backdrop of bushes and trees lining the shore. She belonged here. He did not.

When she disappeared from view, he began tidying up his meager campsite. He doused the fire. What was it she wanted to do with this property once the mansion was razed? He'd forgotten to ask for details. Okay, maybe he was too focused on his own agenda. Wasn't being hunted by a madman enough reason? Not for Laurel. She had changed a lot. Where had all that fiery bluster come from? And her desperate need to control it? She was putting on an act, too.

To listen to her, he wasn't capable of love. Didn't he and Lisa Shaw have a good relationship? Lisa owned the dive shop he frequented. She'd been pressing him lately for something more permanent.

He groaned. Good one, Cole. Tell Laurel you're stringing along a blonde in Miami as proof you're the loving kind. Laurel would laugh her guts out.

What about his son? This sobered him more quickly than he would have liked.

He sank to the ground and stretched out the leg. Laurel would never understand that he'd been forced to give up much of the raising of his thirteen-year-old son, Tyler.

Tyler's welfare now loomed in his mind. After his divorce, Cole had started concentrating on the racing circuit and developing the reputation that would bring the Wescott brothers—and their children— a secure future.

Cole wanted to make sure Tyler never wanted for anything. Tyler understood that, didn't he? Mike must have helped him understand. Mike had raised Tyler along with his own Timmy. Mike must have explained this all to Tyler. Didn't he?

Cole hated these self-doubts. He hated thinking too much. Thinking messed up instincts. He needed his instincts to be keen. Tyler's fine, he chided himself.

But he heard her voice again. *You go your merry way.*

Flopping back, he squinted at the clouds. Just what he needed. A sexy, know-it-all woman who could doctor wounds and spout wisdom that bred guilt. She'd become too good to be true over the years. Too good for him.

A claw of anxiety squeezed his heart.

Something wasn't right about Laurel. Why was her disdain for him so deeply imbedded after all this time?

He shook his head. If he allowed himself to solve the puzzle of Laurel's past, he'd drift from his purpose. He vowed to the heavens and to the image of his wailing mother at Mike's funeral that he'd avenge his brother's death and save his family.

The echo of the footsteps and gun retorts in the railyard haunted him. Rojas wanted blood. Rojas had a lot to lose. What was it?

How many days did Cole have to find out?

The three-story, square mansion loomed as a menacing challenge. It hid the key to a murderous mystery. With its rotting floors, boarded windows and falling-down ceilings, the old house held its own brand of danger.

He paused to gently knead his pulsating leg.

The fragrance of new green growth and pines swaying in the breeze soothed his nostrils and lungs. The place lulled him back to a time when he and a seventeen-year-old powderkeg rolled in sweet timothy grass not too far from here. By the pond behind the mansion, in the meadow, he'd stolen a kiss to the muted buzzing of honeybees dipping into the dandelions next to them. As he'd dipped his mouth toward hers, tasting—

He bolted up in a sweat, not caring how much his leg hurt. His eyes darted back to the bay.

A dot of scarlet, she strutted along the same path they used to take, hand in hand.

Anticipating? What was theirs for the taking in the meadow?

The path hugged the curve of the bay, then followed up the tiny stream feeding the bay and Spirit Lake. It led into the woods and to magical places. The glen. The downed tree trunk among the bed of ferns. The high ridge and the scenic lookout. The little church. Their church.

Sweat trickled down his neck.

Disgusted with himself, he grabbed his backpack and unzipped it. Work beckoned. He rummaged around, pushing aside books and maps, the outdated deed, the box from his dresser, odds and ends of plastic containers and packets of dried food. Finally, he found the plastic bag with Mike's bank box contents. He plucked the photo out.

The photo showed an unknown officer wearing a circa World War II uniform. On the back, Mike had written, "Aunt Flora has the key to everything about M.R. Look under her skirts, but don't tell Langley, V."

Flora was long dead, so Cole had no idea what to do about finding her "skirts" unless the old house possessed a hidden closet. He hoped it would be that simple.

Cole knew "M.R." stood for Marco Rojas. He glanced again at the unknown, handsome fellow in the photo. What was the connection between him and Rojas? An official red stamp smudged one corner. Langley, Virginia, was CIA headquarters. Mike had been deathly afraid of even the CIA getting its hands on the mysterious evidence. Why? Why hide it here? In addition, what would Cole do once he found anything, or this man?

"If only I hadn't been so involved in my life and had paid attention to yours, dear brother. You might be alive and our Mister Rojas would be behind bars."

You just go your merry way.

A new kind of sweat broke out on his upper lip. It was the residue of remorse, sorrow and guilt, the deep love for a brother, the condemning voice of a woman he had no business connecting with now. It all bombarded his head and gut with a hurricane force. He understood the pressure would only dissipate one way: bring down Rojas. Put him away for good, or be six feet under himself.

He set off across the weedy yard toward the mansion.

LAUREL HURRIED back down the path for her cabin, swiping at her face and the anger pressing hot all over her. A good brisk walk helped relieve the tension of being with Cole. Was she afraid of him? Yes. He had the power to unravel her way of life she had so carefully carved over the years.

She tore through the cabin's front door, ducked into the kitchen to splash cold water on her face. She imagined Cole swirling down the drain and out of her life.

She needed to also change every stitch of clothing to rid herself of any trace of him. Once in her bedroom, she sucked in her breath. His blood stained her bluejeans.

Pushing them off in a flurry, she kicked them across the room, then bounced down on the bed. She'd kissed him like a teenage ninny. And he threatened to stomp around in that house—and her heart—chilling her to the bone if she allowed it.

She slipped on fresh jeans and a bright yellow flannel blouse. She bought the cheery blouses by the gross, her mother liked to say with great sarcasm. But Laurel found flannel something injured animals liked to snuggle up to. When a shirt wore out, it retained its soft nap, perfect for lining nesting boxes for baby birds fallen from nests or baby rabbits washed from burrows in summer downpours.

Her time in the basement with Cole, his haggard, but handsome face—flashing before her now—stilled her fingers.

Recovering, she attacked the buttons, feeling comfort with every closure.

She flicked a gaze to the framed photographs resting on a corner of the dresser. In one, her father held up a huge fish. In another, her father and Sheriff John Petski beamed with stringers of bluegills. Her parents' wedding picture sat tucked behind and alongside Kipp O'Donnell's.

She picked up his photo. He always cocked his head when he smiled. He'd been a big man, as tall as her father, different than Cole...but tall as Cole now. She rubbed her thumb over the glass, clearing away the haze of dust. Kipp's eyes were hazel, not the deep chocolate coals she thought suited a man named Cole. Both men's eyes held a devilish twinkle. She'd never thought about that singular similarity until now. She stared wide-eyed at Kipp. Why had she been about to marry him? She was embarrassed to realize enough time had passed that she had to think hard about it.

Her father approved of Kipp from the moment he strolled into town looking for a job. The two men hunted and fished together, and she remembered a certain wild edge about him...that matched Cole's. But unlike Cole, Kipp would leave on trips and always return. When he promised her a family, a home and a good way of life here on Spirit Lake, she needed to believe him. He single-handedly patched the rift between her and her father over Cole.

Simply put, Kipp could do no wrong in her father's eyes. If she occasionally had doubts about loving Kipp as deeply as she should, she would tuck them away. He was "steady," a man that a woman would be a fool not to try and love. Even her mother had agreed Kipp represented everything that Cole was not.

Then the fishing accident stole Kipp and her father. Both of them drowned in the blink of a cold day. All the doubts about Kipp were never played out. The wedding dress was returned, the VFW hall rented out to someone else's party.

Her heart feeling heavy, Laurel put the photo back. Maybe she should be glad Cole charged back in her life. His presence was a reminder that she'd gotten on with things. Her life held no room for men overloaded with testosterone. Men like Cole were interruptions in a woman's life, that's all. That's what her father had claimed all along.

She hurried out to the shed behind the cabin, taking the long way outside instead of through the breezeway to grab a stout twig on her way. She would fashion it into a perch for the owl. When she arrived at his cage, she found him huddled in a corner.

"My poor little Owlsy. At least you're standing up a bit perkier."

A brown-flecked broken wing hung crooked. She would tend to it once he'd acclimated himself more. She fastened the branch across the inside of the cage, raised the heat lamp and slid a water dropper bottle in place between the spaces in the hardware wire mesh. He jumped back, opening his beak to threaten her. Her heart tharumped for him.

"I'm going into town now and when I get back, we'll see about wrapping that wing. And I want you to try that perch and consider how good this water will taste. You hear?"

She moved on to clean the other cages and replenish food. Rusty the fox licked her fingers through his wires and gulped down his soft dogfood the moment she slid the bowl through the wire hatch on the front of the cage. Laurel giggled, then an intrusive thought sobered her. She couldn't help but think about Cole over there with dried food and nothing else to eat. She shook her head, though, wishing away the distraction and quelling her nurturing instincts. Let Jim Swenson offer him a meal.

She finished up chores, tossing hay to the deer and ground corn to her small flock of chickens that shared the pen.

In her minivan, she drove the five miles southwest along Spirit Lake to Dresden. The wildflowers crowding the edges of the road kept reminding her of Cole. Not now, but back then. In their meadow.

She punched on the air conditioning. When had it gotten so hot?

She stopped at the bank first to cash a couple of checks from the wildlife foundations that helped support her. The checks were meager—and she wondered why her father had been so stubborn as to send back Cole's checks? Or not tell her about them?

Chiding herself to quit thinking about Cole, she then went to the post office to retrieve her medical supplies shipped from a Superior veterinarian clinic. Would Cole get to the doctor without her?

After putting the supplies in her van, five small children accosted her with smiles. She wondered what Cole's son was like, now in hiding, not in the sunshine, and probably not smiling. It made the pit of her stomach ache.

A little blond cherub bounced up and down. "Laurel, Laurel, we have baby ducks in our backyard."

"We call them ducklings," Laurel said, tousling the girl's blonde curls and giving her a quick hug.

"Yeah, baby duck ducklings. Quackers."

The kids screamed with giggles. Laurel grinned. "Anybody here want a taffy apple?"

They hopped up and down, arms stretched high. "Me! Me!"

"Come on then."

Laurel herded her brood down the sidewalk crowded with vacationers, then into the small grocery operated by her friends Una and Ted Watkins. She and Una had met in college. After visiting Dresden, Una fell in love with its quiet pace. When the grocer retired, Una and Ted bought it the same day.

While the children picked out the apples coated with the most caramel and nuts, Laurel found herself wondering how tasteless dried soup mixed with lake water would be? Hadn't he loved her fried egg sandwiches once upon a time?

After ringing up the apples and scooting the children back into the outdoors, Una asked, "You gonna tell me what's making you look like a ghost today or do I have to drag it out of you?"

Laurel picked up a shopping basket and headed for the fruit aisle. She grabbed a fat orange. "Can I get a crate of these? My orioles love them, but I discovered they seem to perk up baby squirrels."

Una crossed her arms. "They're on special. As is my listening. Now tell me what gives."

Laurel set her basket on the cantaloupes. "Cole's back."

Una's eyes grew wide. "The guy you couldn't talk about in college without grinding your teeth? The man who..."

"The same." Laurel's heart grew heavy as stone. She related Cole's story to Una.

Una whistled. "Holy cow. Don't you think you ought to tell all this to David?"

Laurel frowned. She and David Huber graduated the same year from high school. He was one of the few who hadn't shunned or avoided her after the fateful summer with Cole. He insisted she hang onto a dream—any dream. When he went off to college to become a lawyer, he insisted she come along, even if she'd spent her last dime bailing Cole out of jail and paying for property damage they'd caused, and paying her father back over the ensuing years. And while many young people got jobs in other towns and didn't return, David had. She liked that about him. With him here, she felt she could also return. She knew their friendship could develop into something more if she'd let it.

"No," Laurel said, rubbing her hands against her sleeves, "You know David worries worse than my mother."

Una frowned. "Then you haven't seen David recently?"

"I've been too busy and the sheriff delivered an owl this morning that needs attention. Why?"

She didn't like the way Una swallowed before speaking. "It seems a couple days back someone wrote an anonymous letter asking that the township not raze the old mansion. David stopped in this morning for a can of coffee and mentioned to me he got another letter just yesterday asking about the deed, and that he'd need to talk to you."

Laurel froze. "Cole couldn't have written those letters."

She handed her empty shopping basket to Una, fear pelting her to a numbness. "He can't move back into that place. I won't have it, Una. He'll find out everything. I can't re-live that. I'm happy now. Very happy."

"He won't move back. David will think of something."

Laurel left the store to find David.

Out on the street, a prickle crawling up the back of her neck halted her. She turned, and there Cole stood anchored across the crowded street, leaning against the corner of the stone building that housed the drugstore.

His hawkish gaze meant only one thing. Cole knew something he was aching to discuss. With her. Now. And he wasn't particularly happy about it either.

"LAUREL!"

Cole saw the mane of red hair toss when she spun and headed in the opposite direction. By the time he limped into the fray of the sidewalk and watched for a break in the traffic he'd lost her. He cursed to himself, then supposed confronting her could wait. He had to adjust to new worries.

He'd followed her advice about getting medical attention, but the officious Dr. Donna Corcoran mumbled something about certain injuries being reportable to the law. Before he knew it, Cole ended up with a date to see the sheriff later. Cole then visited the local weekly newspaper office before picking up the antibiotics the doctor prescribed. What he had read fueled his confusion.

The messy Dresden Chronicle's morgue yielded a yellowed edition from ten years ago. Its front page story about her engagement to a Kipp O'Donnell proved Laurel had fallen in love after Cole left town. Why then had she made it seem that Cole had ruined her life forever? It was a lie. Lies weren't part of the Laurel he had known. That niggled at him. To him, Laurel was like an exquisite vase. To find a crack in perfect beauty sent the owner in a rage to know who did it and how it happened.

Her friend who had given him a ride to Dresden revealed little. Jim Swenson talked about the new beaver pond built upstream from the Tilden place, and the return of eagles over the past few years. Cole took note of the reverence in Jim's voice when describing how Laurel helped release a young pair of eagles off the scenic cliff near her cabin. It was the same cliff where he and Laurel had once watched nighthawks chase the moon.

Cole shook his head. While she flew with eagles, he dealt with turkeys like Rojas.

He glanced around. Could he forget Rojas for the moment? Under the sunny sky and a backdrop of whispering pines, far from oceans and gunshots in trainyards, perhaps he could. He needed to ask Laurel all the questions he'd failed to earlier. About her family, her life, everything. He needed to prove to her—no, first he needed to prove to himself and to his son—that he cared about the feelings of others.

He scanned the bobbing heads in hopes of spotting her. When his gaze hit the hardware store he remembered Laurel mentioning a Gary Christianson. Perhaps Gary could fill in the blanks about Laurel's life.

A STEP INSIDE the store brought smells reminiscent of his brother's marina and a catch caught at his heart. The pungent odor of oil and grease mingled with paint and hemp ropes. Everything had its place above a spic and span gray tile floor. Mike must have appreciated it. Had he been in this store? Probably, Cole thought, tamping down an icy finger of darkness threatening to mist up his eyes. Whoever said big boys didn't cry was a fool.

A stout man with a thatch of blond hair and flushed cheeks strode up the aisle carrying a towering box of flags. Cole noted "Gary" on the embroidered shirt pocket.

Gary plopped the flags next to the counter and grinned. "Howdy. The Fourth's 'round the corner. Ever seen our little town gussied up for it?"

Cole's heart tripped a beat. He'd forgotten about the parade and fireworks he'd watched with Laurel. "No, I haven't," he lied, feeling an odd pang of resentment that he needed to lie.

"Then you're in for a treat. Stayin' that long?"

"I'm not sure." He imagined not living with fear for a partner. Instead, he and Laurel would sit side by side on lawn chairs and watch a parade, with Laurel waving a flag and smiling at him. The Fourth was almost a month away. Did he dare stay that long? What if Rojas showed up? Cole didn't like thinking about a shootout on Dresden's Main Street.

Having more doubts again about prying into Laurel's past and getting involved, Cole muttered about needing tools. Gary hopped to the task of finding the best brands and selections, from a crowbar to a battery-powered stud finder. Cole pulled out the last of his cash.

Gary asked, "You must have quite the building project."

"More like tearing down."

"Where at?"

Cole found himself grasping. "Laurel Hastings hired me to help salvage odds and ends in the Tilden mansion."

"Almost forgot that old gangster's place is going to be fire department tinder any day."

"Gangster's place?"

"Yup. Lots of these big mansions on lakes in northern Wisconsin were built around the turn of the century by the Chicago crime families. Kind of a getaway," Gary said, chuckling.

"How appropriate," Cole muttered. But what about his great-aunt? "I thought a lady lived there for many years."

"Sure did. Rumor is she was romantically involved with a gangster. Some say he gave it to her as a gift."

While Gary took tags off the tools, Cole stood silent, barely managing to contain his questions. Was any of this true? His parents never uttered a word, but why would they? Was Flora the family outcast? Had she married into the mob? Was that why the property had been abandoned or forgotten by his family? Had Mike discovered anything about this rumor?

He asked Gary, the talking tourist brochure, "Do you think there's a vault out there?"

"As in something built underground? With loot?" He rang up the tools. "Not likely that after all these years you'd find buried treasure."

"What about blueprints? Historical society or library nearby?" Cole was desperate.

"No, but you might ask the town clerk, Attorney David Huber. He and Laurel likely discussed the rumors."

"Why's that?" Cole asked.

"David tells me they talked about refurbishing the mansion at one time but Laurel discouraged him."

"Because she wants to return the land to its natural state. Jim Swenson explained that she received some government grant. Something about creating meadows to bring back the elk population."

"Deadline's end of this summer for using the grant. She has to raze the old mansion and plant a truckload of aspen saplings or return the money. If that happens, somebody else could step in and always buy the estate right out from under her. It's prime property for developing into lakeside condos."

A deadline soon? Condos? No wonder she was rabid about his leaving. His presence and ties to the property threatened to spoil what was more dear to her than even him—a patch of barren land. Why she felt such a kinship to a few acres of dried weeds he'd probably never figure out but it intrigued him.

"You mentioned she and Huber went head to head over the issue of refurbishing the mansion?"

Gary's gaze dipped away. "It's my hunch, or at least my wife's, that their disagreement was her way of putting his marriage proposal off again in a polite way."

"Marriage proposal? Again?" The pang of unexpected jealousy hit his gut.

Gary shook his head. "Don't push the lady. She needs to hide out a bit in her woods. She's been through a lot and deserves her peace."

"What happened?"

Gary shrugged. "Lost her daddy and her fiancé Kipp O'Donnell a few years back on Christmas Eve day. Ice fishing. A soft spot under the snow gave way, they think."

Cole's stomach knotted at the things he'd said about her father. "I'm sorry."

But Gary smiled, incredulously enough, and waved him off. "Don't you worry about that woman. She picked herself up and has made quite a life for herself. Always got a cheery hello."

"But she lives out there alone, with animals. I mean, she can't do that forever." It sounded too damn lonely!

Gary skewered him with a squinty eye. "Laurel's served on about every committee you can think of. She does school presentations whenever they want her. The kids thinks she's a second mom and she loves driving kids out to see a new eagle's nest. She gets kicks out of raggin' at the governor to lower taxes on our rural property. She's got a whole town wrapped around her. And maybe that's all she needs from life."

Soundly chastised, Cole nodded. "I've got a lot to learn about her." He stared at the tools then. "I'm embarrassed. Can you deliver? Jim Swenson dropped me off. I don't have a vehicle and I don't know where Laurel is." He couldn't rely on her offering a ride anyway. He'd hitch back if he had to.

Gary reached under the counter and handed him a set of keys. "Here. Take my old truck out back."

"Just like that? You don't even know me."

"You work for Laurel. If she trusts ya, so do I. Keep it long as you like. Return it with a full gas tank when you're done workin' for Laurel and we're square."

"Thanks."

He was heading out the door when he felt compelled to grin and add, "You have a nice place here. Cleanest windows I've ever seen."

Gary nodded.

Cole loaded the tools into the back of Gary's dented maroon pickup, then limped back down Main Street. He didn't see Laurel, but he knew where she might be—Hastings Bait Shop, two blocks away.

Cole paused to scan the sidewalks. He wasn't only looking for Laurel, he reminded himself.

He withdrew the photo from his pocket. The guy would be in his seventies, even eighties by now. Cole stared at the eyes, light gray in the black-and-white photo. They could be hazel, blue or gray in real life. Distinctive, they looked right through a person. Cole had to find the owner of those eyes and see why Mike thought the guy knew something about Rojas. Before Laurel got hurt.

HALF THE TOWN seemed packed into the tiny bait shop. Cole recognized Madelyn Hastings, though she paid him no heed. Relief trickled through him. He found his gaze lingering on her. He knew why instantly. Years from now Laurel would grow to be as beautiful as this woman.

Madelyn's smile spread wide and sweet, made more enticing even with the slight age wrinkles framing it. Her hair, once as flame red as her daughter's, was pinned up in a thick bunch of waves the color of a pleasing sunset. Cole shifted his weight. A sense of loss flowed through him. He would never see this stage of Laurel.

At the other end of the counter, several men and women engaged in a spirited discussion about a fish being weighed on a scale. Cole recognized Buzz Vandermeer, the newspaper editor he'd met as Atlas—earlier in the day. He was a jovial retired teacher from Minneapolis with a buzz cut and a love of language. The hefty fish was about to receive glorious inches in Buzz's Dresden Chronicle before being wrapped in same for a freezer. Cole smiled at the Norman Rockwell scene.

Then he glimpsed the scarlet hair. Laurel sat in the alcove at the place's only table, next to a coffee pot and a side door—an escape hatch. A dozen children surrounded her like a protective moat. Her radiance stilled Cole's heart, but her aura was more than physical. This was not the angry woman who railed at him. This woman's smile bespoke patience. She inspected a kitten, petted a frog and winked to make the cherubs giggle. Laurel held them spellbound.

Guilt slammed into Cole. *What about your son?*

He leaned against a display case to find his balance. In all his life he couldn't remember sharing something as silly as a pet frog with Tyler. He hadn't been there much, but with good reason, right? He raked his hair with a hand, trying to let the doubts go.

Suddenly he lost interest in questioning Laurel about her past and why she'd lied to him. Prying seemed stupid to him now.

He edged toward the door, but when she lifted a puppy to her cheek, Laurel's gaze captured Cole. A bolt of electricity changed the air between them, staying Cole in his tracks. Like the kiss by the bay, or the long ago day in the glen, they peered together across a chasm, inviting, trying to deny a hunger, trying to deny how intimately they knew each other.

Then her gaze returned to the children and the moment passed.

Her carriage grew erect, guarded. She handed the puppy back. An arctic blast blew through Cole. Then shooing the children on their way, she ducked toward the back of the shop.

He followed, recklessness overpowering him.

She stood over the minnow tanks, her back to him, hair cascading forever until it met the rounded shape of her bottom in her tight jeans. His body reacted before he could hold himself in check. The throbbing in his bad leg seemed to have moved up. He despised his lack of good sense and control because she expected that out of him.

Wishing like hell he could touch her hair, he cleared his throat. "You're a regular mother bird these days."

She whirled around, a haunted look blanching her face. "Whatever it is you want from me, I refuse to discuss it. You didn't have to hunt me down out there on the street for all the world to see. And to come into my father's shop—"

She whirled back around to the tank with its gurgling water. His mouth went dry, but he sidled up next to her. He stared at the minnows darting about. With her face reflecting in the water, he found it difficult to focus on the fish and not her electric eyes.

"Those kids reminded me of the time you showed me how you could feed chickadees from your hand. I was never as good as you around animals. Or children."

She dipped a small net toward the tank bottom. "It's never too late."

"I'm not sure my son would want me to teach him about chickadees."

"How would you know?"

Hot prickles stabbed his face. His whiskers itched. "I suppose I deserved that." He watched her dip toward the tank bottom. "Treasure hunting?"

She picked a penny out of her net and set the coin on the tank rim.

"Kids love to make wishes. If we had a fountain in this town, my mother wouldn't have this trouble."

"Fountains are for big cities and they get dirty anyway. You don't want one."

"For once I agree with you. I'd rather work on keeping the lake clean for the kids here."

He wanted to shout for joy at that. "You understand them so well. Ever think about having kids of your own?"

Her hand slapping the water echoed throughout the bait shop. The icy tidal wave drenched Cole from head to foot, especially the one stuck yet in his mouth.

"Ever think you no longer have rights to ask me such personal questions?"

Chapter 6

WITH HER HEARTBEAT erratic, and a slow-burn over Cole threatening her common sense, Laurel marched to David Huber's law office on the side street past the drugstore.

Now he was making her angry as well. "What do you mean we can't get a restraining order to keep Cole Wescott away from me?"

David thumped his pen on the file in front of him. "His merely finding you to ask a question doesn't qualify as stalking. Did he threaten you with a weapon?"

She went to stare out the window overlooking the village's bustling lakefront pier and boardwalk. She thought about the jagged-edged knife still sitting on her counter.

"No." If anything, she'd threatened him. "But what about the letters Una mentioned? Those must be from him."

"Did he say so?"

She turned around. "I didn't ask and he didn't offer. But why should he if he's after the property? He wouldn't want me to try to stop him."

"These anonymous letters might. They question whether the property was properly condemned. The author wants to know whether the township made enough attempts to find the owner. They want copies of tax liens, official ads run by any governmental entity looking for people owing taxes, the lady's will. This research could take weeks."

"Weeks?" Panic burned through her. "I'll lose my grant for the wildlife refuge and for my rehabilitation work if I don't raze that place and get to planting the trees I promised the State. You know how hard it is to get donations. I was counting on that money and the job. Without it I'll have to stop taking in animals. My center is the only one in this part of the state. You can't let Cole do this."

"Slow down. We don't know it's Cole." He sighed and folded his hands over the file. "I have a few letters asking me to find anything I can on Flora Tilden and the mansion. That's it. Why don't you confront him?"

"That sounds like a fight, not peace."

"Have you ever really been at peace since he left?"

With his pointed look cutting her off at the knees, she muttered, "You get to the heart of things quickly."

"Isn't that what you want? Maybe that's all Cole is asking of you."

Burning now from the memory of splashing Cole for "getting to the heart of things quickly," she left David's office vowing to somehow get a look at those files. She wanted to fling the letters in Cole's face for putting her in a tailspin. And he'd only been back a day!

TUESDAY MELTED into Friday and Cole remained at the mansion. Each day gave her hope that he'd find his buried treasure and leave, but he became part of the wildlife she watched through her scope at the picture window.

Each day, he forced her to consider their past. The unfinished business called honesty. It gave her chills to think that total honesty about certain things she'd done in the past fifteen years might be the only way to get rid of Cole and move on with her own life. Their quick parting of ways was the only future possible for them both.

Future? What they would always have would be more like an accommodation on the planet earth. Like two wolves from different packs, keeping themselves hundreds of miles apart with their secrets and distrust.

At work in the animal shed, she fluffed an aged flannel shirt around two young bunnies snuggled in a wood nesting box. They'd arrived yesterday after a mischievous dog stumbled through their nest and his owners rescued the newborns. These babies were palm-size and nearly hairless. Smiling at them wiggling in their sleep, a sigh stole through her.

For a moment, all troubles fled. Would she ever have children? She couldn't deny the soft desire that blossomed with Cole's question of her. She wanted the peace of their laughter, dearly. She wanted the completeness of adding that sound to her life.

Moving on, she patted Rusty on the head, took note of Owlsy, now patched and quiet, the fawn with its splint and the chickens scratching around without a care in the world. She reminded herself of how contented she was here.

But was it enough? Yes, she insisted. Contentment had always been enough, until Cole reminded her of all that it meant to be a woman. But she could control her wayward desires, couldn't she? The ragged edges of womanhood that slapped in the night like laundry forgotten on the line, begging for someone to come and rescue it?

Drat him! But she would find someone again, someone suitable for marriage and children. Someone steady, someone she could always count on to bring in the laundry with her.

Outside, to escape such barbarous thoughts, she took stock of the verdant, neat garden. Lush—because of her steady hand, because of its predictable, responsible rows.

The breeze blew fresh and warm, gentling her even more. Humming, she stopped to weed the quack grass popping up around her tomato plants, then thinned the short radish row and noticed early spinach begging to be picked. The oniony, sweet smell from purple-topped chives lulled her into a broad smile while she fussed about the plants.

Then she stopped. It was too quiet. Even for contentment.

For almost three days, Cole had attacked the old mansion like a crazed woodpecker, his hammering and pounding relentless. Now, the silence slithered in around her, ominous. She sheltered her eyes with a hand against the brilliant sky and squinted across the bay.

The old maroon pickup Gary'd loaned him still sat parked next to the verandah but the usual morning campfire was missing. Where was Cole?

She hated her curiosity, her penchant for worrying and tending things. Especially living things, because they were dependent on her. That part of her was so much like Cole that long ago she'd recognized it as a weakness to be corrected.

But when had she last heard the pounding? Maybe midnight. His ratta-tat-tat robbed her of sleep at least until then.

Had Rojas spotted Cole in town?

The breeze didn't feel warm anymore.

Darn him for doing this to her again.

She stalked into the cabin. She'd fix breakfast. Food cured a lot of ills for mere animals. Let it shake her blues. But the oatmeal tasted bitter despite the maple syrup she poured on. Shoving it aside, she took her coffee out to the front steps.

She heard nothing.

Had he really left? Had he given her three days of excitement and then vamoosed? She'd had so many pent-up questions to ask him yet about his life, his son, his brother. David's advice niggled at her. Had she been unfair? Unforgiving even?

Cole had complimented her way with children. Didn't a good mother need to be forgiving of a lot? With all her heart, she wanted to experience the trouble of children.

Until Cole's re-entry into her life, she hadn't realized how much on the surface that yearning was. At times, it burst like a river from out of an underground cave, crashing into the sun with its message. At times, it ushered forth as soft and joyous as a dandelion seed pod, its feathery wings set free to blow across a soul, to plant themselves in a heart in order to grow.

When the sun began throwing afternoon shadows on the silence and there was still no sign of Cole, Laurel's defenses grew weak. She carefully packed an insulated luncheon box, looking twice at what she put in there and wondering whether he'd know the significance of the succor she brought. Then a tremor rolled through her. Would he even be alive to appreciate the surprise packed in this box? She grabbed her first-aid kit and a coil of rope and headed for her fishing boat.

Outside, she felt as if someone were watching her, beckoning her with a powerful force that vibrated from the earth's fiery core. She peered up at the round window across the bay. Its bleakness mocked her. It seemed to know she couldn't resist giving into curiosity about Cole. Even if danger, or death, lay waiting.

SHE CHECKED HIS tent first. Finding it empty, she hurried along the deer path, the weeds whipping against her bluejeans. She stepped onto the verandah, her hiking boots clomping on the floorboards.

"Cole?" She rapped on the sliver-ridden carved door. "It's me, Laurel."

After shoving the door open, and putting down the cooler and gear, she eased toward the hole she'd fallen through earlier in the week.

"Cole?" He wasn't down in the basement.

With ginger steps and ears attuned to cracking in the wood, she inched through the first-floor rooms. In the parlor off to the right, light streamed through a couple of windows now freed of their plywood. They flanked a dusty fireplace, spider webs spewing down from its mantle and fluttering in the quiet breeze like white sheers. She saw evidence of Cole. He'd chopped holes about the room and there were chunks of plaster piled in corners. The tracks in the dust seemed fresh. Her heartbeat quickened.

"Cole?" she called again, but to no avail. She licked her lips against the cottony fear settling in her mouth.

Searching the kitchen across the hall, she stepped over buckled linoleum. The pantry was empty and dark, as was the library with all its empty shelves, which was as bleak as the family sitting room.

She stumbled out onto the screenless back porch, looked around the yard, then hurried inside and headed for the back stairway.

Fear climbed with her. Her heartbeat tripled.

On the second floor she inspected five bedrooms, their doors screeching on rusted hinges. She found nothing but dust, a few ugly knickknacks that seemed to hold up the walls and a four live brown bats huddled in a dark ceiling corner of one room.

She then stepped into the master suite with its glassless window overlooking the lake. A shutter slapped haphazardly with the breeze. A rusted iron bed with springs sat off in a corner. An oak dresser with cracked porcelain knobs collected leaves and debris near the window. The dressertop was a carved masterpiece attesting to the teenage couples who'd snuck here for a tryst over the years. Laurel ran her hand over the rough notchings of names, holding her breath, thinking about the futures discussed here and oh, the families started, too. Why did she feel left behind by history? What an odd sensation. Lonely. Barren.

She backed away, her nerves taut as fishing line battling a monster pike. If she and Cole had gone ahead with their marriage, would they have lived in this house? They could have carved their names here. And filled the empty shell with their children. That haunted her everytime she came in here.

The stale air suffocating her, she rushed to a stairwell, stumbling several steps before she realized she was going up and not down.

Stopping, she floated a hand over her heart to quell its overwrought response to her ragged thoughts. Could love survive for fifteen years in empty spaces?

Dreaming of what might have been only imprisoned a woman in her own history. *I can't still have those kind of feelings for him. I won't allow it.*

With logical thinking back in place, she decided to proceed to the top floor and get this silliness over with.

She shouldn't have.

Inside the cavernous, peaked attic room with the porthole window, she found him. And she knew—instinctively—that she was about to walk into deep, deep trouble.

LIGHT FROM THE lowering sun now poured through the round window onto his shoulders. He slumped over a rickety wood table, his face buried in his hands.

"Cole?"

He sat on one of several rusted tubular kitchen chairs, most of which were collecting dust and artful spider webs.

When he groaned, she rushed to him and gripped his shoulders, thinking the worst. "Are you hurt? Was Rojas here? Let me see. I'll help. I'm sorry about—"

Snaking out an arm, he startled her, but he used it to rub his face through another moan. She stood still behind him, not daring to breathe hardly, watching with an ache at the way his shaking fingers clawed through his thick, dark hair. Then the same hand, warmed by his face and hair, sought hers at his shoulder, and she obliged, leaning against his back, her fingers entwining with his. The stark neediness in him bound her to him.

"The other day, when I asked for your help?" he ventured. "I overstepped the bounds between us." His elbows rested on what looked to her like maps. "It's wrong to want your help with something like this. Go home. I can handle it."

Stepping back, she folded her arms against both the sudden chill of not being a part of him and her own indignation. "I was worried about you."

"I've been doing a lot of thinking about you."

Heat scuttled up her spine, prickling onto her cheeks. "Be careful. You don't control my mind or my will anymore."

"The drenching in the shop made your point."

"And I hate the way I turn into a fool around you to make my points. That's not me anymore."

"Did Kipp only control your heart because he was your father's best buddy?"

The words scalded. "How dare you—"

"Ask the truth? The editor showed me several photos from hunting trips they took without you. And then there's David Huber."

His obvious penchant to play detective on her personal life sparked a whollup of agitation. "Are you doing a thesis on my friends and my dead fiancé? Kipp controlled nothing about me, nor did I control him. Our relationship wasn't like that."

"And what was it like?"

She opened her mouth but discovered it was the first time anyone had asked her about it. Not even Una or her mother said much about Kipp. Certainly not David. "It was normal. And how dare you grill me."

"Normal? That's it?" He turned toward her. His face was beet red.

"Are you feeling well? What's happened, Cole? You're acting very odd."

Turning back to smooth the crinkled maps, he muttered, "What's happened?" he repeated. "Do you mean in the last fifteen years or since yesterday? Life moves along in this great big space but there's one thing we have to grab."

"Grab what? Don't talk weird."

"I'm not. It's all related. I'm talking about love."

The air grew stifling. "Whose love? What love?"

"Did you love Kipp? I mean the bone-rattling kind. The kind that transcends temporal spaces and events in our lives?"

"Bone-rattling? Transcends? Kipp would have scoffed at such hogwash. I was going to marry him."

"I suppose love comes in varying degrees. I'm only just learning that, you know. Brother love. Son love. Friend love. Love of truth weaving through it all like some surly snake you can't catch and maybe don't want to."

She cocked her head. "How long have you been up here? Maybe you've got a fever—"

"No fever. I discovered why what you and I had once wasn't enough for either of us."

The blood left her face. After all these years, was he deciding to tell her now that he never really loved her? Or that he believed he did once? That was preposterous. "You're drunk."

"I rarely drink. Just the champagne after a race."

"And you always win."

"Not at love. There was you. Then Stephanie. Lisa wants to get married but I can't seem to figure out if that's only friend-love."

"Maybe she knows about surly snakes like I do," she scoffed. "Or, did you forget to—as you say—transcend?"

His chuckle surprised her. "No. The truth is I didn't know what love was until my brother was taken from me. And I haven't had a moment to think about it until I came back to Dresden, until I saw you. I finally came up here last night to think about it."

She was stunned. "You waited three days to come up here? Yours and Mike's pirate ship?"

"I was scared, Laurel. I thought I'd hear his voice. I wasn't sure I was ready to hear him, to see the visions of him and me playing up here, lining up chairs to make seats on our ship, stacking chairs to peer out the window with a dimestore plastic telescope our aunt had bought. We were tough, invincible brothers who wanted nothing more than to sail the seas together when they grew up. Am I crazy? To be afraid of those voices?"

She stood there for an eternity watching dust motes float across the sunbeam blanketing his shoulders. The only sound was his shallow breathing.

He rubbed his palms against his eyes, then raked his dark hair. Wrinkles pinched his forehead.

Finally, she couldn't deny his agony any longer. She went to him, stood behind him and placed a shaky hand on his shoulder, massaging the kinks away, an automatic thing, remembered by her hands after a lifetime apart.

She whispered, "No, hearing his voice isn't crazy." She swallowed hard against the rising throb of her heart in her throat. "It's probably the most human, loving thing I've ever heard from you. He was your brother. He'll be your brother forever."

One of his hands reached back and covered hers. The heated dampness sent the years lost between them crashing into the dust at her feet. It frightened her to be drawn to his grief, yet her heart felt light as a flower in bloom, and against her will it opened to him. Overpowering, his pull was too much for her to refuse.

He clung to her hand, then edged around to look up at her. His eyes were the liquid darkness of a creekbed hidden under shade.

She could only find a whisper. "I've never seen you cry."

His jawline trembled. "How could you stand it, losing Kipp and your father at the same time?"

And so much else. "I couldn't. For a long time."

"How much time does this take?"

"What? Filling in the hole in your heart that's left behind when someone leaves you?" She quaked inside.

"Hell, yes," he said, dropping his hand from hers and pushing off suddenly to go to the porthole window. Had he been watching her earlier? She shivered again. He must have.

In his wake she noticed he'd left behind a small, wood box darkened with age. A wet stain marred its top. His tears. She tried to swallow but her throat had gone dry as paper. She flipped open the box. It held a rainbow of crayon stubs.

She frowned. "You discovered this box up here?"

He didn't turn back from the window, just nodded. "Last night."

"You've been up here ever since?"

"Couldn't sleep."

"Because of this box?"

He took the two long steps back to the table and plucked a crayon out. "He planted these here, on his visit over two weeks back."

"Planted?" Was this another act? A game?

"These are my brother's crayons from grade school. My mother gave us each a wood box for Christmas when we were six or seven. Who knows what I did with mine, but Mike, he was fastidious to a fault even as a kid. He always shared and watched out for me. When we'd be on a plane for Chile and we'd hit bumpy skies, Mike would open up this box and we'd color like crazy to take our minds off crashing."

Laurel watched his long, muscled fingers fondle the crayon stubs one by one. The only sound in the attic room was their gentle plop back into the box. She thought about his apparent fear of flying and how he never revealed a weakness to her before this moment. This couldn't be an act.

"Why would he bring the crayon box here and leave it?"

He sighed. "A signal that he's watching out for me? He knew if I saw this I'd have to keep going after Rojas no matter how bumpy the ride. Mike knew he'd be killed. He lived for a while, knowing that." He crushed a crayon in his fist, the pieces dribbling down into the box. "My brother knew he might die and he never asked my help."

Laurel's stomach twisted but a window in her heart opened further to him. She understood the power of familial love and how it drove people and shaped them. She had been about to marry Kipp— even David—for her father and to bring peace to the family, just as Cole would chase after Rojas for Mike's sake, for his family.

"Do you want lunch?" The question sounded so insipid it embarrassed her.

"Not really hungry." Cole stood staring at her with a forehead furrowed and eyes blinking back tears. "I miss him, Laurel. It's so damn lonely."

Her heart lurched. "I understand," she whispered, seeing in her memory loved ones she'd laid to rest, wishing she could see more clearly, recapture their voices more fully, but knowing time helped. She wanted to help Cole understand it all, but how? How to shrink time for him?

She thought about backing away and running, but he blinked and a teardrop trickled down his whiskery face to his jawline. She rushed to him, wrapping her arms around the tremors racking him.

Nuzzling her hair, he muttered, "I'll never bother you again, Laurel, but I did love you in my own way, and I need you right now. In every way. You feel good, steady."

She closed her eyes against her own confusion. She should be angry. Here he was again making promises. Her heart wanted to burst from the ache, and yet her emotions sizzled like never before—even hotter than she remembered with him. This wanting him was wrong, dead wrong and dangerous, but she saw a man fighting for his very breath. For life. For a chance at redemption.

When his lips caught the shell of her ear, her breathing grew ragged along with her common sense. He needed more than a shoulder to cry on. She wondered if it was possible to make up for lost years during a single moment in a musty attic. She tilted her head, pressed her lips against his neck and drank of his heat.

"I hated the loneliness, too. I hate it now when I forget to be strong and it steals over me. Cole, it will get better. I promise. The black-and-white world evolves into rainbows eventually. Trust me."

A large hand tucked her even closer to him. Heat and ice coming together, resistence melting.

She listened to his heartbeat and to her own voice of reason. He was a lost man driven to find surcease from the ache. She should run to find her hiding places, but her legs would not respond.

His mouth found hers and she became as lost as he, transcending time with him. His breathing spilled onto her face in jagged rhythms, but she remembered the breeze on a hot summer's day. Her hand caught his long hair, fingers recalling the soft strands of timothy grass cushioning their ardor back then.

He was a rock to lean into, his chest and shoulders massive, warm and drenched with an inviting earthy, woodland smell. Her soul felt in need of rest against such a rock. Her back arched to close the gap between their bodies.

A growing thunder of heartbeats echoed within the attic.

His tongue darted into her mouth, exploring, rendering her to a delicate state, making her want to taste of him more, as if she'd been thirsty all her life and he was a clear, cool stream.

She attempted to shut the window in her heart she'd opened for him. Dangerous as a storm blowing through, he could turn her heart inside out again, then leave destruction behind for her to clean up.

She teetered on an abyss.

He kept pulling her back.

The heat grew stronger as he deepened the kiss. Her heartbeat raced way beyond normal and into a red zone, and way beyond what she'd ever experienced even with the Cole who lay with her in a meadow. This Cole was different. Strong yet vulnerable. Aching. Wanting her because of that admission. The new awareness of him bowled through her and begged her to take another look.

His lips skated in a dance across her skin. Feathering a cheekbone. Suckling an earlobe.

The years washed away and down her arms. Like opening the box of crayons, she could see rainbows again.

He lowered her with him to the floor, shedding his shirt and managing to push hers only down her shoulders before reaching their destination. When his thumb flicked apart the front hook of her lacy undergarment, heat crashed through her, tainted with the fear of the unknown. Had they ever made love?

It didn't seem possible.

This felt like the first time. Delicate. Intense.

His eyes were like the hawk, his arms like its wings, wide as the horizon and ready to swoop down and lift her into the skies. Laurel quaked inside, an itch taking up residence in her center. She could answer it by running away. Or by staying to explore.

Cole lowered himself, the hawk riding down on the drafts of jagged breathing to its prey. He nuzzled aside the curtains of hair tickling her shoulders, then the clothing to expose her.

With doubts and fear trembling below her surface, she hesitated to run, her arms pinned yet in her own clothing. Had he planned it that way?

"Cole?"

The hawk trapped his prey by tangling it in the tall, meadow grass. He held it between his talons until it succumbed.

He whispered, "All these years, I've missed this. I've remembered this."

Then he lowered himself to suckle a nipple in exquisite torture. The hawk lingered, and when a moan escaped her involuntarily, he flicked his tongue repeatedly across her ever-tightening bud with the power of rapid wings beating at air currents.

Her heartbeat pounded out of control, her breathing growing so deep that it drew his attention to her heaving breasts. His eyes held a fire in the center of their darkness and yet he waited above her.

He was offering her the choice. Leap away from the fire and run into the darkness, or give in to the hawk.

Her soul reminded her how tiring it could be to struggle against the tall meadow grass, how undignified it was to deny the natural order of things. Her heart reminded her of how lonely and empty that house was inside her.

Did she dare feel this wild again?

Why, with him now, did she think about believing in a future?

She drew in air filled with his spice and the memory of clover and sundrenched earth beneath her. She knew the itch threading through her veins now would never go away of its own accord. So like a small bird, Laurel arched her back, and closed her eyes in repose to welcome what her hawk must do. What she wanted.

In a frenzied capture, they satisfied great hungers. They explored, skin against skin, one heart in syncopation with the other. They borrowed time, not knowing if they could ever be together long enough to pay back this happiness.

Atop the soft flannel of her blouse and his shirt, in their own nest, Laurel forgot that loving could be dangerous.

Chapter 7

THEIR LOVEMAKING was like a brushfire sweeping to the edge of the lake. What started in tender fury found it had no place to go.

Both Laurel and Cole disengaged from the last kiss without a word, though Laurel could not quell her ragged heartbeat or stop her eyes from watching him or measuring his every graceful move.

He tugged on his shirt too quickly, she thought. Her lips could still taste the salt of his skin, the bubbling warmth of the flesh over his pounding heart.

She struggled to breathe when he reached over to slip the top button on the front of her blouse back into place. His obvious hurry to obliterate any evidence of what they'd done sparked confusion inside Laurel.

Why had she succumbed? Why did she already wonder if there would be a next time to succumb?

He'd allowed himself a full range of emotions with her, from sorrow to rage to tender love and tears. When he let down his guard, he was a complicated man. Something she'd never before experienced with him. Certainly not long ago. She was outright attracted to this man. Her body wept to be in his arms. Her mind gloried in the memory of his gutteral whispers, the shared thoughts of needing each other.

His sigh stirred the air. "I'm sorry. I'll leave right away, get to D.C. and work from there."

Panic ripped her. He wanted to forget their slip from grace, their taste of each other.

Her mind raced, confused. What about his brother? The evidence?

Raking his hair back into place, he averted his gaze from her, then twisting around, took stock of the attic.

She sensed he hadn't found what he'd come for.

He reminded her of a lone bear in spring, hungry, thrashing about in the woodland on a search for sustenance, but disoriented with no clear direction. Laurel could not run from that plea for help, even if it was dangerous.

She had to be honest with him, no matter how much it made her stomach ball into a knot just now. "I took what I needed, too. If you're even thinking about being embarrassed—"

His soft smile robbed her of breath. She shoved her blouse back into her jeans.

Adjusting his stance to relieve his bad leg, he said, "There was a time I had no worries. I'd give anything to feel that again."

The attic smelled musty again, old. It made her tired. Looking into his eyes beseeching her in the soft light, she allowed, "All I am, all I do for my job, is worry. Constant worry is a lonely thing. Find a way out of it."

The eyes softened, the lines around them relaxed, and his smile rose like the sun. "I'm glad I have you to talk with. Laurel, you're a fine person."

His tall frame loomed over her, wrapping her tight against him until she could feel nothing but the oneness of their warmth flowing back and forth.

Her heart fluttered. She breathed in the earthy tang about him. "We'd all like to be young again for a few moments now and then. To be free, with the sun on our face, and nothing planned beyond that feeling of sublime warmth."

She hugged him, and he hugged her back.

She committed the elegant simplicity of it to memory.

When she sat down on a chair to put her hiking boots back on, he knelt down and began lacing the hooks for her. "It's more than recapturing youth," he said. "My dad would say it's a marketing thing. It's about us wanting to be heroes, but losing our audience. What does a hero do when he has no audience? Without one, he has nobody to play to, like an actor on a stage without anyone to please."

"Heroes sure don't have it easy."

"No, Laurel, they don't."

Laurel fought the urge to dig her hands into his hair and to bring his lips back up to hers. This was the old Cole, the solicitous one, the kind and charming man and she could fall for him fast. If it weren't for something bothering her.

"You always liked the easy life," she ventured, "but when we grow up, nobody respects people who get things too easily."

His confused look threw bedlam into her heart.

Stiffening, he stopped lacing her boot. "I'm sorry," he said for the second time, "but what's that supposed to mean? I made love to you because, ah, hell, forget it."

Lumbering up, he shot an expletive into the air and steadied himself on a chair.

She bit at her lower lip, not wanting to talk about what they'd just shared, and yet, it was there. Still, they had to disengage, to give each other permission to move on. "I'm making a mess of this. You're trying to be nice, trying to help us over the embarrassment of making love like hot teenagers again—"

"And all I'm doing is bringing back bad memories."

"No," she said, surprising herself. "There were good things you did, but that was then. It's...nostalgia. And that's how we should keep things between us."

A flicker sparked in his eyes. "What was good back then for you?"

She thought a moment. "The way you listened to me talk with your quirky smile on your face. You seemed so absorbed in me, as if I were...special, though I know now you were only plotting new crazy trouble to get into."

He chuckled. "You were smart. I was enthralled, jealous. I knew nothing about fishing and you knew the difference between a plug and a fly. Though I admit you were the cutest thing in the county and that may have been influenced my attention factor."

Heat prickled up her neck to her cheekbones. She should be wary of this silly talk, and yet, it brought sweetness to the air they breathed.

He crouched down again before her and continued lacing up her boots. She let him.

She felt as if they'd walked part way across the bridge from the past and could now see the other side for the first time.

His smile was almost quirky. "Remember those boat rides?"

"You were careless and stupid," she said, but the memory brought a sigh. "We went so fast it sucked the air out of my mouth."

"And you got bugs in your teeth."

"Did not."

"Did too," he said and she almost giggled. He plunged on. "The best was that time in the boat when we sprayed that couple of tourists all decked out in those beer can hats and matching plaid outfits. They'd shoplifted the rubber worms."

Laughter whipped her insides fresh as sheets on a line in the breeze. "We hid behind the counter while they stood there sopping wet in the bait shop threatening to sue my father. He handed them the bill for the worms."

Cole laughed harder. A brilliant twinkle danced in his eyes. "And because they'd never gotten a good look at you, you hired out to them as a fishing guide that evening. They gave you a ten dollar tip."

"Which we promptly spent on more gas for the boat so we could drench our next victims," she said, catching her breath, "though that time my dad didn't much like it. Wasn't the guy a mayor?"

Cole nodded. "You were quite the devil in those days."

"I was, wasn't I?"

Impulsively she reached out to comb through his dark hair with her fingers. It seemed thicker than she remembered. She let her hand slide down along his jawline, so firm and ruggedly stubbled with whiskers he proudly shaved in those days. To touch him now was to emerge from a dark cave into sunlight.

She pulled back her hand and got up. The late afternoon air held a chill in its shadows. "I need to tend my animals."

"Don't go yet. I want your opinion about this." He ran his palms over the maps laid out on the table. Her mind recalled the hot feel of them roving over her body only moments before.

Again she could not resist his entreaty. She convinced herself a look at the map was harmless. "Railroad lines?"

"Yes. Mike and I had marked my railroad adventure out with big Xs on the western states and up through Wisconsin. Up until last night, I thought the last X was here in Dresden, at the house."

"But I don't see any other Xs."

"After finding the crayons, I began going over this again." He tapped a place near Milwaukee and then Chicago. "See those tiny dots?"

She leaned closer. "Yeah. They're made in pencil."

"Mike's sharp accounting pencil. The dots go on. I almost need a magnifying glass to see them, but they go all the way to D.C."

"He wanted you to see someone there? Who? This is a break!"

"Laurel, he made these marks only days before he died. I worked on the map before that and they weren't there."

An awakening trundled ice down her spine. "This is big?"

"More than a chat with our Congress rep, I'm sure." Then his eyes lit up. "Come with me, Laurel Lee. I have to show you something."

He grabbed her hand. They fairly tumbled down the staircases to the bottom floor. When he spotted the cooler in his way at the front door he scooped it up and gave it back to her outside.

"What's this?"

Sheepish, she said, "Egg sandwiches?"

"My favorite. You're the best. No, wait, you used to say, 'you're the cat's meow.'" The twinkle in his eyes warmed her all over again. "Wait here. We'll eat while we talk."

He half-walked, half-skipped with his bum leg across the yard to his tent and was back in no time with his duffel. They sat on the top step to the verandah. The low sun bathed them in surreal lavender light. He fished out his wallet, then pulled out a photo.

Eager and breathless, he asked, "Do you recognize him?"

The photo was hazy with age. "No. Should I?"

He sighed, but said, "Look on the back."

She flipped it over and read aloud, "Aunt Flora has the key to everything about M.R. Look under her skirts, but don't tell Langley, V." She glanced back at Cole and shrugged.

"The man was a naval officer, World War II era. That much I know from the uniform. But Langley, Virginia is CIA headquarters. Whatever the connection is with this old man, Mike's warning me to be careful with the information."

"And he lives here? He'd be in his seventies or eighties, maybe older. Finding an old man based on a fifty-year-old photo will be like needles in a haystack."

"I know. That's why I need your help. Maybe your mother would recognize him."

Now a chill rattled her. "How dare you even think of involving my mother."

She soared from her perch on the step and stood in the weedy grass facing him. "Is that why we made love? Have a little sex with lonely little Laurel Lee and she'll be eager again to be your partner in crime? I had almost believed you'd changed."

His face blanched under its whiskers. "That isn't why I made love to you and you know it."

"Do I? What do I believe about you?" She thought about the letters he must have written to attorney David Huber. Why couldn't Cole tell her about them? "Maybe you made this whole story up about Rojas. Maybe your brother isn't dead—"

He rushed to her, his hands gripping her upper arms. "That bullet you took out of my leg was real." He shook her, his eyes glazed with dark fury. "I loved him. He's dead because of me. I have a son in hiding because of me, which you skewered me with a few days ago.

Now make up your mind which Cole you believe in. The kid who left you or the man who's scared as hell who needs your help despite his better judgment."

He let go of her, sank back onto the top step, raking his hair several times.

Laurel's heart ached with the reality of how far apart they could be. "We're no longer carefree kids. I can't help you with this...murder. And you could die, too. I feel as if you're not real because we're even talking about such things."

"You didn't make love to a ghost moments ago."

"But I did. I've just realized it. And I need more, much more, from a relationship. I want it all, Cole. I want my heroes to live. The man in my life has to live, and want to live. I want promises of a future."

His eyes mellowed to a bronze glow, his jawline sliding into a hesitant rumination. "I need much more from me, too, Laurel Lee, but I won't apologize for wanting you, even if it was misguided. I loved you once."

"You fell into the memory as if falling into a lost well."

"You don't believe a man can be seduced by the romance of bygone days?"

She blinked several times in disbelief. She'd forgotten how driven he could be, how convincing, and then how swiftly he could change course and be gentle, seductive. "No, I don't think you work like that. You hate going back into the past."

"Which means what I feel for you isn't just a memory."

The smoldering intensity of truth sent her heart rushing. Could the old bonds be rekindling this swiftly?

Determined to deny such a bond that could only be temporary anyway, she held her long hair back, then leaned forward to retrieve the fried egg sandwiches with the other hand.

Somersaulting butterflies cut loose in her stomach as she watched him bite into the sandwich, savoring it, a sublime countenance kissing his face. One of his eyebrows crawled into a lazy arch. It always did back then, too.

"Enough catsup on it?"

"Perfect." But he was staring at her lips. "Do you think Flora could have a vault here?"

It was her turn to raise a brow. "The basement looked ordinary."

"Yeah. I couldn't find a weak spot in any of the walls."

"Many of these old places have cisterns or root cellars built away from the house. Maybe Mike found one."

His eyes lit up. "I never thought of that. But then there's the thing about her skirts."

"That's odd to me, too. She hasn't lived here for years. I went through all the bedrooms earlier looking for you and didn't see a single old garment hanging anywhere. Just a piece of junky old picture frame or doo-dad here and there on the walls that even hobos or teenagers making out didn't want for souvenirs."

Cole sighed. "The place used to be so gorgeous. Flocked wallpaper, shiny floors we'd slide across in our socks, fires in that grand fireplace—"

"You're not thinking of—"

He shook his head. "This place is beyond repair, even if I had plans to stay. I'll keep stripping out the good lumber for you while I'm here. Should be able to find enough to expand your animal shed if you need to."

The gesture touched her. "Does it make you sad to see it this way? You spent a few summers here as a boy."

"Yes and no. It used to be a living place. Vibrant, with my aunt swishing through it. But you can't turn a clock back, can you?"

Despite her resolve, the heated imprint of their lovemaking undulated across her body. She thought about being upstairs, her hand running over the dresser with the carved initials of teenage lovers. She and Cole had let life slip past them somehow, like the mansion slipping into disrepair. Sadly, it was too late to fix things, so she squared her shoulders and thought about the here-and-now. "My mother has always sewn a lot. Maybe she remembers something about Flora Tilden's dresses."

"You'd do that for me?" He stopped mid-bite.

She wanted to laugh, for he looked innocent for once in his life. "We've got to get you out of Dresden. Alive. So what should I ask mother about?"

"About where she thinks Flora Tilden bought her clothes, or if she donated anything to a charity or museum."

"A museum?"

"Even as a kid I recognized her ballgowns were special works of art. Mucho dinero."

"Expensive ballgowns? In Dresden? I doubt she was a prom date."

"But Gary said there're rumors about her being some gangster's girlfriend. I vaguely remember my parents mentioning she had interesting connections. It's likely why they weren't excited about coming back and claiming the property. They probably figured Flora's mob friends would have swooped in and who wants to argue with the mob."

Laurel had to smile. "Evidently we were too clean-cut and boring around here for them."

"Never boring." He winked at her and she dove into another bite of sandwich to avoid his teasing. "It's possible Mike could have found where these dresses are and hid something in them."

"It's a long shot but worth looking into I suppose."

He licked catsup off his little finger and she found it the most sensual act she'd ever witnessed.

He asked, "Then you'll ask your mother about what she remembers?"

Laurel gave him a slow nod. She had no intention of involving her mother.

"You're a gem, Laurel Lee. Thanks."

A modicum of guilt at lying hit her stomach. Why did she suddenly feel like she was being sucked into a drain with no way out? She reminded herself of the letters that David Huber had received, presumably from Cole. It bothered her that she couldn't trust Cole completely. It bothered her even more that she desperately wanted to.

"I have to head out," she announced, needing to escape the tension of their lies, the dance they were insisting on playing.

"Could we get together later tonight?"

Her heartbeat tripped, but she was glad she'd planned to visit the graveyard to plant flowers that had long ago outgrown their plastic store pots. "Not tonight. I'm busy."

She rushed off down the deer path toward her boat, breathing deeply of the fragrant summer air.

He called out behind her, "Didn't mean it like a date. We can't go to a restaurant anyway. I'm outta cash. You'd have to buy."

She licked her lips against a threatening grin, then shook her head and trudged on.

ACTING ON Laurel's idea about cisterns and root cellars, Cole poked around the yard until well after darkness set in with brackish shadows that made further treasure hunting impossible.

Near midnight, after washing up in the lake, he finally collapsed inside his sleeping bag under the stars. He watched a pair of raccoons skitter through his meager camp, lick clean the used yogurt container then head into the mansion. He meant to ask Laurel about them. The raccoons visited every night and acted as if they owned the place and he were the interloper. Wasn't he?

He sat up. Why had he made love to her? The question hit with a bang in his head louder than any of Rojas' bullets.

How stupid could a man get? She was embarrassed afterward, but hadn't he felt her want him just as much as he wanted her? Or was that his ego speaking? A fever stormed over him. He'd taken her so fast his hands barely had a memory of her. He'd give anything—

Stop it, man. Laurel vexed him. She never used to. When they were teenagers, they laughed and made love. A simple, joyous existence. Now she was complicated, foreign, a woman who needed subtitles for him to understand. First she hated him, now she was helping him. She yelled at him one minute, then smiled the next.

A sudden, small, glowing light flickered across the bay. Laurel? He watched the glow progress past her cabin, then on down the path that led deeper into woods. What was she up to? And at this hour?

He remembered the cliff off down that path, that it was a long way away and secluded, dangerous.

He climbed out of the sleeping bag. He had to find out what his Laurel Lee was up to in the dead of night. An overwhelming need to keep her safe sent him after her.

LAUREL RESPECTED night's gentle pace and peaceful song. She hadn't wanted to be so rude as to bring artificial light along, but tonight she'd need the lantern. She'd bought the geraniums days ago, but with Cole's arrival hadn't gotten a chance to plant them. Already the poor things were dropping petals and threatening to die on her. She'd had enough of death in her life. Perhaps she was planting them in defiance of Cole suckering her into his own deathtrap. How could she have let down her guard with him? She had to feel in control again.

She glanced across the bay. This time, the porthole window seemed to wink at her with moonlight, taunting her about making love with a hunted man in the privacy of the dusty attic. The old mansion seemed to vibrate under its moonglow halo as if it'd been brought to life by what she and Cole committed under its rafters.

Breathless, she began to trot along the path, hurrying out of sight of the hoary old place. She tried to convince herself that Cole was not at the root of her aching head and limbs.

Earlier, Jim Swenson had brought by a pair of orphaned coyote pups, and the entire shed had gone into an uproar. Even Rusty seemed affronted that a dog cousin would deign to share his digs. The upshot was, she was forced to build a new outdoor cage for the pups. She had been grateful for the handful of lumber Cole had already delivered, but she'd also pounded every nail with extra punishing blows to assuage her guilt for making love with a man she shouldn't—no, couldn't—want.

Being with Cole today had changed something within her. She felt more than an agitation, almost a fear of the unknown. Cole was forcing her hand, spinning her toward an unknown future. And she found herself craving a new, more mature relationship with him.

She'd have to make choices soon if he didn't leave. To tell him things. To keep her own sense of honor intact.

She rushed now.

Crossing the small bridge over the creek that fed the bay, she thought she heard a groan. She stopped, glancing into the shadows. Nighthawks screeched. The breeze moaned through the pines, bringing the perfume of the trees and wood violets in bloom.

She headed up the pine-flanked path that led to the cliff. Then as usual, about halfway up the steady climb she chose the fork that allowed her to traverse the ridge for several yards before dipping down the other side.

Laurel paused at the curious snap of a twig, but pushed on. The graveyard was in sight now, its moonlit gravestones throwing long, inky shadows behind them. She drew in a shaky breath. Flashes of Cole flitted through her. Him laying with her in the attic, holding her as if they'd never left their meadow. His heat taking the chill off the fifteen years they'd been apart.

She could not afford to love him again. And yet, to make love in their meadow again...no woman could forget that. Laurel wanted it again. Even if she couldn't trust him....

She couldn't deny the yearning. They had been in love then. Happy. So damn happy. So innocent to the danger of it.

COLE'S LEG WAS killing him. Twice he almost stumbled over tree roots trying to keep Laurel in sight. Both times she paused, forcing him to duck into the underbrush. The pressure on his leg bandages tortured him. Then there was the matter of those two raccoons following him. What were they up to? Watching out for Laurel? He almost believed it.

It was that ethereal quality that kept him from abandoning his spying on her. Laurel strode through the night as if it beckoned her. She owned the night.

The brush was so thick he had a hard time keeping his bearings, but she knew every step to take to avoid a bulbuous root, a branch and bramble. Or did the plants bow to her, whisking out of her way on their own accord out of respect? They seemed to.

When he finally positioned himself behind a tree where he could pull a branch far enough down for a clear look, his breath caught.

The church! What was she doing here? He hadn't realized he'd walked this far. This was their little church. His heartbeat thundered in his chest. His palms turned clammy.

She approached the place, her long hair swaying back and forth across her back. Cole squinted. The glow from her lantern illuminated the rungs of a wrought iron fence. The graveyard. Of course. Her father must be buried here.

Just then, the raccoons decided to chitter about his feet.

"Who's there?" Laurel called.

He shrank against scratchy bark and his heart raced. Certainly she could hear its tom-tom beat.

Then she chided, "Roxy, Roger, what're you doing over here? Long way from your usual digs."

Roxy and Roger? He let out his pent-up breath and grinned. With the raccoons' noises providing him cover, he edged around the tree enough to watch Laurel.

She pushed open the creaky iron gate, then picked up the lantern and basket, walking past several rows of headstones before stopping. She began unloading the basket. He thought he recognized the shapes of geraniums. While she set up to begin her planting, he used the opportunity to edge closer. A tall, woody lilac bush flanking the corner of the graveyard camouflaged him perfectly and gave him a close-up view.

Laurel was planting flowers in front of not one, but two headstones. The big monument had to belong to her father Gerald, but whose was the smaller one? Her fiancé? It had to be.

Then her softly-spoken words confirmed it for him. "Oh, darling," she said, "you'll always have a place in my heart, no matter what."

A ball of ice slammed into Cole's stomach. Had Laurel made love to him because she was longing for Kipp? That didn't seem like Laurel. She told him she'd gotten on with her life. Or was she here because she felt guilty for making love to Cole? Cole couldn't stand the thought. The lovemaking was his fault, not hers. Guilt wasn't something Laurel bought into anyway. Cole bore the guilt in their relationship if anyone did.

He watched her plant the last flower, then linger, surveying, touching headstones. Her movements ebbed silently in the night, covered by the breeze now and then rattling the maple leaves overhead. When she packed up and left, closing the squeaking iron gate, Roxy and Roger scrambled after her.

At the fork in the path, Laurel chose the way to her cabin. Cole almost followed her, then thought better of it. He turned up the hill toward the cliff.

Standing on the rocky shelf hundreds of feet above the valley, the view overwhelmed him in the same ethereal manner it always did when he and Laurel met here. The rocky precipice jutted right into the stars. He stretched his arm out and tapped a shining speck with his fingertip. He imagined Laurel reaching out the same way, to the same star, until their fingertips touched. They had done that every time they came here. His breathing grew ragged.

Cole withdrew his hand quickly. Why should Laurel's feelings toward him matter anymore? Because he had loved her once. Because her living alone didn't seem right to him now.

Suddenly he couldn't bear the thought of leaving Dresden and Spirit Lake until he discovered the secrets of her heart—the shadow garden she tended. For that's what Laurel was doing, tending the shadows of her past as if they were living, breathing things. Planting flowers in a graveyard. Living in her father's cabin.

Guarding memories. Keeping people away. More specifically, keeping men away, including himself.

Why?

He turned and limped back down the path, feeling like the true Atlas. Weighed down.

Once upon a time he had loved her for the way she shared all of herself—body, mind, heart and soul. She no longer seemed to like to share. She preferred being alone. She admitted she worried all the time about others, animals certainly as part of her job.

None of it seemed right to him. There were puzzle pieces here, but they didn't quite fit together for him.

A part of him, deep down, inside a cave of dormant emotions, felt as if he were following a light now. Wanting desperately to make sure the light didn't disappear before he caught up to it.

And the light was life itself. Love. A part of him wanted to love Laurel. The whole, complete, sharing way.

If he were still that reckless.

THE WEEKEND exhausted Laurel. She was glad. Otherwise she'd be tempted to fill the cooler and visit Cole. She felt sorry for him, to her chagrin. He hammered and pounded away relentlessy at the old mansion, looking for clues from Mike. In between, she spied him turning the sod over in several places. He worked like a madman with no letup. She knew he must be in pain, too.

While she tended her animals, feeding them a variety of sweet fruits, milk, grains, she couldn't help but wonder about Cole. He said he had no cash. Was he still eating dried food mixed with lake water? The vision of him devouring the fried egg sandwich stayed with her. Sometimes she imagined him sitting at her kitchen table, the two of them eating a meal together. Or having a cup of coffee together on the front stoop. Or a late-night bowl of ice cream in the living room by the fireplace. Still, she remained home alone, cleaning pens, feeding animals, bandaging wounds and doing paperwork.

Early Monday evening she spotted two boats motoring into the embankment at the Tilden place. She trotted inside and swung the scope on target. The sheriff? Now what?

John Petski climbed out of one boat and some high school kid she knew was doing community service as penance for breaking windows jumped from the other. What was John up to with Cole?

Then Cole waved to her.

She jerked back from the scope. Darn him. He'd just made her a joke in front of her friend and some kid. Whatever happened to her happy seclusion?

Laurel leaped into her minivan, sprayed gravel and headed for Dresden. She'd get him his answers about Flora from her mother as promised, then send him on his way.

THE BAIT SHOP was crammed. She slithered around tourists' elbows and gawdy T-shirts to the register where she helped bag for her mother.

"This fishing contest is making it nuts, dear," Madelyn said. "And my cottages. I even had to rent the unfinished one, though I got some curtains up. The man insisted he needed a place to stay here."

"That's nice, mother. What've you heard about the sheriff's doings out at the Tilden estate? I saw him and the Bowman kid tying up with two boats."

Her mother skewered her with the eagle eye only a mother owns. "Gary says John found out Atlas knows about boat engines. Your hobo is earning a few bucks tuning up the sheriff's patrol fleet."

Cole and the sheriff? Why would Cole get buddy-buddy with the sheriff so willingly? Unless....

Her stomach churned. Unless they thought Rojas was coming here. Her imagination exploded. Cole was in danger. They all were. A shudder ripped its ice down her spine.

"What do you remember about Flora Tilden?"

"Flora?" Madelyn threw her a frown. She pulled boxes of hooks and purple rubber worms across the bar code reader, then handed them to Laurel for bagging. "Having second thoughts about burning down her old mansion?"

"Of course not. David mentioned something about trying to find her will. We need to make sure the deed to the land is free and clear before we can raze the place."

"That's odd, dear. A will would have been filed in Wisconsin probate court. David could find it in no time."

So why hadn't he? David knew something. What was in those files? "But what about a title to the land? Those are at the county courthouse."

"Not necessarily. If a piece of land's been in a family for years, especially before records were computerized, those documents could be buried in a vault."

A vault? Cole had asked about a vault. Had he been talking with David, too? She fumed.

"It seems I've been out of the loop." She suspected on purpose. It would be just like Cole to hatch some adventuresome plan to catch this Rojas, and try and protect her by not telling her about it. Well, she'd show Cole. She could play detective, too.

Laurel flashed a weak smile. "Did Flora Tilden ever date anyone here?"

Madelyn snickered. "Rumor was, the woman was like a pot of honey. Always a swarm of men around her."

"Anyone in particular?"

"I don't know. Maybe. Rumor was she was married once, but she moved here soon after the War. Maybe she lost her sweetheart in it."

"But I heard she wore beautiful gowns here."

Madelyn handed her split-shot and bobbers to bag. "If she did, it was in her own parlor. She rarely showed her face in town. Most of us called it 'uppity' back then. Your father warned you about that family—"

"Don't, Mother. This is about the land, not me." She winced at her white lie. "Where'd she live before here?"

"I assumed out East. At that time everyone came from the East to settle in Wisconsin."

Laurel lit up. Thinking about Mike's cryptic note, she said, "I bet she lived in Washington, D.C." She hugged her mother quick and planted a kiss on her flushed cheek. "Thanks, Mom. You just gave me a tremendous idea."

Chapter 8

SHE RACED HOME, fired up her fishing boat and motored across the bay.

It was for naught. Cole wasn't there, and only one of the sheriff's boats remained tied at the hastily shored-up dock. If Cole were testing and tuning an engine, that meant he could be anywhere on Spirit Lake. Deflated, she motored back across the bay to tend to evening chores.

She worked late, up until ten p.m., the hour for the final feedings and final checks on the baby animals. About to gather up medicines and formula, she sighed at the phone interruption.

Cole's voice sent her heartbeat into a rollercoaster ride.

She squeaked, "You're where?" She could have sworn Cole said "jail."

"Jail."

"Dresden's?"

"Same old one. Same lousy cots, latrines and paint job. Your mother should do some curtains for this place."

"That isn't funny, Cole. What happened?" She thought of Rojas. Her fingers shook.

"Got in a fight."

Her breath caught in her throat. "With Rojas? Are you all right? Did he have a gun?"

Cole chuckled. "Slow down. It was some old drunk. He's snoring next to me now. I'll tell you about it when you get here."

"Get there? Me? What for?"

"To bail me out."

She felt like a marionette dancing on the end of Cole's strings. Anger welled inside her. "Put John on the line."

"Can't. The sheriff's pissed enough at me."

Her hand gripped the receiver. "So how much is your bail?"

Cole quoted a hefty four-figure sum. She almost fainted. "You realize at this hour I'll have to post a property bond. My cabin and animal shed and boat to spring your hide."

"And I appreciate it, Laurel Lee."

She slammed the phone in his ear. But she put on a sweatshirt over her flannel blouse, grabbed her keys and headed to town. It was time to take charge of this relationship with Cole. He was getting her in deeper and deeper. Sucking her down that drain with him.

SHERIFF PETSKI hollered, "You can't go in there."

She charged right past him.

Cole sat on a cell cot reading *Time* magazine as if this were the most natural way to spend an evening. It made her furious. Another man snored under a blanket on the other cot in the cell. Cole looked up with an uneasy grin on his face.

"Please, don't even try to be ingratiating," she spouted, but an unsettling urge to fling her arms around him unnerved her. He was all right, thank God.

"You came to bail me out. I knew you would. Thanks."

She took note of the grin frozen in place. A bit artificial. What was he up to now?

John met her at the cell bars.

Laurel hiked a purposeful brow at him. "You didn't advance a loan to your new boat mechanic? When were you two going to let me in on your big secret of working together?"

Cole stepped up and wrapped his fingers around the bars. "We could talk outside, but you haven't posted bail yet."

"Forget it until I know more about what you're up to. John, let me in."

John shook his head. "I can't let you in—"

"Why not? Are these dangerous criminals?"

The corners of Cole's mouth twitched, forcing her to control mounting confusion and indignation. "Don't be so smug. This story better be real good to get me here at this hour."

Backing away, Cole stuffed his hands in his pockets, though she thought she caught him trying to control a know-it-all smile. On her glare, Sheriff Petski relented and let her inside the cell, then left them alone. The outer door to the front office closed after him.

Crossing her arms, Laurel scrutinized Cole standing beside the cot only a few feet away. A low-watt overhead lamp in the hall cast meager light into the dark cell. He stared back, looking handsome, but forlorn, crooked in his stance to favor the bad leg. His hair hung dark and disheveled, a shadow of whiskers claiming his chin, a simple white T-shirt bucking its threads against the muscles of his broad chest.

Behind them, the man under the blanket snorted into a long snore.

"Lovely companion," she spouted. "At least it's not your Mr. Marco Rojas."

"We wouldn't be talking if it were."

She shivered. "What happened?"

Easing onto the cot, Cole stretched out his bad leg. "I stopped for a burger at a tavern down by the public dock after running the boat down here for the sheriff. This guy was getting loud in the place and I asked him to shut up. He punched me. I asked him to stop and he punched me again. I finally took him by the scruff of the neck and sat him on a chair, which he then picked up and threw at me. Can you believe it?"

She refolded her arms and eyed him with suspicion. "Yes, I can. Trouble follows you. Can't you ever just get up and walk away from trouble?"

His gaze went soft. "I've tried that. I've heard it sticks in a person's mouth, like an aftertaste."

"Touché, but damn you. I was worried. I am worried. First I'm scared that you're getting killed over at the mansion, and in the next minute you infuriate me so much that I wish you were dead."

He came to her on a heavy sigh. She leaned the back of her head against the bars, his rough hands clasping her arms, rubbing them like tinder between them, the heat ebbing into her. Even through her sweatshirt and jacket she could feel his warmth. She needed the calming effect.

"I like that you worry about me," Cole whispered, "but I worry about you getting so upset. I've always been truthful about having a job to do here, and it could get uglier."

"Like that goose egg at your hairline?" His mussed hair and a couple of scratches on his chin didn't help his appearance. Or her control. She yearned to cradle him, like some wild animal she could patch up and send on his way.

A smile erupted on his face. "I bet I look like something the sheriff usually drops off at your place."

Sighing at the way he could read her mind, she could only nod.

He gave her a slow grin. "Old Wiley's wicked for his size."

"Wiley Lundeen did this? That's the town drunk over there under that blanket?" Then a worry blanketed her. Leaning closer, she whispered, "His mouth can shoot off. I hope this doesn't make the papers. Your cover could be broken."

"With him?"

"Shh." Inches from his face, her gaze took in the cuts and bruises. They tied her in knots. "You're not in much shape to ward off a seasoned hit man."

Leading her over to the corner away from Wiley, he fenced her in against the bars, whispering, "He's going to come eventually. So I have to begin planning for it. I don't have much of a choice. These leads Mike left me are going nowhere. If only we'd talked before..." His face took on the darker edge of hidden pain.

Despite her resolve to not get involved, her heart went out to him.

"I can help," she whispered back, almost shaking from the turnabout from only days ago, but his pain spoke to her. "I saw Mother today and something she said gave me a hunch about Flora and this photo of Mike's."

"What?" He raked a hand over his head and came up wincing.

Nudging the thick hair more gently into place for him, she realized touching him always took her breath away, no matter their circumstances. His neediness wound around her heart. "That's a doozy. You got a headache?"

"You mean I'm not hearing the echo of hammering?"

She smiled at his sense of humor, giving up even more of her resolve to be tough on him. "If this gets any bigger, you're going to look like a walking eggplant."

"That reminds me. Never did finish that burger. Don't happen to have another egg sandwich on you?"

She caught his gaze. The twinkle in his eyes sent shock waves down to her toes. When had being with him become so easy? His firm lips twisted into a silly grin that she had the greatest urge to kiss. She blamed their lovemaking. That's what this "easy" feeling was, just sexual attraction and nothing more. Silliness. She could control this.

"Did Flora live in D.C.?"

"I never asked her," he grunted. "I don't know, and my parents never said much about that part of the family."

She sank back against the wall in their corner, thinking. "She had a ton of money, and Mike says to look under her skirts, whatever that means. You're sure you don't remember some code you and Mike had as boys? Maybe this is a cryptogram or something."

Cole shrugged. "No secret languages I'm afraid."

"Doesn't it seem odd she'd move here just after World War II? If she was a society lady, something had to make her want to hide out here. But what?"

A snort from the cot behind them caused Cole to lean in closer, his gaze locking with hers. He tucked a finger under her chin, starting an electrical storm skipping across her, putting every folicle on alert. "I ask that about you all the time. Why, Laurel, do you choose the existence you do?"

Her temperature sizzled. "We're not discussing me."

He had her cornered. "But we are discussing a woman who could have been just like you. Maybe there's a clue here, if we consider the psychology. You're good at psychology I've found."

"You should have been a salesman."

An eyebrow arched, sending tremors rippling through her again. "Why would my great-aunt Flora hide out from the world? What would she hide under those skirts?"

His body pressed close. Laurel swallowed hard. "Maybe she had a lover she lost and it took all her courage to start over again. Maybe she didn't want other people to see what she'd become. Maybe she was embarrassed to have loved so foolishly."

His eyes darkened to black coals. "Embarrassed?"

She trembled under his gaze. "A woman has pride. To have lost herself in someone else's heart and soul, and then to have him taken away by his own deeds, leaves her empty. All the world can point at her as if she were an abandoned house, and simply pass by. They pity her. It's too much to bear, so she goes into seclusion at first."

"We are talking about Aunt Flora?"

"Of course." But the fluttering in her stomach wouldn't quit.

"Could a woman like that take other lovers?"

She could see every whisker, every scratch, the fine lines in his firm lips only inches away. "Yes, but a woman like that would demand a lot of a man. She would take her time finding the right man, and she would die if the next man she loved with all her heart left her."

His eyes shimmered. They took on the reflective look of the porthole window. "Now I understand Aunt Flora a lot better."

Then he backed away and she could breathe again.

Shaken, she fought to calm herself. "How much longer do you think it'll be before Rojas finds out about your property here, and about Mike coming here in May?"

"Not much. He could have people skulking around already. There are ways to find people. Tax records. Any credit cards Mike might have used to buy a ticket might leave a trail for a good detective, though it appears Mike covered himself with great care on this one."

She registered the profound sadness that overwhelmed him when he talked about Mike. His face wrinkled, with the light in his eyes dimming. Cole was a man without a home, a man on a lonely journey. She could identify with lonely journeys. She'd survived one.

She offered, "My plan isn't fleshed out much, but I know if you stay here overnight you'll get front page in the local weekly. Editor Buzz Vandermeer loves to list names. He's always telling my mother that a weekly is built on names. You'll be a sitting duck for Rojas."

Shuffling wearily to the cot, Cole eased down. "I'll be fine. Seems I owe for a few chairs, not to mention mailboxes. John said because of the witnesses it might be prudent for me to spend the night, since I don't have cash on me."

She scoffed. "John Petski's honesty gets me down sometimes. That man is perpetually running for office."

"He's a good egg."

"We'll see about that." Whipping around, she called out, "John? I'm ready."

The sheriff entered the room and unlocked the cell door, but Laurel didn't step out. John frowned. "Are you coming out or not?"

She swallowed hard against her rapid heart rate. Could she do this? "Would you place Cole under house arrest? At my house?"

FOG ROLLED IN behind them when Laurel led Cole up her front stoop to the door. Her fingers shook on the doorknob.

He noticed. "You're nervous? How long has it been since you asked a man to share your bed?"

She turned to him in the darkness, knowing she'd find a grin pasted on his face. She matched it with a warning frown. "For someone who could have shared a cell with Wiley Lundeen, you're sounding rather boorish."

"Just being honest. It's what you want from me, isn't it?" He reached over her shoulder and pushed open the door. "I'd also like to know why you don't lock your house."

Where his arm grazed hers, a firestorm started that swept across her body. Walking inside, she said, "I'll take you home in my boat after we have a chance to finish our discussion. I never meant for you to stay here overnight."

"You lied to the sheriff?"

Guilt peppered her, but she held fast to her resolve. "He'll forgive me. I want to know what you're up to."

But he wasn't about to divulge anything, darn his ability to stay focused and in control.

They both removed their jackets, and she hung them on the hooks by the door. When she turned around, he'd already wandered into the living area toward the sofa by the fireplace that still glowed. His muscular silhouette engendered hot memories of being consumed by him in the attic tryst. His eyes were soft coals, patient tinder.

Shivering, she offered, "Should I fix us something?"

"No need."

Her mind reeled. She shouldn't have brought him here. She walked around to the other side of the sofa and flung open the glass doors of the fireplace to poke at a dying ember. The fire provided the only light.

"It's just as I imagined it," he said, his voice gutteral, his gaze appraising the cabin's interior. "A perfect, cozy nest for a mother bird."

Mother bird. He'd made the same reference in the bait shop.

"That leg must be throbbing pretty good after tonight's workout with Wiley," she said, thinking how warm it could be in Cole's arms.

Settling into the sofa, he smirked, "You don't have a plan, do you?"

His eyes reflected the ember's growing intensity, with the firelight highlighting chiseled good looks. The room grew close. She reminded herself she had wanted him here. To settle things. Not to stir them up.

She poked at the fire. Sparks spit at her, then full flames danced, illuminating the room.

She planted the iron poker on the hearth. "You could really use a shave and a fat steak on that goose egg."

"I'd rather eat the fat steak."

Shaking her head, Laurel crossed in front of the sofa and headed for the kitchen area, where she turned on the soft light above the sink. "I'm afraid you'll have to wait. I've got animals out back that need a nighttime feeding and medicines worse than you, believe it or not."

"I'll help."

"Maybe you could. I've got to make sure all the heat lamps are on. It's raw out, and it's going to rain so the temperature's not going to rise too quickly."

"Ah, Wisconsin." He leaned against the kitchen door frame. "I do remember huddling under blankets in my bed at great-aunt Flora's. And cuddling under a blanket with you in the car when we went to the dump to watch for bears."

She stuffed her flushed face in the refrigerator to look for formula. "You like how I finished off the cabin?"

"It's great. I like the open floor plan."

She wished for walls and doors to shut out the gaze that followed her every move. He watched her get the formula out, then the syringes and droppers from the cupboards.

Finally, when she drew another glass bottle from the refrigerator, she looked him square in the eyes. "You're like having one of those cheap velvet religious paintings in the kitchen."

He laughed. "The ones with Elvis's eyes following you everywhere you go?"

"Yes."

"May I turn on more light?" he asked.

"I like it this way."

"You never used to."

A feeling scuttled through her that she didn't care for. He was probing again and she didn't like it. She yanked at a bottle on the refrigerator shelf, but a loud crack outside startled her and the bottle slipped from her fingers in a punctuating crash. The wind kicked in then, rattling the windows.

After flicking on the light switch, Cole admonished, "Don't. You'll cut yourself. Let me help."

"I'll have it picked up in a jiffy. Just sit somewhere."

He hovered over her instead, his shoes inches from her hand and the glass. "Can't you allow your friends to help you?"

"What's that supposed to mean?"

"It means give me a little credit for wanting to help you." He pointed to a chair at the kitchen table. "Sit."

"I'm not some puppy you can train."

Before she could yelp, he swept her up in his arms and plunked her in the chair by the kitchen table. "You have to start thinking about your own welfare for a change, instead of saving the rest of us from harm's way without a thought." Corralling her with outstretched arms, he said, "Now stay."

She sat, but her thumping fingers rattled the table with a force that rivaled the brewing storm outside. "I can see why Wiley hauled off at you."

A churlishness clouded his face. "Where's the broom and dust pan?"

She pointed to the slim closet, then watched him sweep. She realized she'd never seen him do anything domestic. It begged for questions about his lifestyle now. Did he cook? Did his dive-shop friend Lisa cook for him? Or ex-wife Stephanie? She held her tongue. Why should she care?

He stood before Laurel with the pan full of glass. "Where do you want this?"

"I'll get you a bag."

"Sit. Where are they?"

She pointed to a cupboard and he dispatched the glass in a bag, then put the bag next to the front door. Back at the table, he asked, "What do you drink at this hour of the night? It used to be smuggled beer on the cliff, but dare I say it's a tad wet out there for such a foray?"

"Herbal tea," she sniped, heated by the memory he'd induced.

"Should have known."

"Now what does that mean?"

Already he was filling the pot with water at the sink. He plunked it on the stove and turned on the burner. "You have it all down."

"Have what down?"

"The act."

"You're always the one with the act." But his turning the tables on her intrigued her. "What act?"

He leaned back against the sink. "Living in the woods, liking the dark, caring for wounded animals. You haven't cut your hair for years. Then of course there's that carefully-practiced scorn for associating with men. If I didn't know better, I'd think I was in a family movie replete with fuzzy animals and you were bucking for an Oscar. And the theme of your movie is, how to hide out from life."

"It's my life and I happen to like it fine." Anger welled in her. "So I don't live a fast-paced, glamorous life like you. At least I don't have someone chasing me down. At least I don't have a living, breathing son who's lost to me anyway because of my choices." She sucked in at the hurt slapping across his face.

Pivoting to the kitchen sink, he stared at the rain sprinkling the dark window. "You're almost too right. I keep in touch with Tyler through the sheriff, and tonight I found out my son ran away already."

She wanted to die inside. She went to him, her heart rallying to him, her hands shaking as she lay them on the wall of his back. "I'm sorry."

"His cousin Tim ran away, too. And of course Karen had no way of contacting me directly."

The teapot whistled, making her jump. She shoved the pot to the next burner and flicked off the heat. "But they found the boys?"

Like a lone wolf, Cole stepped further away from her. "They found them right away, fortunately. They were going to camp under a viaduct for the night, then hitch."

"To find you."

"Who knows. Maybe. If he doesn't hate me."

She watched him cling to the sink rim, the icy whiteness of his knuckles wrenching her heart. There was nothing worse than a lost child. "He knows only one thing. He loves you."

A muscle jumped at the corner of his eye.

"You doubt your son's love?" she asked, her heart swelling at the incredulity of the notion.

"I hate to think what would happen if Rojas..."

She went to him, smothering his icy hands against her stomach to warm him, but he trembled. "Your son is safe. You said so."

Reaching up, she pushed stray hair back off his furrowed brow, being careful of the ugly wound. She attempted a comforting smile. "Listen to me. You're going to win."

"Win what?" He turned and peered at his reflection in the window over the sink. "I don't know that man in the window anymore. I don't know me."

Scrutinizing their reflections, Laurel saw a shared weariness masking their faces, making them appear alike and ghoulishly older tonight, like some married couple, worrying about a child out too late. The thought stunned her, throwing a fright into her that she needed to tamp down. She couldn't afford this type of closeness with Cole.

"You're just tired," she finally said.

"Maybe I could sneak back to Florida, see Tyler, retrace things."

She busied herself with taking clean bottles from the drainer and putting them away. "You can't go flying back to Florida right now. That would be the old Cole, acting reckless, and I won't have it."

He gripped one of her arms as if it were a lifeline. His eyes bore into hers, then softened. "Reckless?"

"It's true. The old Cole Wescott would leave right now, barrel right to Tyler in that old singular focus, leading Rojas right to your family's doorstep. You'd be killed and where would that leave your son? And damn you, if you really are that reckless underneath, I'll come after you myself. For the sake of your son."

Peering down at her with eyes gone wild with awakening, he released her arm as if to say, you're right. "But it's the old me who hopped the train."

"Who promised his brother a legacy for his son as well as your own. What's wrong with you? Stop taking the easy route. You don't have to be the 'old' you. Accept what you're doing and becoming, because believe me, you have no choice. Nobody runs for his life or hides out and remains the same."

"Is it why you changed? Is living out here alone, and becoming a mother to animals what I made you do?"

"Yes," she confessed, her nerves darting like needles. "But don't make it sound so hideous. It's just the opposite. Life surrounds me. Yes, at first I wanted to be left alone. My father was in a rage. My mother was upset. Everyone was talking about you. In college I found I could hide from the prying eyes and the pity. But I should thank you because it forced me to make choices. I didn't have to stay in college. I didn't have to study animals and plants. I found I liked it. For me. I'm strong and I'm doing something lasting."

"But you're missing out on being loved yourself."

"I'm loved here," she sniped, but her heart cried out.

Every fiber in her itched to tell him everything. Itched to tell him she longed to be loved in the way he'd loved her one summer. Fully, completely, in wild abandon that tickled, smelled of clover, came and went softly on the wings of the wind, and returned to stay. Cole would not stay this time either.

He had a child.

She did not, and she could not deny the jealousy tugging at her. It gnawed at her, unbidden in her belly, a secret pain devouring her like some mad disease that sooner or later would consume her with fire and send her running through the woods for relief, and the relief would never come.

Heaving back her shoulders, she said, "I'm not going husband hunting just to fill a gap in my life as you see it. That would be like buying any old chair just to fill a corner in a room and I'm not that kind of person who worries about what other people think."

"Noble of you. Maybe they'll build that fountain you talked about after you meet your maker, and they'll put up a comfortable plaque saying, 'dedicated to the extinct Hastings family.'"

A chill spiked through her. "You lost your right to show such disdain the day you left and never looked back. Dresden and Spirit Lake have been good to my mother and me. This place has been constant, there for me, like you promised to be but never were. This is home."

He limped out of the kitchen.

She chased after him.

He crossed the wide, open room to stare into the fire. "It's been one hell of a night. Laugh, cry, fight. We never used to fight."

Her heart took a right-angle turn his way. "Maybe we should have. It was a movie back then, too."

"Trouble is," he harumphed, "I believe in the values. You do, too."

She lurched. "I believe in the tranquillity here."

"Dresden would be a great place for Tyler. It'll never come to pass because of me. You see, I don't have the power to make choices with my life like you did. It's out of my hands because of Rojas."

"Don't allow pity to be your guide," she said, coming to stand at the back of the sofa. She rearranged the pillows mindlessly. "I think it was the reason I almost married—"

Cole whirled around, his angry look scalding her to silence. "You mean you were going to marry a man you never loved? Then why did you plant flowers on his grave the other night?"

Her insides turned dank and drafty as an ancient cave. "You followed me?"

"When I saw you leave the cabin so late, I was concerned."

"Stay out of my life."

"You ordered me here tonight, remember? House arrest."

Escaping him to put a bottle of formula in the microwave, she punched hard at the timer buttons. A thunderclap made her shoulders flinch. "You always had to be right. Grow up."

"Am I right? About Kipp O'Donnell?" he asked, coming into the kitchen.

She shuddered, not daring to look at him. "Don't, Cole. It's been ten years since he died. Of course I must have loved him."

"Must have?"

Thunder rolled torrents of rain against the windows. "Please, Cole. I'm not in the mood. I was supposed to feed my animals at ten or so and now it's past midnight."

He let go a gusty sigh from behind her. "What have you convinced yourself about me all these years? You could have tried to stay in touch with me, too, but you didn't. Was I...a trophy boyfriend?"

Turning to him, the violent need swirling in his hawkish gaze startled her.

"A trophy?" she mused, but her throat clutched. "Yes. I loved you so much then that I wanted the whole world to see you with me. Maybe it's just a girl thing."

"Nothing could replace the way it felt back then to have you in my arms. Maybe that's just a guy thing. Trouble is, I've never outgrown the need."

Old feelings for him welled up inside her. Budding. Hot. Forbidden yet bursting to be free of the cave, to find light.

Cole's eyes burned into her like liquid fire. Laurel rushed to him, flinging her arms around him and pressing her head to his chest. His heartbeat pounded strong and fast.

Was she falling in love with him all over again? Her head said "no," but her heart still had that window open to him.

Eager to extricate herself from him, she grabbed the bottle from the microwave too fast. It slipped to the floor with a crash, milky formula splashing in a puddle. Before she could stop him, Cole reached down, nicking his thumb.

His blood pooling in the milk, Cole swore, "Damn Rojas. Both of us with nerves shot because of him."

The icy knot clawing her stomach agreed. She would not have a life back until Rojas—and Cole—were gone. "I'll get a bandage."

She rushed from the kitchen, wishing she could run forever. Just like Cole had done to her years ago?

She focused on finding the bandages. Cuts she could deal with, not heartbreak.

Chapter 9

COLE NEEDED THE short respite alone in the kitchen while she hunted up a bandage. He was worried about her, and his son and Karen and his nephew Tim, but did he need to unload it all on her shoulders tonight? After she was daring enough—kind enough—to spring him from jail and invite him into the cabin?

It bothered him that he couldn't tell her that John hoped she'd do that very thing. If she got harmed because of this crazy plan of his and John's, a planned hatched with an old drunk....

He thought about the attic, old days of summer...making love to erase all else. Love? No. Try sex, man, pure and simple. Feel your reaction to her? Don't you listen? She just got done explaining you were fooled back then. You thought she loved you and it all started from some ambition of hers to have a trophy on her arm. Hmm. Sounds like some of the reasons you dated a few women along the way since Laurel. So why does it frustrate you so much to have the shoe on the other foot?

Because the attic tryst had been special.

Making love with her had come naturally, as if they'd never been apart. Obviously it hadn't meant as much to Laurel.

He'd dreaded returning to Dresden because he was afraid his need for Laurel would ball up inside him again. He had always liked protecting her, feeling part of something worthwhile, and damn but the woman was worthy. Of love. Of a man more together than he! He'd just have to get over it. Focus on his tough side. Keep Laurel out of danger and no more of this chitchat about feelings.

Blood dripped off his finger and onto the milk-splashed floor. Everything in his life was a mess, right down to Laurel's floor.

Then Laurel was there, wide-eyed and stoic as ever, blotting his thumb and bandaging it with swift efficiency.

He muttered, "Be nice if we could put something like that on fifteen years, huh?"

"A patch? It doesn't work for emotions, buddy," she said, eyes steady on the task of securing the bandage. When she went to the table to check the syringes and bottles, he felt he'd been set adrift in the Arctic. "So what's your thought about Rojas?" she asked, and he knew it was a diversionary tactic. She hated talking about Rojas.

"I suppose I've got to come up with something."

The bottles clinked under her inspection. "What if he just chose to make you run forever? What if that's his cruel plan for you?"

The acid in his gut threatened to come up. He hadn't thought of that. Life would become focused on one thing—running. He'd never see his son again, never...see Laurel again, never hear her voice, never feel her passion driving him toward relief, never feel her strong fingers patch his perpetual wounds.

A raw emptiness swept through him. "I can't run forever. I want to make a life for my son."

Her answer was to grab a towel to finish daubing milk from the floor, but he swore he spied her eyes grow shimmery instantly. Her long, red hair kept tumbling over her shoulders, threatening to dip into the milk. He walked over and gathered it in his fist. He noted she didn't try to pull away, and that relaxed him a little.

When she rose, even facing away from him couldn't hide a teardrop escaping the corner of her eye. He let go of her hair reluctantly, his heart pounding for her, wishing she'd not feel sorry for him or his son. He wished he hadn't brought this hurt to a woman so fine. It made him want to carry around a basket full of stones on his back, just to show how much he wanted to keep the burden solely his.

At the table he helped her pack the bottles and syringes in a basket for a trip to the shed. He admired her silent intensity.

"You really like doing this, don't you?"

Her brief smile was all he needed, but she said, "I've worked hard to get this far. It's been my dream to have this clinic."

"Who gets all this formula?"

"You're really interested in helping?"

He didn't care for the doubt clouding her eyes. "Of course. Remember the kittens we found in Johnsrud's barn? I held onto them while the vet put some gunk in their eyes."

She smiled and shook her head. "I'd forgotten. You'll meet Rusty the fox. He came from Johnsrud. Found him in a trap that didn't quite work. And I've got a new batch of baby bunnies."

"The fox doesn't see the bunnies as hors d'oerves?"

Her stricken look melted into another smile. "Never you mind the jokes. And take a couple of aspirin for that goose egg. They're in the cupboard by the sink."

She always seemed to be one step ahead of him, doctoring him and forgiving him. He admired her clear sense of herself, of knowing her direction and purpose.

"You think you could ever put up with me if I were healthy?"

This time, he didn't care for her ruminating scowl. "Not sure. It seems the only thing keeping us together is me doctoring your wounds."

"So I have a nurse fetish."

"I don't have that kind of license, so I guess that lets me off the hook."

Well. She certainly let that roll off her tongue too fast, he thought. Still, she was right. She deserved someone she didn't have to doctor all the time. She was intelligent, gifted really in what she could perform with animals and children. What could he do? Race a boat, spout drag quotients of waves under wind conditions, or bring old artifacts up from the deep. What did any of it matter when compared with what she did with her life?

"The bunnies," she was explaining, while nuking another small bottle in the microwave, "need several feedings because they're so small. And special antibiotics. Rabbits have bacteria in their stomachs not found in other small mammals and it's always essential to check them often when you have sick ones like this to start with."

"I see." He didn't at all. "What can I do?"

"We need a couple of towels and we're set."

We. That little word sent his blood rushing to already pulsating points in his body. "We" sounded warm on a rainy night.

He asked, "You have heat in the shed?"

When she leaned down to retrieve towels from a kitchen drawer, her hair swished about in thick torrents, making him long to race over and bury his face in its richness, to smell its wildflower essence. It always filled him like a breeze. He was hungry for that rush. It scared the hell out of him suddenly to know that a woman in a little cabin in Wisconsin could give him a charge as powerful as any racing boat going full-tilt across an ocean. Had she done this to him that summer? Was she the reason he took up racing with such a vengeance, and diving and anything dangerous? Had he been in search of this feeling of being with her?

Oh, yes.

Fortunately she was busy talking, ignoring his silent epiphany.

"I've got several heat lamps on. The animals are probably more snug than we'll be." He heard her intake of breath. "I mean, than I'll be."

"My tent will do me fine."

"I have a slicker you can borrow. And blankets."

"No need. A little rain won't hurt me. Once I'm in my sleeping bag, I'll be snug as a bug in a rug." It sounded cold, wet and miserable.

He followed her through the formal dining area, past the viewing scope, which made him smile. Once in the breezeway, she halted and he almost ran into her.

"What's wrong?"

Slamming the basket of clinking bottles at him, she raced at the shed entrance door. "No light under the door. It means the heat lamps are out. My new babies!"

Cole limped after Laurel. Inside the shed, he watched her almost fly about like a distressed bird, flicking on lamps, reaching for animals.

"I must have forgotten to turn them on before I left," she shrieked. "I can't believe I did this."

Cole's stomach turned leaden. He wondered if the sheriff's plan was already working. Was someone tracking him? Lurking about? "Tell me what to do to help."

"Find Rusty. I've got to adjust these lamps. Oh dear. This one's got a broken bulb, too."

He peered in a cage. "The fox seems fine."

"Take a look at Owlsy. He's newer."

Owlsy sat on a branch with a white bandage wrapped around one wing and half his body. His yellow eyes blinked back at Cole in utter confusion over all the commotion. Cole admitted to confusion, too. Forgetting something as important as these heat lamps wasn't like Laurel. Someone had meant to do harm to Laurel or to Cole through her. A hoary anger crowded his already pounding head.

He asked, "You want me to start feeding?"

"No!" She rolled up her sleeves and was reaching in a small box. "You can't feed baby animals until they warm up. They can't digest anything when they're cold."

Laurel had tears streaming down her face. He'd never seen her like this. He felt as if she'd just plunged a knife in his heart. Reaching out to try and soothe her, she quaked in his arms, like a wounded animal herself.

"Laurel Lee! I'm sorry. Don't go hysterical on me. Put me to work. Let me help you, damnit!"

She reached into a box filled with fluffy tissues, and before he could blink, she plunged two small gray creatures inside the open "V" of his shirt. They tickled his chest.

"Hold them there, against your skin and on your heartbeat."

He peered down. Two silken baby rabbits, their eyes mere slits and their tails only a notion, snuggled between his palm and chest skin. They felt cool to his touch and fragile. He stood still, awed by his unexpected responsibility.

"Now what?" he asked.

"It'll take a minute or two for their nest to warm up. I'm going to go outside and check on the coyote pups and the fawn—"

That's when they both noticed the far door ajar and banging suddenly amid the thunder. Cole didn't like this at all.

"Get in the house," he ordered.

"Why?"

All of the dread that had followed him for days, even weeks now, whooshed in around him with the force of a Florida hurricane.

Laurel's face went chalky white. "Someone was in the shed."

Someone who wanted your animals to die in order to mess with me, Cole thought. Then he had an even uglier thought. "The front door was open. Someone could be in your house right now."

Her eyes, growing large, beseeched his. "It could be a neighbor. Right? Tell me there is no Rojas."

His heartbeat gathering against a storm, he held fast to the innocent baby bunnies, regret slashing through him.

"I DON'T CARE a rat's ass how late it is, Sheriff, we have to find him," Cole said, limping back and forth in front of the fireplace.

Laurel wondered how he could ignore the deep wound in his leg.

She slumped in the rocking chair, wrung out. Before the sheriff even got to her cabin, Cole had scoured the house with Mike's hunting knife in hand. She stayed in the shed, shutting doors and settling the bunnies back in their nestbox. Now, her insides were a volatile cocktail of fear and anger, all of it centered on Cole.

Sheriff John Petski sat on the edge of a sofa cushion, fresh from his inspection, coat still on and dripping, hiked behind his holster. He held his plastic-covered hat in his hands. "I don't see how he could get here that fast."

"Hell, the man owns a jet."

"According to Dade County, Marco Rojas was attending a

diplomatic reception only four hours ago. It's possible, but nobody flies in this stuff."

A measure of relief settled into Laurel, reminding her of the hour and how tired she was. "Maybe I really did forget the lamps."

Cole scowled at her. "The door, too? No way. I know you. You love those animals more than anything, more than people."

She flinched at the unsettling and offhanded accusation. "I was in a hurry, and distracted today. The more we talk about this, the sillier it makes me feel. I must have thought I closed the door and turned on the lamps and never did."

Cole glanced at the sheriff. "You found nothing over at the mansion?"

Laurel watched the two men exchange an intense gaze. She didn't like the feeling it gave her.

John said, "Nothin' there except a leaky roof and creaky wood. You already looked in the duffel and said everything was there. Even the jewelry."

"Thanks for bringing my stuff over," Cole said, turning quickly toward the fire, his back to Laurel.

Jewelry? Laurel would have to ask about it later.

John stood. "Maybe you two just got spooked talking about Rojas and his rich lady friend from Texas—"

"Sheriff," Cole interjected, stepping forward and slapping a hand on John's shoulder, "Laurel and I have done enough talking about Rojas for one night."

Jewelry? Lady friend? From then on, John avoided her gaze. At the door, he turned to Cole. "Stop by. We have to settle up with the tavern. Wiley'll be sober in a few hours."

"Sure thing," Cole said, closing the door against the rain.

Laurel didn't care for the odd glint in his eyes when he turned around. "What're you two up to?"

"You need sleep. I'll be fine out here on the couch," Cole said.

"Don't treat me like I'm still seventeen. I don't need a guard dog on duty. Rojas isn't here, but you two clearly expected him. He was all you talked about, not an ordinary burglar or tourist committing a heist."

"We can talk in the morning."

"I won't sleep until we talk." She stomped over to him, grabbed his arm and dragged him to the couch. "You and John know something you don't want me to know. Why not?"

"I'd like to think I'm protecting you by not wanting to scare you at every turn."

She threw up her arms. "Like I wasn't scared tonight? Like I wasn't scared the day you arrived here and told me you were going to be killed? Like that didn't bring all the scary feelings back when my father went into a rage—"

Her body went slack. She's said too much. Her throat tightened. His eyes grew wide, beckoning like the lake, waiting for her.

He offered, "I don't want to talk about the things your father did back then."

Licking her lips, she sighed, thankful. "He loved me. He couldn't help what he felt about the situation of you and me. But sometimes I feel I'm like him. Stubborn. Fulfilling his mission to get rid of you."

She blanched, the truth delivering a tremor down her spine. Was she really doing that? Repeating the past? Trying to justify all the meanness her father showed toward Cole fifteen years ago?

He patted the cushion next to him. Because of the gravity on his face, she sat down next to him. He put an arm around her, drawing her against the same warm spot on his chest where the bunnies recovered earlier. His heartbeat pounded erratically. The man was afraid!

"Cole, I'm sorry. I hate being at odds. I hate worrying."

"I'm nothing but a bastard, just as you called me, if I bring you into this then tell you nothing." His voice resonated through his chest. Her body rose with his deep breath, settling in.

"Sheriff Petski got some information off his communiqués tonight that aren't pretty," he began, sending new tremors through her. "It involves a woman I dated a couple of times, who ended up in the arms of Senator Milo Goetz."

"What about this woman? And who is Goetz?"

"Goetz heads the CIA oversight committee. Has for years."

Shivering, she stared into the dying fire. "Your brother said not to go to Langley. That's CIA. Did Mike know something about Goetz and Rojas?"

"My hunch is, yes."

"But if they're involved in anything illegal together, that means high-ranking government officials might be part of it. The implications of all this—"

"Are enormous."

Looking up at his face, she watched the firelight's reflection flicker in his dark eyes. "What about the woman, Cole? What's the connection?"

Cole eased her back against him and dropped a kiss on top of her head. There was an urgency about it that added to her worry.

"Goetz messed around with her on a yacht in our marina, near a slip Rojas used. The sheriff says she was last seen boarding Rojas's yacht."

Her mouth went dry. "He killed her?"

"No. According to Sheriff Petski, Interpol's involved. She comes from a very rich family who's making this a national human interest story. Authorities figure she was sold into the white slave trade in the Mid-East."

She shivered. "That really exists?"

"According to John, hundreds of young women disappear every year, not only from the U.S."

More icy tremors tumbled through her. "You believe Rojas would use a woman to get to you, don't you?"

Closing her eyes momentarily, she forced herself to add, "You think he'd kidnap me?"

The fire hissed, almost masking his reply. "Yes."

Shook by the simplicity of the horror, she slipped from his protective arm, got up and closed the glass doors on the fire.

A fire of her own stoked inside herself. "I refuse to be afraid anymore. Nobody messes with...us."

"Us?"

"I've been thinking about what you said about me hiding from life. I can't do that with you, not with you here. You're a friend. And I must help you because that's what I do for friends."

He laughed, an odd disjointed sound in the shadowy seriousness of the cabin. "What's your first step partner?"

Warming to the new balance in their relationship, even tenuous as it was, she smiled back. "You think Buzz remembers meeting Mike? We don't know much about Mike's itinerary here—"

Cole's face lit up. Sitting back against the sofa pillows, he nodded. "But it has to lead us to the goods on Rojas. I need to start talking to people. Mike would have gone to the bait shop. We'll start there."

"You're not asking my mother a thing." Her head throbbed instantly.

"I have to. If what Mike left me isn't at the house, then it's in town somewhere."

"Look, I found out about your engagement from my mother. She came to me triumphantly with a clipping from one of her magazines she sells, but I didn't need to look at it. She was reading it aloud to me as a not-so-gentle reminder that I was too young to know what love was and that you had other fish to fry. She wants nothing to do with you."

"Other fish to fry?"

"It's a turn of a phrase my mother uses. She meant, you were never lacking for women, and the story of your engagement within a year of leaving here seemed to prove that."

Rubbing the back of his neck, he curled his mouth into an obvious twist of disgust. "I already told you why I married Stephanie."

He began rearranging the pillows on the sofa.

"Is Lisa waiting back there for you? Did you leave behind someone who really cares...too much?"

After a pause, he put down the pillow in his hand and turned to her, the muscles playing on his face. "Since my life is bound to dribble out on newspaper pages, you might as well know, Lisa Shaw's the one who talked about marriage, not me. She owns the dive shop where I get my equipment."

For some reason, she welcomed that news. It felt less messy to know he was unattached right now, that he wasn't abandoning another woman. An unexpected concern rose, though.

"Are you afraid for Lisa?"

His face took on gruesomely gray shadows. "Yes. The same way I'm afraid for you. I never told Rojas about Lisa or her shop, but he's a sick man."

Laurel trembled from her epicenter. "Sheriff Petski has always watched out for me."

"I'll watch out for you tonight. I'll be here, on the sofa, until the sunrise. Get some sleep, Laurel Lee, please. I worry about you."

With her common sense threatening to leave her, with her heart wanting her to stay with him, she rushed from the room with a "goodnight."

But then in her room, the darkness settled around her and she longed to be back in his arms.

The lightning crackled, illuminating the dresser photos of her father and Kipp. She sought their company, but the frames felt cold, not what she yearned for tonight at all.

Quickly readying for bed in a favorite soft T-shirt and climbing under the blankets, she thought about how the men she loved became elusive for her. They were never permanent. The man sleeping in her livingroom—Cole Roberto Sanchez Wescott, the hunted and the hunter—was a prime example. He'd left her after vowing they would marry for real someday. Then there was his commitment to his son—or lack thereof—that still bothered her. And he'd divorced his wife. Now there was Lisa Shaw, whom he couldn't commit to.

Could Cole commit to any woman? Laurel's good sense warned her "no." But then she remembered his chastisement of her not allowing him room to be her friend. Maybe he was ready to risk love again if only she would let him take that risk.

Was there a place in her heart for Cole, or not? Was it more up to her to answer that question, than up to Cole?

The questions were beginning to crowd her, and she didn't like it.

IN TYPICAL Wisconsin weather fashion, morning flipped back to sunshine and a verdant world scrubbed clean by rain. Laurel's garden was flush with rainbows in the mist between the rows.

Cole had risen before her and was out back shoring up posts around the deer pen that had loosened with the rain.

She pushed in tomato stakes that had loosened, taking pleasure in hers and Cole's parallel activities.

Then she glanced across the bay.

The porthole window, which faced west over the fanning lake, was still in shadow. A brooding menace, it reminded her she had only about a month to resolve the ownership issues—and Cole—or she'd lose her grant money for creating the wildlife refuge on that land and for continuing her work here. Without that major influx of cash, she faced the prospect of being forced to dispose of her animals because she wouldn't be able to maintain them. They would go to zoos, maybe university programs or other wildlife rehabilitators in the country—if they had the budgets and room. She'd have to pick up odd jobs to support herself and start all over again writing proposals to wildlife foundations and the government. It exhausted her to think about it.

Later, on the drive to town to begin their investigations, she and Cole spoke of everything but the jewelry. She thought about asking him about the jewelry John mentioned but then decided she shouldn't care. Was it some memento of Lisa Shaw he toted across country for good luck?

Dresden was crowded, eliciting a comment from Cole as she slowed the minivan. "Glad I'm not trying to be quick about this little matter of life and death plaguing me. Looks like there'll be lines everywhere."

His quick laugh lightened the mood as it always served to do. That part of him hadn't changed and she secretly hoped he always retained that sense of levity about him.

Pressing the minivan through the sluggish traffic, she noticed his frown. "Problems?"

"It's such a nice day. Why are all these tourists just shopping? Isn't there anything to do around here?"

"After a storm the campgrounds and golf courses tend to be under some water for the morning. The lakes and streams get a bit murky so you have to wait for them to settle out before you can fish."

He pointed toward a bunch of boys playing tag by dodging in and out of parked cars beside them. "I'd forgotten. The ball diamonds are wet. Recreation for kids kind of ends there, doesn't it?"

A cloud descended over her and she resented his implications.

"Miami must have a lot more happening than this little place. Tyler never has a chance to get bored, does he?"

He only shrugged. "He and Timmy are into trick water-skiing."

"I'm afraid we don't have ski jumps on Spirit Lake. There's a fish ladder over by the dam to help the fish swim from one level in the flowage to the next. I take the high school classes over there. The kids seem to get a kick out of watching that."

"Sounds exciting."

"I'd like to think so."

Silence hung in the air then inside the van. So what did he expect here? Didn't he remember what Dresden was like? Friday night fish fries with neighbors, ball games when the diamond dried out, and bicycle rides through pine-scented back roads? She gripped the steering wheel harder. Darn his hide for doing this to her. One minute she enjoyed his humor, then the next he wiped her nose in their differences.

When Cole dug out the faded photo of the Naval officer, then offered it the tiniest flicker of a smile before putting it away again, she asked, "You found your mystery man?"

"Not sure."

His staring thoughtfully out the window caught her attention then. She kept her hands firmly on the steering wheel, but she felt her ire toward him withering. Instead, curiosity ebbed in. Concern even. He settled back in the seat with a resigned sigh, his hand over the pocket holding the photo, fingers drumming lightly, fidgeting.

Venturing to disturb his thoughts, she offered, "Mike wouldn't have put this photo in the bank box unless this person wasn't important."

"Maybe I'm just confused as to why Mike thought certain people were important to me in a small town I barely know."

"Let's hope Buzz can shed some light on it."

SHE PARKED THE minivan at the newspaper office, but it looked quiet. "Buzz is probably at the bait shop collecting first-hand storm damage reports and tips on where to find fallen trees that would make front-page photos."

Finding the office door unlocked, they went in but met up with nothing more than a messy desk with stacks of newspapers.

She surmised, "He could be a while. There are my mother's muffins he's collecting, too."

"The devil." His chuckle tickled her back.

"Don't encourage him. Please. Your habit of questioning me pales with his. The thought of spending Christmases with him at my mother's already sends icicles down my back."

Cole laughed out loud. And she joined him, sharing the laugh back out onto the sunny street. She could become addicted to this mood. It felt as soft and nice as one of her flannel shirts.

They decided she'd drop Cole off at the sheriff's office while she ran errands. They would wait for Buzz to return to his office so they could talk with him alone.

Outside, Cole asked, "Maybe we could catch lunch together?"

Standing in the shade of the one-story office building, he took her breath away. He'd showered at her cabin and shaved, so the shade brought a granite, chiseled look to his face. A blue polo shirt he'd dug out of his bag did nice things for his chocolate eyes, coppery skin and dark hair brushing his shoulders. Though Laurel had never met his mother, she knew this man had inherited the best genes Chilean people had to offer. How Laurel wished they could start over.

Shocked with herself, she plastered on a smile. "Catch lunch? As in go out and get it with hook, line and sinker? We'd starve."

"Hmm. I take that as a challenge. You might want to take me out there sometime on Spirit Lake, but for now I'm thinking about something quicker and tamer."

"Oh sure. Like a burger at the local tap? Wasn't that last night's folly?"

"Come to think of it, the sheriff didn't even give me bread and water. Never got my steak and eggs from you, either. Hospitality's running thin around here."

"I'm sorry. I forgot an errand. Can you be a good sport and grab a sandwich on your own? Then I'll meet you here in an hour."

He saluted to her in a ridiculous fashion, then sauntered down the sidewalk, his limp giving his backside an interesting personality that brought a hike to her own brows.

Striding in the opposite direction, she marveled at Cole's ability to ride the ups and downs in his life with such humor. In the past few years, she'd insisted on keeping her life on an even keel with no surprises. She'd had laughs, but when had they been this frequent? When had someone tickled her belly with mere words or the crook of an eyebrow? The answer was too unsettling: when she was with Cole. Then and now.

Laurel paced past Gary's Hardware to the grocery.

She found Una checking the mist sprayers above the vegetable displays. Una almost started a cabbage avalanche upon hearing Laurel's update on what had transpired.

Recovering, Una said, "So he stayed overnight at your cabin? You didn't tell him—"

"No. And I never will. My plan—his plan, really—is for me to help get his hide out of here before it becomes Swiss cheese with bullet holes."

Una smirked.

"What does that mean?"

"I've never seen you so alive, so wound up. Are you falling for him again?"

Choking, Laurel stuffed her hands in her pockets, then remembered Cole did that all the time and yanked them out.

Una laughed. "How can I help, you ninny?"

"Be there for me. Keep your ears perked. His brother Mike was here about a month ago for only a few days. Cole thinks Mike had some goods on their boss, Marco Rojas. Cole's sure that Mike hid evidence in Dresden somewhere."

"Wow. A giant treasure hunt."

"Yes, very appropriate, considering his boss owns one of the world's biggest ocean salvage operations. Cole's a diver for him. Or was."

"How romantic."

"Una!"

"Sorry. I'm a slow learner." Una went back to rearranging broccoli. "What did Mike look like?"

"Probably tall as Cole, dark complexion, but not quite as muscular."

"I don't recall seeing a hunk like that a month ago, but there was a man in here the other day who was dark, very neat. Didn't look much like a tourist, but then it was probably his first day in town. But come to think of it now, he seemed nervous, flighty, kept dropping his cans of flavored coffee."

Cole's boss? Laurel's hands and forehead perspired. "If you see the man again, call me. Even if he's at your register, excuse yourself to check a price on something and call me."

Chapter 10

UNA'S NEWS ABOUT the man rattled Laurel so that she decided to seek out attorney David Huber. By hiding something in those files pertaining to Cole's property, David could also be in danger.

The office was closed. She peered through the windows for good measure. Then she remembered. He'd gone down to Madison for a university seminar and other business. And she had a key. David had offered her the use his office computers before she'd recently acquired her own.

She looked up and down the narrow cross street. People passed by on Main Street, but nobody glanced her way. Taking a deep breath, she slipped the key in the lock, then rushed inside, locking the door behind her. Since the windows had no shades, she'd have to be alert.

With blood pumping hard through her veins, she raced to the file cabinets. Locked. "Dang," she muttered.

She rifled through his desk, and finally found a key tucked under a tissue box in one drawer.

"Come on, David, that's not very creative."

The key sprung the cabinet drawers lickety-split. With fingers shaking, she homed in on the "W" files. No Wescotts. Disappointment rattled her until she remembered. "Try Tilden. Flora Tilden."

She found the file immediately. She wanted to whoop with her discovery, but instead crouched on the floor to hide behind the desk, out of view of the window to the street.

After opening the manila file, the first thing she saw was a brief note to David's part-time secretary. "Anne, no charge to W. for this work. Pro bono."

W? As in Wescott? And David was doing it for free? She needed to confront Cole with this.

She glanced around, looking for David's copy machine. It had a note on it: Anne, needs toner. "Can't you men do anything on your own?" But she couldn't find the toner either.

She folded up the note signed "W" and stuffed it in her pocket. With the other notes in the file, she figured David wouldn't miss one.

She thumbed through the remaining file items. Most were facsimiles, sent to David from libraries across the country. Some from the Wisconsin State Historical Society showed the Tilden mansion in its heyday, replete with artwork and grand furnishings. In one, a woman stood on the verandah, blowing a kiss at whoever this photographer was. She was beautiful, tall, with penetrating eyes...like Cole's. One photo of the woman was marked, "D.C."

Laurel frowned. Cole had acted as if he didn't know where Flora had lived, yet he knew about this file. Or did he?

A frosty chill skittered across her skin. Could Rojas have hired David? But that didn't make sense.

The pieces weren't coming together as neatly as she first thought they would when she saw the file.

Then she forced herself to draw in a deep breath. Here she was again, suspicious, thinking she could find the answers on her own and not ask for Cole's help. Was she becoming as obsessed as Cole? What was right and wrong anymore? What's more, who was right?

Feeling queasy, feeling disappointed and disturbed about her new confusion brought on by Cole's challenges to her, she replaced the file, re-locked the cabinet, returned the key under the tissue box, then let herself out onto the street.

Footsteps startled her. She turned, and a man dashed around the corner to Main Street. Or was she getting carried away?

She hurried toward the other end of the short street, toward the town pier.

"Oh, no," she muttered, when she spotted the sheriff and Cole with heads together conspiratorially. "Now what are they up to?"

ON THE PIER, under sunlight teasing fishermen to load up their boats and set forth on mighty missions, Cole leaned over an engine. "I can do a tune-up for you in no-time," he told Sheriff Petski, standing next to him, "but if you don't mind, I want to stop by Gary's Hardware for new locks for Laurel's doors and windows and get that taken care of first."

John nodded. "I hope Laurel didn't get too frightened about last night."

"She got upset with me, but we talked. Things seem good now."

"I'm glad."

But the sheriff started walking away, forcing Cole to limp fast to catch up. "I need to ask you a few questions."

"Suit yourself, but I'm in a hurry to file reports for folks and their insurance companies on storm damage."

They headed off along the boardwalk, their booted footsteps echoing under the treated wood planks. More people were filtering down to the piers now, leaving for a day of fishing on Spirit Lake. Cole drank in the carefree atmosphere, wishing he could wear it like a coat whenever he needed a balm.

He glanced at the older man next to him, noticing the worry lines crinkling the eyes and forehead. He felt sorry for John, who wasn't sure about his role in all this. Be mad at Cole? Protect Laurel? Or work with Cole to land a big fish—Rojas? Any choice would cause John ulcers.

Cole ventured, "Does Laurel have a gun?"

The sheriff grunted. "She abhors the things, what with the accidents she sees."

"Owlsy with his shot-up wing?"

"Too many like that. But she would still have the old hunting rifle of her dad's."

"Ah, yes. Nice little number. The one he used to express his opinion about Laurel and me marrying ourselves in that little church."

Anger flared across John's face. "You haven't been out there, have you?"

Considering John's look and the ugly tone, Cole thought better of mentioning the visit to the graveyard. John obviously was still protective of his best friend's daughter after all these years. "No," Cole said, "I haven't been near the place."

"Good. Laurel wouldn't like you tramping around out there by the graves."

Cole knew when it was wise to steer the subject in another direction. "Do you think Wiley's going to be okay with this plan we've hatched with him? His drinking could get in the way."

"I've never seen him sober up so fast. He took quite an interest in your story about Marco Rojas."

A shudder traveled up Cole's spine. "Laurel won't be relieved if she ever finds out I'm working with Wiley, of all people."

"But he offered a good idea on how to help draw out Rojas."

"And he's an old Naval officer." He patted the pocket with the photo of the young man in uniform. "How could I turn him down, right?"

"It won't matter," the sheriff said, pulling his hat down against the morning sun, "if you come up dead after all this."

Cole reached out and stopped the sheriff. He looked the older man in the eyes. "Tell me the truth, Sheriff. Would Laurel be better off if I were dead? Has she said anything about me over the years?"

John squinted toward the sun. "Some things just aren't talked about."

"Because Kipp came along? She alluded to feeling she had no choice but to marry Kipp." He froze in his tracks, thinking over the reasons people marry. "I've been stupid not to guess this, right John?"

The sheriff's horrified look stopped Cole.

Swallowing against a sense of hollowness in his gut, Cole persisted, "She didn't just lose her father and Kipp. She lost Kipp's child, too, didn't she?"

The sheriff averted his face. "Please, son, don't say anything to her, or to anyone, about the baby. It's a private sorrow she's put behind her."

"Of course. I understand. I have a boy of my own now. Was it a boy?"

The sheriff's nod left his gut knotting up. Then John leaned into his day and left Cole standing on the boardwalk alone.

Remorse overtook his soul like a purple shroud.

What a clod he'd been. He'd mocked Laurel about hiding from life and living alone, and he'd galloped in with talk about a thriving, healthy son. His heart ached for Laurel.

He wondered if Mike had uncovered Laurel's background, including the child? Probably. Why hadn't Mike told him? Why did Mike appear to purposely want Cole to come here? To re-connect with Laurel?

The notion hit Cole with more power than a locomotive going full bore down a mountainside. Darn you, Mike! You don't know her at all. Or me!

He couldn't offer her what she deserved, or what Mike may have thought she deserved. And Laurel wouldn't survive loving and losing again. He'd seen that fragility in the way she held her baby animals, in the way her eyes darkened whenever she looked at him, in the way she'd insisted they just be friends. Nothing more. Just friends.

Sweat trickled down his back, and he stuffed his hands into his pockets before limping on to go find her.

FLUSHED FROM spotting Cole and the sheriff with their heads together again out at the public pier, Laurel raced into the bait shop to ask her mother about anything she might know about Mike's visit or John's current cases. Her mother was in aisle two and up to her elbows sorting a shipment of bobbers into the appropriate trays. The Bowman kid was tending the register.

Madelyn beamed at Laurel. "Just the person I was about to call. There's a man I want you to see. The guy in my cottage."

"Mother, please. I wanted to ask you—"

"Hold this." Madelyn shoved an empty tray in Laurel's arms and proceeded to fill it with red and white bobbers. "He's very nice. I know you'd like him. He bought a new graphite rod and a tacklebox, and two pairs of those fancy leather gloves, the thick kind so muskellunge don't bite through them. And oh, the giant minnow cages. I sold one to another man a few weeks back, and now this nice man bought two of them. Can you imagine? He's been asking so many questions about fishing that I hoped you might go out with him, to give him pointers."

Laurel shook her head. She must not have heard right. "What kind of retail specials are you running these days? Buy a hundred dollars worth of equipment and get a free date with the Hastings' daughter?"

"Why not invite him to dinner tonight? I told him about Al's on Hwy. N, and he nodded."

"Because he probably couldn't believe you'd be trying to set him up with a date. He could be an ax murderer."

Madelyn rolled her eyes. "Not here, dear. Not in Dresden."

"You'd be surprised," Laurel muttered.

"You could meet him there, then it wouldn't seem so much like a date. Just talk about fish, over fish."

Laurel plunked the bobber box back on the display shelf. "I don't have time for your matchmaking."

Madelyn looked genuinely hurt. "He likes my curtains."

Laurel had forgotten about the curtains. "Oh, Mom, I'm sorry."

"When was the last time you went out on a real date?"

In pure frustration, Laurel blurted, "I already have a date for tonight."

"Who?"

Right. Who? "Atlas."

"Your hobo help? Talk about ax murderers."

"Bye, Mother." Laurel pivoted, stomping out of the bait shop before her headache grew to gargantuan pounding.

Her mother called after her, "He's going to be there. At seven."

Dashing down the sidewalk, dodging tourists, strollers and dogs,

Laurel ran smack dab into Cole. The bag he carried busted open, spilling hardware at their feet.

"Sorry!" Laurel yelped. She bent down to help him pick up his purchases. "Window locks?"

"I put it on your account with Gary. I'm putting them in tonight."

"We won't have time." She plucked a screw up off the concrete.

"Oh?"

"We're going out tonight." Her heart pounded to match her head.

"What brought this on?"

"I'm asking you for a date, okay? Dinner, drinks, talk about the weather. Now shut up and be nice about it and accept, darn you."

Cole stared at her gape-mouthed. He scooped up the last of the hardware, then stood. "A date, when we're mad at each other?"

"Get over it." She started walking away.

Cole caught up. "Where're we going on this date?"

"Al's on Hwy. N. Pork chops and sauerkraut on special. Get your choice of mashed potatoes and gravy, or home fries. I'll buy."

"Hmm," he grunted, "a serious date."

"At least make it look that way. And fair warning. My darn mother's likely to be there, hiding with some 'nice' blind date to spring on me from behind the stuffed black bear that stands next to the bar. That thing has lice."

"Her date for you, or the bear?"

She flashed him a frown and pushed on through the throng.

He laughed from behind her. "Doesn't sound like your favorite place."

Shuddering, she stepped out of the foot traffic, looking him square in the eyes. "Al's on Hwy. N is where Kipp proposed."

He almost dropped the bag of hardware. "Want some of my aspirins?"

"I'd love a couple."

LIKE A SET OF dominoes, the faces lounging at the bar in Al's Supper Club turned Laurel's way when she walked in. She knew it was because of Cole.

One by one, the men elbowed each other down the line. The air conditioning lacked enough oomph to overpower the heat pressing her cheekbones. Still, one of the dark, empty spaces inside her filled with a glow, a thrill really at the idea of being out with Cole, as if a fifteen-year separation never happened.

When one of the men slammed a dice cup on the bar, the remainder of the curious turned back to their betting and Leinenkuegel beer.

Cole touched her elbow to move on, igniting yet more heat. "Our worry over anyone recognizing me was certainly a waste. Doesn't anyone ever feed those wolves?"

Laurel realized it was a back-handed compliment. She glanced at her nondescript jeans and ordinary pale yellow blouse with eyelet stitching on the front placket. For the life of her she didn't know why men would—

"No man can resist watching the way your hair moves with you," he said, winking at her. "Not even me." He brushed a few wavelets back off her shoulder. "And I've always enjoyed your moves."

"If we turn around now," she muttered, feeling hotter than Hades and foolish to boot for even being here, "we could go home and I'll fix you a sandwich."

"No way," he said, nudging her toward the "Wait to be seated" sign and dining room. "No egg sandwiches. I'm looking forward to clogging my veins instead with those pork chops."

Craning his head in every direction, he added, "Don't see your mother yet."

"I'm betting she won't even show up. One of those wolves, as you call them, is probably going to a phone right now to report in."

Cole laughed. "Your mother as the ringleader in an intrigue is a different side to her."

"Whatever you do, don't encourage her strange behavior."

"Strange? Wanting her daughter to date, marry, have a dozen grandchildren for her, sounds almost normal."

Was this his way of telling her she'd allowed life to move on without her?

The restaurant suddenly smelled stale and looked drab in its mauve carpet and pine paneling. The man beside her seemed too powerful, a scary unknown in her life. She didn't want to be here. She wanted to be home with her animals, with Cole all to herself, working as—what did he say? As partners?

"I don't think I remembered to turn on the heat lamps."

"You checked them when I picked you up. Twice."

"Oh."

Then they were attacked by the clown, no, it really was a waitress, Laurel concluded. The overly-made up woman wearing an elaborate

German costume that left pillowy cleavage peeking out of her peasant blouse smiled and said, "Just the two of you?"

Cole hiked a brow at Laurel. "Should we save a seat for your mother, just in case she chooses not to hide behind the bear?" He winked.

She relaxed. Boldly plunking her hand in the crook of his arm, she replied, "Let Mom fend for herself. Tonight's our night."

THE WAITRESS'S pillowy chest jiggled. "The bear?" the waitress quipped. "We moved him 'cause of losing his fur, but we have Al's bighorn sheep."

The head of which they sat under, next to a window overlooking a miniature golf course with a mangy-looking stuffed bear straddling Hole 13. Two little boys and their parents knocked white balls at the bear's feet.

The waitress disappeared.

Cole grunted. "Some ambiance. Want to leave?"

She gulped at her water. A tiny room in that house that was her heart wanted Cole to enjoy something of hers, even if it was a tattered tourist trap of a restaurant. "No. Besides, I'm starved."

"I can't eat until we clear the air. You and Kipp came here often?"

Surprisingly, she found herself smiling. "He liked the cheap specials, and he met friends here for cards. I came with often enough, but looking back I suspect he just felt obligated to bring me along."

"The man wanted to show you off. Can't blame him for that. I share the desire."

Liquid heat spilled down her skin. "Thank you. But he also appreciated talking about hunting with his buddies here, including my father."

Leaning toward her, his eyes twinkling, he whispered, "I don't hunt. Is that okay to admit that around here?"

"Sure. But watch what bar you're in and don't say it too loud during hunting season."

They laughed together.

The purity of the sound, the shared secret of nonsense, the simple joy of being here with him, all of it unnerved her.

"Kipp and I never had a peaceful meal in a restaurant or local bar where he focused just on the two of us. He was always hopping up and down to greet some buddy of his."

She worried her hands in front of her on the table. "Don't get me wrong. I appreciated that people liked him, but—"

"There's something to be said about a man focusing his attention solely on the woman he's with."

The way his dark eyes burrowed into hers took her breath away. A wellspring of renewal washed through her. She realized, maybe for the first time, the value of the way this man focused on one thing at a time. A thrill threaded through her for the second time this evening.

Feeling coy but daring, she said, "Am I still too much of a tomboy? Should I have worn a dress tonight?"

He leaned forward again, invading her space, eyes growing wide, an eyebrow softening into a sexy slouch. The air hummed between them. "You're pretty on the outside," he ventured in a husky tone, "but I always liked you because of what was on the inside. Don't pretend to be what you're not, not for me or any man."

His reference to "any man" reminded her that what they had was at best a tenuous friendship built on nostalgia. And hormones. Oh, yes, that she would admit to inwardly.

Wanting to keep the conversation on the light side, she said, "Try the sauerkraut here. You'll look like a local."

He pointed out the window. "Like him? Nothing beats the look of a man in plaid shorts and knee socks playing miniature golf."

"That's no local. I'll bet he's a retired speedboat racer from Florida slumming up here in the summer," she said, poking fun at him. It felt freeing to do so.

His broadening smile crinkled the corners of his eyes. "No way will I ever wear plaid shorts like that. Or the matching knee socks."

"Wait until you hit seventy. Proneness for plaid shorts and knee socks to keep you warm is on one of those mysterious male genes. You watch. Scientists will soon discover that men can save their virility by wearing ugly shorts and socks."

His laugh almost visibly illuminated the room.

A giddiness skipped through her, opening windows, beckoning in fresh air for her soul. If she chose to tonight, she didn't have to remember anything about their past. They could sit here...like a couple in love talking about growing old together. Talking about a future.

The new winds swirling around inside her dusted off her heart and got it pumping again. A fever followed the rush through her veins. She never felt this with Kipp. Never. Why not? Was it that he was more comfortable being with his buddies? Had she liked it that way? Was it safer for her heart to allow people to think she and Kipp were in love? So that they would allow her her peace? Had she always been yearning—waiting, saving herself—for the true bliss that came with Cole's attention to her?

Heat settled onto her cheekbones. She had to be careful the winds of emotions didn't turn into destructive tornadoes. Opening her heart was dangerous. Love was impossible for them.

Turning his knife over and over, he smiled over at her. "You're the bravest person I know."

Her mouth went dry. "By taking you in?"

"Of course that." He shrugged. "Also, by coming to this place, knowing it was special to you and Kipp. We could have dodged your mother another way instead of coming here."

"There aren't that many supper clubs. She's got her spies here somewhere. She belongs to every club in a five-county area."

A man in a red shirt and dark hair, half hidden by his menu and their waitress, sat in the far corner. His gaze caught Laurel's then dipped back to his menu.

Laurel glanced back to Cole. "I may have found my mother's spy."

When he went to turn, she quickly said, "No, don't look. Let mother think we're having the time of our lives. She'll hate knowing I'm falling for a hobo."

"And are you?"

His question shocked her heart into a faster beat. "Decidedly no."

But heat pushed at her cheeks again, this time from confusion and memories scorching her.

She nodded toward the corner of the room. "That man is sitting where they always put the Christmas tree. Day after Thanksgiving, a big deal. Kipp ordered T-bone steaks for us. He finished his and half of mine. He was so nervous."

She'd said too much, but Cole blinked expectantly so she finished. "He'd forgotten the ring."

"As in engagement ring?"

"What it amounted to is that I dragged the question out of him, now that I think about it."

Cole frowned, obviously confused. "Kipp still brings a smile to your face?"

She peered into Cole's tanned face, her eyes following the gentle lines etched from years of work under the sun. Cole was the reason she could put perspective on Kipp. That era was indeed done, faded, because Cole had returned now and he was real. Her heart was free to make choices. Slip into the darkness, or come into the light. Her life lay before her in new, clear delineations.

"Yes," she said, her body growing lighter, some of the burden of the past evaporating, "I can smile. For all the good times."

She secretly thanked Cole for allowing her this affirmation.

A new waitress appeared then, with the same revealing costume as the first and with an even bigger valley dipping toward Cole in a way that made his eyebrows arch and Laurel smirk to see his discomfort.

With pen twitching, the waitress winked at Cole. "Name's Jenny, Jen. That's a northern pike over in that fish tank. You guess the weight by Friday night and you get him filleted by Big Al plus a gallon of Al's special German potato salad. I deliver it to your house."

Discombobulated by the presentation, Laurel and Cole wrenched their heads away from Jenny and in the direction of her pointed pen. A built-in fish tank created part of the wall separating the pine-paneled dining room from the waitress station and restrooms.

Cole said, "Mister Pike looks comfy in there. We'll pass and order something else."

Laurel stifled a guffaw. "The special'll be fine for me."

"Me, too," Cole said.

The waitress scribbled. "Out of home fries. Mashed okay?"

"Hold the gravy," Laurel said.

"Pour it on for me," Cole told Jen, winking.

Laurel rolled her eyes at him.

The waitress cooed, "Excellent choice. Anything to drink, sir?"

He was staring at her cleavage, and said, "Whatever's on tap."

"I could be later," Jen quipped, sashaying off.

Cole gawked after her. "Do you think she's serious?"

"During the fall hunting season, maybe. I'd forgotten how awful this place is."

"I've got an idea. When she comes with the food, let's have her box it up and we'll go on a picnic."

Her nerves rode a roller-coaster down her spine. "I haven't been on a picnic since—"

It was more than the sudden cock of his head that stopped her. His grin grew lopsided, flinching at one corner. Then his dark eyes grew beyond mellow and sexy. They became knowing.

Cole picked up her hands, sending panic sizzling up her arms. "We haven't been on a picnic since the one in the meadow as teenagers. Let's go. Just for fun. We both need it. One night, let's be kids again, Laurel Lee."

The eager grin on his face weakened her will. What harm could come from it? One night, he'd said. He always lived his life that way. The focus on one day, one night at a time. Nothing more. She must keep reminding herself of that. And oh, she needed him. His steely arms around her, his confident mouth pressing hers, his bronze skin scorching her paler limbs. Had the quick attic tryst ever been real, or was it only a recurring dream teasing her, leading her on down a path. Like Gretel, going too deeply into the woods for her own good.

"A picnic it is." The explosive yearning overruled her common sense.

They soon climbed into the battered maroon pickup borrowed from Gary. Laurel held the dinner boxes on her lap.

When Cole winced, failing to start the truck, she asked, "Your leg? Want me to drive?"

"Nah. It comes and goes."

"It should be healing by now."

"It's fine."

"I didn't take that bullet out under the best of conditions. I could—"

He braced one arm atop the steering wheel, plunking the other along the vinyl seatback behind her. His dark eyes mellowed. "You take good care of me, Laurel Lee, but you've got to stop worrying about me. About any of this. I don't want to remember you with that frown after I leave."

"After you leave."

The air stilled. His beautiful dark eyes took on ragged edges.

Cold perspiration sheathed her. She clutched the boxes. "It will be lonely without you." There, she'd said it.

Could he possibly feel anything for her beyond the refuge she offered for him?

"And I'll miss you," he said, his eyes steady.

Her heart lurched. Screwing up her courage, refusing to allow the evening to disintegrate, she declared, "We'll go to the old mansion and eat there. I'll help you look for clues again. There has to be something we missed. Mike left the crayon box there, not somewhere else for you to find it. A new pair of eyes, a new angle in different light, and we might see the clue and you'll have what you need to put your Mr. Rojas away forever."

A corner of his mouth twitched. "You're one hell of a woman, Laurel Lee. You're sure?"

"You hungry?" she asked, groping for courage to mask her reservations.

"Starving." His eyes told her he wasn't talking about food.

He started the truck, then pulled out of the parking lot and onto Hwy. N.

Laurel rode in silence, listening to him chatter about the scenery and the clear sky, glorying in his companionship in the truck cab's cocoon.

This is only one night, she reminded herself. What harm could come of being with him?

THE MAN FROM the corner table emerged from Al's in time to see the maroon pickup heading south, back toward Dresden.

Grinning, he got in his rental car, and was soon driving south, thinking how he needed to trade in this four-door for a van, something enclosed and private, big enough for the giant minnow cage he'd bought. Laurel Hastings would be cramped traveling and sleeping in it, but it would only be temporary, until they left all this far behind. He'd keep her like a pet, for her own safety.

Driving along, catching sight of the pickup every so often, he cracked a self-satisfied smile, even looked at it in the mirror. He'd covered his backside by calling his boss in Miami as he was supposed to. Now, he'd steal this woman right out from under all their noses. Hadn't he already done that with the Texas chick? Of course, she'd died enroute. But it wasn't his fault. Putting her in the coffin had been clever. He was sure she'd have enough oxygen in that big thing for the trip north with him. But he wouldn't make that mistake again. That's why an airy minnow cage would be just right for Laurel Hastings.

Chapter 11

LOOKING FOR HIS scissors, Buzz Vandermeer shuffled through the stacks of press releases, hand-written recipes from the locals, computer disks and other such items that eventually he'd have to get into the new newspaper layout software he was trying to learn. He was still trying to live down Una's grocery ad that was supposed to come out "Mr. Lucky Chicken Fryers, $1.98 a Pound." The "F" in Fryers got switched with the "L" in Lucky. For a retired English teacher, the episode gave him the hives every time he thought about it. Now he double-checked everything on the screen, spending longer hours at that and less on keeping a clean office. He finally found the scissors.

The *Minneapolis Tribune*, which got tossed at his office door in a plastic sleeve every morning, had run an intriguing photo on an inside page. There was a couple in it, a shapely blonde he didn't recognize, and a man who looked vaguely familiar.

The story said the blonde came from a prominent Texan family. She hadn't been seen in days after being spotted at a Miami marina. Another woman, a Lisa Shaw who worked near the marina, was missing too. But the bare-chested man in the photo intrigued Buzz the most. He was Cole Wescott, champion hydroboat racer and treasure diver. He also hadn't been seen in days and the article insinuated he was about to be charged with kidnapping or murdering the two women. Wescott's boss, Marco Rojas, said he last saw his employee with the women.

Buzz placed the photo in his scanner, then watched its pixels materialize on his computer screen. He stared for a long time at the eyes and the mouth. What was it about them?

He began altering the photo. Lighten the eyes. No, that didn't do much. Bring the mouth out of its smile. Hmm. What about hair? The photo was obviously some advertising shot, with the hunk's hair clipped short and airbrushed. Put some hair on him....

Buzz sat back. It was the hobo, Atlas, who had come to riffle through his morgue a few days back. And he lived with Laurel, the daughter of the sweetest woman this side of Spirit Lake.

Her sweet smile stuck with him the whole time he printed the enhanced photo of Atlas and walked out the door and down the street with it. Madelyn's daughter was in danger. The photo shook between his quaking hands. If Dresden had a serial killer in its midst, Buzz Vandermeer was about to crack the biggest story of his career. He hoped the sheriff was in.

HUNGRY, THEY had decided to eat on the verandah steps of the old mansion.

Cole leaned forward now on the top step, arms slung casually over his bluejean-clad knees. He wore the same blue polo shirt she'd washed for him, and it made her think he should really stay in one place long enough to accumulate more shirts.

Putting down his plate, he announced, "What if it's the meadow Mike wanted me to see? It's full of colors, like his crayons. Remember the flowers there?"

A flush painted her body with raw heat. "Of course I remember."

They'd first made love there. He had been consumed with the need. Heat niggled her core.

"You go ahead," she said, "I should get home."

But he hauled her into his arms before she could protest, cradling her head against one shoulder with fingers splayed against the back of her head. His heaving chest pumped warmth into her. He was so alive. "I'll miss you."

She gloried in his admission. "Rojas can't have you," she whispered.

"I won't let him win, Laurel Lee."

A shiver undulated down her body. "You always have to win," she said, lips barely able to form the words against his shirted shoulder. Winning and conquering were what he was about. It dawned on her now...had he merely conquered her once upon a time? Having power over someone was not love, she reminded herself.

"Please come to the meadow with me. Don't go home yet," he pleaded.

In the meadow they'd always felt free. It was a sanctuary. The best hiding place.

"We'll find something there," he said. "I can feel it."

Her heart flip-flopped again, giving in. "I'll go." If he was never coming back, she could go with him to their meadow. One last time.

But oh the memories....

They used to meet where the two paths forged into one, breathless, energy pulsating in their loins, fingers tugging impatiently at buttons and belt loops as they tumbled along.

They started off toward the meadow, walking steadily through the overgrown path Cole must have taken when sneaking out under his Great-Aunt Flora's nose. Laurel would slip away from helping her father build the cabin.

Starting from behind the mansion, Cole never hesitated, even with his limp. He moved by rote through tall grasses and around spiky sumac and scrub oak growth. He pushed hard, almost breaking into a run when brush gave way to stubbly grass for short stretches.

Dread kicked up in her stomach. He needed to be in the meadow too desperately, she thought.

He would hide behind the trees, chasing, hurrying her.

They skirted the bay with its bullfrogs croaking.

Cardinals darted through the leafy brush, their chipping call and loud whistles alerting woodland neighbors of the lovers' approach. She remembered it well.

Laurel felt herself swallowed up in the primal world. Yard by yard, it insulated them from the noises of reality, the voices trying to control what was in their hearts. Didn't people know how lonely they were when not together? How each felt like one shoe without its mate? That's how this secret garden had courted them then, too. It told them in every hush behind a leaf parted with tenderness, in every dewdrop poised on a fern frond, that being together was right.

The wilderness was their playground. They were free to go wherever their hearts led.

When the path joined up with the one she took to the cemetery, Laurel almost turned back. Her heart rolled in terror behind her breast. Would he question her again about the graves? Cole pushed himself faster, though limping. The pain must be excruciating. Had he read the gravestone's inscription?

It was clear he wanted to make love. The light in his eyes would dance, and he would turn his face up to the sky like a wolf, calling her name until it filled the woodland. Laur-el Lee. Come to me.

Before reaching the fork in the path that led to the gravestones and little church, Cole veered off, descending the hill. Air entered her lungs again, and her heart fluttered with less trepidation.

Laurel hiked after him. Branches whipped at her face.

"Cole? Cole, slow down."

Cole, please hurry, or someone will see us. Innocence, transparent and flimsy as lace, was enough then. It tasted sweet.

Twigs snapped, brush rustled. A hawk cried overhead. Laurel followed, fear driving her. She never wanted to lose Cole. To her, he was the only worthy opponent for the healthy barbs of the arguments her stubbornness brought. She wanted to draw him close.

But he kept hurrying now, breaking from the brush and into the open. She panicked, her heartbeat swelling torturous thoughts in her head. His boss—that damn Rojas—could pluck Cole from her anytime, the madman's talons drawing blood, purging Cole's last breath, feeding on the flesh that she knew as strong, enticing, protective.

"Cole!" She wanted to protect him!

The hill fanned into a gentle slope. Cole broke into a run, swooping down the incline, ignoring her. Or was he leading her?

Laurel ran. Blood throbbed at her temples.

He stopped abruptly. She almost tumbled into him. Capturing her hand, he tugged her along beside him until they reached the break in the trees and brush.

"Our meadow. Our meadow could be the place for everything to change," he said, his voice so guttural it painted pictures in her mind of wild things, wanton acts.

She lay trapped in the tall grass, and yet welcomed its shelter as he hovered over her. It was the first time for her. It was a matter of the hunted depending on the hunter to take his time.

THE HAZE OF the summer's evening softened the sunlight to a golden glow across the waving grasses and wildflowers. Brown-eyed susans, pink clover and queen anne's lace bowed in the breeze. Laurel stood motionless, knowing she'd been wrong to allow Cole to bring her here.

This was where she'd fallen in love with him. *A girl born free taking up with a boy gone wild.*

His fingers squeezed hers, sending heat shimmering up her arm and into her heart. Staring out across the landscape, his dark eyes flickered with a primitive energy, slices of yellow light tinting them.

Then a muscle twitched in his jaw. Furrowing his brow, his gaze scoped out the faraway treeline. He was hurting her hand.

"What's wrong?" she whispered, her body tensing in unison with his.

"I thought I saw someone."

A tremble chilled her. "Who?"

Rojas? The man in her shed? The man watching her in town, then running? Her mother's spy—the tourist in the restaurant?

Clutching at his arm, she meant to reassure herself as much as him. "He wouldn't come here. He doesn't know about this. We're only guessing it's what Mike wanted us to do."

"He followed us tonight."

"Nobody followed us." *Don't do this to me, Cole!*

But her nerves empathized.

The muscles steeled in his forearms, his hands bending into tight fists. The hawkish gaze, the yellow-tipped eyes, frightened her.

He was gentle, devoted to her. The grass cushioned her back, cradled her wrists when he splayed her arms out in the sunshine to take her. His shadow rode over her. A whisper of muscle entered her, and she cried out.

Across the meadow, against the opening in the trees that led to the pond and stream feeding Spirit Lake, a doe and her fawn emerged, twitching an ear at them. Laurel sensed Cole's sigh of relief with her own. Then, the doe and fawn flipped up their white flags for tails, on alert, and bounded into the thick cover of protective forest.

Even before she could seek his protectiveness, Cole had grabbed her closest hand and rubbed it. "You're shaking."

"Can't help it. This place...hasn't changed at all since then."

"You never come here on your walks?"

The question pricked her heart. "I give it a glance on the way to the graveyard."

A breeze parted the waist-high grass, and he stepped into it, as if eager to leave her, then stopped. His shoulders heaved up and down slowly under the blue shirt, changing the air in the meadow. "It's wrong the way I want you."

There was no mistaking the yellow glint in his eyes, the narrowed gaze, the uneven heaving of his chest in its ragged attempt at control.

The birds went silent, as if waiting for a decision that would change their world forever.

Chaotic emotions darted around her heart, a fiery yearning swirling inside her, but a warning creeping in. Was she being foolish?

"What are you trying to tell me?" she ventured, mouth dry, all senses on hold.

"That there's something about this place," he muttered, "no, about you in this place, that makes me want you so badly it hurts."

Her breathing stopped again. "Are you ever afraid of an emotion that asks everything of a person?"

"I'm only afraid for you." He backed off from her. "But emotions? You're strong. Whatever life asks of you, I believe you're strong enough to find an answer for it."

Her heart fluttered. "I might not be as strong as you think."

"You're very strong these days. And you never used to question me. Now, you question me."

The same breeze that fluttered his long hair cooled the perspiration on her forehead. She leaned on the breeze, flowing toward him. "That bothers you?"

"No. Our differences can be very becoming on you." After a flinch hit his jawline, he turned away, sucking in the fragrant evening air. "The quiet serenity, for example, becomes you. I don't belong here."

"But I do? You make it sound like I'm in a rocking chair watching life go by."

Coming back to her, he reached out and grazed her cheekbone with his knuckles, sending rivers of velvet heat pouring from his touch. "Oh, Laurel Lee. You used to look this flushed with life every day, falling for my stupid challenges and adventures. Don't you see, you're doing it again."

"I came to the same conclusion recently." The window in her heart had opened so wide that she was having trouble closing it. His spirit kept rushing in to join hers, refreshing her like spring air ushered into a musty winter house. "But what choice do I have, to borrow your phrase? Rock in my rocker instead? Alone?"

He turned his face up to the golden sun, and its light spun sienna threads through his deep chestnut hair, but his hands were balled into fists.

"The difference is, we're smarter now," she offered. "I can't lay aside your latest adventure as if it were a book I can close and come back to again. And I can't see you suffer, just as you say you don't want me hurt. Caring about you is...what defines me. Mother calls it 'worry and tend.' I could bottle it and sell it."

His eyes flickered like burning coals. "Yes, you are smarter, more caring, more everything that's beautiful."

Oh she was lost. The window inside was stuck open and he poured in, filling each floor with the sound of his voice, the laughter, the good times and his strength.

Cole strode on into the meadow, then began to jog with a hitch in his stride, dragging the bad leg. The weeds and wildflowers whipped in his wake. Then to her horror he slumped into the grass.

Panic halted her. Fear curdled her stomach. Had she missed the sound of a bullet?

"Cole?" She tore through the tall grass, fighting when she got tangled in stalks of queen anne's lace. "Answer me! Cole?"

"It's the stupid leg."

When she caught up, he appeared grumbly as a black bear with a thorn in its paw.

Shoving up his pant's leg, she unwound the pressure bandage. "Your leg's awfully swollen."

"Saw it off, doc."

Shaking her head at him, she chided, "The way you're going with this, your boss only has to wait until you die of fever. Where were you running to anyway?"

"The pond. It can't be far and that cool water will feel damn good on this leg. Remember swimming in the pond?"

Her gaze met his, remembering all too well.

The icy water made the dry, flat rock in the middle of the pond feel all the warmer. His tongue dipped into the hollow of her neck. He wanted to strike again. She could see it in his eyes.

Heat splashed her face, trickling down her neck and the rest of her body. "I remember," she said, secretly pleased he had too.

"It puckered you in a couple of places."

Sucking in her breath, she punched his shoulder. "If I remember right, something of yours shriveled."

His laughter echoed across the meadow. "We're goin' in, even if it's to prove to you that your memory's lousy."

Excitement escaped her heart before she had a chance to close the window. Reality reeled in the emotion. "You're not too steady on that leg and those rocks are slippery."

"You'll steady me, won't you?"

Her hands grew clammy. "We'll get wet."

"We'll take our clothes off."

"Cole!"

A grin spread across his face. "So we won't take our clothes off. We'll get wet and you can go home and change later, and I'll drip dry all night in my tent. They'll find my body with moss and mildew eating away at its—"

"We're not going in." But she was smiling again, darn him.

"My leg's throbbing. So is something else."

A tingle spread between her legs. Another memory. "That's it. Ice water here we come. I'm taking you in, with your clothes on, but no funny stuff. The rocks are too slippery."

He minded her at first, hobbling next to her through the meadow, letting her take his shoes off, then leaning on her to edge into the icy pool of clear water. Laurel's feet ached at the cold. "It couldn't have been this cold back then."

"Wimp."

But Cole let go a primal scream on entering the water.

He waded in further, up to his knees. "Come on," he said, looking over his shoulder at her. "Laurel Lee, the sissy."

He knew she hated being called that, and she knew he was baiting her. When he splashed toward her, his eyes twinkling, she panicked, but a thrill also coiled inside her. "No, Cole. No way."

With his arms held high, he roared, "It's the pond monster, coming for you. Grrrrr."

Swallowing back giggles, she pushed through the water for the shoreline. Her feet slipped on the rocks though.

"Gotcha!" he declared, grabbing her from behind with strong arms encircling her rib cage.

In short order, he picked her up in his arms, swung around and lumbered out into deeper water. She clung to his neck in desperation, her hands entwined in his thick hair heated by the sun.

"It's too cold," she shrieked.

"Grrrr! My leg feels great, doc!"

She laughed, despite her nervousness. They'd played this a thousand times that summer so long ago.

"Grrrr." A raw hunger swirled in his gaze.

Electricity bolted through her.

Their clothing abandoned, he chased her through the meadow again, until they both tired, and he lay poised in the weeds, waiting for her to want him enough to come find him.

She peered down at the water. "Take me to shore. Now," she insisted.

Splashing to shore, the clumsy, limping monster carried her up the grassy slope, then lowered her to a warm patch of dry grass near their shoes. Cole sat down next to her, panting from the exertion.

Laurel's breathing was ragged as well, but for another reason.

Every fiber of her suddenly recalled how it felt to be wanted by the devil-may-care Cole Wescott, how it felt to be made love to by him when he was focused on only that one thing. In the attic, he'd been focused on using their lovemaking to help relieve his grief. She'd shared that emotion, and let it carry them into old ways, let it be the excuse. But what if his focus now were only on her, on them? Could she stand that kind of passion, and then let it go?

She reached for her shoes, but his arm snaked out to stop her. "Don't be in a hurry."

A shadow swooped across his gaze, and his lips parted. He hesitated, caught mid-thought. He needed to tell her something. What? He'd been that way all evening, and she knew he'd blurt it out in his own time. Could she be patient? She had to be. She wanted him. Very much.

"I've got to get back for chores," she muttered.

"We had good times here." His eyes reflected days gone by.

"We dreamed, Cole. It wasn't reality, remember?"

Picking up a fistful of her loose hair that met the grass, he played it between his thumb and forefinger. She didn't expect the way his simple action pressed a glow into her breasts and deeper into her soul.

"We shouldn't have come here," he whispered, torment flitting across his eyes, "because it's too hard to leave."

Collecting her quaking hands in his big ones, he brought them up to his face, pressing her palms against his stubbly cheeks. His cool skin startled her. Confusion lurked in his brown eyes. A hurt flickered, died, then flared again. What did he want to talk to her about? Laurel's curiosity took over. To stoke the fire, she drew him to herself, into a kiss.

Their pains—her memory of her losses and all their regrets and fears—blended, but they were not fierce enough to win over this exhilarating moment. Flesh against flesh, firm promises that could never be kept, but oh, the bliss of allowing the instinctual fire to roar. Laurel understood this time together would have to last them forever.

Laurel gloried in the way he touched her, soft as a bird's wing, demanding as a hawk sitting on its prey. He needed her for survival, and she was sure it was love. With his fingers, he encouraged her to open for him, and she blossomed with the flowers, trusting, feeding his insatiable desires.

Laurel leaned into him, hungry. Parting her lips for him, he entered her with a gentle thrust, his tongue exploring, dipping deep, reminding her she was wholly a woman. Not a girl. Not a tomboy. Not lonely.

Shimmering temperatures rose inside her. She grew impatient with his hands merely clinging to her arms. She lay a hand across one of his, moving him to the memories.

Obliging, he cupped her breast, kneading her through the fabric of her blouse and the thin cloth restraining her underneath. The nipple pebbled to a hardness she'd never experienced, its tingling pressing to be set free. Let go. Be together. Don't be lonely. Reaching up, she unbuttoned a couple of buttons on her blouse.

"I want you," she whispered, eager for his breath to fill her lungs, to sustain her. She had to have him, to know that he was more than a dream all these years.

Theirs was a special journey. Lovers at first sight. He was strong, limber, worldly. And he knew everything. How to do it. How to make it feel good, how to be romantic. Nobody else had thought of "doing it" in a meadow, she was sure then. They stayed there all day. They had plenty of time.

There would never be another time for them.

But was it a mistake?

Couldn't he hurry!

Unbuttoning everything to the fading dusky sunlight of his gaze, his fingers dragged lightly across the swell of a breast, sketching lines of sparks in their wake.

"You're like a flower," he said, lowering his head to the fire erupting in her breast, spreading in a storm through her body, unsettling her in the way it begged for the hawk's mercy.

She ground her hands into his thick mane, holding on. Flinging her head back and closing her eyes, she drifted into weightlessness. He eased her back onto the grass. It smelled of clover and more promise, and of his mounting heat torching her skin.

She wanted to imprint this sensation on her mind for lonely nights to come. She heard a dove coo, a robin chirp, Cole's sharp breaths. The sky faded to pink overhead, nothing but soft color mingling with rainbows in her heart and the sheen of his skin. In the future, all she'd have to do is close her eyes, and they would be here, together. Reality imprinted on dreams. Dreams to last forever if reality could not.

At first, the hawk showed a mellower side. He came to her like the male dove, settling softly down upon his mate in the grass, their bodies quaking in blissful come-hithers. Their limbs fluttered, hers weakened by the force of his need. Her eyelids closed against the swirling colors and the spark of subdued sunlight collected in his eyes.

A rush of doubt unsettled her, of not knowing how long he would keep her. How long could he keep rising with her into the perfume of the clover? How long would she hear the music of his moans and low whispers escaping the lips tugging at her earlobes, nipping at her breasts, tasting the sensitive places between her legs?

She was about to protest, to regain reality, but the male dove—no, the hawk now—pounced, cleaving her to him.

He took off in winged splendor, flying higher, so high she would fall unless she held onto him.

His strong rhythm of flight, coursing higher, thrusting from air current to current, spun them through dizzying clouds.

Away with her he soared, faraway, until she was lost to everything and everyone but him.

All his. Captured and branded with his seed. She did not worry. For this was how it was meant to be in a wild meadow. Their meadow. No harm could come of anything so natural as the interplay between the hunter and the hunted, could it?

THE DRIFT OF HER clothes back over her skin startled her. Evidently they had dozed. Shaking off a sweet muzziness, Laurel looked up with a smile at the source of the clothing toss.

In the dim light of dusk, Cole was already dressed and striding off, but toward the pond. He halted at the shoreline, his back to her.

"What's wrong?" She sat up, pulling on her clothes. "Cole?"

He swept her up against him, his heat abating the iciness clawing at her. She bathed in his body's hum, one heart throbbing against the other, matching the rhythm, quelling their ragged breathing to whispers.

Pressing his lips on the top of her head, he whispered, "No matter what happens, know that I care."

"I'll be..." Not all right. Alone again. Betrayed again. She had to stop loving him. "I'll be careful."

He grunted, crushing her even closer to him. "Remember? I'm the one who had to buy you window and door locks so not every Tom, Dick and Harry wanders into your cabin."

"Or Cole?"

"You're an innocent."

She couldn't deny the secure comfort his steely arms provided, or the flush of fever still coursing through her body from their lovemaking. "Maybe I haven't been innocent since that first time we came to this meadow."

"And neither have I," he said, sighing.

They stood entwined in the gentle breeze for several moments, serendaded by the coos of whippoorwills and loons on the far side of the pond.

Rubbing her back with the flat of his palm, he whispered, "It's too perfect here. My brother couldn't have dared hide anything here. It's sacrilegous."

The whippoorwill cooed again, and she wished she had answers for Cole.

She drew him to the grass, where she could snuggle under the crook of his arm and they could watch the pond.

"See that movement?"

"What movement?"

"On the pond. The circles."

"Maybe a fish jumped. What's your point?"

"That you skip over details. That you don't notice tiny ripples, or you dismiss those little ripples in life. Things happen right under your nose and you don't notice."

"Like what?"

Like the love growing again between us, our need for each other, our avoidance of talking about the mistakes of our past and what really happened!

Leaning against him, reassured by his chest rising and falling in a steady rhythm, she went on. "Mike saw details. He would have noticed that the pond wasn't interrupted by a fish, but it was a muskrat working the shoreline, playing."

"A muskrat?" He nuzzled her ear from behind.

Her temperature rose. Where was the breeze when she needed it? "You've probably let a hundred clues go by because you're so focused on finding something big, like a treasure chest or a big X mowed in the meadow."

"I was too busy making love to you, Laurel Lee." His tongue laved the outer shell of her ear, causing a stormy disturbance to descend through her body. "For me, nothing else matters when I'm making love to you."

Licking her lips, she gathered her strength. She reminded herself that he could make love, but so far she saw no evidence that he would ever be able to see beyond to the details of a commitment. They had to ease away from this growing attraction and need for each other. She, too, had to remember his purpose for being here.

"Maybe all you need to do, Cole, is look below the surface. Mike trusted you to find something. It has to be here."

Clutching her shoulders, he kneaded them in a luscious way that made her melt. "You're not suggesting I start digging up your meadow?"

"Maybe." She drew in her courage. "But what I'm suggesting you do is dig deeper into your relationship with Mike to find clues. You say you hurt for him, but it seems to challenge you to nothing deeper in your actions."

He scoffed.

She turned to him, a breathtaking move to be so close to powerful eyes like his. They compelled her toward deep currents. She wanted to know, "You love...?" *Me? She swallowed it back.* "Do you feel love for your brother?"

"Love?"

Exasperated, she pressed, "What's your definition of love?"

A frown creased his coppery skin. Pink sky reflected in his dark eyes. "It starts with honesty and trust."

Which they were forever seeking. She swallowed for courage again. "For me, love is also responsibility."

"You already know I feel responsible for this mess."

"But love is also the taking of responsibility, and that requires a steady commitment, like the way nature paints the colors of flowers a person sees year after year, guaranteed, without fail. That color gets into your every fiber and attaches itself. And stays."

"I cared then. I care about you now."

Her heart began shutting the windows in her heart. "You care because you have to. Anything less would bring guilt."

"Is that bad?" He caught her chin in a tender grip. "I like taking care of you. You mean a lot to me."

"But that's so easy to say, and you say it all the time. Mike meant a lot to you, too. How well did you know him? Really? How much can you slow down to appreciate the detail of a person? I'm a friend, too, but what do you really know about me? To love someone, you have to commit the time to truly understand them."

He dropped his lips onto hers, and her heart fluttered, winging away with the hawk again, but warning her to stay strong.

Chapter 12

HIS KISS DIDN'T tease or taunt. It affirmed how well they meshed on several plains. Deep down, they understood how much they needed each other to soothe the loneliness. Friends, yes. A balm for the ache, oh yes. Laurel allowed the warmth of their lovemaking to move back in. She had him close for the moment and she'd make the most of however long he'd be in Dresden.

Drawing her up from the ground, he brought her close and she felt as if she were going to the well. Being one with him refreshed her spirit.

With one hand splayed hot on her back and the other toying with the nape of her neck, Cole said, "Save our meadow as part of your wildlife refuge."

She smiled into his shirt. "If you hand over the deed."

He eyed her curiously. "I'm not pursuing the title search."

The flat statement caught her off-guard. "You and David Huber aren't researching your great-aunt's past?"

"No. Right now I don't have time to stop my life for genealogical curiosity. Why do you look so surprised?"

She stepped back, rammed her hand in a pocket, then handed him the paper from the file. "Here. It's what I hoped we'd get to over dinner at the restaurant."

A puzzled look crossed his face, but she thought she detected a flare of recognition. He shook his head. "Somebody else is interested in the property. It's not me, Laurel."

"You're not the 'W' in this note?"

"Where did you get this? Huber's in Madison."

"I broke into David's office and took it."

"You what? Don't go making headlines on your own without consulting me."

His sudden ire stunned her. "What headlines?"

"A person of your stature breaking into a law office because you're curious about an old gangster's house, which happens to belong to an Eastern lady with ties to the disappearing Wescott brothers? How does it sound to you? Why not take a gun and shoot yourself, because something like that puts an X on your chest for Rojas." He spun in the grass, raking his hair. "I thought we were in this together."

Laurel swallowed hard. She hadn't thought it through to that extent. "I'm sorry. I want the truth about what's going on."

"So do I!" he snapped with fire-stoked eyes, clasping her until her body trembled in unison with his.

And then he released her.

"This partnership isn't going to work, this friendship you want," he continued in a voice coming from deep within him, "because of the truth."

Agony scorched across his face and he backed off, several steps, turning away from her to limp a few feet off into the tall grass, allowing a couple of expletives in his wake.

"Something's wrong." She swallowed hard. "You better tell me."

Shaking his head, he turned, his face resigned to a sullen pallor. "Why didn't you tell me about the baby?"

Laurel wanted the dark earth to open up and swallow her, to steal her away from this poacher's eyes. "What baby?"

"Yours and Kipp's."

Her palms perspired, the blood thundering through her. "Why Cole? Why do you make love to me one minute, then turn on me like some rabid beast?"

"Because with you I'm made to confront emotions that I don't like, remember? I speak gut-level truth now and you fault me?"

Feeling dizzy, she turned away, slipping a hand to her forehead. The iciness startled her. "Lies are what you live by, Mr. Atlas, the man who didn't even have the guts to tell me who he really was when we first met weeks ago."

"The baby you had with Kipp was real. How can you not tell me about this? Damn you, Laurel, you're keeping me on the outside, feeding me crumbs."

"And you can't stand not having every piece of the puzzle so you can put it together yourself. Driven, as usual."

"I can't stand the feeling that for every step forward our relationship takes, you seem intent on going back a step. And it has to do with sharing—"

"You have no right to my memories about Kipp or my son."

His gaze fell fallow, tracking into the dim sunlight and away from her. "I have a son. To lose him, well, I can't imagine what you've been through. I only know how it hurts just thinking of such things."

Rippling fear engulfed her. She didn't want to relive it all. Not now. "Please don't worry about me. I appreciate that you care, but..."

Squeezing her hand, he sighed. "But you don't trust me."

Taking her hand, clasping his heat around her quaking fingers, he began leading them back to the mansion through the tall grass. For a long time, they took their time, with him limping, the weeds rustling against them, the birds crafting their thoughts. She was grateful for his respectful silence.

When he stopped to rest his leg, he raised her hand to his lips, planting a firm kiss on every knuckle. "You are strong. I was right about that at least. You've moved forward. I respect that. It's what I have to do with Mike, move forward beyond the grief, the blame."

"The blame?" She grew hot, hoping he wasn't leading to another of their disagreements.

"It's what comes between people. Blame. It's between us, for example, like a fence. A fence with no gate, no way over." She wanted to pursue his words, but the quick brush of his lips on hers sent a tremor rippling through her. He muttered, "I'm going to kiss you more often. I love what it does."

Her heart tharumped. "What does it do?"

"Makes your eyes the color of the ocean on a sunny day. That warm, frothy green that looks so inviting."

His gaze defied the sunset, but the intensity held her captive and uncomfortable.

"What?" she asked, fearing his need for truth, fearing the emotion of losing her child sweeping through and debilitating her as it used to.

But Cole didn't respond in a predictable way. Instead of words, instead of a challenging answer, he drew her against him so that they could watch the puffs of clouds now tinged with lavender and pink scuttle across the horizon over Spirit Lake. Her breathing soon matched the cadence of Cole's, his heat seeping through her back, warming through to her stomach, relaxing the knot a bit. He even smelled new, freshened by the grasses they'd lain in and the spring water they'd splashed in.

On a cardinal's raucous intrusion, he asked, "You always deserved contentment. Did Kipp bring you that?"

A chill rattled her. "How would you define contentment?"

Squeezing her against him more tightly, he muttered against her hair, "For you, it's walks in the meadow and watching sunsets."

Laurel glanced at the red line on the horizon. Searching her memory, she couldn't recall Kipp sitting still long enough to watch a sunset. Instead, he'd be off playing cards with her father and a bunch of guys down at the bait shop.

She looked at Cole. What habits would he settle into someday with a wife? She would never know. "Kipp wasn't all that talkative about sunsets."

As they stepped onward through the queen anne's lace, clover and grass, Cole clung to her hand again, swinging it between when space in the path allowed. "I like the idea that your loved ones are buried nearby. My parents have already bought plots in England where dad's from, and the whole idea of oceans between us bugs the hell out of me."

She allowed a smile. "Sometimes I'd love my mother to be an ocean away."

His chuckle eased the strain of their conversations. "But you love her."

"My mother says it's silly the way I pretty-up the graveyard all the time with flowers."

"But there's nothing more beautiful than to drive by a country churchyard, seeing the flowers, knowing someone cares."

"Why Cole, you sound positively wistful. It's not a side of you I see often enough."

He growled, planting a firm hand at her waist and tugging her against his side for a moment of rest. "I remember every moment of marrying ourselves in that church. We made promises to help each other through thick and thin."

The sweet surprise of his memory wafted fresh as the breeze whispering off the lake. "You remembered saying that?"

"You refused the stuff about 'obey,' so we did the 'thick and thin' routine." The breeze tousled his dark hair, lifting it off the hint of worry lines that the years had etched.

"Maybe the vow didn't take because we didn't use the right words?"

"Nah. Eloping and marrying ourselves probably wasn't the way for us."

"We did it too fast?" she asked, anxiety creeping in.

"Probably like everything else. And you know what they say."

"Haste makes waste?" she offered. "Maybe it was the witness part. We only had one and I think we're supposed to use two."

He slipped his arm up around her shoulders. "Come to think of it, she was a bit stiff about the whole thing."

Allowing herself a smile, the anxiety scuttled away. "Mary *was* a statue in the corner behind the altar."

"She just stared at us the whole time. Maybe she should have objected?"

Laurel lived for these light moments with him. His humor was a perfect counter-balance to her seriousness. When had she grown so serious? She used to be...so devil-may-care, just like Cole. Regret niggled her. A promise, too, to think about this more.

She'd give anything for this day to never end. Because she knew she wanted to share more about herself with Cole. For a long time she'd carried burdens, secrets. All alone.

"If it matters," she ventured, "I'd like to tell you what it was like after you left."

"Of course it matters."

"I left town for a while."

She appreciated his shocked look of disbelief. "I needed to get away. Everyone stared at me, and never seemed to get over what you and I did."

"What didn't we do. Start with the car."

"My father never stopped reminding me about the new car we wrecked. It became symbolic. What he meant was, I'd been stupid."

Robins chirped, heralding the impending sunset. Her courage flagged. The meadow grew dank-smelling.

Cole offered, "It must have been hard to start relationships again with the populace of Dresden looking on."

"Yes." She'd never admitted that to anyone. "I felt small, as if I'd shrunk before everyone's eyes."

"Back in Florida, I wrestled with Mike, who gave me the cold shoulder, even more than my parents about the whole thing. He liked you."

She hiked an eyebrow at him. "I thought you two were inseparable."

"Mike may have only been a year younger, but he acted the role of the big brother. He was probably why I got on with my life so soon. I loved my brother and couldn't stand him not respecting me."

She smiled again, but it was bittersweet and for him. "We all need special people in our lives like Mike to give us direction."

"It must have been easy, now that I think about it, to choose between a joke like me and someone like Kipp."

Her forehead grew hot. She was glad for the cover of evening's shade. "Loving Kipp wasn't about you." A partial lie. "It was about getting on with my life. I was prepared to make it all work."

"So was I with Stephanie."

"But you divorced."

"My racing schedule." He swiped up a few grass blades to twirl. "And when the weather was right on the seas for salvaging, I had to go. Before I knew it, Tyler was spending all his time with Mike and Karen and his cousin Timmy. He didn't know me."

Her heart lurched for him. A breeze kicked up again. A nighthawk began an early serenade.

Clearing his throat, he added, "Tyler and I were spending more time together lately because he's taken an interest in scuba diving. I hired Lisa to give him lessons so that Tyler would be around the harbor where I work."

"I bet Tyler thinks that's cool."

"Lisa and the diving, yes. Me? I still had the damn job that I couldn't let go of." He twirled the grass between thumb and forefinger. "Ever feel resigned to your lot in life?"

"Resigned?" The notion scalded her fierce pride. "Do you view me as resigned? About what?"

Licking his lips, he took his time, too much time. "I just keep remembering that tomboy I used to know, that woman who crashed cars, laughed, looked life in the eye."

"That's still me."

"Is it? Or is that part of you only allowed out on good days?"

"Cole?"

"Ah hell. I'm the same way." He tossed the grass stems aside. "Forget I said anything."

But she couldn't. They went on, the weeds rustling against the rhythm of their hips. Had she neglected that crazy, tomboy part of her? What kind of woman was she to allow that to happen?

He was limping on, leaving her behind in the meadow.

She rushed to catch up, took a bold move and plunked his arm about her shoulders while snaking the other around his waist. He flashed a glance her way, but they moved on in silence, thoughts of their impending parting for good tearing at her. Even without his boss and Mike's murder, she recalled what he'd said about the blame between them being a fence. No relationship had a chance when blame lurked in their hearts, and it did. It seemed neither of them knew how to get rid of it, either.

Finally, when he'd sighed several times, and she realized it wasn't about his leg, she asked, "What is it, Cole?"

"I'm thinking too much."

"About what?"

"My son. Do you think my son will ever love me? In that proud way? I saw it once. He'd just learned to ride his bike, and when he rode it toward me, wobbling and ready to crash any moment, all that mattered to me was his crazy grin and the light sparking in his eyes when he looked at me. That's a look a father never forgets. It's a look a father wants back again."

Tears stung the backs of her eyes. Before this riveting tender side of Cole could swamp her, she attempted levity. "A teenage boy saying 'I love you' to his dad? You might be setting yourself up for disappointment at this stage."

"Especially with a dad who drops out of sight." He snorted. "A few years, he'll be getting a driver's license. Then he'll have a car and I won't see him again."

"Gee, let's just wish the rest of our life away."

He flashed her a toothy smile. "You're good for me Laurel Lee."

"Don't read too much into it."

"Deal!" he said with a bravado that lightened the mood. "I should bring Tyler up here sometime. Maybe with Timmy. Could I do that, Laurel?" Pinpricks of light from the ebbing sunset illuminated a dance in his eyes.

Could she stand to have him visit again? Especially if he brought along his living son? Would it bring the pain of her dead son back to her? She thought it might. She didn't know if she had strength to face that.

When she looked at Cole, the dance in his eyes tripped over into her, tapping up a storm in that empty house of a heart, filling her head with memories of laughter, warmth, walks amid fragrant summer flowers. A visit every so often would be better than never seeing him again. She was strong, right? She had to prove she was.

"When this is all over, we can talk about Tyler visiting."

Reaching out with an index finger, he lifted her chin. Electricity zigzagged down her middle and into her toes.

He was a massive silhouette to be reckoned with alone in the wilderness. She whispered, "We need to be getting home."

"I can't leave without giving you what I found in the lockbox," he whispered hoarsely.

"Then you did find something." Disappointment laced her elation. "Why didn't you tell me about this until now?"

"It's not what I expected. I...need to show it to you. It's not something I can explain. Like the way I feel right now." He drew her close, the air between them crackling, smelling ominous as a storm. "Can I stay the night?"

The nighthawk cried. Birch leaves rustled. A dankness arose around them, promising fog would roll in soon off Spirit Lake. The mesmerizing depth of darkness in his eyes hushed the rapid beating of her heart.

Was that a thumb tempting her lips in a feathery touch, or just the nighthawk dipping past?

Cole was doing it again. He wanted a night. He couldn't promise more. She shouldn't expect him to promise more. It was time to move on and accept what she had with him. Could she?

A shiver skittered across her heated skin.

His hand slid down against her neck, the thumb pressing against the heartbeat in her throat.

"Laurel?"

"I want you to stay." *For all time.* "For the night."

SHERIFF JOHN Petski sat in his office, sweaty and tired from chasing two loose riding horses down a highway with tourists still attached. He didn't need Buzz snooping around looking for news tonight.

Standing over the desk, Buzz sniffed. "Big story?"

"Aw, darn tourist fell from his horse and got up just in time to step too close to my squad car. I ran over the man's foot."

Buzz grumbled, "I missed a good photo?"

"I don't think you'd be able to use it," John said, pen scratching through the report he had to file. "Guy wasn't wearing a stitch of clothing."

That caused the editor pause, but he recovered, slapping a photo and news article down next to the sheriff. "I got a better photo anyway. You know who this is?"

The computer-enhanced photo threw a chill into John. He didn't need Buzz turning detective and spoiling the game plan he and Cole had cooked up with Wiley. "Dang it, Buzz, of course I know who this is. Atlas. I hired him to tune up some motors on my boats."

"This guy looks an awful lot like the famous Wescott murderer."

"What murder?" John swiped up the article. His veins ran cold. It was Wescott. Damn. They'd have to step up their plans. But he couldn't let on to Buzz, not the town crier. "Just a coincidence. I checked Atlas's prints already."

Buzz harumphed. "I'm taking a ride out to Laurel's anyway."

"Now, Buzz—

But the editor was out the door, slamming it so hard two of John's award plaques for bravery in the line of duty crashed to the floor.

Hurrying to grab his hat, John knew time was running out in more ways than one. He only hoped Buzz would play into their plan instead of messing it up. Or got somebody killed.

COLE MELDED WITH the shadows and the faint light bathing the room from the cabin's fireplace. The budding flames sputtered in the centers of his chocolate eyes, while his skin took on the coppery patina of the aged pine walls.

Laurel sat in the rocker on the opposite end of the hearth, watching him search through his stuffed backpack. "Why don't you just turn it upside down on the floor."

Firm lips parted into a smile when he looked up at her from the rag rug. "That'd be too easy. Besides, this is special. I don't want it hitting the stone in the fireplace."

She was intrigued all the more. During the entire long stroll back from the meadow, he'd remained mysteriously quiet. Focused on some secret. He didn't even respond to her comments about the owl in the tall maple calling to Owlsy in her shed. Without a word, he'd followed her through a quick check on the animals.

Now, he withdrew his hand from the bag, and Laurel thought she glimpsed metal. "Jewelry? What the sheriff referred to?"

He nodded. Still hiding the treasure, Cole stood, giving her a crooked grin that pushed a dimple in one cheek. Hiking an eyebrow, he looked to her like a boy about to give his best girl his best frog.

She didn't know whether to giggle or play it straight. She erred toward the latter, nudging him with, "Well, what is it?"

"You can't let your eyes land on it unless you say you'll accept it first."

"Is it something you found in the ocean?"

"No." Stepping toward her, he tucked the hand behind him. "It's a silly thing. Embarrassing, really."

"Something you and Mike shared when kids?"

He shook his head.

"But Mike kept it for you," she said.

"He's the detail man."

Every nerve ending in her body itched to solve the mystery. "I can't stand it. Show me."

Like the boy with the frog, he stepped over, dropped the object in her lap gingerly, then stepped back, waiting.

Laurel didn't expect the weight of it. Her eyes opened wider in awe.

The locket was the size of a quarter, its gold lid glinting in the splash of firelight which showed off a ring of roses and a garden gate artfully carved into the face. It had no chain.

Cole said, "It was Great-aunt Flora's. She loved her flowers. She never told me where she got the locket. She just said it was time to pass it along where it might do some good."

When had the fire ever thrown so much heat? Laurel licked her dry lips and peered up at Cole. "I can't accept this. It's a family heirloom."

Stuffing his hands in his pockets, Cole shifted his weight and looked decidedly uncomfortable. "There's a problem with that. You see, I can't really give it to anybody else, and I know it's time for me to move on, and well, loose ends have to be tied up—"

"Cole, you're blathering. Why do you want me to have this?" It rested almost too-perfectly in her palm.

Taking his hands out of his pockets, Cole reached down, and in slow motion, twisted the ancient clasp. The face sprung open.

"Oh my," she said, amused. "You and Mike?" They were two urchins locked forever in time in a yellowed photo the size of her thumbnail.

Cole nodded. "I suppose you have one of these lockets laying around already."

"No. I don't." Her own words sounded vacant, lonely. Shouldn't all mothers have a locket?

"Maybe you could find a photo of your baby, and—"

Her eyes misted over.

"What a clod I am," he said. "I'm sorry."

Her heart weighed so heavy it seemed to fall into her stomach before pounding double-speed. "No, Cole, that's so thoughtful, but really, I can't accept this."

She pressed it toward him, eager to be rid of the emotions swirling inside her.

His hands closed over hers and the locket.

Then he took it out of her hands. Holding it out to her, he said, "You know how kids are. Some exchange rings. Earrings these days, according to Tyler. When Aunt Flora gave me this, I did something really dumb."

Turning the locket over, he placed it back in her palm. When he whispered the inscription, "To Laurel, from Cole," she swallowed hard.

So simple and timeless.

All breath left her. "You were going to give this to me then?"

"About a thousand times. I had it engraved at Higgins Jewelry Store."

"Old Higgins must have loved that. Did he tease you?" Laurel could not deny the jets of heat coursing through her veins.

"Mercilessly. It's probably why I kept putting off giving it to you. You were always so on the go, so sure of yourself, not sitting around and into frilly things that I was finally convinced it didn't seem to fit you."

You were scared of the commitment. "Where did it end up?"

"Mike and I had a secret board in the attic. When I left in a hurry that summer, I left it there. Mike kept it, or maybe he only found it himself back here in May. Secret boards are too easy to find and he probably didn't want Rojas pilfering it."

Rojas. It sullied the atmosphere of the room. The fire didn't smell as sweet. The glow ruptured into violent flames.

When she got up to tend the fire, her gaze caught a flicker off to the side—a visage in the window.

The locket clattered to the wood floor. "Cole," she whispered, "someone's here. Someone's sneaking around and spying on us."

HE LEAPED toward the front door. "Call 911."

After doing so with shaking fingers, Laurel raced for the back door that led through the breezeway to the animal shed.

Flicking on the overhead lights, she saw that the heat lamps were undisturbed, and most of the animals blinked up at her from their nocturnal activities ranging from sleep to feeding. Rusty sat up, questioning the intrusion. Laurel reached into a coffee can for a dog treat and gave it to the fox.

She checked the far door. The new locks held it securely, to her relief.

Back in the house, she hurried to all the windows, letting her fingers rework all the locks and seals. She shut the window in her bedroom she'd only opened when she and Cole arrived home about an hour ago. Ready to leave the room, her gaze caught an oddity, stopping her in her tracks next to her dresser.

The photos of her family had been laid face down. Had she done that the other night? Or, had someone broken in?

A tremor rolled through her.

Racing to her closet, she tore the clothes aside, frantic in her search. Her hands found an empty wall behind her clothes. Where was her father's rifle?

Panic climbed into her chest. Someone had stolen the rifle. Someone had been in her house and her bedroom.

Her feet flew out of the bedroom. "Cole?"

She remembered his knife. She headed for the kitchen counter, but was stopped by a ruckus outside.

"Cole?"

The front door banged open against the interior wall. Laurel sucked her body back, fear tumbling over her.

Cole thrashed in, tossing a man in a heap in the middle of the livingroom. The man rolled and landed up against the back of the sofa. He was an unrecognizable pile of coat, fedora and tan gloves. Cole charged at him.

"Cole!" Laurel screamed, backing off, "you got him? Rojas?"

"No," he growled, grabbing at the heap on the floor, "but I got one of his henchmen spies. Stay back, Laurel." Then to the heap, "Get up, you foul-smelling—"

The heap on the floor groaned.

A new bluster blew through the open front door and in hustled Buzz, camera in hand. "Let me at him. I want a clear picture. I saw it all."

"Buzz?" Laurel gasped, amid flashbulbs snapping, blinding her.

The editor almost knocked her down in his hurry to capture the scene. Instead, he shoved Cole down onto the struggling heap.

From the tussle on the floor, Cole shouted, "Get out of the house, Laurel, before you get hurt! Run!"

She groped through the dizzying lights, finding the open door and outside air. Racing off her stoop, more lights assaulted her and for a flicker of a moment she recognized the red and blue bubble lights behind the headlight beams. Sheriff John Petski trotted her way, gun drawn.

"Hurry, John! Cole's got a man in there!"

"Get down, Laurel!" he yelled. "Get down!"

Reeling from the protective shove he gave her, Laurel fell between the tomato rows in her garden near the front door.

Then a gunshot split the night.

BREATHING HARD, the man from the restaurant clambered into the small aluminum boat anchored a few yards below Laurel's cabin and out of sight of her dock. He wiped his brow. That had been too close for comfort. Where had all those people come from? And who was that guy throwing on a disguise just before the sheriff arrived? Sure made no sense. Didn't matter. He'd gotten a good enough look at Laurel Hastings through her window.

Oaring fast, he considered the cage stretching from his feet to the other end of the boat. She'd fit in there, he was sure.

Paddling off in the dark, he turned his attention to the task at hand. Getting rid of the Texas woman's body, now hidden under an abandoned dock up the way, floating inside the other cage he'd bought from Madelyn Hasting's bait shop.

Chapter 13

LAUREL SAT TRYING to brush mud off her face when Cole's long fingers gripped her arms, heaving her out of the tomato rows.

Sheriff Petski poked his head around Cole's shoulder. "You all right?"

"Thanks, John. No scratches. What happened?"

"Gotta go. There's another call and I have to drop off my handcuffed human baggage first."

He trotted off, then the squad car rolled out of her driveway, its back tires spitting up gravel. Laurel stared after it, then back to Cole, dumbfounded.

"Who is that man you found looking in my window?"

Briskly swiping the last bits of leaves, dirt and tomato leaves out of her hair, Cole said, "Don't have bad dreams about this. John knows what he's doing."

Indignation reared inside her. "What happened in there?"

Buzz stepped out of the cabin then, interrupting them. "That's what I want to know. Never did get a good look at the character." He twitched a pencil over a pad of paper. "Now what was the guy's name?"

Cole's eyebrows twitched in minor frustration, but he turned to Buzz. "We're not sure. Just report him as the alleged right-hand man of Marco Rojas."

"Alleged," Buzz said, scribbling, "yes, that's good. My biggest story ever. Gotta get it on the wire services."

Then he took off down the driveway.

Shaky, Laurel frowned after the man toddling down her driveway. "Where's he going? Where's his car?"

"I don't know. Maybe he left it out on the road when he saw John's squad parked here."

"But he was here before the sheriff."

Cole slipped an arm around her shoulder too quickly, she thought. "Who can figure out former English teachers. They talk in riddles and love mysteries."

Laurel didn't buy it. "What's going on?"

"Looks rainy. I'll fix the hole in your ceiling."

He ducked indoors way too quickly, she concluded. She followed him.

Her shoulders sank at the sight. Her home—her sanctuary—was a disaster. The arm was broken off the rocker.

"That was my father's favorite chair," she muttered, smarting from knowing it'd never be the same.

Her breathing labored. She could get angry, or resign herself to...what? Cole?

There was a slash in the back of the sofa, plaster dust everywhere, and a gaping hole in the old plaster ceiling.

Anger began to win out. "Someone could have been killed here."

He began righting chairs, kicking plaster into a pile here and there. "Nobody got hurt. It was a warning shot."

"Don't touch my things. Stop it." A tremblor began deep inside her. It roiled, a bomb wanting to explode.

"Look, Laurel. I'm sorry this had to happen, but if this man spills his guts, my business here is done."

Staring at him, she realized that's what this was for him— business as usual. It sickened her. How could a man make love to her so tenderly, then take joy in creating havoc?

"Another one of your damn adventures."

"No, it's not."

"Get out," she ordered, throwing a sofa pillow at him. "Somebody could have been killed tonight and I don't find it entertaining."

She picked up another pillow from the floor and tossed it at him, then stopped, remembering the locket must be on the floor somewhere. Delicate, the inscription—her name and his—might have been crushed under foot. Sinking to her hands and knees, she started searching, sick at heart. Feeling foolish. Angry. No, mad.

A freneticism overtook her. How dare these men come in here and crush the life out of her things.

Cole could come in and shoot up her house—and prove he didn't love her, but she wanted the locket after all. She cared about delicate things, helpless things. Things lost.

With her head pounding, and her breathing growing sharp and shallow, she thrust her arms under the sofa, then began lifting up the cushions, searching.

"Laurel, what's the matter?"

"The locket. It's gone."

Gripping her wrist, Cole stayed her search. "I'll ask the sheriff to frisk Rojas's weasel we caught. He could have it."

"Lifted it in the middle of your fight?"

He forced her to sit on the sofa. "I'll get it for you from John. I promise."

Then she looked into his dark eyes, and saw a sadness, a pain she didn't recognize. She realized he must be thinking her nuts to worry over the locket she'd given back to him only minutes ago. They had been saying good-bye. How cruel of her to hint to him that she cared for the locket too much. But no man took a family heirloom and engraved your name on it unless he meant something by it. Did he? But that was long ago. And here she was balled up inside ready to blame him again.

"No, don't bring it back," she relented, allowing her weariness to drip out. "I got caught up in...nostalgia," she said, a bit too tartly, she knew. But looking around her cabin...it looked like her insides felt.

After looking at her long and hard, Cole got up and slung his backpack over his shoulder. "I'll ask the sheriff. It won't take anything for me to stop tomorrow."

She panicked. "No. It's Friday. I need to prepare for the weekend. They always get busy."

"I'll come by to help you clean up this mess."

"Please don't." They had to sever their ties. They always came to ruin.

He leaned against the door. "I'll be over at the mansion a few more days. Working things out with the sheriff."

"Like the last time you left Dresden."

"This time, with the guy we just caught, we might be close to nabbing Rojas."

"Gee," she snapped, "congrat's. Mount his head and we'll put it on the wall at Big Al's for you to brag about."

"This isn't a game." He said it so quietly it gave her the shakes.

But he slammed the door. In his wake, plaster dust spewed down in front of her. Her insides now felt the same way. Dry dust.

A deadly silence descended on the destruction. Laurel stood there, alone, her heart feeling as splintered as the rocker. This was not how she envisioned their last night together.

COLE SAT NEXT to his tent until the moon moved from one side of the mansion to the other, watching Laurel's cabin across the bay. Her lights had gone out long ago, but he knew she wouldn't sleep much tonight. Neither would he.

He never came to Dresden to hurt her, but everything he did seemed to go haywire. Even giving her the locket turned into a disaster. The fake shootout hadn't been planned for tonight, and Cole had lobbied for it happening anywhere but Laurel's place, but the sheriff suggested they'd have to leap at the first chance Buzz gave them. They had kept Buzz innocent of their plan because they knew the editor would never fake a story knowingly.

What Cole and the sheriff wanted was simple. They wanted to draw out Rojas or any of his men he might have hired to come after Cole. At Wiley's insistence, Wiley would be in disguise, and then he'd stalk Cole and get captured by the sheriff when they knew Buzz would be around. From there, the sheriff would verify for Buzz that they had captured a Rojas henchman and Buzz would send it out on the national news services. It was all a plan to put heat on Rojas and end the mess.

But something about tonight bothered Cole. Laurel was right. Buzz showed up before the sheriff. Had the editor been the man in the window? Buzz was snoopy, but it didn't seem his style.

It couldn't have been Wiley in the windows. He was too much of a klutz not to have been heard beforehand. Cole found him at the side of the house. Wiley said he'd been dropped off by the sheriff. They'd quickly gone into action, pretending Wiley was a spy for Rojas. But if Wiley had just arrived—presumably with the sheriff—who had shown his face in the window of Laurel's cabin?

His gut told him there was someone dangerous out and about. Someone they hadn't counted on. He could smell it on the fog, taste it in the tinny fear flaking inside his mouth, feel it in the mounting dread fueling the rapid beat in his heart.

Cole wished like hell he was standing guard in Laurel's cabin tonight, but then Rojas wanted him, not her. Better to stay away from her, especially now. Just keep watch. Be her watchdog. The hair rose on the nape of his neck.

Cole's eyes scanned the fog-blanketed land around him, the murky bay, the opposite shore. Private piers jutted from out of the patchy fog. All was quiet.

Too quiet. From Laurel he'd learned to listen for the nighthawks cry overhead, the frogs bellowing from the lowland, the occasional owl. He heard none of that. It meant there was movement somewhere nearby. Out on the water?

Then he turned around and considered the old mansion, its attic window catching the moonlight. Was someone watching him from up there, from his and Mike's pirate ship? Was someone keeping watch over Laurel's cabin?

Cole started off through the tall grass, his leg paining him badly all of a sudden. He'd much rather be curled up with Laurel in his arms in a warm bed.

Pushing on through the cold, damp grass, he took courage from the object in his pocket. When had he begun to feel he was doing all of this for Laurel? Hadn't he come here to avenge Mike's death? Now, he wanted it over with, just to bring peace back to Laurel's life.

He cared too much for her. He knew that. Was it love? He shuddered. Love would mess up everything. To love her openly would put her in danger. Rojas meant to kill him. Rojas would feed on any distraction, any weakness.

Love brought complications to a man's life, and a man had to be ready to shoulder the responsibility. He knew that more than anyone. He knew it because Laurel demanded that love mean accepting responsibilities. But he felt responsible for everyone and everything. Where did he start?

And did any of these challenges matter when he needed to erase the quiet sadness in her eyes? He accepted that responsibility automatically because it spoke to his soul, where a part of him said he still loved her, even if he didn't see a way to a future for them.

Shoving on toward the old mansion, he realized he had no weapon on him except maybe the flashlight.

In the side pocket of his jeans, where normally he carried the knife, his hand clutched the locket. His best weapon was his conviction. Nothing could harm Laurel. He wouldn't allow it.

DOUSING THE flashlight, he held his breath to listen. He hadn't really expected to encounter anyone in the old mansion, but now he stood in the dark halfway up the final stairsteps to the third-floor attic, wondering who was in the pirate ship.

Soft shufflings emanated from the pirate ship, then scraping noises. Someone was moving the old boxes or discarded kitchen chairs around. Cole clenched his teeth, but sour fear trickled down his throat. Had he found Rojas's henchman at last? The window spy? Was it the bastard himself—Rojas?

Cole was about to ease back down the stairs, when a loud crash made him shrink against the dank wall. Beads of sweat sprinkled his forehead.

Miles and miles of memories fast-forwarded through him. Of sunshine and flowers in her red hair, of swimming, riding fast boats and cars together, of the way she looked up into his eyes, so trustingly. He couldn't die this way, like a trapped rat in this old house. Laurel needed him. And he needed her, to hear her question him, to push him to greater things, to hear her ask about his son and to talk about her lost son and family....

Easing with one foot, he began edging down the riser behind him. He was too late.

Thundering, thumping lumps bounded through the murkiness, and in his hasty retreat, Cole stepped backward onto the bad leg. With a sharp needling pain it gave way, toppling him backward down the steps to the second landing.

A powerful force bowled into his hip and leg.

Cole cried out in death-defying anger.

He came up swinging madly in self-defense, but to his surprise, met with empty air. He grappled about for the flashlight, flicked it on just in time to catch sight of two fuzzy tails scurrying down the steps, heading for the front door.

"Roxy and Roger?" Cole snorted relief, then sank against the wall to catch his breath and swipe the sweat off his brow.

What a life I lead. With his butt and back killing him almost as much as the bum leg, Cole wanted to....

...Go home and climb into bed with Laurel and forget this.

He chortled at that. Because something dawned on him. He had never made love to Laurel in a real bed. This unforgivable detail suddenly nagged at him. What would he do in a warm, soft bed, with Laurel under him and nobody knocking on the door? Would Laurel accuse him of thinking it boring? Nothing with Laurel had ever been boring. Not her smile, her wit, the way she made love.

Fool. He looked up toward the attic. The woman deserved a lot more than the trouble he always seemed to bring her. His son deserved a better legacy than this.

And so did Mike. What kind of father had Mike seen in Cole? The chill of truth gripped him. If a son couldn't even count on Cole, maybe Mike felt he couldn't either. And so he'd come here alone, ascending these stairs only weeks ago. A breeze rushed up the hallway.

Mike's ghost? Leading him?

Rubbing his leg, agony gripped him. A longing for Laurel's healing ways overwhelmed him.

Thunder punched at the old mansion, rattling the walls and his bones.

He remembered Laurel's repeated offers to help him with the leg. He'd pushed her away, just as he accused her of pushing him away. Remorse coursed through him. Hauling himself up, he hobbled up the stairs, all the way to the attic...the pirate ship.

He stepped around old boxes strewn everywhere. Roxy and Roger had been curious and obviously playing. They'd even tipped over the old table where he'd laid out the railroad map. He went over to set it upright. Leaning over to catch the table legs, a flash of lightning illuminated something loosely taped on the underside of the table. He trained the flashlight on it.

Cole recognized the object immediately. Picking it out of the tape, fingering its heft and copper and gold machinations, Cole grew excited. A sextant, the device was used by ship navigators to measure the sun or a star from the horizon. With its tiny scope, and half-circle arm with calibrations, it calculated distances to other ships, land or objects out on the water.

On a dive for Rojas this past spring, Cole had uncovered the sextant near some World War II shipwrecks in the Atlantic Ocean. As usual, Mike logged in the treasure, then ordered its careful cleaning before they would complete further documentation on its age and history.

Why was this object from Rojas's prized collection of treasures from the deep here in Wisconsin?

Cole had no answers, but he knew Mike had a purpose. Cole found the crayon box earlier on top the table, but had failed to look underneath. Mike would be shaking his head to know it'd taken two raccoons to uncover something Cole should have found on his first look-see.

"Come on, Mike. So now what do I do with this thing?"

His nerves hummed. He was close to finding something big. The object weighted his hand down, almost begging him to move, to get going and blow Rojas's operation sky high. But how? Why? Why had Mike risked his life for this and lost? He needed to talk with Laurel. She had fresh perspective, even better smarts with puzzles than he.

But he'd promised himself to not endanger her.

With flopsum bathing him, the night air clawed at him with icy fingers. He wanted Laurel's help. She was more than an addiction. They were a team. They found answers together. She'd shown him that. She always demanded he dig deeper. Be smarter.

Laurel had needled him about looking for an "X" mowed in the meadow by Mike before Cole would act. A sextant could measure the distance to a place. What place? From what vantage point? Maybe there was a place in the meadow he needed to revisit, a place Mike remembered meant something special.

Then he swallowed hard. Maybe, just maybe, Mike brought him here because of Laurel. Was something hidden—not in a place special to Mike or Cole—but to Laurel? Could it be the church? That would surely fool Rojas or his henchmen who came looking for the cache of evidence. They knew nothing of the church.

Excitement poured through him.

He hobbled down the three flights of stairs, this time taking the back hallway for a faster exit. Going past the kitchen, the pantry, the old library room...memories flooded back. Laughter echoing. Mike giggling when Cole chased him with a fat ugly toad. Mike teasing him with, "Cole and Laurel, sittin' in a tree, K-I-S-S-I-N-G."

Cole walked faster. Away from Mike's voice. Toward Laurel's.

Pushing through the rotted screendoor, he plunged into the night's storm. The rain drenched him through to his soul. The ditty wouldn't quit. "Cole and Laurel, sittin' in a tree..."

With the sextant gripped in one hand, and the flashlight in the other, he forged back through the wet grass and weeds, past his sodden tent, wishing away the stiffness still in his bum leg. Being careful not to put too much weight on it, he slid down the slick embankment, muddying himself.

He climbed into the sheriff's runabout he'd just tuned up, and started for Laurel's place. Pressing into higher gear, he ignored the wind heaving him at dangerous angles.

FINDING LAUREL'S front door unlocked, Cole panicked. What's more, the lights were on in the kitchen but the place seemed deadly quiet.

"Laurel?"

He glanced back through the door, flicking on her flashlight to see into the yard. The light glinted off the bumper of her minivan. She had to be here. Maybe she'd only been so tired she'd gone to bed and forgotten the lights and door. "Laurel?"

Closing the door, he stood for a moment, listening, sniffing the air, knowing already that something was wrong. The quiet unnerved him even more than the unlocked door. There was a faint odor of cigarette smoke. Laurel didn't smoke.

He tiptoed around the mess in the livingroom, laid the heavy sextant down on the table near the bay window, then turned toward the short hallway that led to the bedrooms. He held the flashlight high over his head, ready to strike.

A creaking caught his attention. He halted.

Then footsteps hit the wood floor behind him. He whirled to see a figure launch from the curtains by the bay window and head for the backdoor to the breezeway.

Cole took up the chase, cussing at his limp, flashlight in hand, wishing he had time to find that hunting rifle of Gerald Hasting's that Laurel kept.

From behind him, Laurel called out, "Cole? I was just outside, I thought I heard—?"

The intruder raced through the breezeway, then into the animal shed.

"Stay put!" Cole called to her. He knew she'd be right on his heels to check out every animal in his wake.

He followed the ruckus of squawks and chittering of creatures disturbed in the shed. Heat lamps pitched every whichway.

The intruder, a lean figure, fled out the back door, through the deer pen, where Cole thought he'd nab him against the high fence. Instead, the man bolted through a new, low hole cut in the fence and headed for the looming forest cover.

Cole cussed, gritted his teeth against his damn leg and made himself ignore it. He had to catch the man Rojas had sent to kill him...or was it Laurel, too, now?

Bile rose in his throat at the thought of losing her. Fury for putting Laurel's life in danger pitched him into the night.

Rain slapped across him in heavy sheets. Slippery leaves caused havoc underfoot, but when his flashlight caught the man's back up ahead, he ran with wild abandon. Nobody was going to get away with messing with Laurel. This was his fight. Only cowards involved women in their wars.

The storm ripped branches off the trees, crashing whitecapped waves at the dock now receding behind him. He could hear the boat banging against the tire bumpers.

Lightning cracked. He felt alive, charged with the same electricity splicing the air. His leg throbbed, but his mind told it to quit hurting. He had no time for such things.

Darting the flashlight about, he glimpsed the man on ahead.

He labored up the hillside's muddy trail, then slid through spongy moss down the other side of the hill. The night smelled dank, perfect for a killing.

The trees bent about in front of him, ominous, as if imploring him to turn around.

He stumbled on.

Suddenly, the lightning illuminated the small, white church up ahead. He stopped, played the flashlight about, but only saw the ragged edges of the iron fence around the graveyard.

The fugitive had to be in the church. Cole's heart drummed. Hatred welled up. The killer had desecrated the place where he and Laurel had exchanged vows. Cole imagined the man hiding now behind the tiny altar, with the Virgin Mary statue watching in fright.

He eased up the few steps to the church door, pausing to catch his breath. Ragged thoughts plastered him between the rain. Laurel had worn wild, brown-eyed susans behind her ears that day. He'd put them there, her hair tickling his fingers.

The memory fueled his disgust at the slime inside. Snapping off the flashlight, he shouldered the door for a moment, then pushed off his good foot, giving the door a good heave.

It gave way, too quickly.

A sharp object slammed into Cole's gut, ripping the breath from him. Cole dropped to his knees in the doorway, and the man kicked him hard in the chin, bowling him backward down the few steps. Cole splashed into the mud, but caught the pant's leg of the man and he went down.

The man scrambled backward toward the graveyard, kicking at Cole's arm. A hoarse voice snapped, "You never learn."

A hard slam down on Cole's arm sent him reeling in new pain, and the stranger ripped away from his grasp, stumbling through the graveyard gate and into the chaos of monuments and shrubbery.

Cole flung himself after him, flashlight flicking here and there, catching a headstone but nothing else.

"Come out, you bastard. I'll stay here all night—"

At a rustle, Cole spied a figure vaulting the fence. Cole took off, but his foot caught in a flower basket and he went down. He pushed up only to hear an engine start. A vehicle roared away on the nearby country highway.

"Son of a..."

Sliding down against a headstone, he sat in its protection from the wind, letting the rain wash over him. The muscles in his bad leg were seizing up around the wound. Losing the vile thug devastated him. All he could think of was Laurel. With that man on the loose, she couldn't be safe. His aching muscles be damned.

He pointed the flashlight about to get his bearings, to figure out the fastest way to wend his way out of here.

The flashlight's faltering light helped him spot the dratted plastic flowers he'd tripped over. He would never forget watching Laurel planting the geraniums. He felt close to her being here, and even with the rain, he found he wanted to linger.

Limping from one headstone to the next, he tried to recall where she'd been planting the flowers. She came here every Friday. This night from hell was a Friday.

Lightning cracked, rippling its residue through his veins and skipping blue light across the tops of the headstones.

Nudging his good leg ahead, the flashlight's beam wavered. Driving white rain splashed back up his legs.

He pointed the failing flashlight about, searching for the right names. It was a crowded cemetery, the kind with trimmed evergreens flanking headstones, flags for veterans, plastic flowers among the real. Despite the storm, the place seemed contented. Settled. He began to understand why she visited every week, why some shadows were good. There was peace in them.

Finally, he found Gerald Hasting's monument. It was a tall granite spire, with a fish carved above his name with the final date of December 24, ten years ago. Christmas Eve. He shuddered to think what it must have been like for Laurel that night. A time of birth being celebrated around the world, and she in mourning.

A few feet beyond was the headstone for Kipp O'Donnell. His was plain, no fish motif. Just "Beloved son of Mary and Kipp O'Donnell, Sr." And the same date, ten years ago.

A hard, clawing guilt overwhelmed Cole. He'd been jealous of this man. Now, he wished the man hadn't died. Laurel had needed Kipp. Maybe Cole didn't buy into the notion of her loving Kipp the way she should, but at least things would have been different for her.

Laurel needed a partner in life, someone to keep her from worrying too much, someone to make her smile, snap and sizzle sexually to forget all those things that worried her.

Someone like himself? "Partner" took a hell of a lot more commitment than mere "friend." So far, they'd agreed only on friends. He dared not entertain other dalliances.

Searching through the rain, placing one foot past the next carefully, he finally found the arc of geraniums around a tiny headstone. The rain drove down harder, smashing the flowers flat to the ground. He shook the flashlight, attempting to keep its beam going. He couldn't read the inscription for the curtains of water whipping past him. That frustrated him, because he wondered about the child's name. Cole had never thought to ask. Wretched regret wound around his heart.

Kneeling down, he poked his head and the flashlight close to the inscription. He muttered, "To Our Dearest Son," before crashing lightning blinded him momentarily. Was it a warning? He had no business here in Laurel's shadow garden. Was she coming down the trail herself?

Cole pressed the flashlight up to the inscription again. "To Our Dearest Son, Jonathon."

Then an especially bright bolt of lightning turned the tiny gravestone white, sending its lettering into clear shadowy relief.

"To Our Dearest Son, Jonathon. You were borne of the Sunshine your Father and Mother shared, and to the Sunshine of God's Heaven we return You."

The gravestone went dark again in the storm.

Laurel used to adore the sunshine. She'd revel in it. The two of them would run through the meadow on sunny days, racing for the pond. Did she enjoy the same with Kipp? She must have. Cole's heart lurched at the discovery.

As he struggled to stand up, the flashlight's weak beam hit the tiny headstone one last time before it flickered out. That's when stone-cold fear gripped Cole and stayed him in his tracks. Something was wrong here.

Cole laid a shaky hand over the carved date, felt the rain washing down the stone and over his fingers.

"God, no. It couldn't be," he cried out, "you've got it wrong!"

In a rage, Cole shuddered, curling one hand into a painful fist that he wiped furiously back and forth over the block lettering and numerals forming the date of birth and death.

"April," he said between clenched teeth. "But you've got it wrong!"

He wiped and wiped, harder and harder, across the indentations. The wind howled louder.

He must have misread the inscription. Lightning flickered. The year was plainly carved to last forever. It could mean only one thing.

Jonathon was...*his son.*

Chapter 14

COLE WISHED HE smoked. He paced back and forth in the cabin living room, glancing across the bay at the round window of the old mansion. Somehow he'd convinced Laurel to try and sleep. He'd lied, told her he'd found a couple of teenagers out for a lark, a muddled story she seemed to buy. He couldn't remember their conversation exactly. He only knew he wasn't ready to confront her about Jonathon. Not yet.

The storm gathering inside him, though, wouldn't let go. He vowed to wait, hope it would abate with the storm outside. He couldn't talk with Laurel in this condition of heat and anger. It would be better to wait for the anger to simmer down to just leaden disappointment.

He'd had a son with Laurel.

All of them—the Hastings, the whole town, and Laurel—hadn't bothered to let him know about it. Something deep in the earth seemed to claw up at him to pull him under.

He'd laid the sextant on the uprighted table, with the crayon box of Mike's and the locket. His life lay on the table, everything that should lead him to happiness. None of it did.

Hollowness surrounded his heart.

He tried to plot what he'd say to her, how the conversation would start. "Oh, by the way, I found out we had a child together." Or, "I was taking a walk in the rain and just happened upon..."

No words were right.

Knowledge robbed him of rational thought. It rendered him raw. Emotions fought like gladiators inside his belly. What would win out? The hurt spewed through him, crashing molten waves of ache, even in his head. The burning hurt was winning.

He wasn't ready to talk with her.

Eventually, he peered in her bedroom. She lay rolled up in blankets, sleeping deeply. His heart flinched. He knew she slept only because he was here watching out for her.

But he had to turn and go back up the short hall because he resented her for that normalcy. She lived and slept happily in shadows.

Damn her. Cole hated being plunged into them like this. No warning. Like watching Mike's boat explode....

And then he knew he couldn't blame her. He had to rise above this anger because he didn't know what had happened back then.

He blamed himself. Guilt racked him. Why did she never tell him? What was it about himself she hated that much?

He stayed up, staring over at the pirate's ship, where the ghost of Mike would protect him from doing something stupid.

He perused the knuckles of his right hand. They were raw from the night's activities.

But Rojas no longer mattered.

Only Laurel mattered. Her betrayal of him, his own guilt. The anger and devastation flipflopped back and forth inside him. He felt like he was wrestling with alligators. Life or death. His secrets, her secrets. Meted out a piece at a time because they both feared the future.

At least he saw it that way. Their futures at stake. Facing her on all this now mattered to Cole. A great deal. *They'd had a son. She hadn't told him.* It gnawed at his soul, crowded his throbbing head.

Betrayal and guilt.

Could they ever find trust for each other again?

THE BRILLIANT sunshine of morning dappling the lake with rainbows sent Laurel out into the yard looking for Cole to ask him about last night. When she spotted him, hands in pockets down at the end of the dock, she retreated to her garden to weed. She knew that stance well. Something bothered him. But the fact that he'd made sure he was out of the house when she awoke said much more to her. Her heart pumped, worrying about the unknown. He knew something. And he was wrestling with how to talk to her about it.

They spent an exhaustive day, but each going their separate ways. Cole worked on a boat, repaired the hole in the fence and brought over yet another load of wood from the mansion, while she tended the animals.

Underneath her efficient doctor's facade, her nerves coiled. She mindlessly bandaged, gave shots, stuffed weak animals in overcrowded cages. What was bothering Cole?

After a lunch of salad made from her garden, in which Cole always seem to avert both his gaze and the subject matter from anything too serious, he took off for a walk, ignoring her admonishments about his sore leg.

When the sun began to droop toward the western horizon to mark late afternoon, Laurel couldn't stand the not-knowing any longer and decided to head off down the trail after Cole.

She stopped when she spotted him emerging from the forest with flowers clutched in his big fist.

"Brown-eyed susans," she said inanely.

"Our special flower." The breeze tousled the bouquet. The rich brown of the flower stamens matched his eyes. She yearned to run to him. She knew he would smell of the richness of their meadow, where he must have picked the tall-stemmed beauties.

"I was beginning to wonder where you'd disappeared to," she said, leading him through the doorway at the front of the cabin.

"I'll get some water for the flowers," he said, making her feel oddly like the guest instead of the hostess of the house. He added, "Iced tea? I feel like something cool after the long walk."

He shifted, but winced, and shifted back again to take the weight off his leg, his eyes not veering from her now.

Shaken, she licked her lips against a sudden dryness and rushed to the refrigerator. "I made sun tea. I'll pour us a glass."

She flicked on the kitchen light.

Putting the flowers in a quart jar, he mused, "You rarely turn on the lights at night, much less in the afternoon."

When he glanced her way while turning the faucet on to fill the jar with water, a flicker crossed his eyes. What was wrong?

She decided she needed to take the initiative or she'd burst. She plunked ice in Mickey Mouse glasses. When Cole raised a brow at them, she was glad for a reason to smile. "The fourth grade class last year. They were a thank you for telling them about small rodents and how important they are on the food chain."

"Suddenly I'm not hungry but I bet the children loved it. You and children just seem to go together."

The way he looked at her then could have chased the sun behind the clouds forever.

Her stomach turned colder than the ice in the glass she handed him. "You know the truth. Don't you?"

He flinched, his coal-dark eyes piercing her. "Why didn't you tell me?"

Sweat broke out on the back of Laurel's neck and in the valley next to her heart.

"Damnit," he said when she turned away to seek the shadows of the livingroom. "Say something. For fifteen years you kept quiet about this. Why?"

Echoing, his voice vibrated through her body, pushing her to reply. Pushing. "Because...I didn't think you cared. And telling you couldn't resurrect him," she whispered, not daring to look at him. "Why did you leave me?"

"Your father's threats."

"Threats?" She whirled around to face him, but he averted his gaze. "What were they?"

"He's gone. It's not important." Raking his hair, he paced to the kitchen window. "Why didn't you tell me?"

"It would also bring all the hurt back to me. I'd have to live everything we had all over again and I wasn't strong enough for that." Heaving a heavy sigh in search of clarifying oxygen, she added, "And I didn't see the point in hurting you either."

When he turned around, Cole's gaze softened. "All last night, all today, I wanted to see his face, to look into the innocence, to breathe life into him, to feel him wiggle in my arms."

He guzzled desperately at the ice tea, downing it before slamming the glass down on the counter.

She lowered her glass to the dining table before she dropped it. "Cole, I'm sorry."

"No you're not."

She came to him, placed a hand on his shoulder. It scorched like fire. "I did what I had to do to protect myself from you."

"From me?" Flinching her off, he limped over to the fireplace where he kicked at the hearth bricks with his good leg.

"I knew you'd be angry. I knew you wouldn't understand."

"But you let me find out by myself." He slammed a balled hand against the mantle. "I'm worried about you, protecting you by chasing a man out of your house last night and then I stumble on the grave and the truth by accident. By accident. As if my knowing anything didn't matter. Do you have any idea what that did to me?"

She whispered, "I do. It's called betrayal. And blame. That fence we have between us, that we can't ever seem to cross."

Seeking the sofa by the fire, wishing it could carry her away like a magic carpet, she added, "Sit down. Let's try to talk calmly for once."

But her own heart pulsated toward an attack, and the cabin's usual sweet fireplace smell only burned at her throat and the lump in it. They settled in, each at opposite ends, with a cushion of space between them.

An invisible wall.

Scared at the sight of her shaking fingers, she clutched them into a fist on her lap. "I can only begin with, I'm sorry. What I kept from you, was awful."

He grabbed a pillow and crushed it between his hands. "I wanted to pull out every damn one of those stinking geraniums you planted. I wanted us to take it all back, to go back in time."

"It was a nightmare." She swallowed hard.

Lunging up again, he tossed the pillow behind him and took up a poker to stir the fire to life. "Get mad at me, damnit, because I'm mad. I want to yell and scream at you and I can't when you look at me like that!"

With his back to her, how did he know she was looking at him with eyes that registered and shared all the hurt in his sagging shoulders? Why was he always able to read her so completely? Why wouldn't he tell her why he'd abandoned their love back then?

"Cole, I'd do anything to make you not hurt. I used to think it would be good to see you in pain, just as I was. Thoughts of revenge felt good for a long time. But I have to face the truth. You even told me that. And the truth was, we didn't love each other enough. You left me because you didn't love me enough, and I didn't love you enough to run after you."

"Stop it!" After slamming his fist against the mantle again, he swung around with eyes glazed, but rimmed with shadows. "This wasn't your fault."

With her mouth gone dry, and her heart stuttering faster in fear, she asked, "What are you talking about?"

"Why I really left. Why I didn't come back. It was your father. It was more than just his intercepting my phone calls to you. He made sure I couldn't come back."

"Why?"

"Because of my careless actions. When I was about to leave, he made it a point to come find me out at my aunt's place."

"He was still mad about the car we wrecked. He could never stop talking about it."

"It wasn't about the car anymore." He limped to the edge of the fireplace mantle and rested an elbow there. His shoulders visibly shuddered. "He was waving his rifle around, pointing it mostly at me, telling me never to come back. My aunt came out of the house then, scared him and a shot went off."

"Oh no." Her heart turned to ash.

"He narrowly missed her. I charged him, ripped the rifle out of his hand and pointing the thing at him, I told him he was a fool. I told him he didn't own you, that what we had was special, that you had a mind of your own and he should listen to you." He shook visibly, wrinkles carving deeper into his face. "I let fly with a shot over your father's head. Just missed him."

It was her turn to shudder.

The fireplace embers crackled. A flicker of flame came to life next to Cole.

Rubbing his furrowed brow, he continued, "It was quite a scene. He didn't like it at all, and when he came at me, I ended up punching him to the ground and we got into a regular fight. Enough to draw blood. I busted your father's nose."

Her body curled in on itself, heavy as stone. She could only look at him, stalking the shadows thrown by the fireplace.

"Evidently my aunt had called the sheriff at the sight of the rifle and pretty soon I was handcuffed and facing charges that could have sent me to prison."

Rippling with cold disbelief, she sunk deeper into the sofa, holding onto her temples before her head exploded. "Nobody told me about this."

"Because that was the deal. Lawyers huddled over the phone lines that very afternoon, and if I left that day and never came back, charges would be dropped and everyone would get on with their lives as if nothing happened."

Staring at her, leaning back against the corner of the fireplace, he tucked his fists in his pockets. "I'm sorry," came the hoarse whisper. "If I'd have known about the baby, I would have stood by you. I told you that when I thought it was Kipp's."

Her calm finally exploded, her hands growing into tight fists of her own when she stood. "Penance is why you'd have come back, out of your guilt. You're doing penance now for not raising your son Tyler yourself! Look what you're doing now to your own living son! He's in hiding and growing up without you. It's guilt that drives you. Not love. I want no part of that guilt from you."

Nerves burning, she slammed back down into the sofa, punching at the tufted arm of the furniture, then picking at the nap, hating the feel of his eyes roving over her.

"I would have married you," he said, showing her the full force of his deep pools. They held fast, not a flicker. "Married you for real."

A flush heated her cheeks.

An ember snapped, fire sizzling in his eyes, dredging guilt out of her.

She rose to meet the truth sullying her, but paused to slake her thirst with the tea. "You would have been a caged animal, with marriage to me like some trap on your paw that you were doomed never to shake off. A wild animal always looking to the horizon, pacing, waiting for escape."

"We could have made it work."

She came back, picked up the afghan, hugging it with fists. "Even if I'd caught up with you in Florida, I would have resented being dragged away from my family. All that strife to live with, it wouldn't have worked. And we were young, awfully young."

"I thought of that, too, when I got back to Miami. Shock set in. I may have been eighteen, but I was fresh out of high school. Time to figure out what to do with my life. You still had a year of high school left. I reasoned my guilt away by thinking we weren't ready. I thought I was helping you, by making the clean break. By keeping your father's secret about me. About what might have happened." He drew in a long breath. "You didn't deserve a stupid punk like me who couldn't control his temper."

The fire spit sparks. Tossing on another log, he glanced back at her. "I've never had such a hard time talking with you," he ventured.

"Because this is about more than truth. It's about us being adults and admitting to things. That takes courage I've discovered." Sinking back, she smoothed the dent in the upholstery she'd punched.

His eyes, framed by the wildness of his dark hair, crackled with energy. "It's hard admitting to mistakes that alter people's lives forever."

He stood tall, menacing almost, his muscles filling out an old denim shirt she'd bought way oversized because she liked them that way. But then he slumped down on the hearth, watching the embers, the firelight assigning a vulnerability about him. "I ache for the loss of our son, for you, for what I missed."

And the way he turned to her, with his face haunted, brought tears ebbing down her cheeks, a freeflow for both of them.

Coming over to her, he sunk to the floor at her knees, clasping hungrily at her hands. The warmth of his firm, strong fingers spiked through her.

"Tell me about him," he said, rubbing his thumbs over her fingers, the reassuring ministrations helping to stop the tears. "I missed everything about him. He was part of me, but I never had a chance to touch him, to smell his baby sweet smell, to press him against my cheek, to lay down next to him and you in the hospital bed and count his toes."

She almost couldn't bear seeing the despair in his eyes.

"Laurel Lee," he whispered, a hand brushing her hair back off her face, drying her tears in the wake of his gentle heat.

When he rose, she followed him, seeking the solid wall of comfort his chest provided.

Then her tears came again, ancient ones, saved up all the years for this moment, mingling with his, with one cheek held tightly against the other, him cradling her head against his sturdy muscles, a hand burrowed into her hair, both bodies trembling in unison.

"All right," she managed in a whisper, feeling a sense of relief pouring out of her, a cleansing. "I'll tell you everything. You deserve to know it all."

THE FIRE ROARED behind them, its pungency soothing. Cole clung to Laurel, wishing he could change the world for her, glad that she accepted his comfort now.

He held her like he'd held the baby rabbits, trying to warm them, make them whole again. He was beginning to understand what peace the animals brought to her heart.

Breaking from him, she led them outdoors, out onto the steps where they could sit side by side to look past the garden and the pines, and view Spirit Lake. Her misty emerald eyes reflected the specks of sunlight glinting off the water.

Confusion and pain welled up in her eyes. "Mother and father sent me away."

"Because of me."

She nodded. His gut wrenched. Lines furrowed her face, and it pained him to see what she'd come to because of him.

"I had a year of high school left," she said. "But I knew by September I was pregnant. That's when I wrote to you."

"And your father found out when he intercepted the letters."

"Yes, but I told him we were married." Her attempt at a laugh fizzled on the breeze. "That we'd promised ourselves to each other in a church already. He had choice words about our promises."

When she closed her eyes, Cole swallowed down the sudden chill of fear. "What did he do? What did you do?"

"I begged him to help me find you, to bring you back so that you could marry me for real. I thought you would."

Launching off the stoop, she poked around at the nearby garden, pulling at quackgrass, tidying up the earth by her cabin.

"The marriage couldn't have happened anyway," she muttered, tomato plants bending to her touch. "Not with your...with your marriage coming at you so soon and with your son Tyler coming along."

Straightening and looking at him with eyes a vibrant hue that made him pay attention, she added, "That's the irony here, isn't it? I wanted something, and it was for the best that I didn't get it. You may not have ever had Tyler..."

"Don't make it sound like you were selfish. You weren't. This was our child you were carrying." Beads of sweat popped onto his forehead. "Once you knew about the pregnancy, where did you go?"

She went back to tending the sturdy tomato plants. More weeds flew. "My mother has a cousin in Phoenix. I went there after Christmas, when I began to show. I finished high school there. I hated Arizona. No grass and the lawns were made of painted rocks."

Cole couldn't imagine Laurel surviving in such an environment. "And the baby?"

She straightened to gaze at the lake. "The baby, our son, was born during Easter break. I was alone. My parents didn't even call."

"I'm sorry." He limped to her, drew her against his chest and into his arms. She didn't resist, and together they looked at the lake, listening to its ripples slapping gently against the dock.

He dropped a kiss on her warm hair. "What happened?"

"I could never eat. I worried."

It registered with him that she needed him. That he knew how to keep her from worrying all the time, that he wanted to scoop her up and carry her onto a cloud. They would fly forever. What a thing to do for a woman.

But she continued, not in the clouds at all. "I searched for answers, who to blame."

An ache swelled in his chest. "I would have given anything to have been there."

Stroking her hair, turning her toward himself, looking into eyes gone dim, Cole felt a purpose rise inside him. To rekindle the light in

Laurel. In himself. To build something together again. Even a family. But his breathing grew uneven, doubts crowding him, telling him to listen first to Laurel.

"My aunt was by my side." She burrowed against him, needy as her little rabbits. "The baby, our baby, was born in a Phoenix hospital on a hot day in April when I would have rather smelled the fresh hint of maple and pine trees budding around Spirit Lake. Three days later, he died."

Holding her tightly, Cole suffocated himself in her hair. "I'm sorry. I'm so sorry."

"They said he had breathing problems. But I knew what they wouldn't tell me. They thought I was too young to understand. I knew what had happened to our son. It was the horrible way I handled my life. I let it happen."

Pressing her against him even harder, Cole squeezed his eyes shut against the vision of her alone in the hospital room. "Don't blame yourself. No teenager should face that kind of stress."

Suddenly piercing him with vacant eyes, Laurel said, "I don't have any pictures of him for you."

A storm blew through Cole, drying up his soul, his heart.

She closed her eyes. "When I need to remember him, I squeeze my eyes shut real hard, and I can visualize his tiny face. He's round, pink as clover in the meadow, with a button nose like my bunnies, with a wisp of dark fuzz for hair."

Cole sucked in, closing his eyes as well. Dark hair. *He had my hair.*

She sighed, limp against him. "My only fear is that someday I won't be able to see him in my mind. Time fades everything."

His gut twisted.

They peered into each other's eyes, lingering in the depths.

A shadow flickered across her face. A doubt? He assured her, "I'm glad you brought him back here for burial."

"I need him here with me. It's all I have left." Then she relaxed into a soft smile, one that soothed the ages and the savage gulf between them. "I need to be held. All the rest of the day and through the night."

"So do I." And Cole drew her under his wings, understanding fully for the first time her need for solitude, wishing he had a way to make this feeling of completeness and peace permanent.

COLE WOKE IN the middle of the night to inky etherealness,

disoriented. Deja vu scuttled in.

He lay in the basement of the old mansion, cold, weary. Sweat popped onto his forehead as he listened to the rolling, rising beat of his heart. His eyes probed the still blackness, searching for escape. About to flail against the weight of something holding him down—the cardboard, yes, the boxes—he caught himself, halting his breath to listen again.

There, in the crook of his arm, Laurel slept, just as she had that first night. Only this time, the flutterings of breath caressing his chest drew from deep within her body. He guessed she hadn't slept well in a long time, not since he'd arrived to interrupt her summer.

Guilt washed across his skin, only to be challenged again by her mere presence. It felt good lying in the soft bed with her, with the woman who meant the world to him and always would. Truth roiled deep inside him. He had measured all other women against her and every last one of them had lost. How could he manage without her? He must.

The specter of loneliness gripped him, peppering him with heat. This lady was in his blood, a part of him. He'd changed because of her.

Because of Laurel Hastings, he'd slowed down, allowed himself to explore emotions with her. Laurel demanded his experiencing highs and lows, joy and sorrow. With her, he was allowed to yell and whisper, get angry, then eager as a pup to please. Her radiant smile never let him forget flowers in the meadow. She'd made him cuddle baby rabbits, and rage over a lost son. She had mustered him to attention like no other woman ever had.

Yesterday, they had visited the gravesite together, smelled the breeze, sweet as any child. They had walked the meadow hand in hand, no words spoken. No words necessary. The sparrows sang for them, and they listened to its innocence.

Being together had felt so right to him. But was it merely the closure they needed finally stealing in? Had they met at his proverbial fence, looked over into each other's secrets, and seeing that crossing over wasn't possible, made the decision to part peacefully once and for all?

Cole closed his eyelids against the darkness. He smelled the hint of sweet pine in her hair that spilled in haphazard, ticklish waves across his bare chest. She felt as soft as one of her rabbits, and was every bit as innocent and needy. She had loved Jonathon with all her heart, enough for the both of them and Cole's soul would always be thankful to her for carrying on, for bringing their son here, for visiting his grave and tending the good memories. Shadow gardens had their place, he decided.

Good memories abounded between them, even with their short time spent together.

The rhythm of her breathing served as a lullaby. As sleep stole over him again, Cole vowed to do everything he could to make her happy in whatever time they had left together. It was the least he could do for the mother of his son.

Chapter 15

COLE'S VOICE USHERED forth with the lilt of the soft sunrise sending scarlet streamers through the window and onto the bedroom wall. "Is it time to get up and feed those animals already?"

Peering at her through sleepy eyes, he displayed a quirky smile on his whiskery morning face. Laurel basked in it, but searched too for any signs of regret.

Lying in the crook of his arm and chest, she had been watching him sleep for several minutes, wondering how they could be this natural together, after all the years. Wondering why it felt this good to wake up. Was it a trick? A dream?

Her heart saved a corner for wariness. Yesterday remained a surreal challenge. They'd confessed to a lot. That accommodation for each other had been designed to bring them peace. But she'd lived with peace for years. It wasn't the same as love.

Under the mesmerizing glow of his sleepy gaze, she reached up and outlined his firm lips with the pad of her index finger. Electricity rushed from the contact, blanketing her body. Touching him in this intimate way set up an ache she hadn't felt since...since that summer in the meadow. Since last night.

"I'm glad you stayed." She surprised herself with the sultriness in her own voice.

Cole gave her a lopsided grin, lighting up the room—and her heart—even more. "You purr in the morning. I never knew that."

Heat suffused her body more, taking hold on her cheeks. "You...never stayed the night before. It's my grown-up voice. You like it?"

"Mmm." He pulled her to him for a kiss that drove her temperature into the ozone. "You shouldn't tease like that."

She knew caution was sensible. Sometime in early morning, after the quiet acceptance of their pasts seeped through their dreams and shadows grew softer, they had awakened in each others' arms, their bodies needy, wondering. They had answered the wondering, searching for the feel of togetherness as ordinary grownups in the very ordinariness of a double bed. Something they'd never experienced before.

To avoid his penetrating gaze now, she burrowed deeper into the nest made by his muscular arm and chest.

The soft joy of lovemaking—the kind that's filled with the quick sounds of dove's wings taking flight—signaled a respect between them. She hoped. Both of them had done their best with the past, and they were ready to move on. Joy tendered to the shoreline around her heart, inviting her to leave forever the vacant house inside herself. A strong beacon was calling her, and she wondered if it were Cole's love for her. Did she dare to trust her instincts?

If she was scared these days, the root of it was not Marco Rojas. No, fear trampled into her heart because there was no ordinary love growing inside her for this man. She'd handled "ordinary" for fifteen years and learned to tend it quite well. This new feeling for Cole demanded a higher level of commitment. The commitment would require surviving a new kind of danger. It didn't threaten to take her to a precipice. It threatened to fling her off! To set her aflight, like the dove to ride the breezes and float on updrafts toward the sun. This love focused on pure joy, on freedom to fly.

Cole muttered, "What's in that pretty head this morning?"

If he only knew, she thought. "Thinking about everything we need to do."

"Like kiss you again?" He planted a peck on a flushed cheek.

"Like solving the puzzles."

"You've always been a puzzle. May I try to connect the dots?"

Sighing, she realized they could not avoid what was at hand. "There's so much to do. Figure out the meaning of the sextant, talk to the sheriff, and I should visit my mother. She'll be worried if she hears of any of this."

"Particularly if she finds out who I really am. And that I'm here to protect her daughter."

Suddenly, she knew why this love for him was different. Ever since coming back days ago, he thrived on listening to her innermost secrets, her fears and desires. He had focused just on her, like a hawk soaring near its mate, always protective.

She and Cole were wild things, kindred spirits. Always were.

They were imperfect puzzle pieces, not fitting with other partners, and yet, in search of a fit of their own.

Still, she needed to be cautious. Theirs was a tenuous relationship shaped by external events that could keep them apart.

"What would you say," she ventured, popping up to look at his wonderful morning face again, "if I made you breakfast?"

"Fried eggs?"

"Over easy, with my own homemade tomato marmalade on toast."

One heavy eyebrow tented, warming her. "How can someone as beautiful and talented as you not have a line of lumberjacks waiting at your door here in the northwoods?"

She teased, "They don't like tea."

"Ah, come on. I apologized for that."

"Maybe I've decided to change. No more earth mother. Give me a rich man to sweep me off my feet and take me to parties in the Twin Cities and buy me frilly designer dresses."

His chuckle tickled her nerve endings. "My Great-aunt Flora and you have a lot in common."

"Two saucy, liberated women? With things to do. People to see. Mysteries to solve."

But he didn't share her levity. When his brows knitted over cloudy eyes, she asked, "What's wrong?"

"People to see. It reminded me that Tyler needs to know. With your permission."

Looking up, she saw the worried set of his jaw. But her own heart pounded. "Of course. They were brothers."

Brothers. The room tilted. Why hadn't she thought about that before? Or had she buried the idea because it sounded like a "family" she had no right to claim? Cole and her, Tyler and Jonathon.

In her heart, they were together, like one of those church photographs in everybody's house. A softness threaded through her. If the image alone could give this pleasure, what would having an actual family with Cole bring? Her breathing stepped up a pace.

Cole's gaze on her didn't help. His eyes were dark pools, rimmed with moisture threatening to spill forth. "I love my son. I plan to say it a thousand times a day."

A mist overwhelmed her vision, her insides yielding, gathering strength for him. "I know you want to be a good father. I trust that about you. Completely."

Laurel escaped the intense moment by slipping from the bed and into her robe. The heated impression of his body next to her lingered on her skin. With palms clammy and fingers shaking, she knotted the belt at her waist and managed to find slippers.

Turning to him, she said, "I want you and Tyler to come back and visit me someday."

Flinching, the light normally in his eyes dimmed. "I suppose I can't hope for something more."

Staring at him lying in her bed, a lump lingered in her throat. "It's not really safe for our hearts, is it, to think in those terms of something more? I mean, there's too much ahead yet..."

He drew in a breath big enough to empty the room of air. "I'd be honored to be invited back for a visit."

Her heart sank. A visit.

Then he plastered on the best fake smile. At least she wanted it to be fake. She wanted him to think about missing her.

"What should I tell Tyler to expect?" he asked.

Relying on that courage they'd talked about earlier, she too put on her best face. "I'll take him on a tour of the new clinic I'm going to build, the educational center, and the outdoor self-guided trails."

"Is that all?" He pimped her again with a broad grin.

Pleasure ebbed through her veins. "Nope. I'm going to write a book, a whole series of children's books based on my experiences with animals. I have to do something with all those reports on hawks and owls I fill out for the State and the feds."

"Whew! Guess I better get crackin' and get on outta here so you can level that old mansion and get on with things."

A shadow flickered across his eyes just as a cloud trundled into her heart. Reality had struck.

She offered, "I won't ask that the place be razed until we find out why Mike hid the sextant there."

"You'll risk your government grant."

"I'll find money somehow."

"Sounds like my tomboy." Sliding from the bed, Cole didn't seem to care that he was naked as a jaybird except for the ragged bandage on his leg. Cradling her chin in both hands, he said, "Did I ever mention I'm proud to know you? How much I admire you?"

Fire erupted where he touched her, spreading in columns of heat down to her stomach and to every nerve ending. "No, I don't think you ever did."

"You've made one hell of a good life for yourself."

Sucking in, she had no reply. She saw a man racing toward a dangerous precipice of his own. His hair tousled on a weathered, tired forehead. A scar branded one pectoral muscle where a bullet had grazed him. His body battered, his mind fighting to stay focused, Cole refused to be afraid. How could she be?

She hurried into the shower, turning on the hot jets full blast.

To know Cole was to know how it felt to have a warm rain awaken a tree's roots from winter.

That's what she would remember Cole for, and it would bring her joy, no matter what became of him. Cole had awakened her to life again.

If she repeated that often enough in her mind, maybe her heart could be happy when he left.

THEY COULD HAVE been husband and wife, Laurel decided soon afterward, with Cole sitting on the table in Dr. Donna Corcoran's examining room and Laurel standing at his shoulder. She liked the feeling. She didn't like that he'd kept another secret from her.

"You could have told me you'd visited Donna before this, instead of letting me badger you about doing it."

He scowled, watching Donna snip a bandage down to size. "And have you worrying even more?"

"I wouldn't have worried. I'd have lorded it over you that you'd followed my advice for once."

The doctor laughed. "You two. Now I need you to hold still."

Wrapping new, snowy gauze up and down his calf, the doctor lectured him to soak the leg in a tub every night, re-wrap it in new gauze, take his antibiotic pills regularly and keep the leg elevated. All things Laurel knew he never intended to do, unless she made him. A bittersweet, urgent tugging nipped at her heart. She could make him well. If he stayed and let her.

Donna tossed suckers at him, then Laurel clamped her best protective hold on his arm and whisked them out a side door.

The peace lasted only until a breathless Una caught up with them at the minivan in the clinic parking lot.

"Buzz is buzzin' about some dead woman found in Spirit Lake."

Laurel was glad for Cole's tightening grip.

Gulping for breath, Una puffed, "The woman's body was inside one of those big muskie minnow cages your mother sells at the bait shop. Buzz even quoted her in his article about your boss Rojas. Said there might be a connection between this woman and Mike."

Cold stones seemed to settle into Laurel's stomach. "My mother's all right?"

Una nodded. "The sheriff came and took her for coffee."

When Laurel swung around to question Cole, he gripped her arm and headed for the minivan, mumbling, "Where's a private place we can talk and sort this out?"

LAUREL NEEDED to steer the aluminum boat just to keep her hands from shaking off her limbs. Spirit Lake was private, but it didn't lull her the way it usually did. The news had tousled her stomach the same way the breeze was tossing Cole's dark hair. She sat back by the motor in the stern, and he sat opposite her in the bow, his coppery skin shining under the full sun.

His gaze scanned the lake, trouble marked in them under the shade provided by his hand.

She shivered. "So he's here. Isn't he?"

"Or a hired gun. Rojas wouldn't be so careless as to murder his girlfriend then dump her under my nose."

"The hired gun could be living in any of those cabins along the north shore."

"But with the story in the paper now, he's scared. That buys us time. Let's try to fit the pieces together."

The boat bobbed against a gust of wind. "As in what pieces?"

"We've found a woman's body, a crayon box, and a sextant."

Her fingers slipped on the throttle, slowing the boat. "The woman on ice at the morgue was inside a big musky minnow cage. This seems like one for John to figure out. Not us."

"Where would she have floated from in that cage?"

Gritting her teeth over getting involved, she did anyway. "The winds tend to come from the west and north on most days, and they switch around from the east during storms."

"Somebody may have rented one of those cabins along that shoreline for something more than fishing. Someone has to have seen Rojas, or whoever this killer is. But who?"

A sinking feeling gripped Laurel. "My mother?"

"Madelyn?"

"She said the guy in her rental cabin had bought a muskie minnow cage." Then she remembered something. "This doesn't make sense. She said there was a dark-haired man in May who bought one, too."

Lowering his hand, Cole straightened. "Mike? But Mike wasn't much into fishing."

"But what if Mike had decided to do a little fishing anyway and left the minnow cage behind? This guy who's been sneaking around my place," she said, fear suddenly clawing at her throat, "maybe he found Mike's minnow cage and used it to try and sink the woman's body for your boss. He may have killed her. But why bring the body to Wisconsin?" That made no sense.

"What if she hadn't just disappeared, as Rojas made people think?"

"As Buzz reported in that article."

"What if she escaped my boss alive with one of his hitmen for me, who brought her here?"

Laurel shuddered. "But why here?"

"To lure me out. Rojas used women and I suspect this is part of the game. When John discovered all of Rojas's girlfriends have been blondes or redheads, Wiley picked up on it..."

"How does a drunk know so much? I noticed he was quoted an awful lot in that article in this morning's paper."

When Cole averted his gaze to the shoreline again, she pressed, "What about Wiley?"

"He's turns out to be the man in my photo."

"The young officer?" She could barely believe it.

"Wiley knows Senator Goetz."

"Who?"

"From Florida, anchors an expensive yacht in our marina, next to Rojas's. Heads the CIA oversight committee in Congress. Wiley's been digging. He found out that Goetz and Rojas are buddies."

The dizzying information befuddled Laurel. "But do power brokers in D.C. let an old drinking buddy resurface to swap war stories?"

"Smart woman. Wiley soon got phones slammed in his ear. Word spread like wildfire that he was fishing for information about Rojas. That's when Wiley got mad. He knows there's something big they're hiding, something so big about Rojas that the CIA oversight committee wants to keep hush-hush."

Laurel recalled Mike's note. "Your brother said not to take this to the CIA. Do you think he said that because they'd somehow tip off Rojas before we catch him?"

"We?" He scowled.

"Yes, we." She squared her shoulders to mask the icy tremors racking her. "But why wouldn't your boss have sent men here to do his dirty work, to just..."

"Snuff me out?" Cole picked up the fishing rod she kept in the bottom of the boat, flicked it, watching the spoon with its several hooks strike the water's surface. "Oh, he likely has sent somebody. Maybe a whole army lurking in the woods, but the problem is, a man of his stature won't openly kill me when I'm with you."

"Me?" Lightning bolts skipped through her nerves.

"Like it or not, you're well-known enough in the environmental fields, what with your governor's awards, that Rojas must know taking me out means risking his own hide."

"You mean I've been your shield all this time?" Tremors radiated through her blood, stilling her heart almost.

"I only guessed it when John and Wiley began putting together pieces about Rojas and Goetz. Of course, Mike may have thought about that, too. It's probably why he thought this would be a safe place to hide whatever evidence he has against Rojas. It's why he probably sent me here."

The boat rocked with a wake rippling from a water-skier and a boat maneuvering off in the distance.

Laurel fingered the throttle, thinking. "But something doesn't add up, Cole. If your Mr. Rojas is truly scared we'll reveal some illegal thing he's up to, certainly he'd have his people find a way to do away with us without anyone finding out."

"Maybe he wants us only toyed with long enough so that he can figure out a way to meet me face to face. Mano y mano."

"He's the bullfighter, and you're the poor animal." Her teeth chattered.

"Don't worry," he replied, his gaze scouring the shoreline cabins and woods. "I might be the bull in the ring that he wants to face, but remember, bulls have sharp horns. We need to work with the sheriff to make sure we lay a quiet little plan to snare our bullfighter."

"Then we have to make sure we have an army planted in the woods, waiting for him."

"John's working on it with the FBI."

Somehow, that news didn't allay her fears. "Let's talk to my friend David Huber. He's back from Madison, and attorneys have connections in high places. Maybe he could find out more about Senator Goetz for us through some Supreme Court judge."

Cole wiggled an eyebrow.

"I like that idea," he said, surprising her. He wound in his fishing line. "There's still a missing minnow cage in all this."

"One big enough to hold a person."

"Don't think about it."

She shivered anyway.

BECAUSE OF THE investigation, the sheriff couldn't meet privately with them until Monday afternoon. After an agonizing weekend with the both of them pacing her cabin, Laurel sat with Cole in the sheriff's office, her heart pumping full and fast, her thoughts oddly on Tyler somewhere off in Florida. Would he have a father when this was all through?

"Deputize us," Laurel said to the sheriff, "and we'll do a house to house search."

She and Cole had agreed expediency was the only way to end this and get their lives back, and those of the people of Dresden.

John glared at them, his face puffy red from little sleep lately. "I'm in hot enough water as it is keeping that lady's body here, against the vile threats of her family in Texas. And the mortician did not appreciate the hint of scandal invading his quiet place of business. And Buzz has all his buddies calling me for exclusive interviews he promised them. Now you want me to let you two knock on doors up and down Spirit Lake? Asking people if they've seen a shady character dragging a dead woman around?"

Laurel winced. "Just call the FBI then and send reinforcements."

"You've already got me faxing the FBI every time I turn around. I've also faked stories, duped our editor, and I've got Wiley living in my house to keep his mouth shut."

Cole griped, "It's that last one that's really gotcha mad."

Laurel caught the glint in Cole's eyes and marveled at it, despite the gravity of things. She offered, "I don't have much use for Wiley either, John, after what he did in my livingroom to fake that story, but it's done and there's no escaping what Wiley's set in motion. He's the 'W' file in David's office and there's no stopping his trying to recapture his Naval spying days."

John scowled. "I thought you blamed Cole for all this."

Blame. It pitched into her stomach like an icy snowball, tearing away her oxygen. She felt the questioning in Cole's dark eyes landing on her, but she stared straight at John, giving herself time to reach into her heart. Was there room in that proverbial house for blame right now?

When she could breathe again, she said, "Tyler needs a father. That's what's at stake here."

"And you two want to play police partners now?"

As a heated flush crawled up her neck, Cole's hand squeezed hers, sending electricity through her. Together, they were a storm of energy that could not be defeated. They had to be. She hoped.

Cole moved forward in his chair. "The article ran in the paper to lure Rojas, but nobody's heard from him. The body showed up the same day as the story. So Rojas probably didn't kill her. This guy in Madelyn's cottage probably did. It's the same guy I chased out of Laurel's house, I'm sure. Probably hired by Rojas. He's not real bright, just faster than me on foot. If we can flush him out, he might give us the information Mike was onto that caused his death."

The sheriff grimaced. "I'm sorry, but my hands are tied. Until we have something more solid to go on, I can't issue a search warrant for properties along Spirit Lake."

Laurel's blood sparked to a slow simmer. "My mother's involved now because of this guy renting her cottage. You have feelings for her, don't you? Don't you want to resolve this quickly, to protect her? To protect everyone in Dresden?"

Babbling something about blackmail, John set about getting them deputized and gearing them with search warrants on behalf of the sheriff's department.

TWO DAYS LATER, on Wednesday, with the big July holiday looming only a few days away, Cole came down with a nasty case of the worries about Laurel.

Cole knew her sleep had been sacrificed. Watching her closely while he helped her check the rabbits and possum babies, she appeared wan, not her usual self around her animals.

He knew he was the root problem. Stress. Her mother had nearly fainted after learning Cole was Atlas. Laurel had spent long hours with her mother, talking over old issues. Then there was the prospect of them actually fighting off unknown stalkers. Being brave in front of the sheriff was one thing; acting brave in your own home was another. They had also spent several hours already visiting at least six cottages along the lake on the search warrant, until the rath of the last two renters forced Cole to call off the search for the day. He regretted the dull shock in Laurel's eyes as she seemed to be making enemies of her neighbors because of their activity. He refused to allow that.

After plunking the baby rabbit back in the nesting box and putting the formula dropper aside, he caught up with Laurel in three long strides that stretched his torn leg muscle mercilessly.

A haunted shadow flickered across her eyes.

Cupping her chin, the trembling there caused his heart to skip a beat. "You don't have to act strong for me," he said. "Nobody's watching."

She planted a quick kiss against his skin, but even her lips proved weak, cool. "I'm fine. Thanks."

"Liar," he said, and she squeaked when he scooped her up in his arms. "I'm tucking you under that quilt on the sofa while I finish the chores."

At that, her lips curled into a smile, and she gave in, wrapping her arms around his neck where they felt mighty fine to him. She whispered, "I'm also beginning to appreciate what a man could do for me around here."

Icy reality stormed his gut. "Then take my advice and find yourself a good one."

Sinking against him even more, she said, "Consider staying."

For an instant, but only that, he entertained the thought of staying on in Dresden. She curled like a baby rabbit against his chest, tugging at his heart. How could anyone abandon a wounded, wild thing? He was beginning to understand why Laurel stayed here. To be needed by a helpless animal was primal, not to be denied.

His mind explored what he could do for Laurel if he stayed. Build the new wildlife clinic. Set up his own marina in Mike's name and finally flex his boating skills beyond racing. He'd keep her boats and Jim Swenson's running smoothly for all those wildlife and lakewater inspections they needed to do.

Maybe with his income, Laurel wouldn't have to worry about scrounging for money all the time. He'd also set up more water sports for the area's kids who adored her. Tyler could help. They could relieve Laurel of the tedium of being tied to this place. She could travel, give more of those talks in schools that she liked to do so much, find more sponsors for it, maybe even bug the governor more about grants. Hell, maybe she'd even run for office herself, what with him and Tyler taking care of the homefront. And she'd make a good politician. People liked her.

All a pipe dream, he realized. For him anyway.

After tucking Laurel in and stoking the fireplace into red flames to warm her, Cole planted a kiss on her pale forehead and escaped back to the shed.

Somewhere between feeding Owlsy and petting Rusty—Laurel's two favorites—the idyllic images blossomed again. They ebbed forth first in sepia tones, then grew brighter, with voices of laughter, with sunshiny days and Laurel in the meadow. Children played around them, their children.

It struck like an arrow. Their children.

He wanted more children.

Maybe he was just missing his son Tyler too much, missing being part of a family. His had disintegrated, what with his parents somewhere across the globe all the time, his sister-in-law in hiding and Tyler a teenager already, about to take wing. Cole had flung everyone far and wide.

But he had the power to pull them back together again! Didn't he? The thought of it—the challenge—scared him to his marrow.

Snatching up a baby rabbit from the nesting box, Cole held it tight against his cheek. It nuzzled against one ear and into his hair. It was so soft, alive, needy and wondrous—like Laurel. Just as he cared about this baby against his cheekbone, Cole was afraid for Laurel. The feeling clawed at his insides, shredding his good sense even. He had to do something for Laurel that meant something, that would last and please her. Sure, he could make something of his no-nothing life, but that wasn't personal enough.

Holding the baby rabbit out in front of him, Cole smiled on the little animal's wiggling, button nose and said, "She loves you, you know. I want you to grow up big and strong in our meadow, you hear? When she takes walks, or visits Jonathon, I want you hopping right alongside, watching out for her, okay?"

The rabbit's ears twitched, sending rivers of delight through Cole. "What do you think if I did this for Laurel?"

When he whispered his idea into the baby rabbit's ear, it nuzzled in reply against his own whiskery cheek.

Cole chuckled. "So you like that notion, huh? Let's hope she'll be pleased."

Soon after, Cole tiptoed past a sleeping Laurel. Picking up the portable phone, he went into the bedroom to quietly ask the sheriff to send someone out to park in her driveway as guard while he went on an errand.

COLE SWUNG Gary's maroon pickup into Laurel's long driveway, mindful that the box of yellow roses didn't slide off the benchseat and onto the floor. Laurel said she preferred wildflowers, but he'd seen the roses in the shop window and they made him think of velvet sunshine. Whenever he thought of Laurel, sunshine came to mind.

But bone-chilling fright took over when Cole soon found himself reaching in around the deputy's body, grabbing the receiver, punching 911. The operator sent the call on through to Sheriff John Petski.

"The son-of-a-bitch is here!" he yelled at the sheriff.

"Where?"

"At Laurel's! Your Hayward buddy fell asleep on the job. Send an ambulance. Damnit, John, where is everybody? The woods are supposed to be crawling with feds."

"Shit. Something's wrong. What about Laurel?"

"I'm heading for the cabin now. Just get the backup."

"You got anything on you?"

"Yeah." Cole spotted the pistol still in the deputy's hand. It would come in handier than the knife sheathed inside his jeans.

He tossed the mouthpiece down beside the comatose deputy, snatched the pistol, then began a crooked canter along the shadowy side of the gravel driveway. His leg hurt bad, but paled to the cutting grief splicing open his heart right now.

Oh, my Laurel Lee. Please be alive.

LYING TRUSSED IN the bottom of a small runabout boat, Laurel fought against the terror strangling her. The boat weaved and bobbed. On the floor behind the driver's seat, she could only glimpse the back of the dark-haired man's head. The hair struck a memory chord. It was the man from behind the menu at the restaurant. Was he Rojas?

"Why?" she spat out, glancing down at her bonds, "why kidnap me? What do you want from me?"

Too easily this stranger had broken through her breezeway and trussed her like a turkey while she struggled to wake from a deep sleep. Where had Cole been? Did this man have him too? Or...was Cole dead already? Chills sprinted across her body. She needed to believe he was alive, or she wouldn't have the strength to survive herself. She refused to become fish bait.

She stared at miles of rope looped around her body. Her hands ached from the extra knots tightened at her wrists. Fear mounted.

Flopping one arm down behind him, he grazed her cheekbone with a gloved hand. Like a vulture, the man cackled from his perch, "My red-haired mermaid, you're all I want."

Laurel wanted to wretch. "You're Marco Rojas?"

"That common thief?" he scoffed.

So this was the hired gun of Cole's boss.

"Where're you taking me?"

"Sweet love, we're going on a nice, long ride so we don't have to worry about your nasty boyfriends."

"Like who?"

"Damn Wescott," the man growled, "Rojas plans to catch up with him."

So Cole must be alive. But how could she save herself? What would Cole do in this predicament? How did he survive being shot at before? He stayed focused! She suddenly rued the first time she condemned him for that. Staying alive was worth focusing on.

"You said Rojas was a thief," she ventured, wriggling at her bonds. She winced at the numbness crawling into her hands. "What did Rojas steal?"

"Everything. Every piece of junk brought up on the dives ended up with black marketers. Even women. He got rich, and I never saw a dime he promised. Neither did the fool Wescott boys."

Laurel shuddered. "What about the women? What do you mean?" Keep him talking.

"My little mermaid, if you only knew how lucky you are to have me rescue you. Wescott would never keep you from the likes of my boss."

"What would Rojas do with women?"

"Not treat them with respect. Not like me. I'd never sell you to any foreigner."

"Sell?" A frigid sheen of fear enveloped her.

The boat sputtered along. "See, I told you Wescott was dumb. He never knew all the years he worked for Rojas that blondes and redheads like you brought more than pleasure to the boss. You'd bring six figures on the international market, sweetie."

She wanted to wretch again, but raised her voice above the engine noise. "What if Cole's brother did find out? What if that's why he was killed? If you can help us get Rojas, you'll be free."

The man laughed louder. "Wescott was too damn cocky for his own good. He never tumbled to anything Rojas was doing. He always wanted to make a name for himself, kept saying his son would be proud of him for the next dive and the next, for the next race."

Laurel's heart ached for Cole.

Trying to sound sweet, she asked, "What's your name?"

"Broderick. Just Broderick."

"You have any children, Broderick?"

His gloved hand reached back to stroke her temple. "You gettin' ideas for us already? I knew we'd be good for each other."

The cool wind did nothing to bust through the fear flushing down her body. "Where's this nice place you're taking me?"

"I was thinking of Canada."

"By boat?" Hope flickered. They'd have to leave Spirit Lake and the transfer to land could give her a chance to be rescued.

"Not by boat, silly mermaid. I'm taking us across Spirit Lake. Got a hidden spot to land all picked out. Then we'll hike over to Deer Creek Gorge. We'll catch the train and head west into the mountains. You ever see the mountains?"

"No." She wasn't getting on any train. She bulged every piece of her fiber against the bonds but they wouldn't give. If only she had Cole's knife. "How can I hop on when I'm tied like this?" She imagined running like a deer as soon as the bonds came off.

From around the edge of the seat, a pistol barrel appeared. "You will do whatever I say."

Like a fog, a chill blanketed her. "Hopping a train is dangerous. I'll need help."

He swiveled to look down on her with his swarthy face. The gleam in his eyes tortured her. Then, he showed her his other wrist. She saw the rope knotting it. He'd tethered himself to her!

"I hop on first," he cackled, "and you either get on with me, or the train's wheels suck you under, splicing both you and the rope, setting me free in that unfortunate event. I have no problem with the plan. Do you?"

Laurel shook her head, hope draining away.

Chapter 16

AT THE CABIN, Cole raced like a madman looking for Laurel. Not finding her, he flung himself back out the front door, where he saw Buzz trundling down the driveway. An ambulance and second squad car pulled in behind him in the distance.

From the other direction, Sheriff Petski hurried up from Laurel's dock after racing over in one of his patrol boats.

Cole demanded, "You see her out on Spirit Lake?"

"No, but there's so many tourists out there fishing and water-skiing that I might have missed her."

"What route did you take?"

"I followed the north shore, since that's where we thought the body came from. Most criminals tend to go back to their hideouts for something."

"Like he'd go pack for a honeymoon with her?" Cole spun, raking his hair in anger. "He had to be here only moments ago. That deputy's wound is fresh. Do your job, sheriff!"

"Get a grip, son. You haven't cornered the market on fear."

"Sorry," Cole gasped. "I checked the cabin and shed. A broken window in the breezeway. Looks like he plucked her up out of her nap, where I put her." A lump rose in his throat. "I never should have left her alone."

John's big hand squeezed his shoulder. "The guy probably has a weapon. If he's the kind to plant bombs on your boat to kill your brother, there's no telling what he showed up with here."

"Bombs." Cole's heartbeat thudded into his stomach. "Don't let anybody back in that place until it's checked out. If anything happens to her animals—"

Another squeeze to his shoulders and John said, "Nothing's going to happen. The FBI should be here any minute."

"I thought you said they were supposed to be planted in the woods before this?"

"They're still not sure this guy is Rojas. They think we've only got a nut case on our hands."

"Like a woman being kidnapped isn't important?" Cole's insides burned with anger.

"Until she crosses state lines, the FBI boys don't think it's their jurisdiction."

"Then you and I better saddle up."

He propelled himself down the lawn's slope toward the sheriff's boat.

John hurried after him. "They're sending a chopper. It'll be here any minute. You can't do much chasin' with that leg anyway."

Cole was already unwinding the nylon rope from the post at the dock. "I don't care if my leg drops off if it means Laurel comes back alive."

"Don't go out there alone. Wait for the chopper."

He blinked at the sheriff's stricken face under the hot sun. "Damn it all, John, Laurel was the mother of my son. Do you really believe I can wait around for a helicopter ride? And for what? What if we spot her being dragged into the trees by Rojas and we can't land? That would be hell for me to watch if I thought I could have prevented it."

Cole climbed into the boat.

John stepped back. "I'll check the old church and get somebody around to Flora's mansion ASAP."

"Thanks." With a nod, Cole backed the patrol boat against the currents of the bay, despising its sluggish surge. He longed for his hydroboat back in The Keys. To get to Laurel faster.

CRACK!

Laurel's blood froze at the rifle retort. Broderick floored the small runabout. She pitched against the seatback, smashing her nose. Blood stained the vinyl.

She hoped the rifle shot meant Cole and the sheriff were closing in.

"Who is it?" she yelled up at Broderick.

"Like I care, sweet thing? Came from that old three-story butt ugly house, but we've left him for good."

The mansion! Cole? The sheriff? But the shot had missed, and she was the new "girlfriend" of a maniac.

But they weren't off Spirit Lake yet! There were people out here who could help her. If they could see her. She pushed harder against the ropes, ignoring the blood.

WHEN COLE spotted a zigzagging runabout, his heart leapt. The crazy driver had to be Laurel's kidnapper. Nobody would speed on this crowded lake unless they needed to. Other boaters, fishers and canoeists scattered like bowling pins in the renegade's wake.

With his guts grinding, Cole pushed the patrol boat to a faster speed. Plumes of lakewater shadowed him.

The kidnapper's runabout ripped an ugly U-turn, almost flipping the boat. Cole wished it had overturned because he could have scooped up Laurel, just as he'd done with fellow racers a thousand times when a boat hydroplaned to disaster. Just as he'd done for Mike. He shouldn't have been in the boat that exploded. They shouldn't have argued. Now, the parallel to Laurel tore at Cole. She shouldn't be out here. The memory of the fiery explosion burst inside Cole's brain, driving him in a fever of terror.

The renegade boat used a line of sleek boats anchored off shore as a shield, turning to head back toward the abandoned mansion. Cole hoped the boat would ride directly into the gun of the waiting sheriff.

Just as he pressed the patrol boat into a clear straight-away, a ski boat darted out from behind the lip of a cove and Cole had to abort his speed and swerve. He lost sight of his quarry.

He circled away from the boaters and into the middle of the lake, losing valuable time.

An angry hunger slammed about inside him, a hunger like that of a hawk spying someone raiding his nest and harming his mate. He had no future without Laurel. His fingers coiled like sharp talons. Wild instinct to pounce jetted through his veins.

He drove for the clear, more treacherous and shallower water near the shoreline. On a sharp turn, water sprayed across his face. Narrowing his gaze, he scoped the lake and land everywhere at once. Where was she? The hawk spotted nothing.

Faster, go faster. The boat's engine grunted. Cole zipped in and out of coves, narrowly dodging rocks and submerged logs.

Just around a finger of land crowded with trees, his boat suddenly snapped up, flung into the air by a powerful jolt.

Clinging to the wheel, Cole flew with the boat as it sailed at a crazy angle before coming back down with a smack!

The boat rumbled, its motor complaining. Then a thin geyser sprayed the back of Cole's neck. Whatever he hit had gouged a small hole through the fiberglass behind the seats.

Where was the sheriff? The helicopter? He saw nothing in the sky but sunshine and birds.

Savage instinct drove him.

Save my Laurel Lee.

With the lakewater spraying in, he glanced around for another option. He spotted three boats about a hundred yards away, tethered together for a party in the middle of the lake. He slammed the gas pedal, but the engine protested again. He hurried for a quick look at the prop, but the engine wouldn't tip up from the damage. Through the frothy water, he saw branches, weeds, twine—all sorts of lake junk trailing off the prop.

With no time to clean it, he sloshed back to the front of the boat and gunned the engine on and off, reverse and forward, to see if he could dislodge the junk.

Laurel needs you!

On the fourth try, the boat moved forward, but at a slow, deliberate speed. Somehow, Cole reached the partiers before the patrol boat became too waterlogged. He jumped onto the deck of a glittery new boat, calling out, "Get off! I'm taking this!"

When a muscle man holding a beer objected, Cole ripped the pistol out and pointed it at him.

Everyone screamed. Cole ordered, "Get your tanned asses off the boat! Now!"

They scattered onto the two other boats, and Cole commandeered the new tri-hull.

Skimming the top of the water, Cole whipped in and out, dodging debris, looking for the runabout.

He spotted it in a thin crescent of red sand shoreline leading into the pine forest. From his vantage point, the boat appeared empty. An ache stabbed through him.

Storming for shore, he rammed onto the sand next to the small runabout and looked down inside it, pointing the pistol. Laurel was gone. His heart busted into pieces.

Jumping overboard, he fell to his knees in soft, squishy sand with stabbing pain. He swore, thinking how he wished he'd listened to Laurel and taken better care of the leg instead of being so bullheaded— his macho act to keep her at arm's length. Everything had backfired on him. His health, his plan to catch Rojas on his own, even his heart. And it hurt far more than his leg. Laurel was his lifeblood. To lose her would be to lose it all. Even Tyler would never forgive him for this.

Nor would Jonathon, looking down, and Cole wanted to believe in angels right now.

Picking himself up, he searched for tracks.

He soon found red stains littering the sand. His breathing grew labored. The bloody trail led off into the thick underbrush.

Cole stumbled onward, the ache welling up inside him at every red, grainy splotch already drying under the baking sun.

"Laurel Lee!"

Only the breeze moaned back through the pines. Throwing himself at the thick brush, he entered the deep shadows, but his leg immediately gave way to a searing jab in the muscles that were still healing. Gritting his teeth, he dragged the leg along, forcing it to function.

SHE TROTTED ALONG in fits through the underbrush, with the man called Broderick yanking relentlessly on the rope tethered to her bound wrists. She was forced to taste her own blood filling her mouth as she sucked for air.

It appalled her that he carried her father's rifle. To see the beautiful wood stock polished to a mirror by her father now gripped in this scum's clutches sent waterfalls of ice into her stomach. He had some other sawed-off thing tucked in his belt.

Branches whipped at her face, the lacerations stinging while she spied every whichway hoping to see Cole lurking in the woods. The nylon rope sawed at her flesh, burning.

"Broderick, please, I can't go on."

He pulled harder. She stumbled, but he dragged them across lichen-etched rocks and through thick ferns. An occasional spot of sunshine up ahead gave her hope that it was the road where perhaps a car would rescue her. But each ray of hope disintegrated into splintered emerald shadows and thick understory.

Could Cole remember this woods enough to find her?

This portion of the woodland was virgin forest preserve, a place left pristine for growing populations of bears and wolves. It stretched into ravines, cliffs and caves, rolling hills, a stream that cut under the road and led to Deer Creek Gorge beyond civilization. Laurel feared that nobody would find her. Ever.

Broderick kept on, manhandling her when she stumbled.

"We can't do this," she gasped hoarsely. "We won't be able to get on the train. Stop, Broderick, stop!"

He thrashed ahead, using her father's rifle like a machete to part briars. "The train'll take us to paradise. You'll do it."

"But the ropes. I can't grab on like this." Brambles clawed at her T-shirt and bare arms. Beads of blood sprouted.

"I'll pull you up, like a fish on a line."

Crack! A rifle shot echoed through the trees.

Laurel ducked instinctvely.

Crack! Then a sharp pain jerked her to the ground.

COLE HAULED UP short against a tree, his breathing ragged. After the two shots, the forest grew silent.

Like a cancer, despair spread through him. He tamped it down. Stay focused. Laurel Lee needs you. If she was still alive.

Don't think it.

Guessing at the rifle shot's origin, Cole crossed a small ravine, dragging his numbing leg up the next incline. With the flesh swelling against his snug bluejeans, the leg moved with all the élan of a pirate's pegleg.

Still, he forged on, desperate to beat the odds. The forest floor smelled dank, like death.

Don't think it.

Branches pushed back, unyielding. He slipped on mossy rocks, getting swallowed up under arching ferns. He wished for the sound of the sheriff's search helicopter, but knew how useless it probably was for spotting anyone in this foliage.

On a rock outcropping, Cole spotted a wide patch of blood. Agony ripped through him. It hurt to breathe the innocent air.

With fists curled around the pistol and the knife hidden at his side, he traveled on.

Beyond a felled oak tree, he stumbled...over a body.

His toe was snagged by the cuff of the jeans on the form sprawled half-hidden in the leaves and twigs. Taking one look brought him to his knees, where it took all his strength to swallow back the bile. He forced himself to look again.

It wasn't Laurel. A man he'd never seen before—Rojas's new right-hand man?—lay with half his face blown away, staring with one crazed eye up at the sky.

Then he saw the sleek wood sticking out from under the man. Recognition flickered. There was no mistaking the fancy rifle that had been pointed at him once. Gripping the stock, he pulled the gun from under the dead man. Though scratched up, the rifle looked in usable shape. He pulled the bolt and checked the chamber. It was loaded, but with only one round left. One bullet. A chance.

Anger spiked down Cole. The rifle shot that killed this goon must have come within inches of Laurel. Rojas could have killed her, too, but had chosen not to. Bile threatened his throat again.

A ferocity of spirit, of destiny, whipped through him. He would take Rojas in his bare hands, then squeeze his traitorous, slimy neck just to hear the man whimper for mercy. Rojas had gone insane for sure. He was a madman, but Cole could match that now.

He breathed fire. Blood for blood. Justice in the end.

Then Cole heard the far-off, long, moaning call of a train. He suddenly feared where Rojas's game would take him.

LAUREL KNEW HE was Marco Rojas, despite the ugly dye job on his hair to disguise himself. She saw it in the sick smile. He was like a cat about to play with its catch before crunching its bones and swallowing it, leaving not a trace.

"You're prettier than I expected," he said, leaning toward her face with curled lips. They sat hidden by a boulder to catch their breaths. "Mr. Sanchez Wescott's taste is finally matching my own. Perhaps my plan will need to change, seeing how beautiful you are. *Que bonita.*"

"What plan?" she said, her mind reeling.

"To kill him while we make love."

Her stomach lurched. "You're sick."

The flesh at the corners of his eyes jerked, his gaze shrinking to hauntingly dark under the cap of spiked yellow hair. A rabid wolf was handsomer. "Not sick," he growled. "Only in control. Not like Wescott. How can he do this to you? To allow Broderick to hurt you like this?"

"Let me go."

The tic at his eyes returned. His gaze lowered to her bound and raw wrists. "I do not care for imperfections, my *querida.*"

"Then take me to the hospital in Dresden."

"Ah, but you are a fiery one. I like that. No, I will take you with me, to my ranch in Venezuela. It is time I leave this country and do other things with my life."

Her bones quivered. "No airline would take a screaming woman aboard."

This time he laughed. The thick foliage muffled the sounds. "My *querida*, I have any number of private planes at my disposal. And besides, you will want to come live with me. If you fight me, I will send someone to visit your mother."

Laurel's chest grew tight. The air so stale. "You'd murder my mother? If I don't go with you?"

His nod was like a match, igniting terror in her.

After he stood, securing his rifle in one hand and the rope connected to her in the other, she had no choice. She got up, put one foot in front of the other, submerging into the deep forest.

HE WASTED NO time in getting his prey to Deer Creek Gorge. Laurel's legs ached from running and her cheeks stung from the branches they'd whipped through. A faint whistle sounded in the distance toward Dresden. A fist tightened in her stomach.

They skirted the woodland, following the railroad bed. Laurel shuddered at the acrid smell of the sun-heated creosote ties and the shiny tracks where tons of steel promised to slide over.

Rojas, with a firm hand clamping her elbow, hurried her over the Deer Creek trestle, then down the hillside toward the creek and flat marshland. They splashed through the icy springwater swirling by, then stumbled along the bank until stopping under an ancient oak tree where the land leveled out near the rail line.

Her wrists aching in their bonds, she looked around for any mode of escape.

Fidgeting with the cocked rifle, Rojas winced and wriggled his shoulder around. Was he hurting? What if he dropped the rifle? Could she run? But he kept the end of her rope twisted in his other fist. Her wrists pulsated, the fingers turning blue.

Looking him in his weasel eyes, she said, "See my fingers? If I fall, it'll be another murder on your hands. You won't have me to serve your every whim."

"If you fall," he growled, "it'll be your fault."

Something snapped inside her. She'd taken enough. She knew her life might be ending and she couldn't let him get away with it. "Like it was Broderick's fault he fell into your bullet? Like it was that Texas woman's fault? You killed her. She was spotted on your yacht and she was found dead after that."

His grin unnerved her. "Nobody found her body near me, remember? They found the body here, Miss Hastings, where Cole Wescott put it."

"Where your hired hitman put it for you!"

"She left my boat alive."

"Like all the other women you sold?"

He began to laugh, but a train whistle masked it, calling louder from Dresden way, though still heralding from far down the line. When it quieted, he said, "You'll like your new owner."

"I'm not going with the likes of you. And besides, Cole won't let you. He's coming. I know he is."

He coiled more of the rope around his hand, then used it to dob at the blood still sliding across her lips. "That's what I'm counting on. He should be here any minute."

Goose-flesh rippled down her body.

Stay focused.

"So I'm the bait? You think Cole is that stupid to just walk out of the woods and into your rifle? Is that all the further you've thought this through? I'd rather have taken my chances with your hired piece of slime, Broderick."

Rojas cuffed her to the ground. Her face smashed into the oily dirt and cinders. When she gathered herself and looked up, it was into the end of the rifle barrel.

WHEN COLE EDGED around a tree and saw Laurel hit the ground, he whipped her father's rifle up. But Rojas yanked her up in front of him, foiling Cole's hope. He eased back behind the tree several yards from Rojas. Taking stock of the situation, he barely recognized the yellow-haired man. Usually impeccably attired, proud of his dark looks and control, Rojas was dusty and dirty, and holding a firearm. He never did his own dirty work, which told Cole how desperate Rojas had become. How dangerous.

When Cole heard the train's whistle from a few miles off as it signaled its way through Dresden, it unnerved him.

He shot the pistol in the air. Rojas whirled in his direction, but didn't see him yet.

Cole demanded, "Let her go!"

"I've fallen in love with this one!"

The man's haughty retort twisted inside Cole like jagged wires. The train's creaking grew louder, the ground quivering.

Rojas hauled Laurel nearer the tracks.

"Rojas!" He ran stiff-legged straight for Laurel and Rojas, sending off a warning pop with the pistol before hauling Gerald Hastings' old rifle into position.

A startled Rojas swung around with Laurel flailing in his iron clutch. He poked his rifle at her chin.

The sight halted Cole in his tracks. His mind spun, dizzy with crazed hatred for the yellow-haired freak holding Laurel. Dirt and blood smudged her wide-eyed face. Twigs and leaves tangled in her loose, red hair. Her chest heaved in a desperate attempt for breath.

When Cole's gaze met hers, lightening bolts sizzled through the air between them. She was trying to tell him something. If it was that she hated him, Cole deserved it. If it was trust, Cole hoped she could cling to it a bit longer.

She called, "Get away! It's a trap! I'll go with him!"

COLE RECOGNIZED what Laurel was up to. She wanted to win this game, too. She wasn't actually giving in to Rojas. She was letting Cole know what he was up to. Her courage stoked Cole's soul.

"Laurel, don't say anything! This is between Rojas and me! Let her go, Rojas!"

The train's engine rumbled toward them, pulling a slow and long snake of boxcars on its way out of Dresden. Once past this curve where the marshland met the forest and gorge, it would surely pick up speed quickly.

Rojas let up with the rifle, hid it, but kept Laurel squarely in front of him. The trainsmen would only think them a hunting party, maybe picnickers. It made Cole's stomach harden.

The engine rolled by, wheels whining. Rojas edged backward with Laurel, pulling her closer to the danger zone where the wheels' vacuum could suck her under. Cole's hand squeezed around the trigger of the useless rifle. He couldn't take a chance on hurting her. She'd kept her focus on him, never wavering.

Against the rumbling of the train, Cole shouted, "Take me. Leave her here. It's me you want. You wanted to kill me with the explosion, but Mike got in the way, didn't he?"

Rojas, his spiky yellow hair tipping back and forth in the train-whipped air, yelled back, "It was an accident."

"The hell it was. But why, Rojas? What did you think I had on you?"

"You tell me. Your brother took off with copies of my records."

But where were they? Cole wondered. "Were you blackmailing somebody? Hiding something? Why kill for it?"

"Are you so stupid? You work for me for years bringing up

bounty from the sea. You could have been rich, ruled the world with me, but instead you turn on me like a common cur."

Cole slid a foot forward. "Ruled the world?" The man had lived alone on his yacht too long.

"I'm the richest man alive. It's just that people don't know it yet. But they will."

Cole licked away the sweat pouring across his lips, then edged ahead a few inches, the rifle still drawn. Laurel's eyes stayed steady. "They don't know it because why? Were you covering up the value of the treasures we brought up? What were some of those pieces really selling for?"

Rojas laughed. "Depends on the country and the currency."

"You weren't allowed to sell the treasures until the government gave the okay." Then Cole's mind tumbled. "If they knew about them. Not everything I brought up from the sunken ships made it to the ledgers, though, did it? Not unless Mike physically saw the stuff and he didn't see it all, did he? Until the end. He stumbled onto a secret cache, didn't he?"

The train ground on behind them still at a walking pace on its journey from Dresden. But it was gathering speed. Boxcar after boxcar slid by, some empty, some heaving with coal and lumber.

Rojas stepped back. "But you know all that, Wescott. You bring the copies of the records, she goes free."

Keep him engaged in conversation, Cole thought. "Like the Texas socialite? Where are all the women who have visited your yacht over the years and Senator Goetz's yacht, for that matter?"

Cole saw the rifle waver. He continued. "Is it just coincidence that the chairman of the CIA oversight committee is anchored next to you? Was the CIA suspicious once? Is it now looking the other way because Goetz's nest is feathered by you? Did Mike discover that?"

A flinch tarnished Rojas's armor.

"Give it up," shouted Cole, "because I'm not handing over the evidence."

Rojas's dark eyes erupted in fire. "You'd let her die?"

Cole noted Laurel remainded frozen. Trusting? Or too traumatized? Sweat poured down his back.

"No, Rojas. Never. But you've been done in. You see, you did kill the wrong brother. Your mistake cost you. Mike hid the copies of your books somewhere and we haven't been able to find them. You've chased me—and now indicted yourself—all for nothing. I can't help you. Let her go."

Rojas responded by hauling Laurel toward the train. Cole squeezed the trigger, but Rojas swung back with Laurel as his shield.

Then Laurel bucked with all her might, her head butting Rojas in the chin. Rojas cried out, letting go.

Cole shot, but Rojas ducked down to grab Laurel, saving himself. Cole tossed the rifle aside and pulled out his pistol, only to see Rojas tip his rifle's barrel into Laurel's neck again.

"Toss it away, far away" he said, "or this is it for her. You're making me do it. You're murdering her, Wescott."

Seeing the glassy terror in Laurel's eyes, Cole knew the man would do it. He threw the pistol off toward the woods behind them.

Rojas began shoving Laurel toward the railcars. Cole ran for him, but his leg went numb and he fell hard. Rojas charged on, half dragging Laurel with him.

Cole staggered up. His leg wasn't working at all.

Then he witnessed the horror of Rojas tossing Laurel at the open door of a boxcar half-filled with pine lumber. Her legs dangled perilously close to the spinning steel wheels underneath. Running alongside the slow train, Rojas tossed the rifle up and in, then leaped up after her.

Cole limped into a trot, not feeling his bad leg. He knew if he didn't catch them now, the train would soon slide on past, circle through the marshland and be gone forever. Rojas would find a way to never be seen again. And he'd have Laurel.

Dredging for his last bit of strength, Cole flung himself at the rocking boxcar, knowing a rifle could stare him in the face.

He landed hard on his belly, but wriggled on in time to see Rojas struggling with Laurel. She fought with the fury of a mother cat against a marauding tom.

Cole spotted the rifle a few feet behind Rojas near the lumber in the shadows of the boxcar.

As Cole crawled forward, Rojas whirled, kicked him hard in the gut. He went down.

To his horror, Rojas pushed Laurel out the open door.

"Laurel!" *Oh, God, the wheels beneath them!*

Cole snapped. The adrenaline rush turned him into a true Atlas. His body surged to a standing position, but he made the mistake of favoring his leg.

Rojas saw it and flew at him with a kick. Cole writhed in pain, going down. Forcing himself up, his fist connected with Rojas's gut, who staggered back against the sway of the boxcar.

Cole seized the opportunity. The two men went down, rolled, fist against fisticuff, growl for growl. When Rojas straddled him handily, Cole discovered that he couldn't fight back effectively with only one leg willing to push. And there was no way he could reach for the knife sheathed inside his pant's leg. Inch by inch, Cole was barely holding off Rojas's attempt to move him to the open door, to dump him into the wheels beneath them.

Chapter 17

LAUREL ROLLED FAST, hands still tied. She spat out dirt. Gasping, she got up to find several boxcars had slipped by. Cole?

The train was picking up speed. She spotted the caboose coming a few cars away. It would take Cole away from her for good. Rojas would kill him.

Her lungs were on the verge of collapse, her fingers were numb, and her legs were jelly, but she forced herself into a wobbly trot alongside the train.

Then the caboose rumbled past, a red flash flickering in her periphery like a cardinal in the woods. It slid on by, but still she trotted down the tracks.

COLE TORE AT the hands squeezing his throat and trying to dump him out the boxcar's doorway to perdition. Wind whipped his hair. The train bounced. Steel wheels seized against steel tracks beneath them, sending off a seering banchee wail.

Twisting, he bit hard on Rojas's forearm. Rojas let go and Cole rolled inside the boxcar on a dead reckoning for the rifle but couldn't come up with it in the rocking shadows. Slammed onto his butt, he pulled out Mike's knife and recoiled.

The madman towered a few feet away, silhouetted against scenery whooshing by outside. "Your Laurel is gone. You made me let go. You killed her, Wescott."

Cole's gut burned, refusing to believe Rojas despite what he'd seen with his own eyes. "She's alive."

Rojas laughed. "You only wish. She and I had lovely last moments together. That you'll never have."

With his last ounce of strength, Cole lunged at Rojas, but the train jerked violently, pitching him and Rojas out.

Hitting the ground hard, Cole gasped for air and rolled just in time to see Wiley charge from the woods in one direction, with Rojas stumbling across the tracks to disappear the other way.

"Wiley! Help!"

The wiry man leaped through the air, tripping Rojas, then straddling his head and neck, twisting an arm back. Rojas let fly with an expletive in Spanish, but Wiley grunted, "Want your mouth washed out with soap, too?" He snugged the arm tighter, eliciting a scream from Rojas, but Rojas was wriggling free.

"Hang on, Wiley!" Cole called, barely able to steady himself on his feet.

A sudden downdraft of wind beating at his hair signaled the helicopter's arrival. It was landing with John Petski aboard. The bright sunlight glinted off the bubble windshield. Two camouflaged men rushed out with him with their weapons drawn.

Cole turned his attention elsewhere, scanning down the trainline for Laurel. He didn't see her. All strength drained from him. A cold wind gutted his insides.

Had he lost Laurel?

Limping alongside the boxcars, one by one, he set off to find her...or what was left of her. The grisliness of the thought tortured him. Why couldn't he have been the one, and not her?

"Laurel!"

He passed boxcar after rusty car. Nothing. Cole backhanded the savage tears threatening to undo him....

And then, a mirage.

Stumbling on, he called again, "Laurel?"

She seemed to take wing, his dove, her visage growing murky.

He was crying. He didn't care.

Then she was there, her long soft hair tangling around him, her throat choking in sobs against his neck, "I couldn't let him take you away. I jumped on the moving caboose."

"You what?"

"The trainman radioed the engineer from the caboose."

Cole hugged her closer, nuzzled the hair adorned with a twig or two. "You crazy woman. The brakes coming on must be why we suddenly flipped out the door. Oh, Laurel Lee."

"I thought I'd lost you," she said, quaking against him, gasping for breath against his neck. "I love you."

Fever gripped him like talons. Words stuck in his dry throat. They had just defied death. The careless Cole of old would have easily taken advantage of this moment and the adrenaline rush, telling her anything she wanted to hear. It shook him to know he was choosing to hold back.

Drawing in a deep breath, he buried the words under the good smells about her: the pines, the floral scent of her hair, and the sunshine polishing her silken skin. To hold her was to glory in their meadow. The peace there. Which belonged to her. Not him, he reminded himself.

Holding her away from him, the sight of her bloodied face and cut wrists brought a catch to his heart. "I'm sorry."

As her smile faded, the lump in his throat grew and he interjected, "I hurt you. Badly. I'm sorry."

Her eyes bore into his, green as the forest they'd run through, beseeching. Did he love her? Always, she was questioning him, challenging him about his definition of love.

Thinking about all that he'd put her through, he knew they'd never be sure about their love if they promised things now.

He could not tell her he loved her. The decision astounded him. It came strong in his brain, like a punctuation mark called wisdom. Be sure, it said. When had he left rashness behind? When had he changed so much?

Laurel tipped her chin up, waiting, not breathing.

He swallowed hard. He wasn't sure enough about his own heart to trust anything spoken about love. Except about his son. He owed his son an "I love you" or two or ten before he'd ever be worthy of Laurel.

Cole's knees almost buckled from the weight of his thoughts, and when she allowed him to gather her to him again, he planted kisses in the soft hair at her temples. Yes, deep down, he wanted her. But even he had fences to mend for his brother, and most of all, with his own son. Those things would take time, maybe years. He couldn't ask Laurel to commit to that waiting. She deserved more. She'd spent enough time waiting where he was concerned.

All she needed from him was to be left to her peace. She had chosen that peace and it had nourished her for fifteen years, making her the best damn wildlife doctor there ever was, making her a vital person in this community. Free of him, she'd become respected again, a thing of beauty. And it wasn't in him anymore to cage a dove.

IN THE DAYS THAT followed, with all the details that needed tending to through the sheriff's office and with the July Fourth weekend bursting the town to its seams, Cole could avoid talking to Laurel about what she'd said beside the train.

But the avoidance became a nervous dance. They grew wary of

each other, nodding politely when they passed each other in town. She kept busy at the cabin. He kept busy splitting apart some of the last of the mansion's dusty lath walls.

He was stacking some of that lumber from the mansion next to her breezeway one evening when she spoke through the screen. "Coffee?"

She had two mugs in hand. What could he do? Run? He told her, "As long as it's not really tea."

"It's really coffee." She smiled then, a tender line of lips made as dramatic as a movie from the gauzy effect of the screen.

They settled side by side on the front stoop. He would miss this with her, the wild moment of waiting before she spoke, wondering what wisdom or challenge would spew forth. It made his heart find the next gear right now. It opened him to a world he'd neglected to notice before coming back to her. He liked the "chip, chip" of the red cardinal and listened for it, and melted at the softness of baby rabbits in his roughened hands. He sniffed the air more now, paying attention to what rode the currents, like the smell of the pungent tomato vines and dill in the garden next to them by the cabin, but most of all he tested for the scent of the woman beside him. Always, heat stirred between his legs just smelling the hint of roses or jasmine or lilac in the shampoo she used to wash the billowing waves of her deep auburn hair.

Uncomfortable with the bend in his thoughts, he seared his lips on the coffee, punished his throat with a slug of it, and asked, "What're you going to do with all these vegetables?"

There were carrots, cucumbers, squash, pumpkins, onions—all of it crowding the sunny spot next to the cabin's front door.

"Do some canning with my mother, like every autumn. Give most of it away in baskets for the needy around Thanksgiving."

She'd be fine, he thought. She knew how to do important stuff. He hadn't a clue what was involved with canning. Or visiting the needy over a holiday. Champagne parties had always been more his style.

On his next sip of hot, earthy coffee, she asked, "You want to leave, don't you?"

Trapped. Like a bug on her breezeway screen under her palm. She understood he had to leave and had skipped right to the emotional nugget. Want versus need.

When he looked her way, he saw regret pushing shadows across her emerald eyes. It spliced open his heart.

"It doesn't matter what I want, Laurel Lee," he explained in as even a voice as he could muster. "I've got to go back to Miami and see if my battery of lawyers can outfox his."

"I understand. It could drag on for years."

She was being gracious. He said, "It could."

The hurt in her eyes would remain burned in his memory.

She drew back her shoulders, basking with closed eyes in the July sun. The breeze picked up her hair and tossed it about her stoic solemnity and summer freckles. Her simple, yellow flannel shirt made his belly flip-flop. Rolled up at the elbows, exposing the fine hairs on her arms and muscles that healed animals and men, he thought her sexy as hell. Other men would be fools not to see the same thing. His stomach churned at the thought.

After a gusty sigh, she said, "What if we went back to the mansion, looked around one more time?"

He thought about making love to her there. He flinched at the ache sparring against his willpower. "There's nothing there."

"You're giving up."

She was testing him. He focused on the steam lazying up from his coffee. "I won't give up until Rojas rots in prison for good."

"But without Mike's proof, he can weasel out too soon for my taste." She took the cup from his hands, setting it down before kissing him full on the lips. Testing him for sure. "Now refuse me one last look around the mansion."

He couldn't deny her. Besides, he needed to get up and move to hide his own embarrassing reaction to the kiss. How long would it take him to get over her? He disliked the way he could still fly full-tilt out of control around her. Hadn't he learned anything from her?

They spent the next few hours searching the grounds of the mansion and the basement again, but it yielded nothing.

They spent a couple of more days at it, starting out with coffee on the stoop each day, mesmerized by Spirit Lake, but sitting too far apart for a stolen kiss. Saying good-bye without saying the word was hell, Cole decided.

Then, to his relief, the case against Rojas tugged, demanding his attention away from Laurel.

The *New York Times* gave Buzz front page billing and asked him to do a series on Cole. Buzz wrote about it all. They'd found Lisa Shaw alive on Rojas's yacht, but Rojas was protesting that everything was master-minded by the murdered Broderick. Authorities quickly proved the Texas woman had died by asphixiation prior to being dumped in the lake, and the coffin with Broderick's fingerprints surfaced at an unoccupied cottage along the north shore of the lake.

But that was that. The story came to its own dead-end as a typical crime case, with no real connection between Rojas and Mike's death. No murder suspected. Rojas almost looked like a good guy for killing Laurel's kidnapper—his own employee.

That enraged Cole. Made him sick to his stomach. Mike would never have risked his life for this. But Cole hadn't found the proof to anything. Was there proof? Maybe he'd misread Mike's cryptic message about the skirt. No matter. The most important conclusion was that Rojas might be freed soon and could endanger his son, plus Mike's widow and son.

Cole wanted to leave.

He made arrangements for a flight out of Minneapolis in two days, that Friday. He remembered that things picked up for Laurel with the animals on Fridays, so he thought it the best choice for hasty good-byes. It also gave him time to return Gary's truck and shake a few hands. How odd to feel the tug of friendships in such a short time. Laurel's friends had been good to him, though, and he counted several already: Gary, Una, Wiley, Dr. Donna, even John Petski. When he got back to Miami, he'd make sure all his debts here were paid finally.

But thoughts about meeting up with Rojas in Miami bothered him. Hell, it scared him. He decided on one last look at the mansion on Friday afternoon before he left for the Twin Cities.

He borrowed the sheriff's boat, wending his way among the tourists on Spirit Lake. The breeze battered the fresh, white polo shirt that had mysteriously appeared in his backpack yesterday. Laurel would always "worry and tend," as she explained once with derision, fearing it a weakness. He now knew it to be a powerful strength of hers.

After tying up, and climbing the steep embankment, he headed through the tall grass, spotting the raccoons Roxy and Roger looking back at him from under the mansion's front verandah. Were they spying on him for Laurel? Watching out for her? Absolutely. He believed it. And smiled.

Inside, he walked through every room, stepping over piles of old plaster and the kitchen's buckled linoleum, then around the hole in the floor of the foyer. He took the slow route to the basement—the stairs—his nostrils flaring at the dankness, his mind reliving perhaps the most important night of his life. Laurel's no-nonsense challenges—punctuated with a two-by-four board, no less—had started him on a journey to become a....

Father. He loved Tyler. Missed him horribly. And feared the look he might see in his son's eyes. So much to patch up. He wished osmosis had given him Laurel's doctoring skills ten-fold.

And as a father, he loved Jonathon, who was certainly waiting for him, too, but in a far different way than Tyler.

But the earthly, real question was, how much did he love Jonathon's mother? Why couldn't he commit? Were all his reasons only excuses? Why was there the fence between them? Because she wanted it? Maybe he had to admit that and move on.

Looking about the basement, he remembered the lightning that night, and the way its spark resurrected its energy in his core the moment he realized she lay next to him.

He couldn't cheat her heart again. Never again would he make her miserable. Go back to your son and patch things up, he chided himself, fist pounding against his thigh. Be a man—and a true father—for the first time in your life.

Move on.

His heartbeat racing, sweat sheathing his forehead, he left the basement, mounting the other set of stairs. Past the second floor. Up to the pirate ship.

The wind whistled through the round window at the far end, its glass broken out by Rojas's attempt to hide while aiming his rifle at Broderick. Rojas had boldly confessed to it all.

Instant anger ground inside Cole like jagged shards of the window pane. To erase the dark emotion, Cole listened to the wind, hoping for voices. What had Laurel said to do? Shut your eyes tight and you can see loved ones? He shut his eyes tight.

And went cold as stone.

He needed to head back to Miami. Fast.

LAUREL WATCHED him through her viewing scope traipsing across the mansion's wide expanse of yard, now festooned with blue bachelor buttons, white queen anne's lace and other flowers in full summer bloom. She didn't like the emptiness that came with watching him move through the wild environment this one last time. It was as if her words of love held no effect on him. Didn't he see that he actually seemed to belong here? He had shoulders she'd relied on as strong as oak trees, a quirky humor as bubbly as the spring that fed the pond and lake, and his focused dedication to bring justice for his brother was as determined as the change in seasons around her cabin.

Yet, isn't that what she'd wanted all along? For him to leave? And hadn't she lectured enough times that he was no real father until he did the honorable thing and return to his son?

How dare she entertain selfish pangs at the thought of him leaving now. Cole was doing exactly what she'd demanded of him.

But she hated winning this way. To win meant someone had to lose. She felt both ends of that spear poking at each other inside her stomach. Already dread filled her at the prospect of living without his interruptions, his plans and plots. He never allowed her to be ordinary. Laurel Hastings tending to her animals in her quiet solitude by the lake. With him she had to make noisy conversation, even lead it and make her points solidly before he backed her into corners of confusion. With him, she had to embrace extraordinary things in life, dangerous things, like saving themselves from death—from death! And he'd made her own up to frailties like selfishness, anger, and pity. And loneliness. Only he understood the quiet satisfaction—the murmur within the heart—of making love in their meadow. Being wild, in wild places.

But life played cruel tricks. She should be happy now, satisfied, complete at last. Instead, a yearning agitation remained. Bordering on the hum she felt whenever around him.

Backing away from the viewing scope she realized it also burned to think that his murderous boss—even from jail—would be keeping her and Cole apart. Without the evidence Mike squirreled away somewhere, Cole would be plagued for the rest of his days. Which meant Rojas was probably grinning even now in his temporary jail cell, knowing he'd ruined their lives and won in the end.

It all gnawed at her. So instead of mixing food for Owlsy, her hands began making a fried egg sandwich, and the action began to fill the hollow rooms in her heart.

Soon after, the aluminum boat's purring motor nudged her across the currents of the bay.

In minutes, she stood in the doorway to the pirate's ship.

He didn't know she was there.

He'd pulled the table over close to the window and sat in the rickety tubular kitchen chair. Sunlight silhouetted the broad shoulders and splashed a coppery sheen on the waves of dark hair feathering the collar of the new shirt she'd spirited into his pack. Her heartbeat sputtered. It needed his gentle fixing.

Clutching tighter to the plastic handle of the small luncheon cooler, she cleared her throat. "Brought you a sandwich."

He jerked his head around, his hands fingering the sextant.

She asked, "Figure it out yet?"

"Trying to."

"We have to figure it out before you leave. We just have to."

His attempt at a smile faded, but she nudged through the dark side of the room to emerge into the light next to him. He went back to fingering the sextant, and studying the old maps on the table with their dots between here and Washington, D.C.

She put the cooler on the table in front of him, just off the edge of the map. "You did what you could for Mike. Even if you don't find it, your boss is in jail for a little while."

"Son of a bitch'll be out in days." After a grimace and a "sorry," he went back to the map. "Fried egg?"

"With catsup on it."

"Thanks," he said. "Those egg sandwiches healed me, you know." The corners of his mouth lifted against the sun coming in the round frame from behind her.

"I know." She shivered against the breeze.

It lifted the hair off his studious brow intermittently. Nudging the sextant across the map, he measured the dots, searching desperately for a clue.

She noticed his pack nearby, ready to go with the crayon box stuffed in the outside pocket. Ready to color on the flight back, she thought, to ward off his fear of flying.

Her heart lurched and she had to find air. At the window she was careful of small glass shards still stuck in the graying wood of the old frame. "It's too bad," she muttered, "that he broke your pirate ship window."

"For Mike and me, it was like a magnifying glass on the world, bringing any adventure closer in our imaginations. Rojas deserves prison just for sullying that memory. The bastard."

Touching the grainy wood of the frame, she thought of the irony of Cole hating that the window was broken when he'd torn apart the rest of the mansion anyway.

"I'll miss the moonlight in the window," she admitted, surprising herself. "It always felt like you were watching me." She drew in the pungent air, then turned to him. "I used to hate that, but I've grown to appreciate your watching out for me."

His black gaze faded against the dry attic shadows. She was losing him. Forever. She could feel it in the prickling of her skin.

His gaze dipped away. "You don't need anyone watching out for you anymore. You're doing just fine."

She should have thanked him for the compliment. It only made her miserable. Why couldn't she just say a clean "good-bye" and leave? Hadn't she learned her lessons from him? To leave the past behind?

Turning back to the window, she plucked a shard off the sill. "I used to be like a china figurine on a shelf. I would allow myself to be dusted off once in a while, but ultimately I was left alone on a dark shelf because people were afraid of me."

"Afraid?" He came to her, smelling of fresh soap and new purpose, ready for his journey home. Taking the shard from her, he held it between his thumb and finger, playing with the afternoon sun as it glinted through the shard, fracturing it to several streamers on the walls around them.

He said, "Even fragile, broken things hold beauty."

"But once they're broken, there's no going back to the way they were before."

Tossing aside the shard, he held her steady with his penetrating gaze. "Even a china doll can be mended, like you mend your animals."

With fear swirling inside her heart, with her stomach churning with desperation, she questioned, "And what is the bandage, the medicine that might work for us? Yes, I understand that individually we can get on with things, but is there no hope for freeing what's in our hearts for each other? Is there no medicine for us? No bandage we can find that would bring us together again?"

With a thumb, he stroked her neck, imprinting himself, breaking her heart because she saw the answer turning his eyes to dull flint. "If there is medicine for getting rid of all the regret and blame we both feel," he said, his voice soft as the sunbeam between them, "I don't know what it is."

HER DESPERATION grew. Just like that he would leave? Forever? That didn't seem possible to her. Marco Rojas couldn't do this to her. To them.

They had finished their egg sandwiches in the pirate ship, and folded the map, and packed the sextant away next to the wooden box of crayons when Laurel thought she'd found the secret that would finally bring them together. She thought she'd found the medicine.

It happened at the window.

"You and your lake are famous now," Cole said, peering out the round hole, his hair fluttering against the sun-drenched gusts of summer air.

"Infamous is more like it," she said on a sigh, wedging in next to him, settling her shoulder next to his, listening to the quiet hum that was always part of them when they were close physically.

Like the ebb and flow of the lake's waves, the energy between them never stilled. It unfurled itself...like the lake in front of them. A deep lake running deep with secrets. Secrets? She stared at the lake in disbelief, swallowing hard, unable to breathe.

"Cole, what did Mike's message say?" Spirit Lake dangled a tantalizing notion in front of her.

"We were supposed to look under Aunt Flora's skirts, which we never found."

With a breathlessness overtaking her, she leaned further out the window, far enough to throw her arms wide and scare Cole.

"What are you doing! Watch out!" he called, snatching at her.

When he hauled her in against his heaving chest, she fought to get to the window again. "See what it looks like? The lake spreads out from the house, like a fan, just like a lady's...?"

And when she turned to Cole beside her, his grin grew wild and he kissed her. It was an exuberant spank on her lips. "Just like a lady's skirt!"

Snatching up the sextant, he positioned it against the horizon again. "Mike put something in the lake somewhere. Of course. We spent our lives diving for treasure. Why not here!"

Laurel's heart leaped every whichway like a thrashing fish in her excitement. "But where? What do you see?"

He groaned. "Miles and miles of lake and a bunch of tourists. Boats everywhere."

"Where does the needle point?"

"To the shore."

"Which shore?"

"That nub of land down the way that nearly did me in when I was chasing after you and Broderick."

"The land that forms the cove?"

"The cove? Wait a minute," he said, sizing up the sextant again.

"When I was racing after you and Broderick, the sheriff's boat caught its rotor on some twine—"

"Connected to a minnow cage?" Excitement erupted in her stomach. "Your brother had to have been the one who bought the minnow cage in May from my mother."

"The proof must be buried in the water. Come on, Laurel Lee!"

AN HOUR LATER, a soaked Laurel followed a drenched Cole in a mad dash into Buzz Vandermeer's newspaper office. They waved their catch—a waterproof cylinder with computer disks inside. Laurel's heart pumped wildly. If this meant putting his boss away forever, would Cole be free to answer the questions in her heart? Did he love her enough to stay? Or at least, to stay on to try and work things out? The unsettled feelings gnawed at her bones.

He hollered at Buzz, "Put this in your Mac, quick."

The shocked editor complied, but he was even more shocked when the first words on the screen were: "*Dearest Brother, glad you found me.*"

Laurel watched Cole go weak and slump into an office chair next to Buzz. She, too, shivered from the wording. "Found me," as if Mike were still alive. Perhaps he was, through Cole. Like Jonathon and the link she'd discovered with his living brother, Tyler. She went weak-kneed, and found herself gripping Cole's shoulders from behind, absorbing the nervous hum rippling through the strong muscles.

"Can't that machine go faster?" he demanded of Buzz's MacIntosh computer.

Her heart ached for him. "Give Buzz time, Cole."

Buzz tapped keys to get further into the menus. "Where'd you find the disks?"

"Spirit Lake," was all Cole could get out, his fingers tapping on the desk.

"In the cove, where the sand collects," Laurel finished for him, "in a waterproof canister inside a minnow cage floating in Spirit Lake."

"Like that thing they found the Texas woman's body in?"

"Just get to the next screen," Cole said, tapping his fingers.

Buzz crowed, "Hot diggity dog, lookee at this."

Laurel and Cole jammed their noses next to Buzz's. The screen flickered. Cole went wide-eyed. "We got him."

Charging off the chair, he hugged Laurel, filling her lungs with the earthy, lakewater smell still clinging to his damp hair. Picking her up, he twirled her about the room, knocking over a waste basket, kissing her fiercely in front of Buzz until her lips went numb. "We did it," he bellowed, "we did it!"

Elation thrummed through her, but all she could think to say was, "Your leg's going to hurt again." Worry and tend.

"Who cares!" Cole said, setting her down. "The proof! What a thing to find right before my flight home!"

He twirled her around again and again, crashing into Buzz's messy desk, dumping stacks of papers in his jubilation. Buzz didn't seem to mind. He just kept going through the disk.

But for Laurel, the world shut down. For some reason, her misguided heart thought that once he discovered Mike's treasure, there'd be a reason to stay. He could relax. He would be assured of Rojas staying in prison. Instead, Laurel realized this discovery was propelling Cole even faster toward new considerations. To home, he called it. How foolish she felt. Silly even. Of course he had to go home.

When Sheriff Petski, Wiley Lundeen and attorney David Huber answered Buzz's phone call and rushed over, conversation swirled, with the men slapping Cole on the back, congratulating him.

Far off against the roar of her disappointment, she heard Cole hooting, "This confirms the second set of books. Wait until I shove them under Rojas's nose."

Her vision blurred. She swiped at her face before Cole could notice. This was not the time for selfish emotions.

She could make out David Huber nodding. "Copy these disks, Buzz, and I'll get the information sent off to the U.S. Department of Justice. The Attorney General will be mighty grateful."

She sat down in a stiff chair, resigned to an odd sense of relief. The adventure was finally over. John was saying, "Those FBI boys are going to be impressed finally."

Wiley nodded toward the screen. "There's enough stolen treasure in here to fuel a war."

Cole's coppery skin paled.

Even Laurel blinked. "War?" Such a word made bones weary.

John nodded. "Try terrorism. According to the FBI, they think Marco Rojas might have been using his U.S. license for exclusive diving rights to the wrecks to fuel terrorist acts here in the States. They just didn't have the proof. Until now. The big boys'll need you in D.C. to testify on this one, Cole."

Raking a hand through his hair, Cole settled a blank gaze on

Laurel. It was as if he'd wiped himself clean of emotions, like...a chalkboard ready for duty.

Her stomach coiled to hardness. He'd said this could take years. Why hadn't she believed him? "Congratulations, Cole. I guess this is the big time for you."

Buzz whistled. "You bet big time! With irony. We journalists love irony. Our government looks the other way while Rojas makes money to buy bombs to use against us." He banged finger pads over the keys. "What's his motive? I need that for graph one."

Cole's brow furrowed over brackish eyes. "Greed. Power. Control. He was the kind of man you never questioned. When I first met him, I thought it was just ego, a man driven to take risks."

Wiley nodded. "Hell, you admired the guy. We all admire guys that have it all."

"But power's a gruesome taskmaster," Cole said with a flickering glance her way. "It makes you go your merry way."

The look—her words spouted back—unsettled her. Was he feeling guilt? Filled with blame? He said that's why he was leaving. Or had he just realized how much he liked his other world of control, powerful boats and fame, things he could share now without worry with his living son? The room spun. She discreetly sought a bookcase to steady herself and escape his gaze.

"Great headline," Buzz declared while copying the disks, handing them one by one to David Huber.

But Laurel puzzled over the tableau before her. "Why would Cole's brother bring this information here and hide it? Why go to these lengths? Why drag us all through this? Why involve Dresden?" *Why involve me?* she wanted to ask.

"The lady who always questions everything," Cole commented. "And they're very good questions."

His bold, public assessment sent heat sizzling up the back of her neck.

Wiley harumphed. "Good thing I'm thinkin' clearly lately, now I'm off the sauce. You folks don't get it. Mike did. He was smart. Do you believe anything coming out of Washington these days?"

Buzz hopped on that bandwagon. "Nope. And if a little town in rural northern Wisconsin breaks the story, that's going to be big news that will echo around the world. They'll believe us. We're honest. We don't like harboring secrets."

Cole's gaze collided with Laurel's again. A draft whisked through her chest. She felt herself desperately trying to shut the windows of her heart to keep the chill out. And that scared her. That shutting down scared her. She was retreating again, like that china doll to her safe shelf. But she had to. Oh the confusion. She'd told him she loved him days ago. He'd never responded to that, yet he complimented her now on something that had always frustrated him. Her questioning him. Always.

When John escorted Cole out of the newspaper office for the trip to the airport, she offered to go along. Begged actually. Right in front of a curious crowd of tourists shoving in to shake Cole's hand. But the sheriff told her they would be riding back with an FBI agent who would be conducting a confidential debriefing of Cole.

When he kissed her good-bye, his lips struck and left with the swiftness of a hawk who needed to escape a trap.

After climbing into the squad car, the man who always spun her life into new directions was gone.

He'd just challenged her yet again to get on with life. To be even stronger again.

But already, she missed the mysterious hum between them.

Chapter 18

AS THE JULY lushness around Spirit Lake turned to the full bloom of late clover in the meadow, and then gave in to an August dry spell of heat and more tourists, Laurel escaped too much thinking about the past.

With the mansion razed, there were no hoary shadows looking down on her. Though loneliness tugged at her now and then, she focused on embracing her freedom from the past.

It helped that she'd become an unexpected hero overnight. By virtue of being the local person who found the key to bringing down an international terrorist, she received a lot of new attention. It kept her busy giving speeches. And Buzz couldn't quote her enough, right next to the ads about "Lucky Chicken Fryers On Sale." Not a misspelled word in sight.

"Mom, warn me," she said in the bait shop one day, "if you hear about anyone wanting to erect a fountain in my name."

Her mother screwed up her face at her daughter. "A fountain? What the bejabbers you talkin' about?"

Laurel smiled. "Never mind, Mother."

Because this time of year brought a lull in animals injured—fewer rabbits born and weeks before hunting and trapping season—she even found herself with time to start a children's book.

The vision of Cole cradling a tiny brown bunny to his chest lingered, inspiring her to create a character called Radical Rabbit. He was the little guy who left the nest early without his mother's permission to race across the lake on the backs of willing, mischievous ducks, causing all kinds of trouble. Buzz had already put her in contact with an old English teacher friend of his who knew an agent. It looked promising, exciting. Scary.

She liked it.

She was proud of herself.

But it was lonely not having Cole to share it with. Oh, he'd called a few times, and she'd called him, but a phone conversation lacked the detail of a relationship. Where they had shared things, she now did them alone.

She tended to the beautiful churchyard in the country. As autumn crept in, with September painting the trees as pretty as Cole's old box of crayons, she raked leaves about the gravestones, planted yellow fall mums in heavy bloom, and apologized to nobody about not dating on Saturday nights.

Frost was in the air on the night in late September when she hauled a basket of tulip bulbs with her down the path. Pausing, she glimpsed toward the open space where the mansion had once been. Five deer fed there—two doe with three fawns between them. One of the does stepped over to lick lovingly at her progeny's ears. The fawn's spots were fading, and in their place came the grayish tone that would camouflage them among winter tree trunks and branches.

Laurel smiled, with a warmth listing into her belly at the sight. The freedom to breathe and to be strong had allowed her to appreciate the raw, emotional beauty of nature in a way that had never been possible. Before Cole. Because he'd come back, because they'd dared to try loving again, she had been set free to think in new ways. Yes, she missed him. Always would. But missing him was altogether more sublime than blaming him, being angry, and mired in self-pity. Because he'd left again, she'd been tested to move on. And she had.

She continued on down the path in the best moonlight she could remember in a long time. In addition to the tulip bulbs, she carried a small animal cage with Owlsy, whom she planned to set free at the cliff after tending to the graves.

Owlsy had experienced a relapse the minute Cole had left. Laurel had taken it as a warning not to do the same. And so she'd stayed strong and focused on babying the tiny owl back to health. Focus. She'd faulted Cole for focusing only on one thing at a time, but she had learned its value. Owlsy thrived because of it. The sense of determination Cole had impressed upon her would serve her well forever, no doubt.

She was digging about in the loamy, cool earth next to Jonathon's headstone when something felt odd about the air. It stirred, then fell still. No birds settling down for the night. No branches clacking in the crisp air.

She shivered. Grew alert. "Roxy? Roger?" The raccoons often followed her down the path. But she heard nothing.

She punched her trowel deep into the earth.

A thick voice captured her— "He'll like them."

Lightning showers burst heat in her stomach. She dared not look up. Her heart pounded.

She reached into the basket, her fingers fumbling, mindlessly taking a bulb and pushing it into the wedge of earth next to the trowel.

"Tulip bulbs?" the voice asked, gutteral as a wolf's growl.

The blood in her veins pulsated wildly, the grip on the trowel loosening. "They take much less work than annuals in early spring."

"The geraniums were always pretty and hardy. Sort of like you."

The pines murmured with the lowing of her heart. Maybe she'd only imagined his voice.

She said, "I...It's good to get out of old habits of the past."

"But I bet they're yellow tulips. Yellow, your favorite color I recall."

She couldn't look up. She was frozen. Looking down at the ground. "I'm going to plant several more perennials come spring. I wouldn't have to come out here so often if I planted more perennials." Her forehead scalded at the sound of that. "I mean, I'll always come out here—"

A big hand stole in and its long fingers began packing down the dirt for her over the bulb. The gutteral voice said, "No apologies. I understand."

The hand grabbed another bulb from the basket, and the teardrop-shaped bud of life looked particularly delicate against his thick fingers. Her heart tripped.

She looked up. She barely recognized him.

The moonlight glinted off Cole's freshly-shaven jawline. He'd trimmed his dark hair to short and sleek and wore a sweatshirt with a snarling animal sports team logo on it. His scent was brisk, pure man and muscle, like someone who'd cleaned up after chores and was now ready for the evening. His black eyes soaked up the blue moonlight, but his gaze flickered, nervous-like, and he escaped to helping her plant another tulip bulb.

Trembling with heat in her middle, she pushed the trowel in, pulled it back in the earth.

He dropped in the bulb. "Lovely night. Cold though."

She knew he disliked the cold weather. "Want my coat?" It was automatic.

"No thanks. You need it."

"Nice sweatshirt. Lions?"

"Wildcats. Tyler's soccer team."

Why was he back? Had she made a mistake in razing the mansion so quickly? Had they missed an important treasure? Her hands perspired. Could he see? Why had she forgotten garden gloves tonight? "Is something wrong?"

"Wrong?" He patted the earth down expertly with the trowel, then flipped it in his hand, delivering the handle end toward her.

She accepted it in shaky hands. She remembered he was good with tools. He'd fixed her boat in a breath, tore apart a mansion with saws and crowbars despite his injury. But he hadn't fixed her heart completely. She wouldn't feel so breathless and expectant now if he had. When had she finally succumbed to wanting to risk adventure with him?

"I mean," she said, realizing she'd questioned him again, "that I wonder why you've come back without phoning ahead. You know I'm busy."

Glancing at her, he grinned. "I read Buzz's articles. I like his new Website. Pretty good for a small town guy to be putting Dresden on the map like that. All at his own cost."

"He's been helpful to me as well."

"Buzz and you?" The next tulip bulb slithered from his fingers and into the cavity in the ground. "You'll have all the guys jealous if the word gets out."

She had to smile. She even punched lightly at his upper arm. "He's helping me find an agent for my book."

"So you are writing that book. That's great. I'm glad."

He flashed her a toothy smile that caught the moonlight and tickled her tummy. How dare he do this to her. "So why did you come back?"

"Wanted to say thanks properly, for one thing."

A fissure of heat wended up her spine. "Thanks?"

Grabbing the trowel from her, he dug several new holes in an arc next to the gravestone. "You could have chosen never to tell me about our son. But you did, you explained it all. And I'm richer knowing about Jonathon and for knowing what you went through. It broke an old pattern inside me, maybe my damn ego, and released something else, maybe my compassion. I never had much of it or much time for it before coming back to you. So, that's why I have to thank you for telling me about him, and letting me inside your heart. That took all your courage. But I think you saved my life by it. Just wanted you to know."

If there was a fence still between them, a thread as thin as gossamer lace from a spider's web just wafted over the fence and between them, niggling for them each to take an end of the thread. But dare she believe it? Could they overcome the elemental conflict between them—the regrets, the blame, the guilt even?

In the dark of night, she watched him, waiting.

Scooping several bulbs out of the basket, he dropped them in the holes, then with his palms smoothed the soil gently over the several spots that now cradled tulips. The bulbs would rest and nurture themselves for new life in spring.

But the way he patted the soil firmly held a finality that unnerved her.

She couldn't take it anymore and stayed his hand. Electricity skipped up her arm under the flannel shirt and jacket. "Why are you here?"

They were crouched on their knees, face to face. The bare tree limbs of the woodlands rattled behind them.

With his broad shoulders pinned against the sky by the stars, he said, "I discovered a loose end I had to take care of. Some business."

"Ah." Her heartbeat dulled. "What kind of business?"

His eyes darkened to match the night's shadows. "Depends."

Frowning with impatience, she began wiping off the trowel and packing the basket next to the owl's cage. "Wiley didn't find out anything else about the deed if that's troubling you? I still can't believe he was the 'W' file in David's office. Wiley, of all people, researching that mansion and your great-aunt."

"But his search did take him to a ledger kept at a local church. He found a notation about a donation Flora Tilden made. It seems my great-aunt had a sense of humor. She donated those sequined gowns she used to entertain her male friends to nuns living in St. Paul. It seems she only wanted to entertain a certain Naval officer."

"Wiley and your great-aunt? An item? Lovers?" Her stomach flip-flopped toward a laugh.

Getting up, Cole reached for the basket. "Let's just say Wiley thinks about those ballgowns and he smiles about getting under skirts. Lots of treasure under skirts."

Her heart racheted into a faster beat.

When he reached out a hand to help her up, she took it, a bittersweet twinge encircling her heart. "What might you remember here? What will make you smile like Wiley?"

"I've been thinking about how much I'll miss helping you with those baby rabbits."

"You could come back next summer."

"Or look you up at a book signing for your first Radical Rabbit book? Buzz tells me they might rush the first printing for next spring."

Pleasure ebbed through her at the notion he'd been asking around about her. "You'll have to stand in line behind all the kids in school. They pester me to death about when my first book will be out."

"They show good taste." He let go of her hand and moved stiffly around the headstone, putting it between them. Like that fence.

"Something is wrong." She knew the furrow in that brow.

"We never finished our conversation."

"Which one?"

"About fragile china dolls on shelves."

A chill galloped along her bones. Rubbing her hands up and down the arms of her jacket, she said, "I'm sorry about that conversation. It was unfair to try pity on you again. And that's what it was. I apologize. Old habits is all. No more."

"That's not my point." He shook his head, and began meandering toward the church, carrying the basket. "I had to come back and talk about fragile things, and fences."

"Fences?"

"Keeping fences up around me hurt my son. And I have to do everything in my power to make it up to him."

Flashing surprise at him, she couldn't hold up against the lightning bolts in his eyes. Did he expect her to congratulate him on making a decision he should have made the minute his son was born?

Groping for the cage on the ground, she picked up Owlsy. The bird fluttered, mimicking her confused heart. "It's getting late."

She took off with long strides, skirting by the church and its bare bridal wreath bushes scratching against the siding.

Pounding the path behind her, Cole blurted out, "Not only did I put up fences, but I put my son on the other side of a fence, thinking I was protecting him. From me. But it's lonely when you're at a distance, detached."

Her heartbeat pressed against her breastbone. She slowed to a normal walking pace to catch her breath. When he eased up beside her, she thought she heard the hum of vibrations undulating through the air toward her. Scooting ahead of the confusing sensation, she said, "Don't blame yourself anymore for anything that's wrong between you and your son. You're there now. He'll come around."

Crowding next to her on the path, he said, "My son is why I'm here."

He'd already made that point. What was wrong with the damn man? "That's your business?"

His response was to lead the way down a steep section of the path. They were quiet for a time while he helped her through the dark, a firm hand at her elbow. He carried the tulip basket.

Tilting his head at her, he said, "No lantern tonight."

She hadn't carried her lantern, she realized, for the first time ever. "It was one of those old habits. And the moonlight's enough."

"I like a night like this."

A wind kicked up with the beat of her heart. The pines moaned, perfuming the air.

"Your son's in some kind of trouble, isn't he? That's why you're here. I said he could visit but if he's—"

"No," he said, setting down the basket. "It's me."

"You? You made all the decisions you had to make. You should feel good about everything and the way it came out when you left here."

He found a log nearby, and sitting down, kneaded his fists in front of him. "I left here for a good reason. And it wasn't because of my boss or Mike. It was because of something you said."

A leaden bolt slammed through her. She set Owlsy down, but remained standing a couple of yards from Cole. "I said a lot of foolish things. But that's past." Didn't he see that?

Staring into the night, he continued, "Remember when you told me how important it was to shut your eyes and remember your loved ones?"

"Yes." She shuddered under her jacket.

"Well I closed my eyes in the mansion one day, and I couldn't visualize Tyler. Oh, he was there, but I wasn't sure of the image. How long was his hair, really? What clothes did he wear, really? And did he go ahead and get the braces or had we only talked about it? I couldn't remember anything. It scared the hell out of me. I knew then, that no matter what, I had to go home. And that you were right. I belonged with my son. I owed him a father. A real father."

"And what is your definition of a real father?"

Looking right at her in a way that stilled the blood in her veins, he said, "He takes action. Words are one thing, but it's what you do. It's what you show your kid that counts."

Like staying with him. Looking at the sweatshirt again with his son's team logo on it, she felt the wind gusting through her. At least he had the sensitivity to come back here and tell her his decision in person. There was no hope to bring down the fence between them. Too much had transpired between them.

Staring at the strong set of his jaw, she said, "Tyler's lucky to have you. So is your nephew, Tim. And Karen."

His gaze zeroed in on her then, powerful. "Owlsy's probably eager to be set free. Come on."

On the pathway again, he said, "Your father would have been proud to see what you've become."

Heat splashed her cheeks. "My father didn't understand."

"He understood completely. A father is afraid of losing his kid's love."

"But to be so obsessed?"

"He was probably jealous of me, the punk kid who seemed more important to you than he did."

"My father only wanted to own everything around Spirit Lake. Including me. To him, it was all about ownership of the land, the lake, the place."

He held a branch out of the way for her to move ahead on the narrow path. "My son's studying the environment at school, saving jungles and such. He told me the other day that even Walden Pond is not about a place. It's about consciousness."

Stopping in front of her, he blocked the path, peering down at her with eyes that reflected the moon. "My son would say that Spirit Lake is all about being conscious of what's important."

"And what would you say?"

"It's about learning how to tear down fences."

With her nerves ravaging her, she shivered. "What exactly are you saying, Cole?"

His answer was his action. He held out his hand and led her onward, the moonlight unfolding the path like a silver runner of silk. Only the reality of Owlsy fluttering in his cage kept her stumbling forward without crumbling under the confusion.

When they reached the cliff overlooking the dark valley below, Cole put down the basket and forced the cage from her hand, taking her quaking hands in his. His hawkish gaze pinned her against the skein of the night.

The hum grew heavy between them.

And then he turned, tucking her beside him and under his arm to look out over the cliff. The moonlight outlined a barn's roofline in the distance, the ragged tops of trees, and a windmill. Laurel smelled the last of freshly harvested cornfields.

"So quiet," he said on a sigh.

When he tipped his head back, she did the same, listening to the hush, floating at the sight of blinking stars on a navy, satin sky.

She glanced at his face, and she was startled by his calmness. What did he want from her?

Then reaching up to the sky, he pointed with an index finger. "Remember how we used to make magic happen?"

Trembling, her hands grew clammy. "Yes. We'd touch our fingers to the same star. We did a lot of silly stuff."

"Let's do it again. Be silly. Make a wish."

She reached up, the pad of her index finger feeling a spark when she touched him and the bright star.

"There," he said, drawing his hand away, "what'd you wish?"

"If I told, it wouldn't come true."

"I can make you tell."

"How?"

"Close your eyes."

"Here? On this cliff?" The darkness lured her, dizzying.

"Close your eyes. I'm here. This won't take long."

Sheepish, she gave in, closing her eyelids against the moonlight.

"Shut them tight, real tight, okay?"

"Cole, for heaven's sake."

A moment later, something smooth and cool slipped into her hand. She opened her eyes. "The locket?"

"I found it stuck in the afghan at your house, and took it with me. But I want you to have it."

Then reality lurched in. "You came back just to give me this? This is the loose end? The business?"

His brow furrowed into deep lines. "Would you open it? Please?"

He looked so earnest that she had to. Her fingernail pricked the hinge, and it sprung open under the moonlight.

The blood drained from her. Her legs went wobbly. Even in the shadows, she knew what she saw.

Her voice was but a gossamer whisper. "Jonathon." She couldn't breathe. "His baby picture. Where—? It is Jonathon, isn't it?"

She searched his eyes for any hidden secrets, for any lies. When he nodded, she cried, hugging the locket to her breast.

Cole engulfed her into the heat of his arms, the locket cradled between their heartbeats. "I talked with your mother right before I left."

"My mother?"

"She was upset at first," he began, a thumb caressing her cheekbone, painting her with his warmth. "But she finally confessed her cousin in Arizona might have kept a photo taken by the hospital. She'd never pursued it because she was sure it would be too painful for you."

And it would have been back then, she realized. Then she felt an ache for him. "This must have been hard for you." When he flinched, she rubbed at his arms. "Talk to me about Tyler. How are the both of you doing? Really?"

She relaxed to see a shadow lift from his eyes. "Feeling safe. We had a long talk recently, about a whole lot of things."

She looked at the photo again, so tiny and fragile lying in her palm under the half-light of the moon and stars. "He's beautiful."

"Like his mother."

"Thank you, Cole."

"I want you to know something."

She swallowed hard under the seriousness of his gaze. "Whatever it is, I can take it. The past is past."

"I found the medicine. That bandage for fragile things."

She leaned toward him and into the hum. "Our medicine?"

Licking his lips, he nudged her chin upward with a callused finger. "When I went back toTyler, he didn't much like me at first. He even told me off, had a few choice words, said he didn't need a bum like me."

"I'm sorry. You've been through a lot it sounds like." Colder air wafted up from the valley.

He gathered her against him. "I told the FBI boys, the newspaper reporters, the racing circuit promo wolves to go to hell so I could spend every day of August before school started with my son."

Warm admiration spiked into her heart. Smiling, she realized they'd exchanged roles in life. While she'd become the one being interviewed with her photo all over the papers and Internet Web pages, he'd retreated to tend to family.

She offered, "I hope you can patch things up eventually."

"Actually, after I followed him to soccer practice for about the tenth time, and after picking up him and his friends to go get pizza for the twentieth time, he told me something pretty darn profound."

"And what was that?" She could hear his heart thrumming in his chest, a fragile thread tethering her to him.

"He said, 'Dad, I forgive you. You're okay after all.' He suddenly made it sound so simple to change things. To make things fresh again he said merely, I forgive you."

"Because he not only needs you, he loves you."

"Yes, I think he does."

Looking up at the yearning in his dark eyes, she asked, "I know he does." Her heart scuttled about. Her mouth went dry.

"That's our medicine," he said. "It's forgiveness. When my son said that he forgave me, something wonderfully free and warm washed over me, as if I were flying. And it helped me see there's a new kind of love out there if I'm open to it. If you'll forgive me. And if I can forgive myself. I think I can if you'll do me a favor or two."

She swallowed around the lump pulsating in her throat. "A favor?"

"I want to bring Tyler back here sooner than we talked about."

"Anytime," she said, breathless. "I want you to visit often. And I'd love to meet him."

"Will you put your finger up on a star?"

She did. He pressed his finger on the same star, his thick finger sparking heat down her finger and arm, through her middle and down to her toes.

He said, "Are visits enough?"

"You're asking too many questions."

"What if Tyler and I came to live at Spirit Lake?"

Shock waves rocked her. "But your business, your racing—"

She began to pull her finger from the star, but he commanded, "No, keep your finger on our star." When she did, he continued, "I figure I still have that crayon box, so I can fly to a race now and then without too much trauma. Of course, I'll need to work out the vacation time with John."

"Why's that?" The heat rippled from their fingers held against the star.

"There's a lot of work to do patrolling the lakes around here. He thinks he could use a deputy, someone who could handle boats and going fast."

She hummed. She definitely hummed. "Cole?"

"Will you marry me?"

Laurel saw the wicked glint in his dark eyes. Lightning must have struck her finger because sparks showered the air between them. Rescuing her heart before she fainted, she brought her hand down. The night air held a pungent promise on it.

She felt a smile bubble up, but she wondered if she'd been hearing things. "You're just lookin' for trouble, aren't you?"

To her delight, he got down on his knee. Raising an eyebrow rakishly, he said, "Have I found it?"

Sighing, her heart aglow, she nodded. "That's your bad leg. You better get up."

"Not until you say you forgive me."

"For what?" Her fingers tingled.

"For being late with this proper proposal."

"There's never anything proper about you, Cole."

"Then you'll say yes?"

"Questions are my specialty, remember?" she spouted.

"Then you'll say—"

"Yes, damn you!" Heatwaves crashed down her.

"I love you, Laurel Lee, and it's not that old kind of love, that stuff teenage boys toss around loosely like cheap bottles of perfume. This is the big stuff, longer and wider and deeper than Spirit Lake."

"Hmm, I'll need a mighty big bottle to hold that kind of love."

"Just a lifetime. I've come home, Laurel Lee. I need you. With you, I can leap fences, tear down fences—"

"And get in trouble!" Her heart swelled and she fell into his arms. "I love you, Cole. You're no good for me, no good at all."

But she kissed him anyway.

LATER, WHEN THEY released the owl, they watched him course high into the sky across the moon, winging onward to their meadow.

And they followed. Hand in hand. They had become a family.

~ The End ~

Christine DeSmet

Christine DeSmet is an award-winning writer who loves fast-paced, visual suspense stories set in wild landscapes that naturally feature both beauty and danger. Her new novel, SPIRIT LAKE, set in the forests of northern Wisconsin, earned First Place in the 1999 Golden Network contest sponsored by Romance Writers of America (RWA). It was a finalist in the 1996 RWA Golden Heart contest under the title SHADOW GARDEN.

She's also a professional screenwriter, and her novels reflect her love of developing visual images and emotionally-charged dialogue. Her motion picture script "Chinaware-Fragile," written with writing partners Peggy Williams and Bob Shill, won the Slamdance Film Festival contest in 1998 and is currently optioned to New Line Cinema.

Christine is a fellowship graduate of the Warner Bros. Sitcom Writers Workshop, a board member of Wisconsin Screenwriters Forum, a member of the Writers Guild of America East, and a member of RWA.

Raised on a farm near Barneveld, Wisconsin, her stories always reflect her love of animals. "I grew up with pets that included gophers, chickens, cows, ponies, pigs, raccoons, the occasional rescued baby bird, and of course parakeets, canaries, kittens, guinea pigs, and many dogs."

She has a master's degree in journalism and leads writing workshops for UW-Madison's Division of Continuing Studies.

Readers are welcome to email her at: cdesmet@dcs.wisc.edu

Printed in the United States
30042LVS00001B/124-132